A Daughter's Duty
PART 1

A Daughter's Duty
PART 1

(God, Country, Family)

LINDA D. COKER

iUniverse, Inc.
Bloomington

A DAUGHTER'S DUTY PART 1
(GOD, COUNTRY, FAMILY)

iUniverse books may be ordered through booksellers or by contacting:

iUniverse
1663 Liberty Drive
Bloomington, IN 47403
www.iuniverse.com
1-800-Authors (1-800-288-4677)

ISBN: 978-1-4620-3121-4 (sc)
ISBN: 978-1-4620-3122-1 (ebk)

Printed in the United States of America

iUniverse rev. date: 06/15/2011

DEDICATION

I dedicate this story to my mother, Eleanor J. Selman, who has been the wind beneath my wings through the most difficult moments of my life. Although she has endured a hard and abusive life, she still continues to give my sister and me unconditional love and beautiful memories.

I dedicate this novel to all the men and women who have served and who are serving our country.

Most importantly, this dedication includes all the women and men who have been abused and victimized by their families.

ACKNOWLEDGEMENTS

I give a great thanks to my little sister, Katrina J. Pavelko, for being my editor. I enjoyed working with her.

I would like to give thanks to Denise Howard Long of FirstEditing. Denise and her editing team are the greatest. I truly enjoyed working with these professionals, and I consider them part of my team.

PRELUDE

I was told that since the Vietnam era, 82% of all robberies, and some types of fraud committed against service members, are done by their own family members. In my opinion, these types of crimes almost always go unpunished and unreported for the following reasons: the service member loves his or her family; the service member doesn't have the financial capability to see that justice is served; our justice system does not see that justice is served; and JAG doesn't have judicial authority to prosecute individuals that commit these types of crimes against the service member, on active duty or not. From my understanding, these are loopholes in our justice system.

This is just one sad tale of the increasing meltdown of an American family's core morals and values—morals and values on which this country was founded. When our family units have lost their way, so do our businesses, our justice system, and our government because they are one and the same. United we stand; divided we will fall.

It is everyone's individual responsibility to instill in each generation personal morals and values of honesty and responsibility, as well as personal liberty.

CHAPTER I

On January 7, 1999, I was sitting on an airplane staring out the window. I let my thoughts wander and I remembered all of the things that my mother had done and asked of me over the years. I thought about how I ended up on this flight. I wondered if I would be able to bail her out of trouble this time. I was flying from Germany, where my husband, Thomas, was stationed to Virginia. We had both been in the Army, but I had left the service because it was becoming harder and harder to stay stationed together. After my discharge, I became an accountant for Army and Air Forces Exchange Services (AAFES).

The phone call I received from my mother the previous night was still ringing in my head. She called around 11:00 p.m. and told me she was turning herself in to the custody of the U.S. Marshals on January 8, 1999. She tearfully told me that she needed me to come home.

I called my boss, Sue, shortly before 11:30 p.m., waking her up. I told Sue my mother was in serious trouble. I didn't know for sure what she had done, but I was preparing to go back to the States. Sue told me to go take care of my mother. She asked that I call her as soon as possible to let her know how long I would be gone. She would hold my position as long as I needed; I was one of the best accountants she had ever had, and she didn't want to lose me. I assured Sue I would keep her posted and give her more details when I knew them.

I was up until 3:00 a.m. making flight arrangements to fly back to the States. I was tired, frustrated, angry, and confused about the entire mess that my mother has gotten herself into, and I wasn't even sure exactly what she had done this time.

In 1995, when Thomas and I had just moved to Germany, I had begun to have nightmares about my mother going to jail. Never in my wildest thoughts had I believed it would come true. I always thought it was my subconscious playing tricks on my mind. Maybe it was what I had heard and what had happened to me that caused my subconscious to play those wicked games with me. I would wake up in the night, yelling and fighting. Thomas thought I was having flashbacks or something, but it was about my beloved mother—nothing else could make me hurt so deeply and profoundly.

*   *   *

My mind drifted back to what I consider the day in October 1997 when all this really started . . .

Mom had called and told me that she and "Big Pete," my mother's husband, were going to file for bankruptcy. She said, "The court needs affidavits from you and Thomas stating all the property in the Daisy house is yours."

Thomas and I went to JAG (the Judge Advocate General's Corps), obtained the affidavits, and mailed them to her. We wondered why the court needed our involvement in their bankruptcy, but we did not want our things involved. I remembered feeling an immense sadness for my mother.

My mother—how do I describe the sadness I feel and why? My mother was born and raised poor. She was smart, and I guess, she felt the only way she was going to escape "the Hollow" was with education and savvy, or by marrying someone from a family of wealth or the potential possibility of wealth—someone in a higher station of life than herself because she was a woman. She was looking for her Prince Charming to come and save her.

My mother was shot and almost killed by her brother, Uncle Poppy, when she was a child. The family covered up the truth with another story: "They were playing cowboys and Indians, and Uncle Poppy shot her in the back."

What really happened was that Uncle Poppy had tried to have sexual relations with my mother; they were both teenagers at the time. My mother tried to get away from him, and he shot her in the back when she was running from him. My mother lost a part of her lung, but she miraculously survived.

The movie *Cinderella* was released around this time, and I believe my grandmother took her to see it when she was better. My mother had been fixated on the Cinderella tale ever since. Unfortunately, my mother did not have a "happily ever after" ending.

2

* * *

After we learned about the bankruptcy, later in 1998, Mom called again. She was in the process of moving some of her things. She said that she had a bad back and could not move them herself. She did not have any money to pay someone to move them, so I told her I would let her use one of my credit cards to hire movers. I assumed she was moving things to the Daisy house. That was a huge mistake. I called the credit card company a few months later and discovered the card had been maxed out. The one consolation was that she was making the payments on time. I felt scared because she had taken advantage of my kindness and spent my credit on things without my permission. I called Mom and told her to send my card back and not to worry about the payments; I would pay it. I told her that she didn't need it anymore anyway. She agreed and mailed the card back to me.

* * *

We called it the "Daisy's house" because it was where my great-great-aunt Daisy had lived. It was located in the middle of the Mills family farm. The Mills' farm was a cattle farm in its hay day with beautiful rolling hills and green pastures. There was one large willow tree located about ten acres behind the Daisy house in the middle of the open field. I always considered that solitude sight breathtaking.

When Thomas and I were stationed in Hawaii in 1991, I received a phone call from my mother stating that she had bought the Daisy house for Thomas and me. When she described it, I told her we did not want it, but we would like to build our own dream home on the hillside on the Mills farm. When we retired from active service, we would live in the Daisy house until our home was built. I told her during this conversation that Thomas and I would pay for the homeowner's insurance and would like to store our things there. Mom had agreed to this. At this time, I did not know that Auntie Bea and my mother could not afford this. They both gave the appearance of having a lot of money, which I now realize was not the case. All the years that had passed, and there was never any mention of needing money. They both were living high on the hog. Later, I found out the entire truth, when I stepped off this airplane on January 7, 1999.

The real history of the Daisy house was quite different from what I believed. My great-aunt Bea Mills (Auntie Bea)—my grandmother's sister who was also my godmother—had bought the house from Ms. Daisy's family when they were relocating Ms. Daisy to a nursing home because Auntie Bea would not take care of Ms. Daisy in 1991.

Auntie Bea had bought the Daisy house because it was located in the middle of the Mills farm. The Mills farm was left to Auntie Bea by her deceased husband, Uncle Herndon, and she bought the Daisy house with the money that Uncle Herndon left her in addition to the property. Ms. Daisy was my great-uncle Herndon's aunt.

According to Auntie Bea and my mother, this is how the property ended up in the names of Auntie Bea, my mother, and Big Pete. Auntie Bea had told Mom to buy the Daisy house for her, and my mother told her she did not need it. Why should she buy another house that was forty-five minutes from where she lived?

Auntie Bea took the money that Uncle Herndon left her and bought the Daisy house which is located on a quarter acre in the middle of the Mills' farm. She went to numerous banks to obtain a mortgage because she needed her money back to support herself. No bank would loan her the money because she did not have enough income, and because of her age, in my opinion.

Auntie Bea went back to my mother and wanted her money back in the bank because she could not afford to live without the income that the CD generated on a monthly basis. Therefore, both women went to my mother's husband, Big Pete. The bank made all three parties sign the note.

CHAPTER II

Later in January 1998, my mother called me.

"Belinda, someone almost broke into the Daisy house again. I'm afraid it will happen again. I don't want you and Thomas to lose all your stuff."

Thomas and I were using the house as storage for our furniture, personal mementos, and the inventory I was accumulating for the shop I hoped to open eventually.

Mom continued, "Belinda, I want to move your Uncle Frank in there. I'm the only one who will take care of him and Auntie Bea. It would be much easier for me if he lived there because Uncle Frank and Auntie Bea can look after each other when I'm not around. After all, the Mills' farm house and the Daisy house are side by side."

Uncle Frank was my great-uncle, my grandmother's brother, my godfather, and Auntie Bea's brother.

I agreed, but with one stipulation. "Mom, he can live there, but his children cannot spend the night, and his grandchildren must stay off the furniture. What is he going to do with his stuff? Thomas and I have the house pretty full with our belongings."

Mom answered, "Oh, don't worry about that, Belinda, most of his junk will stay up in the Hollow where he is now."

I was an artist. I loved working with ceramics, porcelain, sculpture, pottery, and even canvas painting. I had been making ceramic and porcelain figurines for years, and I dreamed of becoming famous from my talents someday. Then I would be able to sell my things with ease; I would become known in the art world.

I had made a variety of items. One of my dreams was to open a shop to sell my creations, as well as the antiques and collectibles that I had collected throughout my travels. Over the past several years, I had been making contacts with different dealers in several countries. I had slowly been buying antiques and collectibles and shipping them home to Virginia.

They were stored in the Daisy house, with the goal of one day being able to open a shop to sell them.

My mother, of course, had known about this dream. A few months after Uncle Frank moved into the Daisy house, my mother asked if I could open up the shop. She wanted to sell some of her things and her husband's things, in addition to my inventory. She said that they were hurting for money and she did not know if they were going to make it. I didn't want my mother living on the street and starving, so I agreed, but with the stipulation that Big Pete would not be part of it. She agreed and so I made it happen.

I opened my shop in Virginia. It was really for my mother's benefit. She was my only employee and ran the shop for me. At this time, Thomas and I were stationed in Germany. One day, I received a call from my mother. "Belinda, this stuff isn't selling fast enough. The store isn't making enough money to support me. If I mailed you some things, could you sell them in Germany for me?"

I answered, "Sure, Mom, I don't have a problem doing that for you."

The first thing she sent was clothing—lots of clothing. It included some of her gowns and other clothing along with her husband's clothing. There was so much. I had Thomas try on several of the jackets, ten of which we purchased, knowing we could alter them. I also bought several pieces of Mom's clothing. I had bought a pad of invoices at the post exchange (PX), and sent her the money along with an invoice and a receipt. I was able to sell the rest of the clothes to my friends. Mom continued sending things, and I continued selling them for her until I was on this airplane coming back home to try to save her.

CHAPTER III

In October 1998, Mom had called me again asking if I could buy the Mills farm and the Daisy house. She said that my great-aunt tried to file bankruptcy, but the judge said she had too many assets and denied her. Adam Greed was the one who picked up the note on the Mills farm. Mom and Auntie Bea approached Adam Greed when they were outside the courtroom after Auntie Bea's bankruptcy hearing and begged him to give the land back to Auntie Bea. Auntie Bea's attorney and Adam Greed's attorney were present for this exchange.

Finally, Adam Greed broke down and stated, "I will sell the note for the Daisy house and the Mills farm to Belinda and Thomas for the amount I picked up the note. If Belinda and Thomas can't obtain a note, then I will give a lifetime home to Bea." My mother told this to me when she called, requesting that Thomas and I buy the Mills' farm and the Daisy house.

I let out a sigh and told my mother to send me the finance documents. I told her that I would put them in my name, and only my name. I wasn't even sure if I would be able to obtain a mortgage because I never had applied for one before. I also told her to tell Auntie Bea and Uncle Frank that they were going to pay a portion of the monthly payment, and that I would tell them the amount when, and if, that time came. Mom sent the finance documents that she had filled out without dollar amounts. I called my mother and asked her why there was not a dollar amount. She explained that the finance agent did not know how much he could get in my name, alone. He needed the information and my income first. It sounded reasonable to me so I made the changes and sent the papers back to the finance agency still without dollar amounts because I did not know what they were.

The question I had was who was Adam Greed? I had never met this man before, and I asked my mother who he was and what his relation was to her and Auntie Bea. Mom only stated that he was a friend to her and Big Pete.

After I had mailed papers back to the finance agency, I received another phone call from my mother. This time she asked, "Belinda, Pete and I are in a lot of trouble. I need you and Thomas to sign a promissory note for our defense attorney. He's expensive, but he can help us." She would not say much more.

I said, "I will have to talk to Thomas before I can give you an answer."

Thomas and I agreed but made it clear that Big Pete would have to find someone else to sign for him. I called my mother back and told her we would pay for her, but not for Big Pete. We received the promissory note from the attorney a few days later. I almost got sick when I saw the dollar amount: $60,000! I called Mom and told her we could not afford this and that we could not sign the note.

She started crying and said we would not have to worry about it. She would pay it. "Belinda, I need you more than I have ever needed anyone."

I talked with Thomas about her situation, and we wanted to protect her, in spite of all the problems she had caused me throughout my life. I felt that even if she was guilty, she still deserved a strong defense. She was my mother, after all, no matter what. Thomas and I agreed to help her out.

We signed the note and mailed it back to her attorney. In December 1998, my mother had called me and stated, "Belinda, my house of cards is going to fall soon."

My first reaction was, "Mom, you better not have opened any credit cards, bank notes, or checking accounts in my name. I mean it, Mom. Don't put me into that position with you again. Please, don't do it!"

She responded, "Oh, honey, I would never do something so cruel to you."

Those words will ring in my ears forever. It had not even been a year since she borrowed my credit card, and I had just finished paying it off.

Mom called me again in December, on Christmas Eve. She said, "Big Pete is drinking more and getting drunk. He is threatening to kill me, and he has been beating on me."

I asked, "What? What do you mean he's beating you *more*? Has that creep been beating you all this time?"

Mom ignored me and said that she could not have any guns in the house because of the bond. This was news to me. I asked, "What bond?"

She answered, "I had to put up $50,000 because of the indictments and pending trial, and under the conditions I cannot have any guns."

I told her, "I don't care about any conditions. Take one of those pistols that I showed you how to fire many years ago and hide it in your bedroom closet. Keep your bedroom locked at night. I know that won't keep him out, but it will give you enough time to get that pistol out and protect yourself. If you go to jail for protecting yourself with a gun, at least you'll be alive. Do you need me to come home and put that creep in his place?"

Mom answered, "No, Belinda, you'll just make things worse."

With concern laced in my voice, I asked, "Mom, can you come and live with Thomas and me in Germany?"

She started crying. "Baby, it's too late for me now, they have already taken my passport. I'll do what you told me to do."

I still did not know what she had done. All I knew was now I was afraid for my mother's life and I could do nothing. If I went home, I could make it worse for her; if I stayed and something happened, I wouldn't be able to forgive myself.

CHAPTER IV

Here I was, on the flight back to the States, thinking Mom should have called and told me the whole truth years ago. I still did not know what was going on, but I knew I didn't know the whole truth.

I prayed to God that I could handle myself without getting into a physical altercation with Big Pete. At this point, I wanted to seriously hurt him for being a bully and hurting my mother all these years. I could not believe I had been blind to the way he was treating her, but my afterthought was always—*That creep isn't worth going to jail and destroying my life for, but I am going to make that creep pay somehow in a civilized way. I want to see him in jail for the rest of his life.*

I believe in following the rules to the best of my abilities. This is why we have laws, but our country has become filled with petty little laws to the point that some of our constitutional rights are taken. It seems our laws change to suit just certain groups of people, and that hurts the rest of the Americans. I'm not a politician, just an out-of-shape ex-soldier, but I do know the difference between right and wrong. My thoughts then wandered back to my first meetings with Big Pete a couple of decades ago. It's a distant dream and a different life for me.

* * *

I knew Big Pete was a crook the first time I met him. When Mom asked for my approval for her to marry Big Pete, I would not give it, and Grandma and Auntie Bea pressured me. They were my elders and felt that I was just jealous. I didn't care. There was something about him that I didn't like, but of course, I gave in and finally granted my consent. I only respected him because my mother loved him. Every time Mom and he would come and visit me in the Army, there was always a fight. He talked to my mother as if she were nothing.

10

I think I was on my third or fourth tour overseas, and Thomas and I were engaged. Mom said she had to come and meet him. She was my mother, and it was my duty to allow her to give her blessing.

I said, "That's fine, but let Thomas and me make the dates for leave. You can come when Thomas and I have authorized leave at the same time, and we will take you around Europe."

I remember Thomas was very excited to meet my mother because I didn't talk much about my family. He seemed to talk about his family all the time, and I enjoyed listening. It only took one day before Big Pete, Thomas, and I found ourselves in an argument.

We were in one of our favorite German restaurant where the owner always served us himself because we were his favorite Americans. Thanks to our big mouths, his business was thriving. The restaurant was in the middle of nowhere, about thirty minutes from post, and Thomas and I had stumbled upon it when we were exploring the surrounding countryside.

From my experiences, communities in many countries and in the United States make a good living around military bases. Within six or eight months, everyone was bringing their dates, spouses, and families to this wonderful mom-and-pop restaurant. Many units, including Thomas's and mine, had been setting up "Hails and Farewells" dinners there as well. I guess business had never been better for our German friend.

On the day of the argument, our German friend did not make Big Pete's drink the way he liked it, and Big Pete started yelling at him. Thomas immediately told him to shut his stupid mouth because they did their drinks that way in that country, and there were many brands of vodka in the world, not just his brand. Our friend was so upset that he brought the bottle of vodka so Big Pete could see the brand. Big Pete started laughing because it had a picture of a moose on it with a straw in the bottle and he gave our friend a 50-mark bill, their currency. I looked over at Thomas, and he still was very angry. When we left the restaurant, Thomas and I stayed back and humbly apologized for my mother's husband's nasty attitude and stated that we would never bring him back there.

Our friend, in his broken English, said, "I know it was not your fault and the only reason I did not kick him out was because of the two of you and your mother, Belinda." We both hugged him and left.

I found out later from Thomas that Pete talked to him in the hotel the night before and told him he had a private investigator check Thomas out. Thomas was still bitter from that, and I told him, "He is nothing but a liar just trying to belittle you and make you feel smaller than him. He is a creep and always has been, just like my mother. Do you see now why I don't talk about my family? And besides, he has never been part of my family to me. To me he is just another husband of my mother's, and I'm praying she will divorce him soon."

When Thomas and I were first married, we visited my mom and Big Pete. We were sitting at their patio table eating dinner, when he started trouble again in front of Thomas.

I told him, "Don't you ever talk to Mother like that in front of me. I mean it this time, Big Pete."

Thomas stood up from the table because it appeared that Big Pete was going to strike my mother.

Thomas asked him, "Did you hear my wife?"

Pete hit Mom right in front of us. Thomas grabbed him and threw him down to the ground. Pete snarled and went inside their house. Mom was crying.

The fight had been over a bottle of wine Mom asked him not to open. He was already drunk. Big Pete had become drunk and mean many other times, but I thought for sure he would never hit her again. He knew Thomas and I would beat the crap out of him. But I knew nothing about battered spouse syndrome. I didn't understand it and never will. I mean if someone hit me and tried to control me, I would protect myself, probably die trying. I just don't understand it. I still cannot understand why my mother put up with it.

CHAPTER V

When I was a child, we were visiting my grandmother after church on a beautiful fall day. I was about eleven or twelve years old and I needed some bugs and spiders for a school project. My cousin, Sam, was helping me because we were best friends then, and it seemed we had so much in common. I was a tomboy by nature. We were over at the old swimming pool, and there was some stagnant water still in it with lots of different types of bugs for the two of us to choose from.

Little Janet had a crush on Sam and was pestering the devil out of us, and she would not leave us alone. I finally told the little girl to shut up and leave us alone. I told her that Sam was helping me collect bugs, and she was distracting us. Then Little Janet ran off.

Little Janet was a foster child that my Uncle Poppy and Aunt Janet had taken in, and they had been taking care of her for about six months. Aunt Janet is my Uncle Poppy's second wife.

About twenty minutes later, Aunt Janet came. She started correcting me for talking the way I did to Little Janet. I told Aunt Janet, "If I did something wrong and need to be corrected it will be my mother, not you." Aunt Janet became angry and left.

Sam and I finally found all the bugs that I needed. We had them in a glass jar with a lid on it. We were just coming around the side of Uncle Frank's trailer, and we heard a lot of yelling. We looked up at the steps that went up the side of the mountain to Grandma's cabin. Uncle Poppy and my mother were coming down the cement steps, and they were fighting. My mother had her hand on Uncle Poppy's crotch and was pulling hard. Uncle Poppy had both hands around my mother's neck trying to choke her. My grandmother and granddaddy were yelling at Uncle Poppy to let my mother go. Uncle Frank was just standing there on his steps to his trailer, acting cowardly. I dropped my jar of bugs, ran up the steps, and jumped on Uncle Poppy's back. I threw my arms around his neck, and I

13

was trying to choke him so he would let my mother go. He then moved his hands from my mother's neck to my hands and was trying to pull me off. Sam grabbed one of his legs, and I think he was biting him. Uncle Frank jumped in it and then Granddaddy. It took all of us to force Uncle Poppy to the ground. As soon as his hands were off her neck, my mother started hitting him in the face, and when we had him on the ground she kept kicking him until my grandmother yelled at her. "That's enough, Jane!"

Then my mother stopped. Grandma yelled at all of us, "That's enough, let him go!"

We all let go of Uncle Poppy.

As soon as he was free, he got up fast and told his family, "Let's go." Mom told Christina and me to get in the car because we were leaving too.

When I was older, I learned from my grandmother and my mother that the fight was over me. Apparently, Aunt Janet went back and told Uncle Poppy what I said to her in front of Grandma, Granddaddy, and my mother. Uncle Poppy said he was going to whip me with a belt for mouthing off at Aunt Janet. My mother told him he wasn't going to lay a hand on her child. What I said was correct because she raised me that way. Grandma and Granddaddy both agreed with Mom. Then the argument started, and they started beating each other. Uncle Poppy broke my grandmother's glass in her china cabinet. He tried to get to Granddaddy's firearms because he said he was going to "finish the job" that he had started when they were teenagers. Mom had pushed him out the front door before he had a chance to get to Granddaddy's firearms and that's how they ended up outside.

Uncle Poppy only had one leg. His other leg was cut off right below his knee and he wore a hollow wooden leg and foot strapped to the remainder of his leg. Everyone nicknamed him Hoppy. As the legend goes, when I was first learning to talk I couldn't say, "Hoppy." I said, "Poppy," and the name stuck.

Uncle Poppy was in the Navy long after WWII, but he would tell everyone that he lost his leg during the war. Anyone who did the math would know Uncle Poppy was just a child during WWII. He lost his one leg saving an officer on board his air carrier. In fact, it was his first tour. The true story is that a ton weight almost fell and killed one of Uncle Poppy's commanding officers. Uncle Poppy saw the cable unraveling and breaking. He ran and pushed his officer out of the way, but it was too late for Uncle Poppy. The weight fell on his leg and he lost it. They honorably discharged him. The Navy had been Uncle Poppy's dream, and it was taken from him at the beginning of his career. He was never the same. I'm not sure that I even believe this version of what happened either.

Uncle Poppy has been a bully and a creep as long as I'd known him. He was not a very nice person, but my mother loved him no matter the nasty things he had done to her over the years. This is just one memory out of many where my mother would fight to protect herself. I just could not understand why she would allow anyone to abuse her in such a manner and yet still fine some way to love that person; but when I think of all the stories of her childhood and what my grandmother and most of my family members have done to her, maybe it's meant to be for her. I still don't understand it. Maybe that's why I was raised to stand on my own two feet and not have to depend on a man for anything unless I choose to do so. I make my own choices in life, and do not have it run by fate and fate alone. My mother raised me so I could break the cycle of mother, daughter, mother, daughter. I'm not sure; maybe my path of life has brought me to this point—the insight that you should have plain old common decency and respect your fellow man. To act against wrong and stand beside right. I wasn't sure; I guess I'd never be sure.

CHAPTER VI

I heard someone talking to me. I looked up from the window of the airplane, and the flight attendant was asking me if I would like something to drink. I asked for two vodkas and one can of tomato juice. I paid the flight attendant, and made myself a stiff one. I looked back out the window of the airplane and started drifting back into my thoughts and memories. Our country was preparing to go to war in Desert Storm. Thomas and I were stationed in Hawaii, and at that moment in time, we did not know if Thomas or I were going or not. I received a phone call from my mother asking if we were going. We did not know the answer because our units were not called.

Certain types of support personnel were being asked to volunteer to go out with the units that were preparing to go, and we had not decided if we were going to volunteer yet. Mom had stated she was following the news, and she thought Thomas and I should obtain more life insurance coverage. Just in case.

Big Pete was in the insurance business, and Mom told me Big Pete felt we should have extra coverage. The military insurance wasn't enough for us. Mom asked if she could put additional coverage on the both of us. I told her we could not afford Big Pete's premiums. She said that was okay. She would pay it, and it would have a war clause in it. I did not think policies were like that, but Thomas and I agreed. She sent the paperwork via FedEx, and we went and did all the blood work. I put Thomas as beneficiary, and he put me as beneficiary. We put our mothers second in case something happened to both of us.

A little over a year later, President George H. Bush turned the reins of our great country's military forces over to our new commander-in-chief, President Clinton. He had already pulled our great military forces out of the Middle East, which at the time, in my humble opinion, was the biggest mistake our country could have made. Most of the military knew, or at least knew in the back of our minds, we would be back. The job was not finished; it was just a matter of time. Thomas and I went home to our beloved Virginia that we had sacrificed so much for, to heal our hearts and minds, to gain our strength once again, and to find peace. During this time, we were visiting my mother and Big Pete in Virginia. My mother gave us the finalized documents of the insurance policies that Thomas and I opened about a year or so prior. I was stunned. My mother and Big Pete had changed the primary beneficiary. My mother was now the only beneficiary listed on both policies. I informed her, with a few choice words, that we did not need it anymore. She said the policies belonged to her and Big Pete, and they were not going to cancel them. She was sure Big Pete must have made a mistake.

I angrily retorted, "Mother, you will change that policy. My husband will profit from my death, not you!"

Thomas told her the same thing. After we said that, we just let it go. We could do nothing, and she was right. They were paying the bill on those policies.

Before we left, I opened another policy, a standard policy that I could afford. Again, I put my husband as my primary beneficiary. I had Big Pete help me open an IRA before I left as well. I listed Thomas as the beneficiary. Once again, however, Big Pete put my mother as the beneficiary. This time, I waited a year and called the company directly, without Big Pete knowing about it, to have it changed. I was able to have the new insurance policy and the IRA changed. I was told that I could not change the beneficiary on the original policies, because Thomas and I did not own them. I would have to go through my agent, who was Big Pete. At this time, I was unaware that what Big Pete and my mother did to us was considered fraud.

CHAPTER VII

I looked from the window and decided I needed another drink, and I opened another vodka bottle and mixed it in my cup with the tomato juice. I took a sip. The plane was full of passengers, and I could hear the sound of numerous conversations. I watched the flight attendants coming down the aisles slowly as they were passing out dinners to the passengers. I thought to myself about how much I hated these long flights. I turned back to my little window and stared out at the fluffy clouds again. I went deeper and further into my memories, thinking about another airplane flight long, long ago.

I started thinking about my grandmother's funeral. Many, many years ago, I had a horrible dream. I dreamed my grandmother was dying. I woke up, and it was 2:30 or 3:30 in the morning. I rushed down the stairs, picked up the phone, and called my mother. She answered the phone in a sleepy tone and became irritated with me. I asked her, "Is Grandma okay?"

My mother answered as she yawned, "Belinda, your grandma is fine as far as I know. I guess I didn't tell you that she is living with your Uncle Poppy. She had another seizure a while back, and she has been with him since then."

I asked inquisitively, "Mom, did you make amends with Grandma?"

Mom didn't answer me. Instead she said, "Belinda, go back to sleep."

I thought, *I should have asked Grandma a long time ago if my mother made amends with her, but I never came out and asked because they always acted as if they were fine when they were in my presence.*

Several days later, I received a phone call from Mom. She was crying and said that she and Uncle Poppy let Grandma go. She had another seizure, and she was brain dead. I had a sneaking suspicion that my mother never had made her peace with her mother. As Mom was crying on the phone, she told me that she would make flight arrangements for me to come home. She needed me, and she wanted me to give Grandma's eulogy. Out of all the cousins, I was the closest to Grandma before she started going downhill. I told her I would do whatever she wanted. That evening, Mom called me back and said she thought it would be better if Mary or Christina gave the eulogy.

I said, "You have to be kidding me, Mom. Neither of them knew who Grandma was and never tried to have a relationship with her. You have already bestowed the honor on me and I will do it."

The following day, I sat down and wrote my grandmother's eulogy. I was very tasteful with the things that I wrote, so as not to offend the living. I didn't feel any emotions or have any sense of loss, maybe because I didn't really know my grandmother anymore. A long, long time ago we had been best friends, but that seemed like a lifetime ago. Damned if I was going to allow Mary or Christina to do it. After I finished the eulogy, I went upstairs and packed my things.

I flew from Fort Polk, Louisiana, to Snobville, Virginia. When I arrived at the Snobville Airport, no one was there to pick me up. I waited about an hour before my cousin Mary, who is my Uncle Poppy's daughter, drove up at the curb. I was very angry that it was Mary and not my mother or my sister, Christina.

While I was waiting at the airport, my thoughts went back to another time I had sat at the airport waiting to be picked up. I had been only a teenager, and I had waited three days before my mother picked me up.

*   *   *

Mary was as skinny as a skeleton because she was an alcoholic. She was tall, flat-chested, and she had big lips. She had blond hair and blue eyes like my sister and my mother. She had gotten pregnant in high school, dropped out, and married the father of the child. She ended up having two children with him. She convincingly told everyone that she had a college degree, but I knew that she didn't even graduate high school, let alone college. I'm not even sure she received her GED.

For the last decade, my mother and my sister, Christina, had treated her as if she were the daughter and sister instead of me. They had always treated me as if I were an outsider, as if somehow Mary was better than I was. Of course, I had been jealous of her because of this. My family should never have treated someone outside our immediate family better than they treated me, but that was what my mother and sister did. In fact, it seemed that for my whole life, there was always someone else in my place. My sister and my mother have always treated me as if I were less human than everyone else was. As I have stated to my sister many times, she acted as if she were of better stock than I was.

When we pulled up into my mother's driveway, Little Pete was standing there in front of the garage doors, very agitated and pacing back and forth. He could not even wait until I got out of the car before speaking with me.

Little Pete was a small black man about five-foot-six or seven. He could not have weighed more than 130 pounds soaking wet. He was skinny. He was around the age of sixty, and his skin was a soft brown. He was a very nice man with a southern accent. We used to tease my mother and Little Pete by saying they were like the characters from *Driving Ms. Daisy.* They were the best of friends, and Little Pete seemed to be driving my mother everywhere.

As I was trying to get out of Mary's rental car, Little Pete was standing right in front of me. He said in a very agitated, concerned voice, "Come on, Miss Belinda, come on."

I said to Little Pete, "Let me get my suitcases first."

Little Pete said, "Alright, Miss Belinda. Alright, let me help you. I need to talk to you, Miss Belinda, in private."

I said, "Okay, Little Pete, okay."

Mary just stood there, looking at us.

Little Pete gestured to me to go around the back of the house and said, "Miss Belinda, your mother is acting crazy! Big Pete, Christina, and Mary have been down in the basement drinking, and your momma is making me bring her buckets of hot water. She's pouring it over the cement around the pool, and even on the deck! She is in her bathrobe using a blow dryer, barefooted, trying to melt the ice and snow. I can't do a damn thing with her. Can you please get your momma back inside? Nobody will do anything about it! Miss Belinda, I'm afraid she's going to electrocute herself, as well as me!"

I replied angrily, "First of all, Little Pete, stop talking to me as if you are some kind of slave. Why are you acting like this? You are an employee, not a slave! You don't need to degrade yourself! You have never acted like this before!"

We were just standing in the front yard talking, and Little Pete said, "You're right, Belinda, I don't need to do that, but I have to around Big Pete. Your mom isn't just my employer, but my friend, and I don't . . ." Then he stopped and said, "I can't talk about that."

I said, "Okay, Little Pete, let's see what we can do for my mom."

We proceeded to go around to the back of the house, and be damned, there was my mother beside the swimming pool with a blow dryer in her hand, which was plugged into an extension cord that was plugged into an electrical socket on the outside of the house. She was barefooted and in a bathrobe. The temperature was two degrees. I went beside her, gave her a hug, took the blow dryer from her hands, and passed it to Little Pete, while I was hugging her. I gave her a big kiss on the cheek and said, "Come on inside with me, Mom. I'm freezing!"

Mom came in with me. I kept my arm around her waist as I guided her into the house. I looked over at my mother, and behind her Little Pete was moving his lips, saying, "Thank you." I just nodded my head and started consoling my mother.

I opened the French doors to the basement. Mom went in first. I looked up, and Mary was sitting at the bar already. Big Pete was standing behind the bar and said, "What's your poison?"

I said, "I need to get Mom upstairs."

I looked over to my left, and my sister, Christina, was getting up from the wicker love seat and walking towards us. She went to Mom's other side, put her arms around Mom, and hugged her.

I said, "Come on, Christina, come upstairs with Mom and me."

Christina followed Mom and me upstairs to Mom's bedroom. Mom decided to take a bath and get dressed. Christina went back downstairs. I went into the main bathroom upstairs and asked Mom if there was anything I could do for her. I could hear the water running into the bathtub. Mom started crying, "I lost my mother, Belinda. I lost my mother."

I felt completely helpless seeing my mother like this, knowing there just was nothing I could do. I said, "Momma, I know, I know."

All of a sudden Mom looked up at me with anger in her eyes and said, "How could you possibly know how I feel! You are always making things about you!"

My eyes opened wide and I said, "Mom, I'm sorry, I didn't mean it that way at all. I just didn't know what to say to make you feel a little bit better."

Mom said, "Just get out of here, Belinda! Just leave me alone!"

I looked at her, let out a sigh, walked out of the bathroom, and went back downstairs to the bar. I was just glad I had gotten her inside the house.

I came down the steps, and the basement was silent. Christina walked over to me and hugged me. I guessed we hugged each other for several minutes. As I let go of her, I looked into her deep blue eyes. They were filled with tears. For one split second, I felt as though I were her big sister again. It was like when we were small children, and I was her hero. Mary said something, and that look was gone again. Christina's attention went back to the bar where Mary was sitting and Big Pete was on the other side making drinks. I watched as they started talking among themselves. I let out a sigh, sat in one of the chairs, and looked at the television screen. I felt so sad and lonely.

I didn't talk to anyone the rest of the evening. I just sat in my chair and listened to their chatter. We buried my grandmother the next day. When I stood up in front of the church to give the eulogy, looked at my grandmother's casket, and started speaking, the tears started flowing.

We went outside and as they carried my grandmother's casket to the burial plot. I knew that everything would change again in my mother's family. It would never be the same. We would all drift even further apart. When it was my turn to lay the rose on my grandmother's casket, I said softly, "Goodbye, Grandma." I looked up at my mother. She must have heard me and gave me an angry look. I just didn't understand why. To this day, I have no idea why she was angry with me.

After we buried my grandmother, we all went to the church meeting hall. All my life they have had dinners and other church functions there. Mom and Uncle Poppy provided food and drink for all the mourners. Mom wanted Christina and me to go to Auntie Bea's house. I think Auntie Bea had left several hours earlier, if she even showed up. I don't remember. All I remember was Christina and I went to check on Auntie Bea. By that time, Christina had drunk several glasses of wine.

Christina had the keys to Mom's old pickup truck, and I said, "Christina, let me drive. You had a few too many glasses of wine and I think it would be better if I drove because I did not drink."

Christina became upset and said, "No, I'm driving."

I let out another sigh, and let her drive. It had been years since I had been home to Virginia, and I didn't remember exactly how to get to Auntie

Bea's house. I don't think Christina had ever been there. I made a mistake and had her turn too soon. It had been snowing earlier in the week. It had melted and then re-froze. There was ice on the roads everywhere.

It only took a moment before I realized we had made a wrong turn. I told Christina she would have to turn around because this was the wrong turn. Of course, my drunken sister was stuck in the muddy ice and snow on the side of the road.

I told her, "Stop, Christina! You're causing the wheels to sink deeper!" I let out a sigh again as I continued, "Now, Christina, listen to me this time, and do what I tell you to do, so I can get us out of the muddy ice puddles."

Christina snarled, "Okay, okay, Belinda!"

I looked around the road and found a couple of medium-sized logs. I was lucky and found a large piece of plywood that must have fallen off a truck. I put everything I had found under the back wheels, which were stuck. My little sister had made the mud holes even deeper, and the tires were stuck at least halfway or more. She did what I told her to, and I pushed with all my strength. We got the tires out of the holes. By now, of course, my good dress I had worn to the funeral was covered with mud, and my high-heeled shoes were ruined because of my stupidity. I should have changed first!

I walked to the back of the truck where I had a bag of clothes: jeans, a sweatshirt, and sneakers. Because we were out in the country, and on an isolated road, I started to change my clothes.

Christina got out of the truck, came around, and said, "Good idea."

She started changing out of her good clothes to her casual ones also. I just looked at her, disappointed. She did not even bother to get out and help me do the dirty work. I sighed again.

Looking back, it seems to me as if I sighed the entire time I was around my family. At this point, I wished I was in my uniform, back in my world. Christina started talking—as if she were some kind of prophet—about my feelings. It was a lot of garbled psychobabble. What I did hear from her babbling was that everyone considered me a kindred spirit to Grandma. People handle their stress in different ways, and there was no need for me to be jealous of her.

I sat there thinking, *You stupid little twit! I'm not jealous of you. I am jealous of your relationship with Mary and everyone else you put in my place. You treat me as if I'm not good enough to be your friend and sister.*

I finally said, "Christina, just shut up! Just stop it! You have had too much wine! If you want to keep driving, I would appreciate it if you kept your mind on the road and stopped talking." Then, there was silence. A few minutes later, Christina and I arrived at Auntie Bea's house. We were only able to visit for about an hour before her phone rang. It was my mother checking in to see if Christina and I were there. Auntie Bea passed the phone over to me. Mother asked if Christina and I could come back to her place before it got too late. So Christina and I said our goodbyes to Auntie Bea, and we both gave her a kiss on her cheek.

When we returned to Mom's house, about an hour later, the driveway was full of cars. We went inside and walked down to the basement. There must have been at least a dozen people there. They were all drinking and having a good old time. My mother was in the midst of everyone, talking and laughing. I didn't know who most of the people were, only Mary, Jay (Big Pete's son), and Christina. I don't think Mom heard us come in because she stood with her back to the stairs, talking with a woman named Jean. As I stood behind her, I heard her tell Jean that I was like a dog that needed attention. I was not really her daughter; I was adopted. I just stood there and looked at her in total disbelief.

Jean looked at me and asked, "Who are you?"

My mother turned around as she blushed. I got the impression she wasn't sure if I had heard the conversation.

I answered calmly, "I'm the adopted dog."

I simply went outside and I walked around the wooded yard wondering, *Why would she say such a lie?* I just shook my head and lit a cigarette. I stood there thinking, *I had better go back to my world. Where it's sane, disciplined, and has some type of order to it.*

About a half an hour later, Jean came out and asked, "Belinda, can I speak to you?"

I thought, *Here we go, more bull.* I factitiously smiled and answered, "Sure."

Jean was a tall slender woman in her mid sixties. She had short salt and pepper hair with deep brown eyes. She was wearing a black long sleeved dress that flowed to her knees. She was wearing a long black wool coat with large gold buttons. She had a checkered black and white scarf that loosely draped down her coat that was still opened, revealing her black dress.

She was having a hard time walking through the wooded area in her shiny black heels. I noticed the heels of her shoes desperately needed repair.

I know she was friends with my mother for several years and I do not believe she ever met my grandmother. I assumed she went to my grandmother's funeral per the request of my mother.

Jean spoke with a soft and patient voice as she introduced herself and explained who she was. We sat down on one of the cement benches that were scattered throughout the wooded area and both crossed our arms across our chests. We were very cold, even with our coats on. "Belinda, your mother explained more to me after you left the room. She said that she meant like an adopted child. She loves dogs, and it was easier for her to explain to me who you are by using the term 'dogs' because she says she relates to animals better than she does people. She didn't mean that you are adopted in that sense. She knows you came from her belly."

I just rolled my eyes as the crap spewed from this poor woman's lips; it was just more than I could bear. She continued, "It must be hard for a soldier to have to relate to civilians in such a manner, and I'm sure you're trained to handle stress a certain way."

I remember thinking, *Oh, brother, the stupid crap and the ignorance of the military coming out of this woman's mouth.*

She started talking on about a relative of hers in WWII and blah, blah. That was all I could take. I finally said in a disciplined and quiet tone, "Ma'am, I'm sorry if this is going to come across rudely, but it's none of your business. I don't really care what you think you know because you don't know anything about this. So please go back inside, enjoy yourself at my mother's expense, and shut your mouth. I have had enough horse crap for one day. Thank you very much for taking the time out to talk to me. I think being compared to a dog speaks for itself. I know exactly what my mother is, and I tolerate it. To set the record straight, when I joined the Army many years ago, my mother thought I was somehow insulting her. She smacked me in the face and tried to order me not to join. She said that people would think I was a freak because I'm a girl, and I'm her daughter. So please, please, I do not want to hurt your feelings any further and say things that will offend you. Just go, and don't worry about my mother and me."

I did my best to keep from laughing. The look on that poor woman's face was priceless. I don't think she knew what to do, or if she had been insulted or not. As I think about it, I let out a chuckle. Believe me, if she had a day like I had . . .

I stayed outside for a few hours and waited until I heard cars starting up and leaving. I went back into the basement through the French doors on the side of the house. Christina, Mary, and Mom were sitting on the love seat, squeezed together. I sat down in one of the side chairs next to the love seat. They all looked up at me.

Mom got up, came over, and whispered in my ear, "I'm sorry, Belinda. You know me. I don't know why I say such hurtful untruths."

I stretched my arms out for her to give me a hug and whispered back into her ear, "I'm still angry with you, but I love you." I looked up at her; she was smiling again. She went and sat in between Christina and Mary again.

I walked over to the bar. Big Pete was so drunk that he had to lean on the bar to keep from falling over. I said, with a smile on my face, "Big Pete, can I have that drink now?"

He slurred, "S-s-s-sure. What do you want?"

I replied, "In your condition, just a beer."

He laughed and said, "You got it."

I took my beer from him, took a sip, and walked back to the chair. By that time, Mom, Christina, and Mary were talking about my grandmother's jewelry. They were talking about who was going to get which pieces and what they wanted. I sat there and listened to the crap for thirty minutes as they gossiped about other relatives taking what, where, and when. Just giggling, giggling, and giggling, and how they were going to take it all. By the time I finished my beer, I could not take any more. I stood up and fussed at them, "Shame on you, shame on all of you! My grandmother isn't even cold in her grave, and you all are already squabbling over what she had! I've had enough! I'm going to bed!" I started to walk upstairs.

Christina followed me. She stood at the bottom of the stairs and yelled up, "Belinda, that's just the facts of life."

I yelled back, "Bull!" I went to bed.

I was woken up from a dead sleep by Mother shaking me. I said in a sleepy tone, "What?" She pushed me over and crawled under the covers with me. I said, "Momma, what do you want? What time is it?"

Mom turned to me and said, "It's late, but I need to talk to you."

I rubbed the sleep from my eyes and turned over to face her in the bed.

She whispered, "Belinda, I love you. You gave a great eulogy, and everyone has been talking about it all day. You seemed to make sure you touched everyone's hearts regarding your grandmother. You told the truth, but you made it sound bigger than life. Your grandmother is proud of what you did for her memory, but I have to tell you something, something bad, and I know you're not going to like it."

Here we go again. I let out a sigh and got out of the bed. I walked over to the light switch. As I turned on the light, I looked over at my mother, who was creeping out of the bed as I asked, "If you're going to tell me whatever it is, I want a drink and a cigarette. Has everyone gone to bed?"

She whispered to me, "Yes. Go downstairs, get yourself a drink, and meet me in my bedroom."

I said, "Mom, I want a cigarette. We will have to go outside."

Mom said, "No, Belinda, it's too cold. I'll let you smoke it outside my window. Just don't tell anyone."

I whispered, "Okay, Momma." I got a beer and went to her bedroom. I hoped that whatever she said, I wouldn't go psycho over it. She cracked the window and proceeded to tell me the wicked truth. Thank God I had a cigarette. She murmured she had not done what I asked of her many years ago.

It's here in my face again full circle. I felt as if I was betrayed again, from the grave, because of my mother. I finished the beer and put my cigarette butt in the bottle. After she finished, I was so angry, I could hardly contain myself.

She told me Grandmother had taken her out of her will because of what she had done with my grandfather. I was so angry, hurt, and disappointed in my mother. I sat there and held my tongue until the right words came to me. It must have been an eternity for her. She sat there looking at me with her eyes wide, waiting for my response. Finally, I just let it all out.

"Damn it woman! I told you after Granddaddy's funeral to fix it and to make amends with Grandma. What you did to her was wrong, and you know it! I don't give a damn what your excuses are now! Grandma is dead! Christina and I have to pay the price, again, for your wicked deception. I'm tired of it, Momma, tired of it! Do you understand me? I have put up with a lot of crazy crap simply because you're my mother! I have told you repeatedly to leave the dirty piece of crap, Big Pete. I have asked you repeatedly if you fixed it, and you told me you did! You lied, Momma! You lied again! I know damn well that you and Big Pete have profited off of Grandma because there is a brand new Cadillac sitting in your garage! The two of you are spending money like its water! I know damn well that you profited from Granddaddy's death too! Now, Momma, you had better fix it! I mean it this time; you better find some way to fix it."

Without saying another word, I walked out of her room and went downstairs. Mom started crying. By this time, it was around 4:00 a.m. I went into the kitchen and started making coffee. I was so angry. Mom came into the kitchen, still crying.

She continued our previous conversation by saying, "I can't fix it, Belinda! I can't fix it!" Her voice had gotten louder.

My voice also was louder. "What do you want from me, Mom? You have taken and taken from me my entire life! Then you treat me as if I'm some type of plague! You come running back to me when you've done something else bad to me and beg for my forgiveness! It's never ending, Momma! Never ending!" She started crying louder and louder. At this point, I was almost immune to her tears.

She sniffled and said, "I'm sorry, Belinda, I'm sorry."

I said in a softer tone, "I'm just tired of all the drama. If you can't fix it, you can't fix it."

By then Big Pete was awake, and he came into the kitchen. He started yelling because Mom had already done the fake heart attack again. Big Pete yelled, "Don't you talk to your mother like that! I'm calling the doctor!"

I retorted, "Oh, forget it, Pete. I'm going home!" I got on the phone and changed my flight for that morning.

I started to call a cab, but Big Pete finally said, "No, Belinda, I'll take you." Mom then started the fake heart attack crap again.

I went upstairs, packed my things, came back downstairs with my luggage in hand, and asked Big Pete, "Are you ready?"

Big Pete answered, "Yes."

Mom yelled at me, "Don't go! Don't go!"

I turned around, looked at her, let out another sigh, and said in a calmer tone, "Momma, one of these days you're going to cry wolf one too many times, and I won't be there." I turned around and walked out the door.

CHAPTER VIII

Big Pete dropped me off at the Snobville Airport. I checked my luggage and sat there, waiting for my flight.

I remembered my grandfather's funeral that took place almost five years earlier. Thomas was along that time, and we were going up to the Hollow in Mom's Cadillac. Mom was driving, I was in the passenger's seat, and Thomas was in the backseat. As Mom was driving, she proceeded to tell me that Grandma was angry with her.

I asked my mother, "Why?"

She told me, "Years ago your granddaddy adopted me and made me his executor and left all of his possessions to me. He did not want your grandmother to know because he did not like your Uncle Poppy. He knew your grandmother would make him adopt Uncle Poppy too."

I immediately became very angry with my mother. I said, "How could you do that? You know you're wrong! You should have told Grandma. How would you like it if Big Pete, your husband, adopted me, made me executor of his estate, and left me everything? Momma, Granddaddy was her husband, not yours."

Mom pulled over to the side of the road, got out, and dropped to her knees. She started sobbing with one hand on her chest, and her other arm stretched out to the heavens. "My heart! My heart! Thomas, could you please get me my purse? My medicine is in it. I think I'm having a heart attack."

Of course, my husband had never seen anyone fake something like that.

I told my mother, in a very angry voice, "Please, Mother, you have pulled that one on me too many times. I'll get her purse, Thomas." I opened up her purse and she had a porcelain pillbox in it. I looked in it, and it had Valium and other pills that she used to get high.

Mom started yelling, "Let Thomas do it, Belinda!"

Thomas looked at me as if I were a monster.

Mom said to Thomas, "Thomas, could you please drive for me? Belinda, get in the backseat."

I said, "Oh, Mother, you only do this when you know you're wrong, and you've been caught. You only fake a heart attack when you can't prove you're innocent. Do you know, Momma, there is a show called *Sanford and Son*? And Sanford always does that heart attack bit to get his way."

Then she started the crying bit. I know her tears are genuine at the time she does it, and I think she is truly remorseful. She never thinks about the consequences of her actions and the reactions of others. My mother is a very self-absorbed individual. Do I dare say spoiled?

I calmly said, "Momma, you will give everything back to Grandma and let her take the helm as executor of Granddaddy's estate. You will tell her you are sorry and beg her to forgive you, or I will stay angry with you forever."

Mom turned around in her seat, looked at me, and then looked at Thomas. She said, "Of course, Belinda, I will fix it. I promise. I just didn't think everyone would go crazy about it."

It wasn't worth a retort. I just simply said, "Good. Just do the right thing, Momma. After all she is your mother, and she didn't deserve this."

Mom said, "You're right, just don't be mad at me anymore. You're my daughter, and I love you."

I said, "I love you too, Momma. Just fix it and make things right again."

CHAPTER IX

I looked up from the window and the flight attendant asked which meal I would like. I chose the turkey sandwich and asked if I could get a few more vodkas and another can of tomato juice. She said that the other flight attendant was behind her, and she would take care of that for me. I said "Thank you" and started eating my sandwich.

After having my drink and finishing my meal, I started thinking of happier times. I was kind of looking forward to seeing some of my cousins after all these years, even if most of them were alcoholics, drug abusers, and just plain white trash. It would be nice to see if any of them had grown up and made something of their lives, instead of wasting them. Sam, May, John, and Samantha were my Great-Uncle Frank's children. They were my second cousins. Uncle Frank, even though he was my grandmother's brother, was closer in age to my mother. My mother and Uncle Frank basically grew up together. I remember her saying numerous times that Uncle Frank was more a brother to her than Uncle Poppy.

My Great-Uncle Frank only had a third-grade education. He was an alcoholic and lied about everything and anything. We would sugarcoat his behavior, saying that he told "tall tales." It sounded better than admitting he was a liar. My memories wandered again, and I started remembering the cousin that I truly loved the most. The one who I thought was going to be someone great—my beloved Gary. I couldn't help but feel remorse and loss for him.

My Auntie Bea had a seventh-grade education. She also lied, but not as frequently as Uncle Frank did. She liked sipping wine from time to time, but she was not an alcoholic. She was more like my mother, pretending to be something more than what she really was, but I guess we all do that from time to time. She had only one son, Gary. It makes me want to cry just remembering what happened to poor Gary. He tried to kill a police officer, and after that, Auntie Bea and my mother put him

31

in a mental institution. He was diagnosed with paranoid schizophrenia and was heavily medicated because it was against the law to perform a lobotomy.

If my memory was correct, he had also thrown Auntie Bea down the stairs, breaking her hip, and he had almost killed Uncle Herndon. There was another time when he had a large amount of cocaine and pot in the trunk of his car, and he drove his car through a police blockade resulting in thousands of dollars in damage. Somehow, Auntie Bea, Uncle Herndon, and my mother were able to keep him out of jail.

They had kept his violent behavior and fixation on the military a secret for many years from the rest of the family and the authorities. When he was finally arrested, he attacked the police officer because he thought he was a Russian spy. They discovered an arsenal of weapons in his trailer. I am so glad that Mom got him off the streets, kept him out of our messed up judicial system, and placed him into a mental institution where he could receive proper treatment.

This all happened long before I met Thomas. I was stationed somewhere overseas, and I had not been home in a few years. One time when I called my mom, just to check in, she asked if I could take some leave and come visit her. That's when Auntie Bea and Mom told me the story of Gary. After hearing it, I wanted to see him. Of course, they conveniently left out a lot about the weapons, his fixation on the military, and much, much more. That's why I just couldn't believe he was like that. The last time I really knew Gary, or had any contact with him, was when I was a teenager.

The Gary I knew had been a very talented young man. He could pick up any instrument and teach himself how to play it. He could play a tune after listening to it one time. It was incredible! He could do so much, and when I was younger, I thought he was very cool. I loved him, and we hung out together frequently when I lived with my grandmother. We were best friends.

Mom and Auntie Bea took me to visit him at the Western State Mental Asylum. Apparently, he had been there only a month or two. It looked like a jail camp when we went into the greeting area. When we walked through the doors, Mom told them who we were and that we would like to see Gary. I had to fill out some forms, and then we were escorted into a room with nothing but a table and some chairs. Mom had one of my hands clutched to her chest, and Auntie Bea had the other one clutched to her chest. At the time, I didn't understand their fear. On the way to the asylum, we had stopped at a country store. Auntie Bea had bought Gary a Big Gulp, and I bought him some fudge. Auntie Bea had the Big Gulp in her hands and handed it to him when he came in. Her hands were trembling. I had the bag of fudge, but I immediately got up, went over to him, and hugged him. He hugged me back and kissed me on my cheek.

He said, "Belinda, are you here to get me out of this hellhole that your mother and my mother put me in?"

I didn't answer him. Instead, I turned around and said, "Sit down with me, Gary."

He sat down in the chair next to mine, and moved it very close to mine. He took my arm, crossed it into his arm, holding my arm and hand tightly across his chest with his arm locking mine in place to his chest. He acted as if I were leaving and never coming back. He asked again, "Are you getting me out of this place?"

I looked at him, took my arm back, got out my cigarettes, and offered him one. He never blinked. He just stared at me. There was something missing from the dear cousin that I once knew and loved. He was cold, and the laughter was missing from him. I started to feel uncomfortable because he was sitting so close to me, staring blankly.

He then answered me, "Yeah, I'll take one of those reds."

He lit both our cigarettes with his silver lighter. I sat and watched as he turned the length of the cigarette into ash with just one inhale. He then placed it in the ashtray to put it out. I had never seen anyone smoke an entire cigarette in one breath.

I said, "I have something for you." I pushed the bag toward him. As he was opening the bag, I looked across the table. Mom and Auntie Bea were both watching us. Their eyes were as big as saucers. I turned around, looked at the door that had a small barred window and saw the back of a guard's head there. I was becoming more uneasy.

I looked back to Gary, and he said, "Oh, good, you got me something good."

I asked, "Are you going to eat them?"

He patted my knee under the table and answered, "No, I'll save them for later."

Just then, I realized that Gary thought I gave him some fudge laced with pot because Gary and I used to smoke marijuana together when I was a teenager. Rather than correct him, I let him believe I had laced the fudge. I shook off the uneasy feeling and started chatting with him. I brought up the time that he and I had spent together. I told him that he had always been my favorite cousin, and that he still was. I would laugh and then he would force himself to laugh because that part of my Gary was long gone. Auntie Bea and Mom then started to settle down and join our conversation. Mom and Auntie Bea kept changing the subject regarding what I was doing then. Garry started asking questions, and before we knew it, three hours had passed, and it was time for us to leave. We got up from our chairs to leave.

Gary grabbed me by my arm with a firm grip and asked, "Belinda, you're not leaving me here?"

I turned and looked at him, but before I had a chance to answer him, he pleaded, "There's nothing wrong with me, Belinda. I did those things because I was drunk and high. Belinda, please don't leave me here."

Tears filled my eyes because of the empathy I felt for my beloved cousin. By now, I knew he was mentally ill. I grabbed him, hugged him as tightly as I could, and kissed him square on the mouth. I said, "Gary, you are sick, and I want you to get better for me so we can go party. You don't think you're sick, but you are. Do this for me. You do what your mother and my mother tell you to do when I'm not here. They both love you. They didn't want to do this, but you have to admit, this is better than jail. Get better, and I'll get you out of here."

He looked at me, stunned. "I love you, Belinda, you're my best friend. If you say I'm sick, then I am. I will get better for you, but I'm not going to do it for my mother or yours. But I will respect them for you."

I said, "That's fine. I'm on leave for a few weeks and I promise I will be back before I leave."

Gary asked, "You promise?"

I solemnly answered, "I promise."

I went to see him twice more before I left and every time I came home on leave. I made it my first priority to see him. I wrote to him all the time. It broke my heart to lie to him because I knew he would never get better. When we left from my first visit, I looked at Mom and Auntie Bea and asked angrily, "Why did you set me up like that?"

Mom chimed in before Auntie Bea had a chance to answer, "Belinda, we didn't tell you that Gary's illness was fixated on the military because we didn't know if he would respond to you. We wanted to keep him from being angry with us. We are all he has, and we don't want him upset with us. We knew if you couldn't keep him from being angry with us, we would never feel safe around him. We know now he will do what you tell him to do because you're a soldier, and he trusts you."

I said, "That's bull, Momma. I was just in there with him. He has no emotions at all. Who do you think you're fooling? He mimics another's emotion."

Auntie Bea gave her two cents. "No, Belinda, he does have some emotions—anger or hostility, I'm not sure which it would be."

Mom remarked, "Belinda, they had just medicated him before we arrived."

I confessed to both women, "Okay, okay, you know more about this than I do." I just let out a sigh, as I shook my head in disbelief.

CHAPTER X

Sam was my great-uncle Frank's younger son. Sam had turned out to be an arrogant and conceited individual. He had nothing to do with a person unless he thought that person could do something for him. At one time, when we were children and teenagers, I had believed he was truly my friend. He thought he was intelligent, but the truth was, he was just a pothead and cocaine addict like most of Uncle Frank's other children. When he was younger, I saw the potential in him to become someone better than what he turned out to be. I guess I loved him and he disappointed me, but I still wanted to see him. I hoped I would find something to change my mind. Sam had joined the Navy but was given a general discharge for not being able to adapt to military life. He had been arrested for domestic battery against his first wife. He had been going downhill ever since. Sam was a few years older than I was, but he had failed a grade or two in high school, and we had graduated high school together.

I first moved in with Grandma when I was a teenager. Uncle Frank's trailer was right next to the old homestead house that my grandmother lived in. That's one reason Sam and I became close. After we had been at the same school for a bit, I discovered from some of our shared friends that Sam had been bragging all over the high school that his cool, beautiful cousin was coming to town. How silly it seemed, as I think back. I've never considered myself beautiful. We hung out all the time when I first moved up there, but of course, things change.

I played field hockey in high school, and I remembered one time when it was canceled, I took the bus home to the Hollow. When I got off the bus, Aunt Janet and Uncle Poppy were sitting on the flatbed trailer of one of the big trucks he owned.

I was mentally preparing myself to hike the two miles down the dirt and graveled driveway when Uncle Poppy, who was lighting a cigarette, asked, "What's your hurry, Belinda?"

I answered, "I'm sure Grandma has chores for me since I'm home early."

Uncle Poppy said, "No, she doesn't because she's headed for the grocery store and told me to tell you to wait for her here."

I said, "Okay."

I don't know why but, out of the blue, Uncle Poppy started his usual tirade. He said, "You know what, Belinda, your mother is a marrying whore and a stupid woman for giving birth to a dyke kid like you."

I scrunched my eyebrows together because I knew that I didn't hear him correctly, and asked, "What?"

He answered, "You heard me."

I said, "No, I'm sure I didn't."

He said it again. I was very confused. I didn't even know what "dyke" meant. I never had heard the word before. I was scared! I knew he was goading me into a fight. I took him on anyway, knowing he was going to kick my butt. I said, "Uncle Poppy, I would appreciate you not talking about my mother that way in my presence. What you just said and then repeated was the most hurtful and nastiest thing you could say to a child."

He said, "That's the best you got? I knew you were a yellow-bellied dyke."

I let out a vicious giggle and said, "Well, Uncle Poppy, I guess it is the best I've got because I don't know what dyke means. Instead of the malicious pretense that you're spewing from your lips, let's get it on. For some unknown reason all you want to do is abuse me. I stand by what I said—don't talk about my momma like that again, or I'll finish you, you sorry jerk. Is that what you want? Bring it on!"

As I suspected, Uncle Poppy started walking toward me and smacked me hard across my face. I took my fists and hit him in the gut. Then I bent down and pulled his good leg out from under him. We kept fighting until I somehow pulled his wood leg off him. He grabbed it from me and beat me with it until I fell to the ground.

Sam and his friend arrived just as I was passing out. They started beating on Uncle Poppy. When I woke up, Sam and Granddaddy were carrying me. They put me into the back of Granddaddy's 1930s Ford pickup truck. My grandmother had a stick in her hand and was telling Uncle Poppy and Aunt Janet to get off her land. I think the only reason she said that was because Sam's friend was there. Sam saved me from being killed that day! I guess it hurts that I have lost him because I did love him so much back then. He was my hero that day, and I never have forgotten that. How people change through the sands of time.

I then started thinking about the time when we were all visiting Grandma. Thomas and I were married, and Christina was married to Chris, her first husband. He was a Navy pilot. In fact, my mother introduced Christina to Chris when he was a student at the local college.

I guess I wasn't the "cool cat in town" anymore because Sam snubbed Thomas and me the entire time we were there. He hung out with Chris, Christina, and Mary. I guess Thomas and I weren't so impressive anymore. Their conduct was outright rude to Thomas and me. Of course, Thomas and I just shrugged our shoulders, did our duty, and visited with the kinfolk.

CHAPTER XI

John was my great-uncle Frank's oldest son. John was, and always had been, a worthless, lazy, two-faced jerk. He was just plain weird and a strange character. He was several years older than I was. He didn't move out of Grandma's house until he was in his thirties. He married Ann, who had an ugly personality. Just another dysfunctional personality added to the mix. They are filthy people living in their own garbage. I remember the time when my other cousin, Samantha, and I went up into John's bedroom. I was living with Grandma at the time, and we were teenagers. We were in John's bedroom because we were looking for something that he had said we could use. I don't remember anymore what it was that we were looking for, but I do remember that there were *Playgirl* magazines under his bed. This memory stuck with me because it had pictures of naked men, and I had never seen a magazine like that before.

Samantha and I started looking at the pictures and giggled like teenage girls do. There were also balled-up tissues and hand cream all over the floor around John's bed. At the time, we didn't know what that was all about. We just knew it was nasty! I remembered another time when Christina and I were visiting my grandmother in the Hollow. I guess Christina and I were about nine or ten years old. I remember that I was playing basketball or something with Sam. Christina was off somewhere in the Hollow with John, Samantha, and May. Uncle Frank called Sam because he wanted Sam to do something for him, so I went looking for my sister and my other cousins.

I found them up at what we called "the rock." The rock was located on one side of the mountains that surrounded the small valley between the mountains. That is why it was called the Hollow. This homestead has been in our family for over two hundred years. The cabin that my grandmother lived in was at least two hundred years old as well. It was surrounded by woods and mountains. It was a very beautiful place, accessible only by a two-and-a-half-mile dirt road that branched off the state road. I believe the mountain farm was about sixty-six acres. Christina, May, and Samantha were lying there, completely naked. John had one of their Barbie dolls and was touching my cousins with the doll where he should not have been touching them. I remember yelling at him that I was going to tell on him. I didn't know for sure what he was doing, but I did know it wasn't a good thing. I also knew Christina, May, and Samantha didn't know any better. I ran back down the path to the cabin, ran inside, and breathlessly started telling my grandmother what I saw. Shortly after that, John came inside.

My grandmother took him outside. I followed them. She walked over to the old, big willow tree and cut a switch off. She made John watch her. Then she started swatting him on his back end with it and yelled that he was a nasty little boy. John started running from her, which made her even angrier. When she caught him again, she started switching harder. John was crying. She stopped after a dozen or so swats, and yelled at him to go up to his room and not to expect any supper. Grandma then turned around, looked at me, and switched me one time on the butt. She said, "That's for being a tattletale."

I just stood there stunned. I started to cry and asked, "Why wasn't I supposed to tell?"

She answered, "Because you were to hit him, make your sister and cousins get dressed, and get away from him." She asked, still angry with me, "Do you understand, Belinda?"

I fearfully answered, "No, Grandma." Be damned if that old woman didn't switch me again.

Then she said, "Stop being a smart ass. You protect your own. You were raised better than this, Belinda. It's called mountain justice. A strong person takes action; a weak person tattletales, which is asking someone else to handle it for them. Only if you cannot handle it yourself, should you seek help!"

In my child mind, I still didn't understand. I thought I had been protecting my own by telling Grandma. To keep from being switched again, I answered, "I understand, Grandma."

She said, "Good. Now go and get your sister and your cousins from their hiding places." I went and got them.

She then gave each one of them a lick with the switch. She told them all, "Don't you ever take your clothes off again for a boy to play with you in that manner. If I find out, I will switch each one of you again."

Be damned if Christina didn't get mad at me, and she stayed mad at me for several days. I didn't know Grandma was going to switch us over it. I thought John was the only one at fault.

CHAPTER XII

The next person I started thinking about was another favorite cousin, Samantha. Samantha is my great-uncle Frank's oldest daughter. I just adored her when we were teenagers. We were close when I was living with my grandmother, and we were close in age. I thought she was smarter than my other cousins were, and she had a very cool personality. She was laid back and self-assured. She talked to me often and befriended me. I don't know why, but I just liked her. She didn't keep in touch after I moved, but none of the others did either.

I chuckle to myself as I remember the stupid things Samantha and I did as teenagers. One thing in particular stands out in my memory from when I was about sixteen years old. Samantha and I had played hooky one day. I think that was the first and last time we did that. Of course, we were caught. Only the two of us could have such luck. Me and my stupid ideas. In those days, Samantha would have followed me to the end of the earth. I had a fake ID and my learner's permit for driving. Uncle Frank was working the day shift, and all the adults were at work. It was a perfect day to get away with something bad. For some reason, Uncle Frank had left his pickup truck home, and Samantha knew where he kept the keys.

"Let's drive to the country store, I'll buy us some good wine, and we can get drunk."

Samantha replied with a gleam in her eye, "Yes, yes," and she started to giggle.

I grabbed some money and a couple of joints, we jumped into the truck, and I started it up.

Samantha asked for one of the joints, and I took it out of my purse and gave it to her. We sat there with the engine running and smoked the joint. By now, I was stoned yet attempting to drive.

As I remember this fateful day, I realize how stupid Samantha and I were. I put the pickup in drive, and we took off down the dirt road. We didn't even make it a mile! The truck was running, but it wouldn't move any further.

Samantha asked, "Belinda, what's wrong with the truck?"

I answered, "I don't know."

We both got out of the truck, and I started looking at the tires.

I frantically cried out, "Oh, no! No wonder Uncle Frank left the truck."

Samantha came around to where I was standing, and fearfully proclaimed, "Oh, shit, we're in trouble now!"

I asked, "Oh, shit, how are we going to fix this?"

Apparently, the tire was already flat. After we drove it down the mountainside on a gravel dirt road, it didn't really look like a tire anymore. There was rubber completely wrapped around the entire axle and the metal rim of the wheel was bent into a bizarre shape. We looked at each other and said it again together, "Oh, shit!"

I said, "Let's smoke this last joint now, before we get into trouble for having it in our possession."

We stood there smoking the joint and saying over and over again, "Oh, shit! Oh, shit!" We then decided to leave the truck and go back to the trailer.

Before we could start home, we saw Uncle Frank's car coming toward us. Our eyes grew wide, and we kept saying, "Oh, shit! Oh, shit! Oh, shit!"

Uncle Frank stopped the car in front of the pickup truck. He got out of the car and looked at us standing there with our eyes as big as saucers.

Uncle Frank yelled, "What is going on here? What is my truck doing here? Why aren't you two girls in school?"

Samantha and I just looked at each other. We didn't say a word.

Uncle Frank walked towards us and looked down at the back tire. He started yelling, "You girls, what the heck have you done? If you were going to take my truck without asking, you could have at least looked at the tires to see if they were flat before taking off with it! Damn girls, you messed my truck up!"

He immediately assumed Samantha did it. He grabbed her by the arm and pulled her over to the messed-up axle. He started yelling at her and said, "You stupid girl! Look what kind of mess you got your cousin in! You are a bad influence on her, making her play hooky! She's going to make it in this world! You're not! You don't need to drag her down with you! She's

Jane's kid, and she is going to go places! Now get your little butt over here, and help me get this tire unwrapped from the axle!"

He continued, "First, you walk back up to the house, get my tool box, and bring it back. Don't expect to get any supper tonight, and expect to get your little butt whipped too."

He just acted as if I wasn't even there. I stood there as Samantha looked up at me with bitter eyes.

I was not about to let my cousin take the blame for something I did! I just wasn't going to allow it!

I said, "Uncle Frank, Samantha did not do this. I did. I'm the one who had her play hooky with me. How dare you talk to my cousin in such a manner? She is your daughter, and I think she is cool! If I'm going to go places, I will take her with me, if she wants." I was very scared, but I stood my ground.

I thought for sure Uncle Frank was going to beat me for mouthing at him, but he didn't. Instead, he got up from the ground, walked over, stood over me, and said in a calm voice, "You disappoint me, Belinda. It's too late for my kids. I know what they are and what they will be. You're better than this, and you just proved it simply by what you just said. Do you think for one moment that one of my kids would stand up for you? I know they would have allowed you to take the blame. You didn't, and that's why I'm not punishing you. Now both you girls go back to the house, and if I ever catch the two of you playing hooky again, you both will get a whipping. Do I make myself clear?"

We both nodded our heads gesturing a yes.

I was ready to say something back to him, but before I could utter a word, Uncle Frank looked at me and said, "Not another word, Belinda. You spoke your mind. Now let it go."

As Samantha and I were walking back to the trailer and Grandma's house, Samantha said, "Thank you, Belinda. I would have done the same for you."

I said, "I know you would have. Don't mind Uncle Frank, Samantha. He's just mad because he got it wrong. He had to lay blame on you somehow. I know he doesn't really feel that way."

Samantha bitterly remarked, "Oh, yes, he does, Belinda."

We walked back in silence. I guess I understood that day why Uncle Frank's children hated him so much. I know I would have. Uncle Frank had no faith in his children, but at the time, I did. I even had hope for old

John. After that, Samantha started to drift slowly from me. She eventually dropped out of high school and married her sweetheart. Not because she was pregnant, but because that was the path of life she chose. I did everything in my power to keep her with me, but I lost her in the sands of time as well.

Finally, I thought about May, the youngest out of my four cousins and the youngest daughter of my great-uncle Frank. I didn't know her very well when I was a teenager because she was much younger than I was. The last time I saw her had been at my wedding. I met her husband Hank Harp. He was a scruffy man and at least twenty years her elder. May was slightly mentally challenged. I hate the word mentally "retarded" because it's such an ugly word. I knew she was a little bit dimwitted, but I didn't see her as being challenged. I didn't know her very well, though. She did graduate high school, but she didn't make it either in life. She's still a pothead, drug addict, and alcoholic. For that matter, Samantha is too, but Samantha only uses marijuana. John never really did drugs or drink; his challenges are of a different kind.

CHAPTER XIII

The flight attendant asked for my trash, and I handed it to her. About thirty minutes later, I heard the announcement that we would be landing soon. I had a transfer flight, so I had to run to make it on time. This was the last stretch of my journey, and it was about an hour long. It was one of the smaller planes, and there were few people on board. I buckled up, and as we took off, I started thinking about my sister, Christina. I wondered if I needed her help, would she give it? I didn't know if our mother had called her. I always had thought Christina was our mother's favorite because of the way she treated each of us. My thoughts started to drift again back into time.

*   *   *

I guess I lost my sister's love and friendship when I was about twelve years old. It seemed that after our parents divorced our relationship slowly began to change. I would take one side, and she took the other. We always flip-flopped back and forth. Even if I was right, she would take the other side. That's the way it had been ever since. She started snubbing me and didn't want me around her. I think I was in seventh grade when she started trouble the first time. We were both living with our mother at the time.

I had worn some of Mom's turquoise jewelry to school without permission. I knew I would put it back in her jewelry box before she came home from work. I was trying to impress some of the rich popular kids. I was trying to become a part of their clique. At lunch, they admired my jewelry and asked where it came from. To impress them, I lied, but there was some truth mixed in.

I explained, "Oh, my daddy has an airplane. One weekend he flew my sister and me to New York and bought some of these pieces of jewelry in an exclusive store." At that moment, I was immediately accepted in their clique, just like I figured I would be. After school that day, I put the jewelry back into my mother's jewelry box without her ever being the wiser.

The next day, those girls would not have anything to do with me. I was told by one of the snobby little girls that they asked my little sister about the jewelry. My little sister told them I was a freak and a liar. She told them that she didn't have anything to do with me and that they should watch their backs with me. I just couldn't believe that my little sister had said such wicked things about me, knowing I wanted to be friends with this group of girls. I may have been wrong in lying and taking my mother's jewelry, but my sister didn't have to be so cruel.

About a month or two later, a female bully in my gym class was calling my little sister a whore. There were rumors going around that she was having sex with all the boys.

I told the girl, "I'm going to kick your stupid butt for talking about my sister like that. That's a lie. My sister is a virgin, and she would never allow that. In fact. my sister is too self-righteous to do that anyway."

She asked, "When do you want to get your butt kicked?"

I answered, "Same place, same time, tomorrow," I told her.

I must have scared the crap out of that bully because she came with a dress on. I beat her up anyway. I guess it took the female tomboy to beat up the female bully of the class. I just chuckled to myself because I was a tomboy, and I have always been able to protect myself. I never messed with her when she made the other girls give her their lunch money, and she always stayed away from me. I guess it took the tomboy to put her in her place. As I remember, I don't think she ever messed with any of the other girls again after that.

That summer we would ride our bikes to the park swimming pool. A little boy that I had a crush on was there. All day he would dunk me, and I would dunk him. By the end of summer he was nowhere to be found, and neither was my sister. One day Christina brought him and his friends home, and we played football. He was wearing my sister's Saint Christopher, and she was wearing his. I could not believe what my sister had done.

When I was around eighteen, and in my first apartment, I ran into him and his friend. I invited him over to my apartment. I asked why he went steady with my sister and not me. I thought he liked me. He answered, "Because your sister said you were a freak and you didn't like boys. She said that she liked me, and she gave it up."

I angrily asked, "What?"

He replied, "Oh, I'm sorry, I didn't mean to hurt your feelings, but that's what your sister said to all of us. I have always thought you were the prettier of the two. I did like you, but I wanted a girlfriend that would put out too."

I thought I was going to vomit.

A few years earlier, when I was living with Daddy, and she was living with Mom, I wrote her a letter. In the letter, I told her that I was dating a boy named Woody, and I thought my friend's boyfriend was cute too. His name was Chucky. Anyway, I called Christina at Daddy's house. Unbelievably, Christina got it all mixed up. She told me that she was dating Chucky, and he said he never dated me.

I said, "Christina, I never said I dated Chucky. You are one sick kid to go after seconds of your big sister; what a freak you are?"

She had been doing that for years, either stealing my boyfriends, trying to steal them, or dating them after we broke up.

* * *

Christina has done a lot of weird stuff throughout my life. She has rejected me and told people I wasn't her sister. The list of crazy things my sister has done to me and to herself is long and truly unforgiveable!

I guess I have always hoped we would have a relationship, but to this day, it has not happened. That's why I didn't know what I would do if I needed her to help with Mom. I believed deep in my heart that we could unite as sisters should. I have always believed, "United you stand, divided you fall."

I love my sister and my mother. God help me because I also believe they are the most self-absorbed, self-centered individuals I have known. With a sister and mother like them, it's no wonder I have such a strong back.

CHAPTER XIV

The Snobville Airport was a small airport. By the time my flight arrived, it was mostly empty.

I went to the ladies' room, which was right next to the baggage claim area. I then went to grab my luggage. I stood there at the carrier belt, waiting for my luggage to come out, and then saw Little Pete waiting for me. I looked over at him. We walked toward one another and immediately hugged each other.

Little Pete chuckled as he asked, "What are those white folk going to think of an old black man hugging on a young white girl?"

I laughed as I answered, "I think they would be jealous, and I don't think people think that way anymore, Little Pete. You're still living in the '40s and '50s."

We both started laughing.

He said, "I'm glad you are here, Belinda. I think you're the only one that's sane in your family."

I laughed and said, "I don't think so! I'm here, aren't I?"

He laughed and helped me get my bags.

I asked, "What are you driving?"

He answered, "My van."

I asked, "Oh, you've been making a lot of money?"

He chuckled. "Of course, I work for your momma."

We both started laughing as we put my luggage in the back of his van.

Little Pete remarked, "I don't normally let people smoke in my van, Belinda. But I know you're probably wanting one, so go ahead and light yourself up. I know you've got that nasty habit."

I cocked an eyebrow up while I looked over at him, laughing at the same time. "Oh, shoot! If you're going to allow me to smoke in your prized possession, what are people going to think we are doing now?"

He laughed at me and continued our joke, "Ms. Star, I'm not that type of employee!"

We both started laughing.

I never did light a cigarette in his van. My habit isn't that bad, except when I come home. In fact, that's when I drink the most as well. "Okay, Little Pete, fill me in with what you know."

Little Pete asked, "Will I be working for you until it's finished?"

I answered, "Of course you will—at least until I can't pay you anymore."

He then said, "I would like to ride the wave until it's over, for your mother's sake."

I said, "I can't promise you. Little Pete, I don't know what's going on or how bad it is. The way you are talking it sounds as if my mother has already drowned, but I give my word I will try to take care of you."

Little Pete said, "That's good enough for me."

I said, "Now tell me what has been happening, and no lies! I want as much truth from you as you can give. You've always kept their secrets. If you're working for me, from this moment forward, I want total loyalty from you. If you've been sworn to keep a secret, you will still share it with me. I understand you will not be able to tell me everything now, and I know you will be reluctant to, but I will have the truth, Little Pete, and nothing else."

He responded, "I understand, but I want to finally tell you about all the beatings that have occurred over the years. That's the most important thing to me. I almost told you about it all when you were here when your grandmother passed away."

I said, "Okay, Little Pete, spill it."

I was so tired that my brain hurt. He proceeded to tell me about the beatings Big Pete had been giving my mother for at least the past two decades. Little Pete said that each beating seemed to get worse. He told me how my mother and Big Pete were verbally abusive to each other. The things he told me made the hairs stand up on the back of my neck. He also told me about the racial prejudice that he had endured from Big Pete and the nasty racial slanders that he had suffered over the years. He said that he had no education and this was the best paying job he ever had. He stayed because he knew he would never get another job like it.

There were many beatings, but one stood out from all the others. It had happened after a football game. Friends of Big Pete's, who were also supposedly my mother's friends, were in the front of the house, drinking and eating at my mother and Big Pete's expense. In fact, these friends never paid for anything. This time Big Pete not only beat my mother, he literally picked her up and threw her down the driveway. Little Pete said those white people looked and went back to their drinking as if it was nothing.

Little Pete said he had enough! He ran inside to the telephone, called the police, and ran back out to my mother. He said she just lay there like a broken doll. He watched the police officers question all those white people. They all tried to say they saw nothing. One police officer was very angry, and he said to the person he was interviewing in an angry tone, "You're trying to tell me you saw nothing, or that you just didn't do anything about what you saw?"

Little Pete proceeded to say it was like pulling teeth to make those white people tell the truth. He said the police officers pulled it out of them in the end. He also stated that one of the officers told him that he had never seen so many cowards bunched together like that before in his life.

"Your momma was taken to the hospital by ambulance. She had a broken arm and a broken rib from Pete punching her. Then your momma tried to have the charges against Big Pete dropped, but the Commonwealth attorney would not drop them."

Not only was my mother victimized, but so were Little Pete and countless other employees over the years. I felt nothing but remorse and shame that Little Pete had to endure all this for a paycheck. Tears started rolling down my face out of sorrow for him and for my mother. All of a sudden, it all started to make sense. I understood why my mother had turned into who she was. It was out of self-preservation. I understood now why Little Pete acted the way he did in front of Big Pete. Everything was falling into place.

My tears and sadness quickly turned to anger and total hatred for this man: Big Pete. I had no empathy or sympathy toward him. I never had and I never would. At that point, I knew my instincts about him from the beginning had been dead on. He was a rotten, greedy, thieving son of a gun, but in the back of my mind, I knew I had to participate in this wicked, deadly game to try to save my mother from this evil man and from herself.

I looked over at Little Pete as we were pulling up into the driveway and said, "Little Pete, act as if you didn't tell me anything. If you can endure this type of treatment for a little longer, follow my lead. Okay?"

Little Pete answered, "I will follow."

I said, "Okay, I'm ready to walk into the twilight zone."

I wondered to myself if it was too late to save my mother.

CHAPTER XV

It was a moonless, pitch-dark night with a bitter cold that crept into my bones like piercing needles. I let out one last sigh as Little Pete opened the garage door and helped me carry my luggage into my mother's house. We walked inside.

Little Pete said, "I'll take your luggage upstairs, Belinda."

Mother said, "Thank you, Little Pete, for picking my daughter up from the airport."

Little Pete replied, "You're welcome, ma'am. I'm just going to put these upstairs for Belinda and be on my way."

Mom said, "That will be fine."

She hugged me, and I hugged her back. We stood there hugging for several minutes. Her entire body was trembling. I took her hands and held them in mine for a few minutes. As I looked at her face and down toward her hands, I noticed bruises up and down her arms and wrists. She was wearing a short-sleeved cotton bathrobe with a white flowered print. Her eyes were glazed over. We just stood there, looking at each other for several minutes. She stopped trembling, but whatever medication she was taking for anxiety did not appear to be working. I assumed she was taking medication because of the way her eyes were glazed. I did not say anything about the bruises. There was no need. I knew.

At that moment, I recalled an incident that had occurred a long time ago when Thomas and I had been visiting. My mother had a large bruise going down her neck, and her cheek was bruised. When Thomas and I were carrying our luggage to one of the guest bedrooms upstairs, I noticed a hole in her bedroom door. I asked her what had happened to the door and how she got the bruises. She had told me that she and Little Pete were moving furniture. They punched the hole in the door with the corner of the piece of furniture they were moving, and she fell down the stairs. I had believed her at the time. I now knew without a doubt that she had lied about that incident and about so much more.

I instantly realized that I had been completely stupid and blind to everything that my mother had been going through over the last two decades. I wondered if, subconsciously, I had allowed myself to be blind because she had been so cruel to me for the majority of my life. A part of me felt that she deserved exactly what she got. I felt guilty for these thoughts because I knew that no matter how she treated me, I should have at least tried to help her, even if it was just giving her a sympathetic ear. At that moment, I just felt guilty. It didn't matter whether or not my feelings were justified. I felt like I should have done something more for her. It was my obligation. A daughter's duty.

I stated, "All you had to do was pick up the phone."

Mom replied, "I was ashamed."

We stood there in front of the refrigerator in her kitchen. Mom said, "Belinda, let's go sit in the Florida room so we can talk."

I said, "Okay." I followed her.

The Florida room was an addition my mom had built onto her house. She had one outside wall knocked out and a room added where the walls were all windows. The Florida room was filled with her beloved flowers. The room also contained a desk, a sofa, coffee table, curios filled with expensive knickknacks, a fireplace with built-in bookcases on each side filled with books and royal Dolton character jugs, fancy chairs, end tables, and the large cuckoo clock that I had purchased for her on one of my military tours in Germany. In fact, she built most of her collections around the pieces or paintings that I had made for her over the years.

Big Pete was downstairs in the basement watching TV and drinking. I could hear the television as we passed the stairway, and I knew he was doing what he always did. We went into the Florida room. I sat down on her sofa, and she sat in one of her big bamboo chairs across from me on the other side of the coffee table.

"Thank you for coming, Belinda. Pete said you wouldn't come. The police will be coming for me in the morning, and I have a lot to tell you before then. You can have everything Pete and I have left to help us."

Before she could go any further, Big Pete walked in. He wasn't drunk, but I could smell the alcohol on his breath when I stood up to face him. He reached over and hugged me. I just stood there.

He stated, "I didn't think you would come. Your mother and I will give you everything we have left if you will help us. You can take whatever you want. I'm so glad you came."

I stood there biting my tongue and looked at him with total disbelief. I could not believe that he actually thought I didn't know about the abuse. Granted, my mother was verbally wicked to him, but she didn't physically beat him.

He then said, in a cowardly way, "Well, I guess I will leave you two alone so your mother can tell you what is going on. Belinda, thank you again for coming."

Then, he left the room, and I watched him as he went back downstairs.

I turned to my mother and asked, "Well, before we start, I need to gather my wits. May I take a shower and freshen up? I really stink from flying for the last fourteen hours. The layovers and multiple planes didn't help. There's also the time difference."

Mom answered, "Sure. I will be waiting for you."

After my much-needed shower, I came back downstairs. Mom was just sitting in the chair where I had left her. She got up quickly and gave me a hug and a kiss on the cheek.

She said, "I have something for you." She gave me a ring box and said, "It was your grandmother's ring."

I opened it. Of course, it was a fake bauble, but it was pretty. I said, "Mom, you don't need to give me anything."

Mom said, "Don't be so dramatic."

I thought, *My poor mother has tried to buy people my whole life. I have watched her do it repeatedly.* I picked up that same habit in my youth, but I realized a long time ago that nobody is worth trying to buy. I guess my mother never learned that valuable lesson. She has spent all her money on her friends and family, especially Christina, Jay, and Big Pete. Thomas and I never took anything from her. I guess because it was never offered. In fact, she had been the one who was always taking from us. I thought about how sad that was, and wondered if she was trying to give the ring to me because she had done something evil to me again?

We sat down. I drank a beer, and she proceeded to tell me about the check kiting she had done and the other types of fraud and crimes that Pete had committed against his clients. She did not commit those crimes, but she had helped Pete cover them up. She had been placed on bond. At that time, Pete was not earning an income, so she had started the check kiting to help Auntie Bea. Auntie Bea helped her with the check kiting and took some of the money that Mom had received from the fraud. Because it was such a large amount, they revoked her bond. She was turning herself in because she had no other choice.

As she was telling her story, she begged me to keep my promise to save Auntie Bea's farm and the Daisy house. She begged me to save Auntie Bea before they found out about her and prosecuted her for her participation.

The telephone rang. By this time, it was late in the evening. Mom asked me to answer it. I picked up the telephone and asked who it was. The man on the phone proceeded to tell me he was my mother's therapist. My mother was on a suicide watch. I told him that I was her daughter, and I had just flown in from Germany. I was livid that my mother was going to try to take the easy way out! I told the therapist that he did not need to watch her any longer because I was there. He asked to speak with my mother, and I handed the phone to her.

As my mother was talking with her therapist, I started thinking about my time in the Army. There had been soldiers who had committed minor crimes and those who committed horrible crimes. Some had been in the process of being summarized or receiving a full Article 15, which could lead to a court martial. They would threaten to kill themselves because their life was ruined and their careers were tarnished. The minor crimes are normally summarized Article 15s that stay with the unit where the minor crime was committed, and they do not follow a soldier to the next duty station. They made these threats in an attempt to escape punishment with the hope that the suicidal threats would make it all go away. The military takes suicide threats very seriously. When someone makes such a threat, they are placed on suicide watch with other soldiers monitoring them to ensure that they do not attempt to harm themselves or others.

I have always considered these soldiers weak cowards because they want to take the easy way out instead of standing up and taking their punishment like strong individuals that they are supposed to be. I know that other leaders and senior noncommissioned officers (NCOs) probably feel the same way. I know when a soldier does this it is in the best interest of everyone to weed out the weak. It doesn't happen often, but it does happen enough that it is a problem for the military. I never thought someone so close to me would be so weak, especially my mother. Indeed, for me, it was a daughter's duty to toughen up my mother.

I heard my mother tell the therapist I was with her and would help her get through the dark thoughts she was having. She hung up the phone. I gave her a hug and sat back down on the sofa. She proceeded to tell me it would be best for all concerned if she just killed herself and was done with it. She called herself a stupid bitch who had treated me terribly over the years, and she claimed that she deserved to die. No one loved her. All anyone had done was use her and try to hurt her. Then, she blamed the whole thing on me! She said it was my fault because when I was young, I had floated one hundred dollars in checks. She said that she was like this because she decided to give birth to me! Her life would have been different if she had given me up. She said it would be just better for her to die because she felt this way.

By this time, I had heard enough! I got up from the sofa, grabbed her shoulders, pulled her into a standing position, and I shook her back and forth like a rag doll a few times. I let go and lightly smacked her with my open hand. She looked at me, and her expression went from sadness to anger, which is what I wanted. I wanted her to be angry with me instead of herself. I wanted her to focus her anger on me so that she would stop thinking about killing herself.

I commanded, "Stop it! Stop it! If you kill yourself, Mom, I swear to God, I will not bury you. Look at me! Look at me! You are going to do exactly what I tell you to do. You are going to stand up like the strong woman you are and take your punishment like the strong woman that you raised. You are going to squeal like a pig. You will tell the United States attorney everything, and I mean *everything*, without any sugar coating that you did. You are going to tell them what Auntie Bea did. You are going to tell them everything Big Pete did. You are going to waive your right to trial because you are guilty. Period. There is no need wasting Thomas's money, my money, and the taxpayers' money for crimes that you committed. You are guilty of stealing. It doesn't matter what type of stealing because there is no excuse for it. None. I still don't really understand how you did it, but it is still stealing, and it's against the law.

"If you don't do what I'm telling you to do, then I will not help you get through this! You should have called me a long time ago, instead of waiting until the last minute when you had no other options. You are going to confess, and after that, you are going to pray to God that the court has mercy on your soul. I want you to call this damn expensive attorney first thing in the morning, before the police come to get you. You will tell him that you will be in my custody, and if they won't allow that, ask for an ankle bracelet to monitor you. They let the rich and famous people wear them, after all.

"Then, you and I will have time to liquidate what needs to be liquidated and move your things into storage in the Daisy house and on the Mills farm. I promise I will get the land back! You are separated from Big Pete as of this moment! I will deal with him so you don't have to. You will not go to jail for him! You are going to jail for what you did—nothing more. You will not take the blame for what Big Pete and Auntie Bea have done! Have I made myself clear?"

Mom had her self-righteous attitude back, at least for the moment.

She replied in an angry voice, "That's fine, Belinda, and if you ever smack me again I will beat the shit out of you. I don't care if you are stronger than I am. You're my daughter, and you will not smack your mother. Have I made myself clear?"

I giggled at her then. I had pulled her back into realty again, and she was standing tough.

I answered, "It worked, didn't it? Yes, ma'am, you have made yourself clear."

With tears in our eyes, my mother and I started giggling with each other. I had my mean old momma back.

Mom said, "I will not give up your Auntie Bea, Belinda. You need to pick up all the checks that Auntie Bea and I did so they will not be so inclined to prosecute her as well. I will also try to make a deal with the U.S. attorney. Belinda, if I give her up, everything that I did will have been in vain."

I said, "Okay, Momma, I will help save Auntie Bea from going to jail with you." I continued on a lighter note, "Momma, I think you need a glass of wine, and I need one too. I'll go downstairs and see if you have any left in the fridge."

She replied, "That sounds like a great idea," and giggled.

I went downstairs. The television was still on, and Big Pete was passed out in his chair. I turned off the television, walked behind the bar, and looked into the refrigerator. There was an opened bottle of wine. I poured two glasses of wine and carried them upstairs. I handed my mother a glass, took a sip of mine, and sat down on the sofa.

Mom then said, "I wish it would snow, baby, so you and I have more time."

I answered, "I wish it would snow too."

We talked a while longer, and I asked, "We need to go to bed and pray that it snows. Momma, can I sleep with you tonight?"

Mom softly answered, "Yes, we need sleep, and I pray it snows for us so they don't come to get me. Yes, you can sleep with me, baby. I guess you're scared."

I was scared. Scared that she would try to kill herself, but I desperately needed some shuteye before the morning. I had no clue what was going to happen to my mother. I just knew I was praying that they would put her into my custody. So I answered her, "Yes, Mom, I'm scared."

Mom smiled and said, "I'll protect you."

I laughed, and we went to bed. As Mom settled down in her big bed, I draped my arm around her midsection to ensure I would wake up if she stirred.

CHAPTER XVI

The next morning, which was a Friday, my mother's alarm woke me up. Mom was still asleep. I reached across her and turned off the alarm, and I looked out the window. I crawled out of the bed as fast as I could and scrambled to the window. It was snowing! It was snowing hard! It was after 6:00 a.m. I went over to Mom's side of the bed and shook her gently. "Momma, wake up! Wake up! It's snowing and snowing hard."

Mom stirred, rubbed her eyes, and asked excitedly, "What!? It's snowing?" She looked at me, looked at the window, got out of the bed, and looked out the window again.

We both started jumping up and down and yelling together, "It's snowing! It's snowing!" We started laughing like schoolchildren. Mom ran down the stairs to the kitchen, and I followed. She picked up the phone and called her attorney. She had a gleam in her eye, and she was smiling from ear to ear. Apparently, she woke him up because she had called him at his home. She told him it was snowing very hard, and because she lived out in the country, she wondered if the marshals could pick her up on Monday instead since today was Friday. She hung up the phone. The smile was gone from her face. She said that the attorney did not know if the snow would stop them. He told her that she should still be ready for them to pick her up. They would take her to the courthouse and then to jail. He said that he would try to deter them from coming because of the road conditions.

Mom and I dressed, fixed our hair and makeup, and put on our jewelry. I went to the kitchen and made bacon and eggs for breakfast. We were sitting at her kitchen table eating when the phone rang. It was around 9:00 a.m. Mom answered the phone, spoke briefly, hung up the phone, turned around, and told me who it was. It was her attorney. He told her that the snow was not going to stop the U.S. marshals, and she needed to be ready.

She had a large plastic bag full of medications. She had her purse packed full of female paraphernalia. Around 9:30 a.m., there was a knock on the front door. Big Pete answered it and led the U.S. marshals into the kitchen where we were waiting. He frowned at me, showing disappointment. He handed Mom's purse and medications to the marshals. Mom started crying. The marshals cuffed her hands behind her back. The female marshal handed the bag of medications to me. She said that Mom could not take any medication with her, even if a doctor prescribed it for her. She said I would have to bring it to the courthouse for her. She also handed my mother's purse to me and said that Mom couldn't have that either.

I told the marshals, "I'm a veteran of the United Stated Army. This is my mother. May I go with you and stay with her as she goes through your process? She is very scared." I pulled out my military ID and showed it to both marshals as proof of my service and my rank.

The male marshal jumped in before the female marshal could answer me, and answered, "No, ma'am, you cannot ride with us. We don't normally allow this, but because you are a veteran, I will allow you to follow us in your own vehicle. That way your mother will know you are close by."

I gratefully acknowledged his kindness. "Thank you, sir. I will be right behind you in my mother's car."

Little Pete walked in as the marshals were escorting my mother to their vehicle. I told him, "Little Pete, the marshals just took Mom. I need you to drive me to the courthouse. We can follow the marshals."

Little Pete rushed to Mom's car and quickly started it. I was walking as fast as possible, out the side door to the garage.

Big Pete said, "Belinda, I just can't go with you. You can handle this, can't you?"

I looked at that cowardly man and thought, *He's the one who got Mother into this mess,* but I said, "Yes, Big Pete. I can handle this because I'm the one who has always been there for her. It's okay, you don't need to come. I understand." I gave him my fake smile, and my "everything is going to be okay" attitude. But I knew that nothing would be okay. I knew that it was too late to save her. I failed before I even started. The only thing left was to do everything in my power to convince my fellow men and women in uniform to treat her a little bit better than they would normally treat a thief. My only weapon was the uniform of respect I once wore. I prayed that it would generate sympathy toward my mother in some form. I felt

I deserved at least that much because I had sacrificed willingly my body, the beating heart that runs it, and the mind that makes it function to the people of this great country. God knows how many times Thomas and I had put ourselves in harm's way for our country, which is something that civilians do not understand. When you take an oath and sign your name on the dotted line, you give your heart, mind, and body to the people. Only fellow brethren that have served in the armed forces truly understand this type of sacrifice, and they truly respect it. I have learned from experience that only those who wear the marshal, police officer, or firefighter uniform, and those who are veterans of the United States military forces understand this type of respect.

Your soul belongs to God, of course, but with this contract, your body is owned by the Unites States government. For example, if a soldier is sunburned during off-duty hours, and that sunburn is so severe that the soldier can't wear their uniform or do their duty, their chain of command can elect to give them a summarized Article 15 because they damaged government property. Tattoos placed on the body where they cannot be covered, men piercing ears, and even dying one's hair an unnatural color, like blue or green, are the type of things that can be considered defacing government property and if the chain of command elects to do so they can punish the soldier. Those who take the oath, who understand that our great country was founded on "blood, sweat, and tears," and are willing to die so others may bask in our freedoms are the only ones who truly understand the sacrifices that are made by men and women in the military. So yes, I do expect that respect from another person who has served. Respect is earned, not given.

On this terrible day, God blessed me. The United States marshal was a veteran of the United States Armed Forces who had traded one uniform for another. I don't think he would have bent the rules for me otherwise. He didn't break them, but he did bend them for me because we were brethren. At least that is my interpretation of his actions. All I know is I was very grateful that he allowed me to do this.

As we approached the courthouse, everything within my sight seemed to become a slow motion scene from a thriller movie. Little Pete was speaking to me, but the sounds that I heard were inaudible. The snow sprinkled on the looming, large four-story brick building with small windows and made it look even more uninviting. The drab, hideous building appeared to grow larger and larger as we approached it. The parking lot that surrounded the courthouse seemed to stretch for miles with a sea of vehicles parked throughout.

When we arrived at the courthouse, the marshal came over to me in the parking lot and said that my mother's hearing wouldn't take place for a couple of hours. He said that when I went inside I would have to ask the clerk which courtroom the hearing was in, and he gave me the name of the presiding judge. I could not go with her into in the building, but the man did allow me to give my mother a kiss and hug goodbye. That was the first of the few gestures of kindness my mother and I received from anyone in our justice system.

CHAPTER XVII

I was in desperate need of a cigarette. We had to wait, so I asked Little Pete to drive to the fast food joint I had seen about a block away. We used the drive-thru. I bought a coffee for myself, and Little Pete got a breakfast meal. Little Pete pulled into a parking spot and put the car into park. The snow had stopped while we were ordering. There was about two inches on the ground. I sat in the car feeling guilty because it was my mother's car. I rolled the window down, lit my cigarette, and sat smoking and drinking my coffee. Little Pete ate his breakfast.

When he was finished eating, he said, "I know this is tough for you Belinda, but your momma did this to herself. She could have left Big Pete years ago when she found out he was stealing from his clients." I looked over at Little Pete with a puzzled expression.

I asked, "Where would she have gone, Little Pete? Grandma and Granddaddy are dead. It seems to me she didn't have any real friends. None of her friends had basic common decency to help her. I'm in Germany, and Christina is just plain weird. Jay just graduated from college, and he's Big Pete's son. Yes, maybe she could have come to Europe to live with me, but you don't know my mother as well as I do. In fact, I don't even think I really know what makes her tick anymore."

Little Pete took a drink of his coffee, looked up at me, and said, "Maybe you're right. All I know is that my loyalties are to her and to you. But I'm going to tell you this, Belinda. Big Pete scares the crap out of me. What are you going to do?"

I answered honestly. "Right now, I don't know, Little Pete, but I do know that my mother isn't going to be the only one that goes down for this. I believe with every fiber of my being that Big Pete has set her up to take most of the fall. I think that's why he has been beating on her more because he's trying to get her to take the blame for all of it, and to go to jail for him too. As God as my witness as long as I have control over my mother again, I will not allow her to do that, and I have told her so."

Little Pete started chatting about his adventures with Mom over the years as they collected the plants in her landscaping. He laughed and laughed, and so did I. I thought that it was good of him to take our minds off what was about to happen. We drove back to the courthouse and sat in my mother's car in the parking lot. Then it was time for me to go into the courthouse.

Little Pete asked, "Belinda, can I come in with you?"

I answered, "Yes, I think my mother would like to see you there because you are such good friends."

Little Pete was funny as he took charge, a typical man. He led the way to the clerk and asked where the courtroom was. As we walked through the hallways to the courtroom, we passed a few people who Little Pete knew. Pete walked with his head held high, and it was my impression that he was proud to show off the people he knew inside the courthouse. I think he was letting me know that he knew people that could somehow help us. I was very grateful for his "take charge" attitude. I guess he wanted me to know that he could help. Whether I needed him or not, I'm just glad he was there for my mother. At that moment, I knew that he was not just my mother's employee, but also her only true friend.

The courtroom was very large and filled with long benches, like pews in a church. It could easily hold a hundred people. It was so empty you could almost hear an echo when talking. Little Pete guided me to the first bench behind the fenced-in area where my mother would be. The benches were separated from the front by a fancy fence that was accessed through a swinging gate that came a little above my knee. There were two tables, one on each side of the courtroom with chairs, and the judge's bench.

Mom was not in the courtroom yet; it was empty except for Little Pete and me. I looked at the judge's bench, and there was a door on the left and right side of the judge's bench. Each door had a small window in it. As I looked at the door to the right of the judge's bench, I saw a head come toward it. The door opened, and I gasped in total shock. They had my mother in shackles! They were treating her as if she was a hardened criminal or a murderer! My first reaction was to jump over the fence; run to her, and take the shackles off. I could not believe that they had her shackled. She was a little old lady! How in the hell could they treat her in such a manner? She stole from banks, not people! According to her, the only reason she stole at all was to take care of my Auntie Bea! Little Pete must have known what I wanted to do by the way I reacted to the sight of my mother in shackles. I didn't say a word, but my face and body must have betrayed my thoughts because Little Pete grabbed my arm and ordered, "Belinda, you can't do that." He told me later that my body had jerked toward the railing.

My mother slowly walked into that courtroom. She could only take baby steps because of the shackles. Her head hung so low that her chin was touching her chest. She was bent over so far that she looked like a hunchback. A marshal different from the one who picked her up escorted her. I heard someone walk into the courtroom behind us. I turned around and saw a man that I assumed was my mother's attorney. He walked through the swinging gate, toward my mother. I proceeded to follow, but before I could reach them, the marshal stopped me and gently pushed me back through the swinging gate.

The marshal said, "I'm sorry, ma'am, but there is no touching or contact with the prisoner."

Before I had a chance to utter out one word, the female marshal who had taken my mother from her home came through the door. She rapidly walked toward us and said, "It is okay. She's the daughter we told you about."

The marshal's face turned a little bit red. He apologized. He said he was told to bend the rules for me, and that I could go to my mother. I politely asked him to remove the shackles. The female marshal nodded that it was okay. They first removed the leg shackles then the ones attached to her wrists.

Mom started rubbing her wrists with each hand as if they had been too tight. She looked up at me and hugged me quickly before the marshals had a chance to react. I immediately walked through the gate to the other side of the fence. I did not want the marshals to get into trouble for bending the rules for me. In my opinion, you should treat a criminal in the manner that fits the crime, and Mom did not deserve to be treated in such a manner. She did not physically hurt anyone, and it was obvious that she did not have the physical strength to attack the marshals. She had already voluntarily turned herself in, so they knew that she wasn't going to run. They did not have to do that to her, and I was very disappointed in my brethren. All they could think about was degrading a person, and they did not even know the crime that had been committed by the person. To me it was overkill on the part of the U.S. marshals. What happened to "innocent until proven guilty"? Confession should be worth a bit of respect. At this point, my mother's character didn't matter. I knew in my heart that this was the worst punishment that could be inflicted on her, and it was even worse that her daughter was watching.

I looked up, and the court officer called everyone to stand because the judge was entering the room. I looked over to my left, and had my first glimpse of the female prosecutor, the assistant U.S. Attorney. She oozed pure unadulterated cruelty and bitterness. She looked as if she had something to prove and the world owed her. I didn't like her. Before she even uttered a word, I knew she was going to use my mother to promote her own career. It was apparent she was intent on prosecuting my mother to the fullest extent of the law; it didn't matter that she was just a little old lady.

I looked behind me, and to my surprise, Big Pete was sitting on the back bench. It seemed that the coward was trying to hide from me. The judge sat down and everyone in the courtroom followed his lead.

He called the court to order, and then Mom's attorney started to speak. He asked the judge to put my mother in my custody. He told the judge that I was a veteran of the United States Army, and I would ensure that my mother would not commit any more crimes before her trial. He stated that I would ensure she stayed here in this county until she was tried and sentenced. He told the judge that my mother was waiving her right to trial, she admitted her guilt, and she would help the U.S. Attorney's office with the investigation against her husband.

The Assistant U.S. Attorney, of course, was not going to allow that to happen. She twisted my mother's attorney's statement completely around. She claimed that my mother would be a flight risk because her daughter was a veteran and had contacts not only nationally, but also globally. She stated that I could easily hide my mother anywhere, and they would never find her again. She said that I could easily change my mother's identity because of my military background . . . .

I thought, *What a stupid woman. That is the biggest load of crap I ever heard!* Then, to my shock, the judge agreed with the prosecution. I could not believe my ears!

Mom's attorney started again. "But, Your Honor, we could also put a tracking bracelet on her as well and there would be no flight risk—"

The female assistant attorney interrupted him before he could finish. She claimed that because of my highly technical training in the military, I could easily disable the tracking device, and hide my mother internationally. She also stated that the defendant, my mother, was a menace to the financial communities of the world.

I then learned that she had committed the fraud in the names of Belinda Star, Jay King, Christina Bishop, Margaret Tate, and Arthur Tate, and numerous other names. I was in total shock! My mother used my name, my siblings' names, and my deceased grandparents' names! I was so angry with my mother because she did do something evil to my siblings and me. I also realized that the judge and the assistant attorney did not connect the dots because Mom's attorney used the words "her daughter" and never mentioned my name. They did not know I was Belinda Star, and Mom had committed the crimes in my name. They did not realize that she had committed fraud against me as well.

My mother looked at me and whispered in her attorney's ear. She kept looking at me the whole time she was whispering. Suddenly, the attorney jumped up and stated, "The defendant requests that the court leave her family alone, and she will willingly cooperate."

I sat there thinking, *What does her family have to do with it? She did the crimes in our names and committed crimes against us.* I sat there dumbfounded and stunned not only because she did this to my siblings and me, but because she was trying to act as if we were a party to it. She was acting as if she was saving us from something that was not done by our own hands, but by hers. I was completely confused. I had no idea what crimes she had committed against us, and to what degree, and I knew that now was not the time to think about that. I said to myself, *I will worry about and deal with that tomorrow. Today, I have to keep my thoughts and wits in this courtroom. It's not about me today; it's about my mother.* I focused my attention on the scene playing out in front of me.

I could not believe the horse crap coming out of the assistant attorney's mouth. Soldiers are not trained in all that crap. We are all specialized in different fields, for Pete's sake. I wanted to open my mouth and call her a liar, but I knew better. I knew the judge was just acting stupidly, and his behavior was just a farce. I knew that he was every bit as determined as the assistant attorney to make sure my mother sat in a jail cell. I was angry and disappointed in our justice system. I could barely contain myself. I guess the Army did discipline my impulsive behavior, as I was able "to think before acting."

I thought, *I wasted my life! I have sacrificed my life for this!* My faith in our country and our justice system flew out the window. Didn't they realize they are talking about a little old lady and a highly decorated NCO? You don't make rank in the Army by being a coward, running away, and breaking the rules. It does not work that way. I could not believe my ears. Why would a soldier who was active duty ruin his or her career breaking the law for someone else? If they did, it would have to be something much more important than this. The words that were coming out of the woman's mouth didn't even make sense. She had no idea what she was talking about!

I knew at that moment, without a doubt, my mother was going to jail. The judge didn't even deliberate. He immediately ruled that Mom was going straight to jail and would stay there until her sentencing. I had heard enough; I reached across the fence, grabbed my mother's attorney's shoulder, and ordered him, "You'd better not let her go to jail! Do something! That stupid little woman doesn't know what she's talking about! Put me on the stand before it's too late. That woman is lying about the military, and I can prove it."

Mom's attorney asked the judge if he could approach the bench. I couldn't hear them, but there appeared to be an argument between Mom's attorney and the assistant attorney. The judge kept looking over at me with a frown on his face as he was whispering. Mom's attorney came back toward the table were Mom was standing, and I was right behind her in the first bench.

He murmured, "The judge said you probably can prove without a doubt that the assistant attorney doesn't know what she is talking about, and that he will probably agree with you. But you have to admit, Belinda, your mother would be safer in jail than with her husband."

I looked up, and the judge was looking straight at me. My mother was looking at me. I let out a sigh because I didn't know what the right choice was. Before I even decided what my decision would be, Mom looked at me and said to her attorney, while she was looking at me, "It would be safer for me to go now, but only if this time will be counted as time served when I'm sentenced."

I let out a sigh of relief. I was so thankful that Mom made her own decision. I knew it would be easier for her to go ahead and get it over with. After all, she was guilty and deserved to serve time for her crimes.

Mom's attorney looked up at the judge and asked if the time would be counted toward her sentencing. The judge nodded and said it would. He then looked at Mom's attorney and me, and to my surprise he said, "If your client would like some time to spend in private with her daughter before I turn her over to the U.S. marshals, she may do so. In fact she can take as much time as she wants."

I saw Mom's attorney look at her and my mother turned her head toward me as he acknowledged the judge, "Yes. She would like that very much, Your Honor."

The judge said, "Fine." He looked over at me and winked as he was leaving the courtroom. Everyone turned to look at me. To this day, I have no idea why the judge winked at me, or why he even allowed my mother and me to make the decision instead of him. All I know is he restored my hope in our justice system. I looked behind me, and Big Pete was walking toward the front where we were.

He then spoke. "I'm sorry, Jane."

Before anyone could react, the courtroom guard approached us and lightly pushed Big Pete away from us.

He said, "The judge only allowed the daughter, not you, sir."

Big Pete angrily remarked, "But I'm her husband."

The guard politely said, "I'm sorry, sir, but the judge only allowed the daughter. I'm sure you heard him."

Big Pete just shrugged his shoulders and left the courtroom. We all watched him leave. The guard then asked us if we would like some privacy. He pointed towards another door at the rear of the courtroom. Little Pete looked over at me and said he would meet me at my mother's car.

I nodded and said, "Okay."

My mother, her attorney, and I sat in a little room with a desk and three chairs. Mom started taking off her wedding rings and earrings. I asked Mom's attorney if she could keep her wedding ring on. I knew how important it was for her to have some type of jewelry. Mom's attorney said that he would ask. He stepped out of the room. When he opened the door, I briefly saw the U.S. marshal standing there before the door was closed. He returned after a few moments. He told us the marshal told him that it would be okay, but he wasn't sure if the jail would let her keep it on.

In front of her attorney, Mom said to me, "Belinda, do not stay at my house with Big Pete. I'm afraid that one of you will kill the other. He has been drinking very heavily lately. Just go back, get my safes and my cars out of there as soon as you leave here. Start moving all my personal property immediately! I know you said you did not want to help him, but Belinda, if you help me you are going to have to help him to some degree."

I told her, "I will only help to keep the peace for as long as I can, but after that, the creep is on his own."

She agreed with me. We all stood up after making plans. I knew exactly what my mission was.

I brought my mother's purse with her medications in it, and Mom was able to take one last pill for her high blood pressure. I allowed her to bark orders and feel in control for as long as I could until it was time for her to leave the room. We stood up again. I hugged her, gave her a kiss on the cheek, and told her I loved her. I acted as if she had done nothing to me, but I knew I was going to have to address the problem eventually. I was just burying my anger. We walked out of the little room, and I stood there and watched while the marshal shackled my mother again.

I asked, "Is it really necessary to shackle an old lady?"

He looked at me as if I were a thorn in his side and said, "These are our procedures."

Of course, it was a different marshal than the first three. I wondered how many marshals it took to guard one little old lady. In the back of my mind, I was truly stereotyping because my mother was an old lady, but she had stolen. She deserved to be punished and humiliated. I guess I resented it because she was my mother.

Once again, the female marshal showed up at the opportune moment and told the male marshal, "That will not be necessary. All you have to do is handcuff the lady's hands in front of her."

She looked at me and winked. I smiled back at her. I could tell the male marshal did not like her giving him orders, but I think she outranked him. I thought, *You go girl!* I could only smile at her. I knew I could not say anything aloud in front of the male marshal.

I waited until Mom was out of the courtroom and completely out of my sight. Then, it was time for my next task. I had a headache from hell! My brain hurt even more than it had when I got off the airplane. It's not easy being my mother's daughter. Not easy at all. Suddenly tears started flowing down my face as I thought of my aged mother sitting in a jail cell, so humbled. I hurt for her because I knew it would not be easy for her at all.

As I was walking down one of the halls toward the elevators, I saw a water fountain. I took a sip and remembered the previous night's conversation. I had told my mother, "If I can do boot camp, you can do jail, because jail is like a walk in heaven compared to basic training."

I chuckled to myself as I got onto the elevator. Maybe now Mom will prove to me that she is tough and can handle it. Once outside, I immediately lit a cigarette as I walked through the parking lot towards my mother's car. Little Pete got out of the car when he saw me.

As we were getting into the car, he asked, "Is your momma going to be okay?"

I replied, "I'm not sure, but I think so."

Little Pete asked, "What is next?"

I told him, "I have been ordered to get the safes, the car, the pickup truck, and my luggage out. Then I need to go to Auntie Bea's house. What I want to do is hook up Mom's car to her pickup truck, load the safes into the pickup truck, and take everything in one trip to Auntie Bea's. You can leave and go home straight from Auntie Bea's to save us a trip."

Little Pete agreed. "That's a great idea."

CHAPTER XVIII

We arrived at Mom and Pete's house. Both of us were praying that Big Pete hadn't returned yet because I knew there would be a physical altercation with him over the courtroom guard. We pulled up into the driveway, and Big Pete's van was nowhere in sight. Little Pete and I did not say anything because we were thinking the same thing.

Little Pete said, "I'll pull the pickup out and hitch your momma's car to it."

I said, "Okay, I'll go get my luggage together and bring the safes out." Did I bite off more than I could chew? That small safe was heavy, but I got it out into the pickup truck along with my mother's briefcase and a two-drawer file cabinet that was located in her office. I found a handcart and used it to get the larger safe out. When Little Pete saw what I was doing, he stopped what he was doing and helped me lift it into the back of the pickup. I went back in for the other two-drawer file cabinet. I loaded that up into the back of the pickup truck. By then Little Pete had the car hitched to the pickup truck and he was ready to go.

I decided I better get those file boxes as well because they had "legal stuff" and "evidence" written on the outsides of them. There were four of them and they were long and very heavy.

I asked Little Pete, "Can you help me get those file boxes I saw in Momma's office as well? I think it will be important for me to read as much of their contents as I can."

Little Pete answered, "Of course."

We proceeded to move those boxes into Mom's car, but I wasn't going to push my luck, so I told Little Pete, "Let's go before Big Pete gets back."

Little Pete said, "You better leave him a note."

I replied, "You're right, I don't want to start out fighting with him."

So I went back inside to my mother's kitchen. I left him a note saying it would not be civil for your wife's daughter to stay with you without her mother also being there, and I just didn't think it would be right. I only wrote things that I knew Big Pete could relate to without getting upset. I also wrote—even though I didn't mean it—that I was sorry the guard had treated him so badly at the courthouse. I added that I noticed he didn't have much food, only liquor, and I was going to try to help him out a little. I put the note and a $100 bill on the kitchen table. I wrote, "Sincerely, Belinda," at the end of my note, knowing that I didn't mean a word of it. I felt two-faced, but I was going to have to play this game until he was finally out of our lives forever.

Little Pete was waiting for me in his van. I said, "I'm hungry! I haven't had anything to eat since breakfast, and it's already 8:00 p.m. Are you hungry too? I can pick us up something in a grocery store. Oh, and I better go and call Auntie Bea because it is getting late."

Little Pete said, "I'll get something when I get home, but they have a Kroger on the way to your auntie's house if you want to stop in there and get something."

I said, "That will be fine. I'll run back in, call Auntie Bea quickly, and we will be on our way."

Little Pete said, "Okay, Belinda, but make it quick, I'm sure Big Pete will be coming up this driveway soon."

I ran back into the house and found my mother's address and telephone book that I had forgotten to pick up earlier. It was in the kitchen beside the telephone. I quickly dialed Auntie Bea's number. Auntie picked up the phone and said, "Hello."

I said, "Auntie Bea, it's Belinda. May I come and stay with you for a while? Mom is in jail. I will explain everything when I get there. I can be there in a few minutes. Little Pete is with me."

Auntie Bea replied in a surprised voice, "What! Of course you can stay with me. Where are you, and how are you going to get to my house from Germany in a few minutes?"

I said, "Auntie Bea, I'm at Mom's house right now. I will explain everything when I get there."

She said, "Okay, Belinda, hurry up and get here. It's gettinglate."

I said, "Thank you, Auntie Bea, I'm on my way. I love you." I hung the phone up, ran back outside, jumped into my mother's pickup truck with her car hitched to it, and followed Little Pete in his van. We had left just in time, thank God. We reached the end of Mom's street, made a left onto the next one, where we passed by Big Pete heading home. I don't think he recognized us, thank God. By then it was dark, and I'm sure he had been out with friends drinking.

CHAPTER XIX

Little Pete stopped at the grocery store as promised. I ran in to the deli, grabbed a sub, a bag of chips, and other necessary items. On my way to the register, I found some wine. I grabbed a bottle and took everything to the register. I paid for everything and ran back outside to where Little Pete and the cars were waiting for me.

We pulled out of Kroger's parking lot, onto the road, and arrived at Auntie Bea's house about twenty minutes later. She had her spotlights illuminating the yard as she waited for us. Little Pete helped me carry the safes into her house. I told him not to worry about the other stuff. I could get the rest. I said that I would see him on Monday. There was no way that I was going to allow him to work on the weekend. I asked for the keys to my shop, and he gave them to me. I asked if he had been paid for the week. He said no, but I didn't have to pay him until Monday. He would be okay until then. We said our goodbyes. Auntie Bea stood there with a puzzled expression.

I went into her kitchen and started cutting my sub. I asked if she wanted some because it was so big, and I could only eat half of it.

She said, "No, I ate earlier. I want to know what is going on!"

I said, "Auntie Bea, let me collect my thoughts, get something to eat, and take a bath. I stink from this awful, awful day."

Auntie Bea said, "Okay, Belinda, but hurry up!"

I guess the reason that I wanted a shower or a bath so desperately was because during the many years I served in the Army, there were many times I would have to go days without being able to bathe. The stench of your own body odor is very humiliating for a female. In my opinion, using a helmet to take a sponge bath just didn't cut it. It was impossible to feel clean, but things in the Army have changed dramatically since my time.

After I was prepared to eat, I realized that I wasn't hungry after all. I decided to put the sandwich into Auntie Bea's refrigerator and take a bath. I collected my bath paraphernalia, went into her bathroom, and started filling up the tub with nice hot water. As I sat there in the hot bath, I focused on collecting my thoughts so I could focus on the next problem at hand: my Auntie Bea. I heard her telephone ring and heard her muffled voice through the bathroom door. I was sure it was Big Pete. Auntie Bea knocked on the bathroom door. Through the door, she told me that Big Pete was on the phone and wanted to talk to me.

While lying there relaxing in the bathtub, I told Auntie Bea, "Tell Big Pete that I will try to catch up with him tomorrow. Tell him I'm tired and in the bathtub."

Auntie Bea said, "Okay, I will tell him, but, Belinda Denise, you have a lot of explaining to do. You didn't need a bath. I think you are avoiding me as well, young lady."

In exasperation, I yelled, "Auntie Bea, please! I hate to stink! You will be too busy fussing at me because of it, instead of listening to me. Would you rather me be clean sitting beside you or smell like a stinky skunk, who is babbling instead of giving you straight talk?"

Auntie Bea retorted angrily, "Belinda, you kids always seem to make a mountain out of a mole hill. Just be quick about it."

As I was drying myself off, I revisited the many battle scars that I have accumulated throughout the years. I normally do not think about how I received them because "technically" I was never there. After all, I am a woman. But as all rules can be broken, they were for me because I am no ordinary woman. I never have been. I shrugged those memories to the dark corners of my mind.

I came out of the bathroom with a towel wrapped around my wet hair, and I put on clean, comfortable pajamas. Auntie Bea was sitting in one of her big overstuffed chairs in her living room. I sat down beside her in the other overstuffed chair. She had already lit a cigarette and was smoking it. I lit up one of mine, let out a sigh, and asked, "Auntie Bea, would you like to have a glass of wine with me?"

She looked at me. She could tell from the question that the news was going to get worse. She said, "Yes, I better have a glass to calm my nerves also."

I went into her kitchen and opened the bottle of wine that I had purchased at the grocery store. As I poured it into the glasses, I thought,

I'm turning into a wino or a drunk. I don't think I have drank like this in years, but I knew wine and beer were better for you than the alternatives. I really needed something to help me relax, and I don't believe in taking pills and all that psycho mumbo stuff when you are under stress, especially this type of stress. I also thought I would rather be back in the Army instead of here in the middle of this terrible situation. I felt like I was a fly trapped in a spider's web, and there just was no end in sight or way to break free. It was like an episode of *The Twilight Zone*; it was just so unbelievable. I thought, *This only happens on television. It doesn't happen in real life, or if it does, it only happens to other people doing stupid, nasty things to others. Not my family. I knew we were dysfunctional, but I didn't think we were crooks and fraudsters.*

I walked back into the room where Auntie Bea was sitting and gave her a glass of wine. She took a sip; I sat down in the chair beside her and took a sip from my glass. There was a table between the two chairs. I set my glass down on the table beside her glass and picked up my burning cigarette.

I let out another sigh and started to tell Auntie Bea everything that I knew, and everything that had happened this day.

The first thing that came out of Auntie Bea's mouth was, "I can't believe Jane got caught. I can't believe she is going to jail for writing bad checks."

I just looked at her stunned, even though Mom had told me some of the story the night before.

Auntie Bea looked at me and said, "Belinda, don't look at me like that. Jane tells me everything, who do you think was helping her?" Then she asked me, "Am I in any trouble?"

Dumbfounded as I was, I answered, "I don't know, Auntie Bea, I don't know."

Auntie Bea asked, "Who's going to give me money? What about my property?"

I sat there shaking my head in total disbelief. I told her directly, "I'm not going to steal, lie, or cheat for you, Auntie Bea. I will keep my promise and try to get your land back for you. I will do my very best to pick up all the bad checks that you and Mom wrote. I will see what I can do with the U.S. Attorney's office about not indicting you as well. I promised Mom that I would do everything in my power to protect you and Uncle Frank, but I didn't know that you were this involved until you told me. I want to know how you lost your land."

Auntie Bea started to tell me the story. "I went to your mom, I guess, in 1991. I wanted the Daisy house because it's in the middle of my property. Your mom would not buy it for me, so I took my CD and bought it. Then I realized I needed the additional income that I had received monthly from the CD. I realized that I could not afford to maintain both homes, so I went to your mom. None of the banks would loan me the money without your mom and Pete cosigning, so she and I went to Pete, and he agreed to do it. Your mom and Pete had to file for bankruptcy in the beginning of 1998. A few months later, I tried to do the same, but the judge said I made too much money and denied me bankruptcy." Then she just stopped. Again, I sat there just shaking my head.

I already knew the entire story of course because my mom had told it to me, but I was still stunned and upset with my great-aunt when those words came out of her own mouth.

She had told me about the irrevocable trust that she nagged Mom into creating for her, and how she had put Mom and Big Pete as the trustees. She even pulled it out of her files. I was so disappointed in my great-aunt.

I said, "Auntie Bea, you are a sexist! I'm your other goddaughter and your blood, but you wanted that sorry-ass creep Big Pete to help you. If you had done it the traditional way, and put both your godchildren on as trustees, this never would have happened."

Poor Auntie Bea, she looked at me and started crying. "But he was rich and you aren't! Because he was married to your mother, I thought I would be living high on the hog without any more worries about money."

I said, "Auntie Bea, it was always an illusion of grandeur. It was never real. They were living off other people for years. I hate to say it, Auntie Bea, but I warned all of you years ago what I thought of Big Pete, and none of you listened to me. You just brushed me off, as always, thinking I was just a silly girl. All you people could see, including my mother, were the fake dollar signs that Big Pete flashed before your eyes. Now you have all turned into crooks trying to save what you originally had, but it's all gone. I'm only one ex-soldier, Auntie Bea, and I'm all that the three of you have left. I don't know if my best is going to be good enough to win this war that you have thrust upon me. Intentional or not, it only proves to me that you were always crooks and fraudsters. The only thing Big Pete did was bring the true crooks in all three of you into the light, and yes, I am referring to you, my mother, and Uncle Frank." I let out a sigh again.

Auntie Bea didn't say another word.

I said, "Auntie Bea, let me go through some of your records."

She showed me the drawers where she kept them. She was a packrat like my mother, and she kept every single piece of documentation. It was all in order and filed in a safe place. She easily located the papers. I had already brought in a box of records recording the indictments and legal proceedings that involved my mother. I needed to sit down, piece together who all the bad people were, and figure out who was the guiltiest for my peace of mind. It was already 2:30 a.m. I knew I had drilled my great-aunt to death since I had arrived.

I said, "I still love you, Auntie Bea, and I will still try to help. Let's go to bed and stop thinking about it today. We will wake up refreshed, and maybe I will have an answer for you in the morning."

Auntie Bea went upstairs. I followed her as she went into her room.

She was in bed within five minutes. I went into Gary's old room. I closed the door so the light would not disturb her. I settled down on the bed and started reading the legal documents. After looking through one file, I checked the clock on the nightstand. Almost 4:30 a.m. I was exhausted. I crawled off the bed, put the file back into the box, and turned off the light. As I walked toward the bed in the dark I thought, *I'll get some sleep now and then decide what action to take next.* As I walked over to the bed, I remembered all the years of specialized training I always volunteered to learn, "psychological warfare." Was this the war I just entered? I crawled into the old musty bed. I think the mattress must have been almost as old as I was. I didn't care. I knew I had slept on much, much worse in my day and in far worse conditions than my mother and Auntie Bea could ever imagine. I closed my eyes and went straight to sleep without another thought, my head still aching horribly. I refused to take any aspirin that my auntie had offered me earlier because the bottle had been dated 1965. When I saw that date, I promptly threw them in the trash. I told Auntie Bea that I would buy her a new bottle, but she was very angry with me for wasting good pills. Auntie Bea—what was I going to do with her?

CHAPTER XX

I woke up and looked at the old electric alarm clock that was sitting on the table beside Gary's old bed. It was 9:30 a.m.! I could not believe that I slept so late! I had not slept that late in years. Normally, I automatically woke up at 5:00 a.m. every day. It didn't matter if I went to bed late or had too much wine the night before. I sat on the edge of the bed, and I felt like I had been run over by a fully loaded tractor-trailer. That feeling only lasted for a second before my adrenalin took over once again. My mind automatically focused on the severity of the mission that I had taken on. I stripped the sheets off my temporary bed, carried them out into the hall, and threw them over the stair rail.

I went back into Gary's old bedroom, grabbed my toothbrush and a clean change of clothes, and ran down the stairs toward the only full bathroom in Auntie Bea's house. I set my toothbrush and clothes on the edge of the sink, went back into the hallway, and picked up the sheets. I put them into the washing machine, added powdered detergent, and started the washer. I went back into the bathroom, freshened up, dressed, and I was ready to start the day.

Auntie Bea lived in an old, white clapboard farmhouse that was built in the early 1800s by Uncle Herndon's great-great-great-grandfather. It was built on the site of the old cabin that was torn down to make room for the house. The Mills farm had been in Uncle Herndon's family for over 175 years and was passed from one generation to the other. Uncle Herndon's father put in the bathroom and plumbing. Uncle Herndon added a mud room that held Auntie Bea's washing machine and dryer, a couple of old chest freezers, and two antique wardrobes. One wardrobe was cedar, and my grandmother had one that was identical. My mother received it when my grandmother died, and she promptly gave it to me. I was storing it in the Daisy house. The other wardrobe was oak. It was painted dark brown and had a full-length mirror on the door. The tiny room contained a toilet, nothing else.

Many, many years ago, right before Uncle Herndon and Auntie Bea were married, the Commonwealth forced Uncle Herndon's father to sell a portion of the farm because it was in the path of the planned Route 901, also known as Burnwood Road. That road split the farm into two sections. There were thirty-three acres on one side and sixty-six acres on the other side. The Mills farmhouse and the Daisy house were located on the sixty-six acres. Uncle Herndon and Ms. Daisy's husband built Ms. Daisy's house. It was a ranch-style brick home with an unfinished basement. It was approximately 3,350 square feet including the unfinished basement. It was built in the 1950s.

My Auntie Bea is a very skinny woman, so thin that she almost looked like a skeleton with skin. The old photographs that she had hanging on the wall in her living room showed that even in her youth she was that slender. She colored her hair an auburn color and wore her hair in a bouffant (teased puff on the top of her head), the style women wore in the late 1950s and early 1960s. She faithfully went to the hairdressers to have it cleaned and styled once a week. She never washed her hair in between the weekly hairdresser appointment. She always had someone who took care of her. She never had to lift a finger to provide for herself financially. First it was her father, my great-grandfather, next was her older sister (my grandmother), then it was Uncle Herndon and his parents, and finally my mother. She never had any money. In fact, neither did Uncle Herndon. Uncle Herndon was a butcher at Safeway for over thirty years. When he died, he left her a modest amount of money, barely enough to support her, but he also had left her great wealth in the land that he had inherited.

Auntie Bea was from the Depression era, and to this day, she still lived as if she were in the Depression. She was very frugal. One example of her frugality was that she reused coffee grounds to save money. Uncle Frank was the same way. My grandmother was the total opposite. Auntie Bea had a seventh-grade education, but I consider her a very savvy lady because she was very good at manipulating people to do her bidding. Maybe that's where my mother learned it.

Auntie Bea loved her cigarettes and was a chain smoker. She didn't cook simply because she didn't enjoy cooking. Her hobby was gossip! She came across as a sweet little old lady, until you really came to know her. For as long as I can remember, my grandmother always warned us about her. She called Auntie Bea a "money-grubbing whore" numerous times. My mother and I thought my grandma was just jealous because Mom paid more attention to Auntie Bea during the last few years of my grandmother's life. Now, I can truly relate to Grandma's feelings. To be completely honest, I didn't know who the bigger crook was: Auntie Bea, Big Pete, or my mother. When I was done with my daily toiletries, I walked into my auntie's family room. Auntie Bea was sitting in her chair. She had a cigarette in her right hand and a cup of coffee on the table beside her.

I smiled and said, "Good morning, Auntie Bea. Today is a fresh, new day."

When I looked out the window, I saw that the sun was shining, and most of the snow had melted.

Auntie Bea replied with anger in her voice, "Belinda, it is not a good day and it most certainly is not a fresh one! What is the matter with you? Have you forgotten what has happened?"

I walked over to my auntie, gave her a kiss on the top of her forehead, and said, "Yes, Auntie Bea, it is a good and fresh day because you and I are going to work together to make things as right and clean as rain again. You're not going to like it, but you and Uncle Frank are going to have to start telling me the entire truth and helping me so I can undo the financial crap you guys have gotten yourselves into because of greed. I don't want to hear another word come out of your mouth, Auntie Bea! I'm going to do everything in order to detach you and Uncle Frank from that sorry-ass creep Pete King, and also my momma."

Auntie Bea's face was in total shock because of the manner in which I had spoken to her and because I had cursed.

Auntie Bea stated in a shocked, angry tone, "Belinda Denise, I am your godmother, and you will not speak to me in such a manner ever again!"

By this time, Auntie Bea had gotten up from her chair and was standing in front of me.

I replied in a low, deadly tone, "Sit down, Auntie Bea. For the first time in your life, you will listen to me. The moment that you stole from me is the moment that you lost my respect. You are damn lucky that I haven't decided to break every single one of your fingers for doing such a nasty thing to your goddaughter. If you want my respect, you will have to earn it back. This time I am not going to give it to you freely. You made a vow to God, and to me, that you would be my godmother! I don't remember anything in the vows that said it was okay to have your one goddaughter, my mother, steal from your other goddaughter, me, for your benefit. I am not stupid! You and my mother have already confessed to me your crimes against me. I promised my mother that I would try to help you and Uncle Frank. Unlike you, I keep my word to the best of my ability. I don't like being lied to, Auntie Bea! It hurts my feelings because I know that you're not telling me everything.

"You have come clean on almost everything you have done. My mother asked for my forgiveness. I have been able to forgive her for almost all of it. Your stories are similar, but there are major differences and huge gaps in them—"

I suddenly stopped and stated, "I'm getting a cup of coffee."

I calmly walked out of the living room into the kitchen. I figured that would give my great-aunt a moment or two to mull over what I had said. I picked a cup out of the cupboard and filled it with coffee. I carried it back into the living room, sat in the other chair, and lit a cigarette. I sat there sipping my strong coffee (I could tell that this was the first time she used the grounds), smoked my cigarette, and looked at Auntie Bea.

Auntie Bea was furious! She had her small lips curled up and she glared at me through squinted eyes. She stated in a measured tone, "I'm sorry, Belinda, that I was part of it, but I was desperate! They stole my land!"

I let out a sigh and said sadly, "Auntie Bea, nobody stole your land. You did this to yourself. Granted my mother and Big Pete encouraged you to help with the rest of the mess, but you made the choice to join them. I am going to help you. I will do my very best to get you out of this mess, and I forgive you for what you have done to me. I am going to tell you the same thing I told my mother. When you dance with the devil, your feet always get burned. You should know this better than I do. Now, I need to start to work on cleaning up this mess and obtaining funds for you to live on. Please tell Uncle Frank that I will be over at the Daisy house later today to talk with him also, okay?"

Auntie Bea replied, "Okay. Belinda, how are you going to get us out of this mess? It's so much money!"

I answered, "I don't know, Auntie Bea, I don't know. But I will say again; I am not going to steal, lie, or cheat for any of you. All I know is that I'll try to save Uncle Frank and you from sinking with the *Titanic* of your creation; it's too late for my mother. All I can do now is try to make it as easy as I can for her because she has already drowned in the financial mess she created."

I got up and gave her another kiss on her forehead. I walked out of the living room and down the hallway to the mudroom. I took the sheets out of the washer and put them into the dryer. I added a dryer sheet, shut the door, set the timer, and started it. I then went back into the living room, and sat down.

I told Auntie Bea, "I just don't know exactly what Momma has done, or how much. I'm still working on finding out all the details. I need to begin my investigation. I'll be back later today. I love you, Auntie Bea, God help me. I love you, Momma and Uncle Frank. It hurts so much! I'm so humiliated and ashamed of all of you."

Auntie Bea started crying. I guess she had just realized that she was as guilty of destroying our family as Momma was. She softly said, "I'm so sorry, Belinda! I'm sorry! I didn't think I was hurting anyone! I now know that I am just as much to blame for this as your mother is. I still blame Big Pete for most of it because I still hold him more responsible for this than any of us."

I just let out a sigh, got up from the chair, and hugged my Auntie Bea. I knew it wasn't going to get much better because I didn't know if I would be able to generate enough cash from my shop quickly enough to fix this. I still had no clue exactly how bad the situation was.

I went back to the mudroom, got the sheets from the dryer, and went upstairs to make the bed. I then walked back downstairs and headed to the door. As I was walking out the door, I gave Auntie Bea a hug and a kiss and promised, "No matter what happens, I will make sure you have a roof over your head and food in your belly."

She smiled, and I think she felt better.

CHAPTER XXI

I jumped into Momma's old pickup truck and headed to the bank in Greenville, which was only a few minutes' drive away.

I asked one of the tellers, "Could you direct me to someone who could assist me in opening a checking account?"

She guided me to a small office that contained a chair and a desk. She asked if I could wait a few minutes and said that someone would help me momentarily. I said "Thank you" and sat down. I waited about ten to fifteen minutes before a middle-aged woman in a business suit came in. I stood up as she greeted me.

I pulled my military ID, Virginia driver's license and an international driver's license out of my purse as I sat down again in the chair that was in front of the desk. I explained that the account was a temporary account, and asked the normal questions on opening and closing an account. The woman answered all my questions satisfactorily, and I accepted the checking account terms and conditions. She proceeded to put my information into the bank's database. She looked at me and said there was a warning not to open another account for me.

I said, "What? I have been living in Germany for the last four years! I have never opened a checking account with your bank before in my life. There must be some mistake."

She replied, "I have never seen this before. I'm going to have to speak to my manager. Can you wait here for a few minutes?"

I said, "Sure." After she walked out, it hit me. *My mother.*

The woman came back with her manager, who also had a puzzled expression on her face as well. I started explaining what my mother did, and that I was sure she did it. I told them the whole story. The manager looked at me with sympathy. She looked at the computer screen, which I could not see and told me that I was correct. It was indeed my mother. The manager gave me the dates on which the account was opened and closed, and she showed me the forged signature card. She said there was no doubt in her mind it was not my signature because my military ID and driver's license had my signature on them, and my signature was completely different from the one that they had on record. It was obvious that someone had impersonated me. She also told me the warning was there because my mother had written several thousand dollars of bad checks. It was some sort of check scheme she had been doing with other bank accounts, but this bank had a ten-day hold on all deposited checks. My mother was angry because they held the checks she deposited for ten days. The checks she was depositing were written from accounts that had no money, and she knew that she would be discovered in ten days, so she closed the account.

The manager told me, "At that point, the manager at the time put a warning on your name. No one knew it wasn't really you." She told me that they could use my husband's social security number with my name so I could open the checking account without any further problems. She promised she would fix it for me. I thanked her immensely because they had bent the rules for me. I believe that was the only way she could manipulate their computer system to open my checking account. I needed the account opened for my business as quickly as possible.

I left the bank and drove up the street to where my shop was. I had never seen my shop, but I was able to find it by the descriptions Mom had given over the past year.

CHAPTER XXII

Mom wanted to call the shop "Cognac's Run." I am terrible at coming up with creative names. Cognac was my mother's beloved dog, and he had passed away from old age. Cognac was a Dachshund, and he was the color of Cognac, hence his name. I had agreed with Mom that was a perfect name for our shop.

The shop was located in one of the original buildings that made up downtown Greenville. It was on the corner of Burnwood (Route 901) and Route 54, which led to Washington, D.C. My shop was one of several stores on this corner; it was between a barn-red, three-story wooden building, and on the other side was a tin building. My shop was also painted barn red because my one wall was adjoined to the other building. It looked like it came right out of an old western movie set in the early 1800s. My shop was the only one with a big window in the front of it. Arched above the window, in large gold letters, were the words "Antiques & Collectibles." I stood there with a smile on my face and let out a sigh. My dream, the one that I had held on to for so long, was alive and breathing right in front of me. Little did I know at the time that my dream wouldn't really come true for me at all. I did not earn one penny from all the years of hard work and money that I had been putting into my inventory to make my dream happen. In fact, I had lost hundreds of thousands of dollars. I stood there and looked at my store with pride, and then tears of sadness filled my eyes. My dream had turned into a nightmare, thanks to my mother.

I let out another sigh and walked up to the door to unlock it. It was already unlocked. I walked through the door and heard the little brass bell tinkle as I opened and then closed the door. I saw Big Pete standing in the middle of my shop. I was livid at the sight of him standing there in front of me.

As I looked to the back of my shop, I saw filing cabinets that were turned backwards. They appeared to have been set up that way to block off one fifth of the shop space. I walked towards the filing cabinets, but Big Pete hurried in front of me and greeted me.

He said, "Well, what do think of what your mother has done with the place?"

I looked at him, and he was smiling with pride. I kept my thoughts and emotions in check as I spoke, "It looks great, better than I had hoped for. You and Mom have done a great job."

Big Pete replied, "Oh, no, Belinda, I can't take credit for any of it. It was all your momma's doings. I just have my office space in the back for my business. You know the same old, same old." He continued, "Oh, I completely understand why you didn't stay at our house last night. When you explained it in your note to me, I completely agreed. It wouldn't be proper because you know how neighbors like to gossip; even when it's none of their business. Plus I know this is probably real hard for your auntie and your uncle."

I said nonchalantly, "Yes, Big Pete, it's going to be very hard for them. Do you know if Momma has paid for this month's rent? I need the name and phone number of the landlord. I also need the records and tax information for the shop, farm, and the Daisy house as well."

Big Pete answered, "Oh, I'm sure she has all that information in this desk of hers somewhere. You may want to get familiar with it."

I started to walk toward the desk Big Pete had indicated. It was facing the back wall of the shop. I started going through the drawers. With Big Pete's help, I found what I needed. She had the paperwork from the bank, tax bills, utility bills, and everything else I would need in the drawers. I found an empty box and filled it with as many papers as I could fit in it. I taped the top shut.

When I was finished, I looked around my shop. There were hundreds of my porcelain, ceramics, and paintings displayed throughout the shop along with some of my inventory: crystal pieces that I had bought and shipped back from the Czech Republic, my pottery from Poland, and various pieces of artwork from Italy, England, Germany, France, and numerous other countries. I looked with pride at the different displays and was amazed at how beautiful it looked. There were many other antiques and collectibles that I did not recognize.

As I was preparing to leave, Big Pete said, "Oh, Belinda, thanks for the money."

He then walked to the back of the shop. I followed him and saw he had his own office back there. Even though he mentioned it earlier, it still took every ounce of discipline to contain my anger. He then handed me a stack of credit card bills. I looked at him dumbfounded and then looked down at the top bill. It had my name on it! I became even more furious.

I contained my emotions and said with a fictitious smile, "Thanks, Big Pete. I'll take care of these if I think it is necessary."

Big Pete simply said, "I thought you might." He then let out a venomous chuckle.

I wanted to reach up and rip out his throat, but instead I calmly said, "Since you are going to be here today, and I need to take care of other business, I'll wait until tomorrow to come to the house to start packing my mother's clothes, if that's okay with you?"

Big Pete looked at me with a puzzled expression. I guess because my reaction wasn't what he was expecting. I just chuckled silently to myself. Big Pete simply stated, "That's fine."

"Well, I better get on my way."

The telephone rang. Before Big Pete had a chance to answer it, I picked it up and said, "Good afternoon, Cognac's Run." It was a recording from the jail asking if I would accept the charges for a phone call from Jane King. I accepted the charges, and I heard my mother's voice.

She started the conversation by telling me how terrible jail was and that I needed to come see her. She told me some of the procedures and where she was. She was in the county jail. She said they did not give her medication, and she needed it. One person told her that I could have the pharmacy deliver it straight to the jail. That was the only way they could accept it. She said that I needed to get the ashes of her beloved dogs. I told her I had already gotten them, and they were at Auntie Bea's, along with her safes. She said I had to set up an account with Western Union at one of the grocery stores, but she wasn't sure which one, and put money on it as well as the phone numbers of Pete, Auntie Bea, Uncle Frank, and Cognac Run's. She told me that when I visited the jail, I needed to find out everything regarding their procedures. I told her that I was about to leave the shop, and I would change my plans for the day and be there shortly.

When she was done speaking with me, she asked if she could speak to Big Pete. I passed the telephone over to him.

As soon as I passed the phone to Big Pete, the little brass bell started to tinkle. I saw Little Pete coming through the door.

I told him, "Little Pete, today is your day off."

Little Pete said, "I know, Miss Belinda, but I thought you might need me anyway."

I asked, "I guess I do because I don't know where the county jail is. Can you drive me in Momma's pickup truck?"

Little Pete's face lit up with a smile. "Yes, ma'am."

I looked over at Big Pete. He already had hung the phone up after talking with my mother. He said that once I learned out how things worked at the jail, he would see my mother too. I told him that I would let him know, and Little Pete and I left the shop. Because Big Pete was at the shop, I asked Little Pete to take me straight to my mother's house instead of the jail. When we arrived, I went to the back door. I put my key in to the doorknob and unlocked it, but that idiot, Big Pete, forgot to lock it. I went up to my mother's bedroom and packed more of her small jewelry boxes. Little Pete helped me carry them out to the truck.

We went into her sheds and retrieved more paperwork that she had stored there. We loaded up the pickup. I didn't know at the time, but I was collecting evidence against Big Old Pete. At the time, I just knew my mother had been a packrat, and whatever I was picking up had to be something that could be used against Big Pete. Once the truck was loaded, I went into the house for one last check to make sure I had everything I needed. I then set the alarm, the one Big Pete forgot to use. Little Pete and I jumped into the pickup truck and headed toward the county jail.

CHAPTER XXIII

While we were in route to the county jail, Little Pete told me that my mother had a storage unit, and he had the keys. He told me that she had opened it about a year ago, and it was where she stored her things that she did not want to keep in her house because of Big Pete. I told him if we had time after visiting my mom in jail, he would have to show me where it was. He said that he would gladly do so. I realized that it was very important to him that I knew about it, but I couldn't figure out why because he hadn't told me about it during our previous conversations.

We pulled into the parking lot of the county jail, and the first thing I thought was how small it was. It was a square one-story brick building surrounded by a high fence with three rows of barbed wire on the top. The only section of the jail that was not fenced in was the main entrance. Little Pete pulled into a parking spot and turned off the truck. We climbed out and walked toward the main entrance of the building. It was around 5:00 p.m. We walked through a set of glass double doors, through the tiny foyer, and then through the next set of glass double doors.

When I entered the main lobby, the first thing I saw was a counter in the middle of the wall I was facing. There was bulletproof glass from the top of the counter to the ceiling. In the center of the glass was a metal circle that had numerous slits through it. There were no other openings in the glass, but there was a small slot between the bottom of the window and the top of the counter. To the right of the window was a door. There were six sets of red plastic chairs scattered throughout the room. They were bolted to the floor and connected to the wall by metal rods. There was a soda machine on the wall to my left and a snack machine on the wall to my right.

I could see people in police uniforms sitting at desks through the window. There was a small, round, white button to my right. I stood at the window for a minute, but no one noticed that I was there. I reached over, pushed the button, and heard a buzzer sound. Several of the people who were sitting at the desks looked up at the window and saw me, but they did not move. After a few minutes, a short, young, overweight officer finally came to the window and asked, through the glass, if he could help me.

I answered, "Yes, sir. My mother, Jane King, was brought here last night. I have come from Germany and would like to see her. I also need to know your procedures for providing her medication and telephone access."

He replied in an irritated voice, "Ma'am, it is 5:00 p.m., and visiting hours for females are Wednesdays and Saturdays between 1:00 and 3:00 p.m. As far as her medication is concerned, you will have to come back on Monday to find out."

He handed me a piece of paper with the procedures for telephone access and said I would have to read it.

The past few days had been very stressful for me. I believed I had done an excellent job controlling my emotions, but his rudeness was the straw that broke the camel's back. My temper flared, but I managed to keep a cool tone and demeanor.

I retorted, "Sir, my name is Belinda Denise Star. I am a veteran of the United States Army, and my husband, Thomas G. Star, is still active duty. He is stationed in Germany, where I have just come from. I have flown from Germany to be with my mother as she goes through this because it is my duty as a daughter. I have not committed any crimes or wrongdoings, nor do I plan to. I do not appreciate you talking to me with such lack of respect. I'm sure you have guidelines for when an inmate has a family member coming from another country to visit. Please have a little bit of sympathy toward this family member, and find out what I need to do so that I may see my mother now."

The little snot-nosed punk and an older officer peered through the window at me. The older man pushed the snot-nosed punk out of the way, and apologized. "Ma'am, I am truly sorry for the behavior of my subordinate. You are correct; he had no right to disrespect you in that manner. Yes, we have procedures for family members in your type of situation. Can I please see your military ID, driver's license, passport, and airline ticket?"

I said in a much softer tone, "Yes, sir, and thank you."

He simply confessed, "I'm a veteran of the Marines myself. Civilians just don't understand."

I said again, "Thank you, sir." I looked at his nametag, noting that it said Sergeant Smith.

As I was digging through my purse to find all the items that he requested, I looked up. Sergeant Smith had left the window and was walking toward one of the desks. I saw him open a drawer and pull out papers. I found everything he requested and put it in the little slot between the glass and the counter. He came back to the window and instructed me to walk through the door to the right side of the window as he took my documents. The door was a gray, thick, steel door. It had a single handle and a very small window at the top. I heard a buzzer sound and the door click as it unlocked. I opened it and walked through.

Sergeant Smith was standing just on the other side, and he guided me to the room that I had seen earlier through the window. I looked back through the window and saw Little Pete in the lobby. He was pacing back and forth.

I sat down in front of Sergeant Smith's desk, and he started filling out a stack of forms. He periodically checked my documents for information that he needed. After a few minutes, he had completed all his forms. He looked up at me and said, "You can come every day, and any time between 10 a.m. through 6 p.m. for the next week. After that, you can only visit on regular visiting days, which are Wednesdays and Saturdays. You will need this form that I have completed in case I'm not here. You will need to sign it. Each time you visit you will need to show the officer on duty this, your airline ticket, and your military ID. You will have a maximum of fifteen minutes to visit with her each time. Okay?"

I answered with a grateful smile, "Okay, and again, thank you so much for your help."

He said, "You're welcome. You will need to go back out to the waiting room, and we will get your mother."

I said, "Yes, sir. Thank you, sir." I walked back through the steel door. Little Pete was standing at the door impatiently waiting for me.

He asked, "Well? Can you see her?"

I smiled as I answered,. "Yes, but I will have to wait a little bit longer before I can see her."

Little Pete reached over and hugged me. He said, "I'm so happy they are allowing you to see her."

Little Pete and I waited in the lobby for about twenty minutes. I heard the buzzer that unlocked the door. I looked over at the door and saw a black female officer step through the door. She called, "Belinda Star?"

I stood up and walked over to her. I greeted her, "Hello, how are you?" She merely grunted at me and scowled. She was even rude to Little Pete when he greeted her as well. Her personality oozed with contempt for us. I had the feeling that she thought I was inferior to her. I did not like her mannerism at all. I noted the name on her badge: "Green." She was a voluptuous, full-figured woman, who wore her uniform pants skin tight, and her shirt gapped at the buttons. I had gained a few pounds since leaving the Army, but I wore clothes that fit me and left some breathing room.

Ms. Green would not let Little Pete accompany me to see my mother. She escorted me into a small room with a row of six booths that were divided by gray painted wood on the bottom and Plexiglas on the top. Each booth had a chair and telephone on each side. I stood there and saw a door on the other side of these booths. It opened, and I saw my mother come through it. I could see Ms. Green walking behind her, and she had her hand clutched tightly on my mother's upper arm. She pushed my mother into one of the chairs and then stood behind her, watching and listening. I slowly walked over to the booth and sat down across from my mother. We both looked at the telephone on each other's side, and we picked up our phones in unison.

I heard my mother's voice coming through the telephone, and through the Plexiglas, I could see her mouth moving. I put my open hand on the Plexiglas, and she did the same. We sat there with our hands together yet separated by the cold, unfeeling Plexiglas that separated us. When I looked at my mother through the divider, I was shocked by her appearance. She appeared to have aged twenty years overnight! There was white slime around her teeth, and white powder around the outside of her lips. Her hair was greasy and unwashed. I could not believe she was the same woman who always had taken such great pride in her appearance.

She told me that she was never given a blanket, pillow, or a mattress. She had to sleep on the springs of the cot. They didn't give her a toothbrush or any toiletries. She was still wearing the same underwear and bra that she had on when she was arrested. She had not had any of her medication because they refused to give it to her. I could tell her blood pressure was up because her face was beet red and her fingers were swollen. I noticed they had taken her wedding ring.

I thought, *What have I done? Was I wrong? She didn't do anything to deserve this treatment. We don't even treat our prisoners of war like this. What is wrong with our justice system?* Cold, nasty people that collaborate with blood-sucking attorneys and crooked judges run the majority of our jails. *What had I done? I would never be able to forgive myself if something happened to my mother. What have I sacrificed my life for?* I saw a cockroach scampering across the floor. I was livid at the inhumane way my mother was being treated. I told my mother I would do my very best to do something about this. I told her that I loved her and I would see her tomorrow.

Ms. Green came back in. Without saying a word, she grabbed my mother by the upper arm and jerked into a standing position. I had now reached my limit. I jumped out of my chair and yelled at the top of my lungs so she could hear me through the Plexiglas, "Stop! I want to speak to your superior immediately!"

She looked at me for a moment. I know she heard me, but she chose to ignore me. That would be the biggest mistake that nasty woman would make. I walked out of the room and went to Sergeant Smith's office. His door was open. I tapped on the door and requested to speak to him ASAP. He waved me in, and I sat in the same chair from before. I proceeded to tell him what I had discovered. I told him that I would camp out on their front steps until my mother was given the basics. His facial expression became angry as his eyes narrowed and he had a furrowed brow while listening to me. I stated that he knew our country did not treat war criminals and prisoners of war in such a manner.

"So why in the hell are we treating our own citizens in such a distasteful manner?"

By this time, his true attitude appeared. He was clearly agitated and angry with me. He stated in a powerful authoritative tone that she was in jail and that she was a criminal. She was now a ward of the state, and the only reason he allowed more leeway to me was that I had done so much good in my life that it offset all the bad things that my mother had done in hers. He said that she was there for a reason and that I needed to settle down and respect the rules.

My anger diminished a bit. "Sir, I follow the rules and I have no problem following the rules and procedures, but tell me this, sir, since you were in the military, if your commander told you to kill a prisoner for no reason, would you? Or would you defy his order? Isn't this the same thing I'm doing? You are treating my mother as subhuman because she was a thief. This dictates to me that you treat all your prisoners in this manner. Are they not still citizens of our country? What gives you the right not to give my mother the basics? Of course, you hold all the power and I have none, but I will go to JAG and find out the procedures to see that everyone in this state knows what you are doing. I will write my Congressman. I will expose what you have been doing to anyone that will listen and let the public make the decision if I'm right or wrong. Granted my mother is a thief and she deserves to be punished, but should not the punishment fit the crime?"

I guess that's all it took, threatening to report him. I knew I was right.

He said in a less threatening manner, "Okay, Mrs. Star, you have made your point. I give my word your mother will receive the basics. There is no more need for drama, and I promise I will discipline the guard."

I said, "You will do it in front of me so I know that you have disciplined her. I will wait here until my mother has a mattress, sheets, blankets, and a pillow. I expect her to have a toothbrush, soap, shampoo, and towels, and for her to be taken to the showers so she can bathe ASAP."

He picked up the phone and requested that Ms. Green come to his office. A few minutes later, she was in front of us. He verbally reprimanded her for using unnecessary force against my mother and disciplined her for being rude to Little Pete and me. He informed her that he would write her up if she did it again.

After she left, he looked over at me and asked, "Are you satisfied?"

I answered, "Yes."

He picked up the phone again and spoke to someone about the necessities for my mother. He hung up the phone and said, "Everything has been taken care of. I'm sure your mother will report everything to you the next time you speak with her. I am truly sorry for the bad experience."

I knew he was full of it and the only reason he met my demands was that I had threatened to go to the media. As far as the discipline, he only gave a verbal warning. I'm sure their rude practices will continue against the inmates and their families. Granted some deserve it, but others do not. I said, "I humbly apologize for my behavior. Thank you for making sure that my mother is provided for." I assured him that I would follow his procedures and asked about my mother's medications.

He said, "There is nothing I can do about that. The only thing that I can do is to write a note on her file."

I didn't dare push my luck with him any further, but I knew my mother needed her medications. I knew I could do nothing else to help her. I realized that I needed my baby sister's verbal skills to make them give her meds to her. At that moment, I knew that I could not handle everything without her. I just prayed to God that Christina would unite with me. I knew without her, I was going to fail. United we stand, divided we fall. It was going to take two strong-willed and intelligent sisters to do this and to do it correctly. I knew my single best, one ex-soldier (veteran), was not going to be good enough this time. There were too many battles to fight in this mess.

I was a damned good foot soldier, and now I was starting to realize that maybe my country was not great enough for me to sacrifice my life, or was it? "Greatness" isn't just a word. It's the interpretation and the idea of the word. Sometimes I think that the majority of my fellow Americans have lost the true meaning of this idea; the meaning that our forefathers believed in. Could this part of the idea mean just plain old common sense and decency to your fellow man? Should this idea apply throughout our communities and our country? To fight, kill and be killed for freedom, common decency, and respect to your fellow man; to stand by right and fight against wrong; when to fight and when not to? When to convict and when to let it go? To treat *all* the people equally? I don't know the answer, only my God does.

I got up from the chair and walked to the cold, gray, steel door. The officer pushed the buzzer; I opened the door and stepped back into the lobby. Little Pete was standing there anxiously waiting for me. I didn't say a word until we were outside the jail and standing beside the pickup truck.

I verbally expressed my thoughts, "I need a cigarette, and I need to collect my thoughts, Little Pete." I lit my cigarette and inhaled.

Little Pete asked impatiently, "How is your momma, Belinda?"

I simply answered, "It was awful." I took a few more puffs and climbed into the pickup.

As I was putting my cigarette out, he asked with concern, "What do you mean?"

I answered him, "They have not given her any blood pressure medication yet."

Little Pete asked frantically, "What? She could have a stroke or something. What are you going to do?"

I solemnly answered, "I'm going to call my sister."

Little Pete said, "Oh, shit, Belinda, you know your sister isn't going to help. I don't think your momma wants her to know anything because your sister is so judgmental towards her."

I said dejectedly, "I don't care. I at least have to try. I need her desperately. She knows how to fight this system. I do not." It occurred to me that I really should have something to eat and drink. My body had been running on pure adrenalin all day, and I knew I had to settle down first. The thought ran through my mind that I wasn't on the battlefield—or was I? It was just a different type of war that was being fought in a more civilized manner—or was it more civilized? My instinct was to protect myself, but from exactly what? And whom? My poor little brain had to figure this out. It seemed like the answer should be staring me straight in the face. I had to call my sister immediately before I did anything else to try to help my mother.

As we were pulling out of the parking lot, I asked Little Pete, "Could you please stop at a convenience store or something? I really need some water and a bite to eat."

Little Pete said, "There is a little store about ten minutes from here."

I said, "That sounds great."

CHAPTER XXIV

We were about an hour and a half away from the Mills farm when Little Pete pulled into the store. We went inside and I grabbed a liter of water and a large fountain Coke. I saw that they had tuna sandwiches in their cold-storage units, and I picked one up. Little Pete showed up at the counter with a fountain soda and a sandwich. We paid for our supper and hit the road again.

As we were driving back, I thought of my baby sister. I was so proud of Christina's accomplishments; I had been my whole life. She was the one who had the book sense, and I was the one with the common sense. School always came easy for her. I always had to study more than she did. I was eighteen months older, and I was two grades above her. I'm a Scorpio; she is a Leo. Maybe that's one reason we didn't get along anymore.

Christina had her master's degree in psychology, and she was a counselor. She worked mainly with abused teenage girls. I think she pursued this field because of the abuse that she and I endured as children, but that was only an older sister's speculation. I didn't know if it was a fact.

In addition to her intellectual abilities, Christina was gorgeous. She had blond hair and the most beautiful blue eyes. When you looked into her eyes, it was like looking at the sky on a beautiful sunny day. With her eyes, she could make you feel as if you were the only person who mattered and that you were all she cared about. When she was angry, those same eyes could make you feel so small. She had maintained her perfect figure, and she still could make men's heads turn. She was just a beautiful woman, and I was so proud that I was her sister. I guess I considered her a goddess of pure physical beauty Even though we frequently disagreed and were not close, I was still proud to call her "Sis-sis," a nickname that I had given her when we were toddlers. She used to call me "Sissy," and she still does from time to time.

In my opinion, Christina was hardheaded. She was so proud and arrogant she would never admit when she was wrong. If she couldn't make you agree with her or at least see things from her point of view, she would just shut the door. She would cut off all communication until she was ready to move on. If you could bring her on your side, she would try to move heaven and earth fighting for your case. This was what I was hoping she would do now. Convincing her would be another story.

CHAPTER XXV

Little Pete pulled up in front of Auntie Bea's house, and I saw that she had her lights on, waiting for me. She came out the side door with her cane in hand. Before I could even get out of the truck, she was at her white picket fence, opening the gate, and yelling at me, "Where have you been? I've been worried sick. Do you know what time it is? You should have called me!"

Good Lord, I thought, *I didn't even realize what time it was.*

I got close to the fence where Auntie Bea was standing and said, "Good night, Little Pete. I'll see you on Monday at 8:00 a.m. sharp."

He said, "Okay, good night." He ran to his van in fear that Auntie Bea would get a hold of him too and start fussing at him as well. I had never seen him run so fast!

I gave my full attention to Auntie Bea. I gave her support as she put her weight on my forearm and used her cane to walk back inside. She started lecturing me.

"Belinda, you have to call me and let me know where you are. I had all kinds of terrible thoughts. I thought you and Big Pete got into a fight, and I didn't know Little Pete had brought his van up here and parked it until now."

I said, "I'm sorry, Auntie Bea, but I was visiting Momma. I think she is going to be okay."

I didn't want to go into details with my great-aunt. It is better that she not know what was really happening to my mother. I felt she could not handle much more stress.

She said, "I'm sorry, Belinda, but I was so worried I called Big Pete. He told me that you must be off somewhere getting drunk."

I said, "Auntie Bea, for goodness sake, I told you what I was doing this morning. Like I have time to go out and get drunk! But while we are on the subject, I sure could use a glass of wine about now."

102

We were in her kitchen by now, and she replied as she chuckled, "After what you put me through, I could use a glass of wine too. At least you bought a good bottle." She became solemn as she continued, "You know, Belinda, you're all I have left."

I was pouring the wine into the glasses. "No, I'm not; it's just a hiccup for Mom. When she gets out, she will continue taking care of you and Uncle Frank. Technically, you guys are all she has left."

Auntie just looked at me for a moment and then went into her living room and sat down in her chair.

I followed her with our glasses of wine and sat in the other chair. I watched her light up a cigarette. She took a puff, laid it in the ashtray, picked up her glass, and took a sip of wine.

She said, "You need to call Frank and tell him you will be over there in the morning, Belinda."

I said, "Yes, ma'am."

I picked up her phone and hit Uncle Frank's phone number on her speed dial. Uncle Frank answered the phone, and he already knew who it was. He started fussing at me as well because I didn't call Auntie Bea or him to tell them where I was. He was angry with me because he and Auntie Bea still did not know what was going on or what was going to happen to them. I told him that I would be over in the morning

Uncle Frank continued, "Okay then, good night, and you better be here in the morning, or girl, there will be hell to pay."

"Yes, sir." I laughed as I hung up the phone.

Auntie Bea said, "It's not funny, Belinda, I don't care if you were a soldier or not. That Big Pete is big, and he can hurt you and probably kill you."

I said, "That maybe true, Auntie Bea, but I don't believe we are at that point yet. If it comes to that, I expect you to put him in jail before my husband finds out."

Auntie Bea said, "You know if he kills you, he will come for Frank and me, and there won't be anyone to put him in jail. You are our last line of defense, Belinda."

I couldn't believe Auntie Bea was treating this like a war.

I said, "Auntie Bea, you don't need to be so overdramatic. You're worse than I am."

Auntie Bea finished her glass of wine and said she was going to bed. She said that ever since I came into town, I had worn her out. I allowed her to be the auntie, and let her feel her self-importance, even though she was partly to blame for this. I stood up, gave her a kiss on her cheek, and asked if she needed any help. She replied that she didn't need any help, and she was off to bed. I told her I was going to stay up for a bit and take a walk outside to clear my mind for a while. I said that I would set the alarm, and shut the house down for the night when I came back in. I looked at the clock on her wall. It was only 8:45 p.m.

CHAPTER XXVI

I found the keys that had "Daisy house" written on the key tag in my mother's purse and ran over to the Daisy house where Uncle Frank had already gone to bed.

I snuck into the closed-in garage that my mother had turned into a Florida room. Uncle Frank had the door that went into the house locked, and that side of the house was made of brick. I knew that Uncle Frank was a heavy sleeper, and because his room was on the other side of the house, he would not hear me at all.

I lit my cigarette and took a sip of soda while I tried to formulate what I was going to say to my sister. I still didn't even know if my mother had called her. I didn't even know if Christina knew anything. After a few moments, I let out a sigh, knowing I was going to have to do this. I picked up the telephone and dialed my sister's telephone number. I knew Christina's time in California was about three hours behind us. I hoped she was home since it was Saturday night. The telephone rang twice and my sister gave a greeting, "Hello."

I said, "Hello, Christina, it's Belinda."

Christina said, "Oh, Belinda, what a nice surprise. How are you and what's going on?"

I said, "Christina, I'm not in Germany. I'm at the Daisy house and I'm sneaking this phone call. I'm staying at Auntie Bea's and Uncle Frank is asleep."

Before I could say anything else Christina said, "What? Why are you sneaking and where is Thomas? What is going on?"

I asked, "Didn't Momma call you?"

She answered, "No, I haven't heard from Mom in a few weeks. What's going on, Belinda?"

Her voice was turning anxious and confused. I decided to just blurt it all out.

"Christina, I need you to come home! I need you! Momma is in jail! She turned herself in yesterday!"

There must have been at least a minute of silence on the phone before she spoke. When she finally did speak, her voice was angry, and then confused, and then sounded like she was going to cry.

"What? She's in jail? What the hell is going on? Belinda, give me the Daisy house telephone number and let me call my friends, cancel my plans for tonight, and I'll call you right back."

I said, "Okay", and gave her the number.

She demanded, "When I call you back you're going to tell me everything and I will make flight arrangements to be there tomorrow."

I said humbly, "Yes, ma'am. I love you, sis-sis."

She said in a softer tone, "I love you too, sissy."

My hands were trembling. I didn't know if being meek and needy was going to work or not. I didn't know my baby sister anymore. I didn't know how I was going to get her here or if she would really come. I didn't even know if she would help. She said she was going to make flight arrangements, but I knew how fickle my sister could be. I had no game plan, and I knew if I didn't do this right, she would not help at all. Uncle Frank had some liquor somewhere in the kitchen, and I knew he never turned the alarm on. I took the set of keys and opened the side door to the kitchen. I turned on the light and there was a bottle of whiskey sitting on the counter beside the sink. I quietly walked over to it, poured some of it into my soda, and stirred it. I turned the light off and locked the door again. I had to keep the light off in the Florida room because I didn't want Auntie Bea to see me from her bedroom window, but there was enough moonlight coming in for me to see my way.

I sat back down in the chair next to the telephone. I took another sip of my whiskey and soda and lit a cigarette. I was very anxious as I waited for my baby sister to call me back. It seemed like an eternity, but it was only about ten minutes before the telephone rang. I picked it up quickly because I knew Uncle Frank had a phone in his bedroom. I got lucky; Uncle Frank never woke up.

I asked, "Christina?"

She answered, "Yes, Belinda, it's me. Now tell me what's going on. I have cancelled my plans for tonight."

I proceeded to tell her about Mom's call and some of what I knew. I told her Big Pete and Momma did something squirrelly with Auntie

Bea's land, but I felt most of it—or all of it—was done by Big Pete. I told her about the living irrevocable trust that Auntie Bea had done with Pete King on it as well, and not me. I told her about the suspected credit card fraud done in my name, but I didn't know how much. I told her about the check kiting done in our names. I told her I wanted her to do a credit report to make sure nothing was done to her. I told her I was angry with our mother, and I didn't tell our mother how I felt. I told her it was just a matter of time before Big Pete and I ended up in a physical altercation. I reminded Christina of how I didn't like the creep. She was the expert in these types of matters, and I felt she could control Big Pete much better than I could. I told her about the jail and how they refused to give our mother her medications. I felt that she knew how to deal with these people better than I did. I told her I desperately needed her before someone was hurt or, even worse, killed over this.

I purposely left Auntie Bea's involvement out. At the time, I didn't realize, but that omission was something that I would regret not telling my sister for the rest of my life. I stopped to breathe. I knew I was jumping from one subject to another because I was not focused, and I had allowed my emotions to run wild. I hoped she understood me. When I finished, there was nothing but silence on the phone.

I heard Christina let out a sigh, and then she spoke in a sympathetic tone. "Belinda, I will try to make flight arrangements in the morning. I will call to see if I can get a flight back home. Will you be at the Daisy house or Auntie Bea's?"

I told her I didn't know which house I would be at because I had to talk to Uncle Frank in the morning. He was next on my list. She said she would call me at the Daisy house again, and I said that would be fine. She continued, but this time there was more anger and disappointment in her voice. "Belinda, Mom flew me home to visit with her for Christmas. I was there for a few days. Big Pete took me to their shop and let me pick out something as a gift. Big Pete said it was their shop; there was no mention of you. She never, ever mentioned to me that there was any trouble whatsoever. In fact, she only became angry with Big Pete for allowing me to take something I wanted from the shop."

I said to Christina in a non-emotional tone, "Christina, I guess you didn't know that I've been the wind beneath our mother's wings for a long time, and I assumed you were as well. If you believe Big Pete, then I can easily prove to you that the shop is mine and always was. It has been a dream of mine for a very long time. Didn't you even notice all my artwork, pottery, sculptures, and ceramics?"

Then her voice seemed to turn towards resentment as she continued, "Belinda, you don't need to prove it to me. I know you're telling the truth, and yes, I knew that was a dream of yours. I guess I just didn't connect the dots, but the point is Mom and Big Pete didn't tell me anything. They acted as if there was nothing wrong. What I'm the most upset over is that she didn't call me to tell me. She didn't even tell me anything when I was there just a few weeks ago. You didn't even tell me, and you have known for at least a year that something was going on, even if you didn't know all of it. I have been treated as if I'm not part of this family. I'm very upset over this, but you are right, you need me to keep Pete out of the way for you to do the right thing. I need to help Mom with her medications. I may be angry with her, but I don't want her to die. I love her too, Belinda."

I said, "I know you do. Just come home and you and I will figure out the best course of action. We can't go wrong with me being an accountant and you a therapist. It's a win-win combination. Together we can figure this whole mess out together. I love you, Christina, and I desperately need you."

Christina's voice softened. "I love you too, Belinda. I'll call you again tomorrow at the Daisy house."

I said, "Okay, sis-sis, I will be waiting. I love you and hope you can get some sleep after this."

She nervously chuckled and said, "I hope so too. Good night, Belinda."

I said, "Good night, Christina."

My brain was hurting again, and I remembered that I never had bought any aspirin. I looked at my half-empty cup, took the straw out, and then drank the rest of it. It tasted bitter in my mouth, but I hoped the alcohol would make me sleepy. I lit another cigarette to calm myself down more.

As I sat there, it occurred to me that my mother had called me last Christmas Eve telling me Big Pete was beating on her. I thought, *Was I lied to?*

I put my cigarette out when it was only half-finished and just pushed the thoughts to the side. I wanted to brush my teeth. I felt like I had an ashtray in my mouth from all the smoking I had done during the day. I hadn't smoked like this in a long time. I looked at my cigarette pack. I had smoked ten cigarettes since I got off the airplane the other night. No wonder I felt like that, but I didn't even care. I had no idea that I would go through several cartons before I flew back to Germany.

I ran back to my auntie's house and I locked all the doors and set Auntie Bea's alarm. I looked over at the clock on the wall and it said 12:30 a.m. I couldn't believe I had talked to my sister for that long.

I went into her bathroom, brushed my teeth, and freshened up a little bit. I turned out the lights as I went up the stairs to the room I was sleeping in. I looked over to Auntie Bea's bedroom and saw that her light was out. I could hear her snoring.

I changed into my pajamas, grabbed the box of files that I was reading the night before, and started reading again.

CHAPTER XXVII

I woke up at 5:00 a.m. I had papers, canceled checks from Mom's and Auntie Bea's checking accounts, and file folders all over me. My head hurt from using a large, old, hardback dictionary as a pillow. I felt like I had not slept all night. My eyes were sore and blurry from reading and trying to figure out who all was involved in these crimes against the banking institutions and against me. I groaned and sat up. I swung my legs over the side and sat on the edge of the bed. I looked out the window and saw that it was still dark.

I sat on the side of the bed shaking my head in complete disbelief of everything my auntie and mother had done over the last year; they had left a mile-long paper trail. I had most of that paper trail scattered all over the bed.

Granted Auntie Bea did not open the checking accounts nor did she sign her name, but she did take the money. Every month she eagerly accepted the money that my mother gave. The accounts that the checks were drawn on were in my name, my sister's name, our stepbrother's name (Big Pete's son), and my deceased grandparents' names. Auntie Bea took those checks and deposited them into her personal account. I know she knew that the accounts were bogus. She had told me the previous night that she was as guilty as my mother was. I guess I didn't want to believe her. It wasn't until I saw the evidence with my own eyes that I realized how involved she really was. I now had to accept the fact that she was just as guilty as my mother was. There were thousands of dollars of laundered money in her checking account alone. What did she do with the money? No wonder she and Mom have been living like there was no problem. These two old women were modern-day bank robbers. They didn't even have to step into the banks to do it, and they did it in other people's names.

There was still the possibility that Auntie Bea took the money because she had no other means to support herself. I also wondered if Big Pete was somehow setting Auntie Bea and my mother up to take the fall for everything. I was not clear yet if my great-aunt actually knew what she was doing or if she was innocently tricked.

My encounter at the bank the day before now made sense, but I still could not figure out how Mom was able to do it. Even if there were no holds placed on a check that was deposited, she would have a ten-minute window to get from one bank to the other. She would have to write a check from Bank A, deposit it at Bank B, and then withdraw it using the ATM before Bank B found out that there was no money in Bank A. The whole thing would be impossible if there were holds placed on checks because Bank B would realize that the check from Bank A was bogus before my mother was able to withdraw the money she had deposited. The computer from one ATM to the other should be catching this. Something was missing. There had to be an accomplice, but who could it be? I did not think Auntie Bea helped with this part.

During my nighttime investigation of the paperwork, I discovered, or at least I thought I discovered, that my mother was telling the truth when she said that Big Pete alone committed the crimes against his clients. Three years prior, she had started helping him to conceal his criminal activity, and about a year earlier, she had begun the check scheme. I also discovered that Mary was involved regarding a bank branch in Pennsylvania.

My mother was trying to make restitution to Big Pete's clients one at a time and helping herself at the same time. She set up the bank accounts in our names and used them to start paying back Big Pete's clients, while at the same time using some of the money to continue living her rich lifestyle. It might have worked if Big Pete, my mother, and Auntie Bea had not been so greedy. He continued to steal from his clients and was spiraling deeper and deeper. From the paper trail, I concluded that my mother and Auntie Bea mainly stole out of pure desperation and to keep up the appearance of their lifestyle. I felt better once I realized that. I had absolutely no problem blaming this entire mess on Big Pete. That nasty man had used my family and then set them up to take the fall. I felt total contempt for him while I tried to clean up the mess that he created, but at the same time, I was completely disappointed in my family members.

It had never dawned on me that maybe my mother and auntie were always crooks, and Big Pete simply brought their crooked ways into the light even though I had already said this aloud to my auntie and to my mother as well. I had always known that both women were the most greedy, selfish people I knew, but they were also my family. Long, long ago, I had accepted the fact that my sister, auntie, and mother were very selfish and very self-centered people. I just never thought that two of them would turn out to be crooks as well. I started to feel bad for the way I had portrayed my mother when I was talking to Christina the night before. Maybe I shouldn't have made my mother look just as guilty as Big Pete. I was glad that I had not told her about Auntie Bea's involvement because then she definitely would not have come. I decided that it would be better not to tell Christina about my discovery until I was sure. I then decided that it would be better if I did not tell her anything else, but I still hadn't decided just how much I was going to tell my baby sister. I would later discover that this decision would haunt me for the rest of my life.

I was very thankful for my accounting background. I could never have dealt with this financial mess without it. So far, what I had unraveled was that Big Pete stole from John to pay Peter. He then stole from Sam, used it to pay John back, and kept the rest for himself. He stole from Henry to pay Sam back and so on, and so on. It was one continuous vicious cycle. It appeared that Big Pete began stealing because he was underbidding on contracts and wasn't making enough income to support his lifestyle. The loop kept growing bigger, and bigger, and bigger until it just could not be hidden any longer. In other words, Big Pete, my mother, Auntie Bea, and even Uncle Frank, were living a champagne lifestyle on a beer budget.

I then remembered 1995, when Thomas and I were PCSing to Germany. We were putting more of our things into storage at the Daisy house. Mom and Janice (Big Pete's accountant) were having issues reconciling the books again, and Mom asked if I could look at them and figure out why that was a reoccurring problem. Pete was out of the office at a meeting, and I sat down with Janice, who had brought the spreadsheets out for me. The account was $95,000 out of balance. There was money that had been withdrawn without explanation. I immediately began calling the banks and asking them to fax copies of the withdrawal receipts. Pete King's name was all over them, and Janice did not have documentation of any of the withdrawals, or any explanation as to where the money went. It took several hours, but I was able to account for every penny.

I started to compare the withdrawals with the accounts payable. Mom and Janet were standing over me, watching as I matched up the entire month's receipts and invoices to the withdrawals. Big Pete returned when I was almost finished. He came over to Janice's desk. He wasn't there very long before he reached out, grabbed the withdrawal slips and other documents out of my hands, and shut the computer off. He angrily yelled at Mom and Janice about having me look at the books.

Looking back, he thought I was on to his dirty little scam. I had thought that Pete was being an asshole, like he always was. Mom was crying again. Janice just stood there very quietly, and she appeared very nervous. Now that I knew what was going on, I understood why he had such a nasty reaction. Who in their right mind passes up free expert help or even a fresh pair of eyes to look at a problem?

As I sat there on the edge of the bed, I realized that I would have to hire an attorney to protect myself from my auntie and my mother. I thought, *That can wait for another day. Maybe I'm just being paranoid.* I pushed all thoughts of an attorney to the back of my mind. For all I knew, I could have jumped to the wrong conclusions. There were still a lot of gaps in the paper trail, and I knew that I hadn't figured everything out.

I looked at the stack of credit card bills that Big Pete had handed to me the day before. I knew that I would have to look at them eventually, but I decided to wait until later. I just didn't know how much more I could take. This was only my mother's second day in jail. God only knew what other crimes I would find out about. God only knew what all they had done.

I decided that I needed a nice hot bath to clear my head. Maybe it would help with my sore neck too. I quickly made my bed and grabbed my shower items and a fresh set of clothes. For the past two days, I had stuffed my dirty clothes into an old military laundry bag. I figured I now had enough for a full load, so I grabbed that too. I tiptoed out of my room and down the hall. As I snuck past Auntie Bea's room, I peered in. It was dark, and I could hear her snoring.

When I was downstairs, I went into the kitchen. I knew it was going to be a long day, and I needed extra fortification. I started a fresh pot of coffee. As it was brewing, I took my clothes to the washer and started it. I then took a nice, long hot bath and dressed for the day. I desperately needed coffee. I returned to the kitchen and found the coffee was done brewing. I got a cup out of the cupboard and poured a steamy cup. I took a sip and sighed. I sat the cup down on the counter and walked to the kitchen door. I turned off the alarm, unlocked the door, and opened it so

I could see what the weather was outside. I saw a cold mixture of rain and sleet pouring down. There was a coating of shiny ice on all the trees and wires. I had a bad feeling that even more crap would hit the fan today. It didn't matter that it was Sunday.

I looked at the clock and saw that it was about 6:30 a.m. I decided to go over to the Daisy house. I wrote a note and left it for Auntie Bea by the coffee pot. I wrote that I was going to Uncle Frank's. I was taking my things with me because I was going to stay with him, but I was going to leave the safes and dog ashes there for now. Then I would go to see my mother and then to the shop. I wrote that I wanted to catch all the after-church folks who were sightseeing around the countryside. I signed my name to the note, grabbed my coat from the hook by the door, put it on, and picked up my mom's purse and briefcase. As I walked out the door, I wondered if Christina would call. I went inside back and forth until I had all my belongings and papers loaded into the pickup truck.

CHAPTER XXVIII

I climbed into Mom's old pickup truck. I was thankful that it started without giving me too much hassle. I drove over to the Daisy house, which seemed the most sensible thing to do considering the weather. I unlocked the sliding glass door to the Florida room and sat everything down on my mother's white wrought-iron sofa. I unlocked the door to the kitchen and turned off the alarm. I went back to the pickup truck, got the remainder of my things, and brought them into the Florida room as well. Uncle Frank's coffee pot was sitting next to the sink, and I made a fresh pot. I tried to make enough noise to wake the dead because I wanted Uncle Frank to wake up. I took my luggage and all the papers to one of the guest rooms where I would sleep. Of course, I took the one that had my king-sized bed and furniture in it.

Finally, after about thirty minutes, Uncle Frank stumbled sleepily into the kitchen and said, "Damn, girl, you made enough noise to wake the dead."

I started to giggle and said, "Good morning, Uncle Frank. I'm sorry. I didn't mean to wake you."

He said, "Good, I smell coffee perking. Did you reuse the grounds?"

I answered, "Ukkk, Uncle Frank! No, I did not. I will buy you coffee while I'm here so you don't have to do that."

Uncle Frank replied, "That's a waste of money! You can get at least two or three pots from the same grounds."

I stated simply, "That may be true, Uncle Frank, but it tastes nasty!"

Uncle Frank said, "Shit."

I just laughed at him as he went to the coffee pot.

He continued, "Damn, girl, you cleaned my coffee cup. The coffee doesn't taste as good when you clean it!"

I teasingly retorted, "Uncle Frank! There was fungus growing in that cup! It was disgusting, so I cleaned it before you got sick."

Uncle Frank said, "Shit."

I giggled some more as I gave him a hug and kiss on his unshaven cheek.

Uncle Frank poured his coffee into his now clean coffee cup with a scowl on his face. He was not one bit happy that I had cleaned his cup, and I could tell he wasn't sure if I had really seen fungus in his cup.

He told me, "You're worse than your momma. I guess you're going to be running things now until she gets out."

I said, "No, Uncle Frank. I'm here to clean up the mess she made and make arrangements so I can take care of you guys from Europe, or at least try to. I'm going to be calling your kids at some point because they need to start taking responsibility for your care and well-being."

Uncle Frank said, "Bullshit. You can't take care of me from over there, and you know it. You know my worthless kids aren't going to take care of me either."

I said, "Yes I can—it's called using a computer, telephone, and airplane. As far as your kids are concerned, we will see. You're still in the dark ages, Uncle Frank."

He barked his command, "But I want you here!"

I said, "We'll see, Uncle Frank, but for now we have a problem, and it needs to be fixed."

He nodded his head in agreement with me.

I asked him, "Where are your checkbook and all your bills?" He replied,

"Your momma has all that. You're going to have to ask her, and I need some of my money. She wasn't here on Friday to give me my money so I can buy my weekly groceries and cigarettes."

I reached into my wallet and took out my last $100 bill. With a sigh, I handed it to my great-uncle. He snatched it out of my hand like a greedy miser, but he did say, "Thank you."

I told him, "I'm not your banker, Uncle Frank. As soon as I find your checkbook, you're going to pay me back. I'm not like Momma. I don't have deep pockets."

He answered, "It's my money, and that's fine with me. That's what your momma did anyway."

I stated, "Okay, as long as we are clear on that. I'm going to get you a debit card and show you how to use it. That way, after I go back to Germany, you won't have to worry about someone bringing you cash.

There is a Kroger up the road. You can use the debit to buy your groceries, cigarettes, and whatever else you need there. The debit card works just like cash. There is also an ATM machine inside the store where you can use your debit card to get cash."

Uncle Frank was about seventy-four years old and lazy. If he had access to alcohol, he drank from the time he got up in the morning until he passed out at night. He had been a lying drunk for as long as I could remember. He lied about everything. He had the ability to make a lie incredibly believable. He could lie to your face in a manner that made it so you would never know he was lying. He considered himself a charmer and a ladies' man. In reality, he was just an old drunk and a dirty old man, but in my eyes, he was a charmer.

Uncle Frank was a six-foot walking skeleton. His clothes just hung on his thin frame. I could tell that he had not been eating well. His pants were held up by suspenders and appeared to be three sizes too big. I knew he had lost at least sixty pounds since I had seen him four years ago.

I looked down at his feet and noticed that he was barefoot. That's when I remembered he was a diabetic.

I asked, "Uncle Frank, where are your socks? You know you have diabetes. Your feet are blue and swollen because it's so cold out here. You're not getting enough circulation."

Uncle Frank said, "Damn it, girl, stop fussing over me. You're as bad as your mother."

I sternly replied, "Where's your socks?"

I was a nurse before I joined the Army many years ago, and I unconsciously slipped back into the role. I didn't even realize I was barking orders to him until he replied in a very obedient tone, "My socks are in my drawer in my bedroom."

I stated, "Good! I'm going to go get them. Have you taken your medication yet?"

Uncle Frank answered, "No."

I said, "Take it now, and if I catch you drinking whiskey in your coffee again, I'll dump it all down the drain! You know I will."

Uncle Frank answered in an even more humble tone, "Okay, okay."

I could tell by the tone of his voice that he would continue to drink his coffee with whiskey, and he would continue drinking all day. I could do nothing to stop him.

I walked back to his bedroom. I easily found the dresser drawer and a pair of thick socks. I grabbed them, went into the Florida room where he was sitting with his coffee, and put them on his feet. Uncle Frank fussed the entire time because I was putting them on his feet for him. I had also found a brown sweater hanging in his closet, and I put that on him as well. It had been a long time since I heard him complain as he did that morning. He was the classic example of a grumpy old man who didn't take care of himself.

I told him, "Uncle Frank, when I leave the Daisy house today, I want you to take a shower because you stink! I have decided I'm moving over here to make sure you start taking care of yourself. I have already moved into the spare bedroom where Mom has my bed and furniture. I guess I'll make this home base."

To my surprise, Uncle Frank welcomed this wholeheartedly by saying, "Well, that's a great idea! You know your auntie is going to be jealous."

I replied with a chuckle, "No she won't. She will welcome the peace and quiet she'll have when I leave. She has already told me that I have worn her out." I giggled, and Uncle Frank laughed with me. I looked in the kitchen at the clock on the wall, and it was almost 8:30 a.m. I knew I could not stick around and wait for Christina's phone call.

I told Uncle Frank, "I have to go visit Mom and take care of the shop today."

No sooner were the words out of my mouth, when I spotted Little Pete again driving his van to the front of the Daisy house. I said aloud, "Damn it." Uncle Frank and I sat there and watched as Little Pete got out of his van and walked to the sliding glass door. I stood up, walked over to the door, and opened it.

Little Pete came in and said, "It's nasty and cold out there."

Little Pete sat down. I got him a cup of coffee so he could warm up.

I stated, "Little Pete, you know that I can't afford to pay you all this overtime."

Little Pete replied, "I know, and it's not overtime. I don't start the clock until Monday, and it's just eight hours a day, Monday through Friday. Don't worry about it, Belinda. I'm just here as a family member, nothing more."

I said, "Okay, Little Pete, but I feel bad because there are a lot better things you could be doing with your time."

He said, "I know, but that's okay. I figure the more truth I get out quicker, the faster you will figure out a solution."

I simply nodded my head in agreement with him. I told Little Pete and Uncle Frank, "I need to head on out. It is going to be a busy day again."

Little Pete asked, "Can I drive you?"

I answered, "Sure."

I looked over at Uncle Frank. I told him that I was expecting a phone call from my sister. I asked him to write down her flight information and to tell her that I would pick her up at the airport.

Uncle Frank asked, "Christina's coming?" he asked.

I answered, "Yes, she said last night when I spoke to her she was going to make flight arrangements and come and help me."

Little Pete was amazed. "Wow, how did you get her to come?"

I didn't answer. I simply said, "Let's go."

CHAPTER XXIX

As we were getting into my mom's old pickup truck, I looked up at the sky and saw that the sun was slowly coming out from behind the clouds. The clouds were starting to disappear and you could see the blue sky once again. It even felt like it was warming up.

As we pulled out of the driveway onto Burnwood, Little Pete said, "I want to show you where your momma's storage unit is because it's just up the road, here in Greenville."

I said, "That's a great idea."

Little Pete drove past my shop and went straight across Route 54. Right next to the burger joint/gas station was the Burnwood Storage. The Burnwood Storage was comprised of one long building made of brick. Large units were on one side and small units were on the other. We pulled in through the open metal mesh gate and up in front of the second large unit. Pete put the truck in park, and as we got out, he pulled out his huge key ring. He found the one he was looking for and opened the roll-up door. The storage unit was huge. It was fourteen feet high, eighteen feet wide, and seemed to go on forever. I had never seen a storage unit so large before. The building and the units were well designed for the different temperatures of the winter and the summer. There were small gaps between the walls and the roof so air could circulate through the units.

I walked inside the unit and was surprised at how empty it was. I spotted my large, bronze Remington that I had purchased from Mom. I had told my mother to hold it for me and not to mail it to me while I was in Germany. There were about thirty china barrels, a few boxes, and a few pieces of furniture. That was it. The rest was just empty space. I had inspected everything that was in there without opening any boxes.

I said to Little Pete, "Let's go."

Little Pete closed the rolling door and locked it with the key lock.

I asked, "Little Pete, would you please give me the keys? You will not need them anymore."

Little Pete became hostile and angrily replied, "No! I will not give you the keys!"

I asked again, "Little Pete, please give me the keys."

Little Pete replied, "Only if your mother tells me to give them to you." His behavior was very confusing. This was not the Little Pete whom I had known and loved.

I responded with anger in my voice, "Then I will have my mother tell you when we go to visit her." I was still confused, but then it dawned on me that Little Pete might be part of this conspiracy. I started to think that maybe Little Pete was not my mother's friend at all, but I shrugged that feeling off as I thought, *Na*. I went to the office, which was located in the front of the concrete building. There was an elderly woman in her mid-sixties sitting at the only desk in the office.

I introduced myself. "My mother has a storage unit with you, and I need to have it changed into my name. What information do you need from me?"

The elderly woman returned my greeting. "Okay, let's see what I can do for you. What are your mother's name and the unit number?" I gave her the unit number and my mother's name, Jane King. Patty went to her files and said the unit is not in that name.

I said, "What? Maybe she put it in her maiden name, Jackson?"

Patty said, "No."

I looked over at Little Pete and asked if he knew what name my mother used when she opened the unit.

Little Pete just shrugged his shoulders and answered, "I don't know."

I looked back over at Patty. She had a bewildered expression on her face, as did I. We just stood there looking at each other. I didn't speak for a moment. My mother had been married numerous times, and I was trying to figure out which name she might have used.

I said, "Well, let's see, the first name would either be Jane, Sara, or a combination of the names. Was the last name Clark? Bishop? Will?" She said no to all three. Then I said, "Oh, there was one other husband. His name was Patrick . . . I can't remember his last name." I looked over at Little Pete. Of course, he just shrugged his shoulders as if he had no idea. Then I remembered, and said, "Lane!" Then I spelled it out.

Patty said, "Yes. Good Lord, Belinda, your mother was married a lot."

I said, "I know." Then all three of us started laughing.

After opening the file she asked, "Can I speak to you in private, Belinda?"

I looked over at Little Pete, and he said, "Oh, I'll wait outside in the pickup truck."

Patty and I watched as Little Pete walked out, and I closed the door behind him. She was sitting in the chair behind her desk as she solemnly told me, "Belinda, your mother has a bounced check for last month's rent, and she has not paid for this month's rent yet."

I said, "Oh, how much is the rent, and I will reimburse you for the bounced check."

She gave me the amount of the rent and the bounced check and said, "Don't worry about the fee for the bounced check. I don't think it would be right for you to pay that because you didn't write it. I'm just grateful that you are clearing it."

I said, "Let me go to an ATM machine and get the money that my mother owes you. I would also like to pay cash for the next three months in advance. That way, you won't have to worry about any bad checks."

She said, "Oh that will be fine."

I said, "Goodbye. I'll be back in just a few minutes to settle up with you."

She said, "Okay."

Little Pete drove me to the bank up the street where I had just opened up a checking account. I took out one of my credit cards. I regretted to have to use it. I never used credit cards except for when we were traveling. I never had a balance over a thousand dollars before; I only had credit cards to build up our credit and for emergencies. Cash advances are very expensive, and this was the first time I had to do a cash advance. I had always believed that you should live within your means. Now it looked like I was headed down a path of nasty debt, one that I hoped I would be able to escape.

I withdrew the maximum from the ATM, but that was not enough. I repeatedly withdrew from other ATMs that Little Pete drove me to until I had enough to pay for the storage unit. I groaned as I thought about all the charges on my credit card. I had used it to purchase a one-way ticket when I flew back to the States as well. My daughter's duty was becoming very expensive.

Thomas and I were not rich. We were just middle class people. Most soldiers live in poverty. That was one reason Thomas and I did not have children. We had heard about many soldiers whose families survived on food stamps. Soldier's base pay started increasing under the leadership of the first President George H. Bush, and then President Clinton continued to grant small increases each year by implementing a cost of living percentage each year. Thomas made more money as a first sergeant than I had made when I was serving. Not to brag, but I outranked my husband for a very long time. Thank God I married a man who was man enough to handle his wife being his superior in rank.

After I had the money, Little Pete drove back to the storage unit, and I settled with Patty. She filled out the new forms for the unit and had me sign them. I then asked her to make sure that she did not give anyone, especially Pete King, any information about my storage unit. I asked that she respect my privacy, and that she contact me if anyone began snooping around trying to obtain information on my unit. She said she had no problem with that at all. We chatted for a bit, and I found out that her husband was a veteran. I told her that my husband was serving in Germany and that I was also in the Army and had been discharged. Patty and I shared something that most Americans lacked: "patriotism."

I told her some of what was going on with my mother, and she reacted as if I were some kind of hero. She told me that my actions demonstrated my unconditional love toward my mother, and that she wished her children loved her the way that I loved my mother. She informed me that she would help me any way she possibly could against this evil monster, Big Pete. I felt sad, as I wished my own sister would have reacted the way this gentle woman, who was a complete stranger, had reacted. We said goodbye, and she wished me luck.

I climbed back into the truck and pulled out the procedures for jail telephone access from the glove box. I asked Little Pete if he knew if there were any Western Unions close by.

He answered, "Yes. That grocery store is just up Route 54, about fifteen minutes from here."

I said, "Good, take me there next, please."

It took about ten minutes to reach the grocery store that had a Western Union. I went inside, found the Western Union, and explained my situation to the clerk who was at the counter. I showed her the address for the county jail. She pulled out some forms and handed them to me to fill out. I put all the phone numbers on the forms, including Little Pete's home phone and my sister's phone number. I used my credit card again and put another $300 on it. Before long, I would soon realize that $300 was like water for my mother and this expensive process. I would soon learn that our jail system is designed to make a lot of money off the family members of convicted felons. I didn't know it yet, but over the next three months, I would spend over $4,000 on the jail's phone scam alone.

While I was in the grocery store, I bought some groceries. When I got back to the truck, I checked my watch and I told Little Pete I would not have time to go visit Mom. I said that I needed to open the shop and work there today. Little Pete said that would be fine. He drove me back to the Daisy house so he could get his van. I took the groceries inside and asked Uncle Frank to take care of them. I got back into the truck and I drove to my shop. Little Pete followed me to the shop. After I had unlocked the front door, and we were standing inside, he asked if he should stick around. I told him there was no need, to enjoy a day of rest. Then the telephone rang.

It was the recording from the jail again. I dutifully accepted the charges.

My mother asked, "Belinda?"

I replied, "Yes, ma'am; I will not be able to see you today. I need to work in the shop."

Mom said excitably, "Okay. They gave me my toiletries last night, some undergarments, and another set of jail garb. They even gave me a mattress, pillow with sheets, and even a blanket last night."

I did not tell Mom about the altercation I had with the head guard last night. There was no need to. I simply said, "That's great. I'm glad they finally provided for you."

Mom disappointedly asked, "But I haven't received my medications, Belinda. Have you called the pharmacy where I have my prescriptions to see if they will deliver them to the jail?"

With everything else that was going on, I had totally forgotten about that. I told her, "I will call them as soon as I hang up with you. I will have them deliver it to the jail today."

Little Pete was still standing there, listening to our conversation. Knowing he was listening, I told Mom, "Mom, Little Pete refused to give me the keys to the storage unit. He will not give them to me until you tell him to. I will need them for when Thomas gets leave. I would like all the other keys that Little Pete has as well."

Mom said, "What? Pass the phone to Little Pete. I want to speak with him."

I passed him the telephone and after a few moments he said, "Yes, ma'am."

I didn't hear what my mother was telling him. All I heard was Little Pete saying, "Yes, ma'am. Yes, ma'am," over and over again. When he was finished, he passed the phone to me with a bitter look in his eyes.

Mom said, "He is going to give you all the keys he has. I don't know what got into him."

I answered as I was looking in Little Pete's direction, "That's okay. I'm sure it was some kind of miscommunication."

Then Mom said, "You need to call your brother today, and have him fly in ASAP." She continued barking orders, as usual, telling me what she wanted me to do. I just let her talk until her time was up. A prisoner is only allowed fifteen minutes on the telephone and it automatically cuts the person off.

As soon as my conversation with my mother was finished, I looked up the pharmacy's phone number and took care of her medication. When that was done, I thought nothing more of it.

Little Pete grudgingly handed me a string full of keys. Each one was labeled.

I said, "Thank you, Little Pete. You need to remember that I am the one who now gives you a paycheck. If you feel you cannot take direction from me, please tell me now so we can go our separate ways. I have no problem doing a letter of recommendation for you and giving you employment verification. I am under enough stress as it is, and I do not need to deal with any insubordination from the lower ranks for any reason at this time. You are either for me or against me. There is no in between. I expect your total commitment to me and complete honesty. Anything less is unacceptable. It appears that you are unwilling or unable to give that to me. I would like to believe that you are helping me out of loyalty to my mother, but I have a sad feeling that you are involved in this mess and have ulterior motives for wanting to stick around. It is up to you whether you will come clean about it to me. I hope that you will stay, but if you continue to have a hostile attitude towards me, it would be better for us

125

to go our separate ways. You have until tomorrow morning to make your decision. If you show up tomorrow morning, then I will take it you are going to respect my wishes, and that I will have your full cooperation."

Little Pete looked at me with a puzzled expression. It was as if he was trying to read my thoughts, and he said, "Yes, ma'am. I have no problem with it. I am sorry for my conduct today. Everything is changing so fast I can't keep up."

I accepted his excuse and said, "I'm glad, and I'm sorry if I spoke too harshly towards you. I will see you tomorrow morning. It will be a new day and beginning for us."

He said with a half smile, "Okay." He went out the back door of the shop to where he had his van parked beside my mother's old pickup truck.

As soon as he left, I pulled out my mother's telephone numbers and address book from her purse. It was a worn white address and telephone book for her personal use.

I looked up Jay's phone number and called him.

He answered, "Hello."

I said, "Hi, Jay. It's Belinda."

Jay said, "Wow, you have never called me before—what is going on?"

I said, "Mom's in jail and she wants me to fly you home. I will fill you in when you get here."

Jay asked angrily, "Oh, shit. What has that creep done?"

I replied, "Jay, it's too much to explain on the telephone. Can you make flight arrangements and find out how much it costs so you can be here tomorrow?"

Jay answered, "No problem, but you're going to have to pay for it because I don't have any money. I am still just working for a pizza place."

I said, "That will be okay. Mom told me which of her charge cards to use."

Jay replied, "I'll call you back in just a few minutes."

I said, "Okay." I gave him the telephone number to the shop so he could call me back.

About fifteen minutes later, Jay called back and asked for the credit card number. I assumed the credit card was her credit card because it had her name on it, and I gave it to him. I later discovered it was in my name with her name as a user. Jay gave me his flight information and arrival time. I had told him I would be at the airport to pick him up and would explain everything to him then. He told me that would be fine and he would tell me everything he knew as well. We told each other that we loved each other, and he said he would help as much as he could.

About ten minutes later, I heard the brass bell tinkle as the front door opened. There were at least fifteen customers trying to get into the shop. I jumped up and greeted everyone. I told them that there was a twenty percent discount on everything in the store. I hoped that would entice people to make purchases, instead of just looking. The afternoon flew.

Before I knew it was 7:00 p.m. already, and the last customer of the day was walking out the door after purchasing one of my masterpieces. I stepped outside, stood in front of my store, and took a deep breath.

I looked to each side of my shop and noticed the other shops had already closed for the day. *Good grief*, I thought. How could Mom not make enough money from this shop to live off of? The location was perfect for tourists and sightseers. Business was booming—and on a Sunday of all days. You would think Friday and Saturday would be better, but my day was great.

I noticed before I opened the shop for the day that the cash box was empty except for about two dollars in change and a couple of checks that were made out to Cognac's Run. I did not understand why there wasn't any money in it from Friday and Saturday's sales, but then I thought, *Big Pete. I'm sure he took all the money. I'm sure one of the reasons that Mom wasn't making enough income was because Big Pete had been stealing from the cash box.*

I counted the money from the sales and put twenty $1 bills into the cash box. The store did not have a cash register, just a calculator and a cash box. The receipts were hand written. I had no problem with that; in fact, I was just fine with it.

After I closed the shop for the day, I checked my mom's desk, and I found the tax coupons that were done every month and sent to the local state sales tax department. At least that was being done. I put the cash box in the drawer and locked the desk drawer so Big Pete couldn't get into it. I turned on the computer that was on the desk and found a spreadsheet for this month's sales. I added the data from my receipts of today's sales and did the standard daily accounting reconciliation. I looked at the receipt pad again and there were receipts for yesterday's sales missing. In fact, it appeared that all the receipts were missing from the pad. I realized Big

Pete could get me into a lot of trouble because I didn't have any data, or any idea what had been sold, if anything. I walked to the back of the shop and looked into his trashcan.

Damned if I didn't find the receipts from yesterday's sales crumpled up in his trash can. I was livid and ready to scream. Big Pete was very lucky that he wasn't there. I might have killed him, I was that angry. The receipts showed a total of $200 in cash sales, and that was just for what he wrote out. God only knows how much he really sold from my inventory. That sorry-ass creep! I wanted that low-life, thieving jerk out of my shop. He didn't even help pay for overhead. He was never supposed to be in my shop anyway. I never gave permission for him to have his office here.

Common sense prevailed, and I knew I wasn't ready to get into a fight with him. The best course of action was to allow him to keep his office here and hope that my constant presence would push him out. I was going to be in that shop as much as possible to prevent, or at least deter, him from stealing from me again. I found a zipper money pouch in one of the desk drawers. I put the cash and checks along with my deposit slip in it. I would make my first deposit the following morning. As I was walking out the back door of the shop, I stopped, looked back into my shop, and started crying. I turned back toward the door and continued walking. When I reached the back door, I turned off the lights and locked the door. I was still crying as I climbed into my mother's pickup, but I made myself stop before I started driving.

I started back to the Daisy house. I drove out the alley and stopped at Mr. T's gas station and convenience store, which was across the street from the shop. They made the best sandwiches in town. I bought sandwiches for Uncle Frank, Auntie Bea, and myself, along with a quart of homemade potato salad and a six-pack of beer.

I pulled into the Daisy house driveway and saw that Uncle Frank was on the telephone in the Florida room. In fact, he was in the exact same chair and in the same position as when I had left him that morning. My arms were full with the sandwiches, potato salad, and beer. I struggled to open the sliding glass door. As soon as I opened the door, Uncle Frank stretched his arm with the phone in hand and gestured for me to take the phone from him.

With a guilty look on his face he said, "Belinda, it's your auntie."

I put the bags down on the floor and grabbed the phone. Before I could get the phone to my ear, I heard Auntie Bea fussing.

I said, "What? I didn't hear you, Auntie Bea. You were talking before I got the phone to my ear."

She repeated, "What is going on? You told your uncle you were coming over here tonight, and you were treating him like a child this morning and he didn't like it. What is the matter with you? I will not have this kind of treatment towards us. You haven't told us really anything that is going on and what is going to be done for us."

I was tired, very stressed, and fed up with selfish people. I lost all patience with Auntie Bea. She was treating me as if I were a twelve-year old child. I guess I couldn't hold her responsible because I had always allowed them to talk to me that way. I never corrected them. I guess I had always allowed my older family members to make themselves feel important and superior at my expense.

In a halfhearted, angry tone I replied, "Auntie Bea, have you seen what Uncle Frank looks like? Did you smell him this morning? Did you forget he is diabetic?" As I was speaking, I was looking at my great-uncle straight in his eyes with a furrowed brow. He could not look me in the eye because he had lied that morning about how I treated him. He was caught.

There was silence on the phone for a moment, and Auntie Bea regrettably said, "Oh, I forgot."

Nothing else had to be said because she knew what Uncle Frank was all about, even better than I did. I didn't even need to see her to know that her face was probably red from embarrassment.

She simply asked, "Well, are you coming over here tonight?"

I replied, "Yes, Auntie. I have already moved my things over here because one of us needs to keep an eye out to what is going on. I will talk with you more after I get Uncle Frank fed. I hope you haven't eaten yet because I got us all those good sandwiches from Mr. T's."

I was careful of what I said because Uncle Frank was listening to every word. Auntie Bea barked her orders, as she answered, "No. I haven't eaten anything because you and Frank have worried me sick. Hurry up and feed him and, Belinda, if you find a bottle of whiskey over there throw it out."

I lied, "Yes, ma'am, I will."

I knew not to come between Uncle Frank and his booze. Auntie Bea and Mom may get away with pouring it down the drain, but I knew I would have a fight on my hands if I tried. Threatening him with it was one thing, but actually doing it was another.

I fussed, "Shame on you, Uncle Frank. What I did for you this morning was necessary and you know it. It was for your own good and you know it. I'm going into the kitchen to fix you something to eat."

He didn't even say a word about it, but instead he asked, "Baby girl, what are you fixing me?"

I knew he regretted telling those fibs to Auntie Bea. I shrugged off my disappointment with my great uncle and answered, "One of those good sandwiches from Mr. T's."

Uncle Frank asked, "Did you get that homemade potato salad too?"

I replied, "Of course."

I went into the kitchen to make him a plate. As I was preparing his plate, I noticed Uncle Frank had a new bottle of whiskey sitting on the counter. I didn't say a word. At least I could monitor how much he was drinking. I was hoping he would not increase his alcohol consumption due to the stress of what happened to his beloved niece, my mother.

Uncle Frank has only truly loved, respected, and listened to two women: my grandmother and my mother. Nobody else could do a damn thing with him or tell him what to do. I took Uncle Frank his plate along with a glass of milk. I put everything on the table in the Florida room. I went back into the kitchen and got my plate and a glass of milk for myself. I sat down at the table across from Uncle Frank.

I watched him take his medication with the glass of milk that I had brought to him and he began to eat. After he gobbled it down, he said, "Belinda that was good. I forgot how good Mr. T's sandwiches are."

I smiled at Uncle Frank and said, "I'm glad you enjoyed it. When was the last time you ate?"

He looked down at the plate and it appeared he was reluctant to answer. When he did speak, I couldn't believe what he told me.

"I guess it's been a couple of days. I don't remember."

I put my hand on Uncle Frank's arm and I spoke with great concern, "Well, then I'm just going to have to do something about that, won't I? I know you haven't had a homemade meal in a long time, so tomorrow I'm going to the grocery store, and I will make you a meal you will love. How does that sound?"

Uncle Frank looked at me with a boyish smile and said, "That sounds good to me, but remember, Belinda, I don't have any teeth, just these false ones."

I laughed at Uncle Frank. "I'll remember. It's getting late, Uncle Frank, and I need to get Auntie Bea's dinner to her so she doesn't pass out on us. I may be back late, so you don't have to stay up, but I'll clean up this mess before I go."

Uncle Frank said he was going into the living room to watch a little bit of television because he was too full to go to bed.

I said, "Okay."

As he was walking into the living room he asked, "Could you lock up for me, baby girl?"

I answered, "Sure, Uncle Frank." I gave him a kiss on the cheek as he walked through the kitchen. "Uncle Frank, did Christina call?"

Uncle Frank replied, "No. I waited by that phone all day, and no one called."

I quickly cleaned up the mess, took my stuff, and loaded it into the pickup truck along with the food for Auntie Bea. I drove next door to the Mills farmhouse. Auntie Bea had her floodlights on again waiting for me. As I was walking to the side door to Auntie Bea's house, I thought it was a lot of work and wished I could just disappear. Everyone had neglected these old people for a very long time and they were very lonely. I could understand why my mother had neglected them for the last several months, but I couldn't understand why Uncle Frank's own children, who were Auntie Bea's nieces and nephews, neglected them. I was only the great-niece. I felt very sad for my great-uncle and great-aunt, but I was still angry with Auntie Bea. Whether she was a victim or not, she had no right to victimize me because of her problems.

I pushed it to the back of my mind, let out a sigh, and walked into Auntie Bea's house. I forced myself to put the crimes behind me for now. I forced a smile and walked into the kitchen through the side door. As I was putting the bags down on the kitchen table, Auntie Bea walked into the kitchen from the living room with her metal cane in tow.

She apologized, "Belinda, I'm sorry for snapping at you on the telephone. What are you going to do about Frank and me?"

I hugged Auntie Bea. I don't know why, but I just started crying and said, "I still don't know, Auntie Bea. I'm still waiting to see if my mortgage for your property has gone through. I don't know anything yet."

Auntie Bea's face lit up with a smile. Apparently, she had not believed that I was really trying to get her land back because she said, "You are really trying to get my land back? I thought you were going to leave me to rot because of what I have done and that you really didn't care about me. I know we never have been close, not like you and Margaret were. I understood because she was your grandmother and I was just your godmother and you never really spent that much time with me. I just thought your mother lied to me about you agreeing to buy my land back."

I just looked at Auntie Bea, shook my head, and said in an agitated tone, "Auntie Bea, I guess you really don't know me very well at all. I told you, or at least I thought I told you, the other night that I was trying to get a mortgage to get your land back, and that Momma was helping me. I'm still angry about what you have done and not even sure you realize what you have done, but you are my godmother and my grandmother's sister. No matter whatever else you are, I have always loved you, and I always will. I'm still very angry with you for being so greedy over that Daisy house and getting yourself into this mess to begin with. Then you opened the doors for Big Pete and possibly my mother to strip you of everything. I told you before that you would not have gotten into this mess if you weren't a sexist and believed that men are better and smarter than women are. You have been proven wrong the hard way. I am the one paying for your mistakes. I don't know why I'm supposed to be held accountable for all this, but it appears to me that there is no one else to step up to the plate and try to bail the two of you out of this mess."

To my surprise, Auntie just laughed as she hugged and kissed me. She simply dismissed the subject. "I'm starving; what did you bring me?"

I just shook my head again, let out another sigh, and started pulling the food out of the bag. I replied, "One of Mr. T's great sandwiches and potato salad."

She giggled and said, "I'll get the plates."

I shook my head, this time smiling at my auntie because I realized just how spoiled she really was. I thought about how much she was like my mother. Auntie Bea gobbled down her sandwich like a ravenous dog. I slowly ate the other half of mine. When we were finished, she helped me clean up the mess. We chatted about unimportant things for the rest of the evening. We both put our problems behind us, for the night anyway.

After Auntie Bea finished her coffee and I drank a well-deserved beer, we decided it was time to go to bed. I locked up, shut the house down for the night, and drove my mother's pickup back to the Daisy house.

I walked back over to Auntie Bea's house and got my mother's Cadillac because I was going to need it to pick up Jay in the morning. I locked up the Daisy house and shut it down for the night. I got into my PJs, grabbed another box of files, and climbed onto the bed. I made a mental note not to fall asleep with the dictionary as a pillow this time. I had learned my lesson from the night before.

CHAPTER XXX

I woke up at 5:00 a.m. I felt refreshed. I know I slept well this time because I was in one of my own beds with a comfortable mattress and nice fluffy pillows. I was ready for a new day.

I went into the kitchen and made a big pot of coffee. I checked out the freezer and found several microwaveable breakfasts. Uncle Frank loved them. I figured that I would make one of those for him when he woke up. I didn't eat breakfast very often. All I needed was a cup of coffee. When the coffee was done, I filled my cup, took a sip, and went to the Florida room.

I pulled out the credit card statements that Big Pete had given me and looked over them again. I still could not get over the amount of debt. Sadly, I knew there was even more debt that I had not discovered yet. I should file charges against my mother for credit card fraud and identity theft, but the thought of filing charges against my own mother broke my heart. I truly did not want to have to do that. I decided that I would have to speak to my mother's attorney regarding the credit card disaster to see if I had any other choices. At this point, I had no idea if the credit card statements that had Uncle Frank's name and my mother's name on them were fraudulent as well. I knew I was going to have to talk to Uncle Frank about it.

I remembered Auntie Bea telling me, the first night I was with her, that Big Pete tried to cash her life insurance, but she caught him before he could do it. He had set up a post office box for his fraudulent activities, but the insurance company accidentally sent the forms directly to Auntie Bea's house. I asked her to show me all of her insurance policies. She kept them in a safe that she said my mother had told her she could use. The safe belonged to my grandmother. Auntie Bea didn't know that my mother had given it to me, and my mother asked me if she could let Auntie Bea

134

use it instead of putting it into storage. I had given my blessing to let Auntie Bea use it for a while.

She went over to get them out, but she could not open the safe, so I opened it for her. My mother did not give it to her and I had to correct Auntie Bea. This is just one lie or fabrication of the truth that Auntie Bea tried to pull on me that night, and she continued to lie to me during my entire visit. I expected Uncle Frank to lie about everything as well. One thing that I knew about both of them was that there was always a little bit of truth in their stories, but they twisted it to suit their needs.

After I opened the safe, Auntie Bea handed over two policies. The first policy was from JC Penney with a face value of $5,000. It was owned and paid for by Auntie Bea. The other policy was a whole life policy with a face value of $300,000. Big Pete had tried to cash that policy.

According to the papers that Auntie Bea had, the policy belonged to Big Pete and my mother. Because they owned the policy, they could cash it in if they chose to do so, but Auntie Bea was correct when she told me that she had to give her permission first. Legally, they could not just arbitrarily cash in the policy. I'm sure the cash value was only the few thousand dollars that they had put into it. I did not know how long Big Pete and my mother had been paying into it, but I did know it had not been more than five or six years. Knowing them the way I did, I could see them opening a policy to get their money back from Auntie Bea when she passed away. I knew she owed them several hundred thousand dollars, most likely an amount that was close to the face value of the policy.

I knew that my mother had to spend a large amount of money to get Auntie Bea out of the mess with Uncle Herndon's estate, and things were starting to click. I understood why Auntie Bea agreed to open such a large insurance policy. It was the only way she would be able to pay them back. They still should have asked Auntie Bea before trying to cash in the policy.

The only reason I knew that they should have checked with Auntie Bea prior to cashing the policy was because they had already cashed the policies that they had taken out on Thomas and me. We were living in Germany when I found out that they had cashed in the policies, and I called the insurance company directly and asked. I was informed that even though someone else owned the policy, they had written authorization to obtain some of the money back that was put into it. In regards to Thomas and me, I knew what they had done was fraudulent. I did nothing about it because it was their money, and I had no problem with it.

I remembered asking Auntie Bea during my first night at her house, "What happens when the leprechaun's pot of gold runs dry?"

Auntie Bea had looked at me and not said a word.

After a few minutes of silence, I gave her the answer, "The magic is gone, and it's time for you to put the gold back into the pot. In other words, Auntie Bea, you have to take responsibility for your own debts and pay them back. The right thing to do is to pay for your own debts and stop trying to blame everyone else for the mistakes that you made throughout your life. But we will not worry about this tonight; we will worry about it another day."

I then remembered that she told me that Big Pete and my mother stole from her checking account. I went through all the canceled checks and then scolded her because the checks were all payments for getting things fixed on her property. There were canceled checks for when she had her house painted, her septic tank drained, and from having her well repaired. According to all of Auntie Bea's records, Mom and Big Pete paid one hundred percent of the upkeep on Auntie Bea's property until the last two years when they started to make her pay for the upkeep of her own property.

As I sat there remembering everything that Auntie Bea had told me, and what her own paper trail told me, I came to a conclusion. There was not a doubt in my mind that Auntie Bea was just a victim of her own demise. My mother and Big Pete helped her for as long as they could. My mother could not say no to my auntie, and that is why my mother started stealing. She didn't steal *from* Auntie Bea; she stole *for* her.

Regarding Auntie Bea's land, I discovered Auntie Bea, my mother, and Big Pete were all to blame equally. What I had discovered was that Auntie Bea gave the thirty-three acres across the road to Mom and Big Pete as payment for the purchase of the Daisy house. When Auntie Bea, Mother, and Big Pete applied for the mortgages, they had the property divided into three parts. The thirty-three acres across the road from the rest of the farm was part C, the Daisy house with a quarter acre of land was part B, and the Mills farmhouse with sixty-six acres was part A. The first mortgage was for the $100,000 on part B (the Daisy house), and the money was immediately put into a CD in Auntie Bea's name at the bank that held the mortgage. My mother and Big Pete mortgaged the thirty-three acres that Auntie gave them for another $100,000 (part C). Big Pete gave Auntie Bea $100,000 of stock from his business and a position title in his company. Big Pete did not have to do this because Auntie Bea gave the thirty-three acres to him and my mother. The only reason Big Pete did this was because of my mother's nagging. After she got the mortgage money, Auntie Bea kept on making mistakes and mishandling her money.

While reviewing the records, I realized that the bank that drew up the mortgages did not specify the amount of debt that was tied to each section of land; they had lumped all the mortgages together. The documentation from the bank had everything listed together, both homes and all ninety-nine and one-quarter acres. That's how Adam Greed received the entire farm and the Daisy house for $192,000. Part A of the farm should have been clear with no debt.

Auntie Bea knew about this mistake, but had done nothing to fix it. My mother did not have the finances to fight the bank once she realized this terrible mistake. The bank foreclosed on Auntie Bea and took her $100,000 CD. The bank picked up the Mills farm of sixty-six acres for zero dollars.

I have already instructed Auntie Bea to go back to the bank today and get the $20,000 that had been paid to the loan. It was such a mess all I could do was buy it all back for the $192,000, which was in Thomas's and my reach. I just prayed Adam Greed honored his word if I did obtain the mortgage.

Now I knew all the facts. I had seen the truth with my own eyes as I looked through the paper trail that my mother and Auntie Bea so thoughtfully kept for me. I had concluded that all three parties were equally to blame, but at the same time, they were the victims of outside forces. Much to my regret, I realized that I couldn't place all the blame on Big Pete. He was not solely responsible for the mess regarding Auntie Bea's land. I now regretted telling Christina the other night what I thought I knew because it was incorrect. I knew the next time I spoke with her I was going to have to tell her that I was wrong and tell her the correct version of this wicked story.

CHAPTER XXXI

Christina had not called me yesterday, even though she had promised to do so. I wondered what had happened, but I was not going to call her again. It was truly up to her. I thought if she didn't call this week I would know that she was nothing but the coward I always had suspected. She had always had a viscous bark, but had run away when confronted.

I decided to call my husband because I had not spoken with him since I arrived, and I knew he was worried sick. I took another sip of coffee, put my cup back, and reached for the phone. As I picked up the phone, I prepared myself mentally for his reaction when I would tell him what my mother had done to me this time. I knew he was going to be very upset.

Thomas answered the phone in a sleepy voice. Before I had a chance to say anything he asked, "Belinda, is that you?"

I replied, "Yes."

He angrily stated, "It's about damn time! I don't even know where you are. I called that stupid creep, Big Pete, and he told me that you were with your auntie, but I didn't have her telephone number, and of course, that asshole would not give me the telephone number. What the hell is going on?"

I proceeded to tell him everything I knew so far. When I finished telling the saga, I had to pull the phone from my ear because Thomas was yelling so loud it was hurting my ear. I had never heard him that angry! Of course, I did not blame him at all. I pretty much felt the same way. I gave him the telephone numbers for Auntie Bea, Uncle Frank, and the shop. He told me to call him the same time every day from now on and report to him, as if I was one of his privates. Naturally, I scolded him for even trying to pull that kind of crap. I reminded him that when I was in the Army I outranked him. That made him even angrier—men.

Then, his attitude changed to complete remorse, he humbly apologized and stated whatever course of action I decided to take he would support me one hundred percent because he knew I had a more level head on my shoulders than he did regarding this crazy "twilight zone" crap. He said he was going to arrange to take leave and let me know the dates. He asked me to call again when I had a chance; of course, I promised I would. We said "I love you" to one another and hung up. I took another sip of my coffee and realized it was ice cold. I got up and went into the kitchen. I dumped the cold coffee down the sink and poured myself a fresh, hot cup. I took a sip—much better. I turned around and saw Uncle Frank standing in front of me with his hair sticking straight up on the top of his head. He still looked very sleepy.

He asked me, "Baby girl, you didn't drink all the coffee, did you?"

I answered him with a smile on my face, "No, Uncle Frank, I didn't. I think there's at least four more cups in that pot. Would you like one of those breakfasts that I saw in your freezer?"

He answered, "Of course! Microwave me one. Let me get my coffee and take my pills first."

I said, "Okay."

I reached into the freezer, pulled out one of the breakfasts, quickly read and followed the instructions, put it into the microwave, and started it. Uncle Frank went into the Florida room and sat at the table. When his food was ready, I put it on a plate and carried it to the table for him. As I walked into the room, I saw him taking his medications with a glass of water. When he was done, I placed his breakfast in front of him. He nodded his thanks and began to shovel the food into his mouth.

As he was eating, I had picked up my notepad and began a list of everything I needed to do and questions I needed to ask. I had found Uncle Frank's checkbook in my mother's papers along with his bills. I took his checkbook and wrote out a check to reimburse myself for the $100 he owed me. Little did I realize that this would become a weekly practice, writing checks to pay Uncle Frank's bills, and paying me back with weekly cash I would give him. Of course, I made him sit there with me as a witness. There was no way I was going to write out his checks without him witnessing it. After he finished eating and I had cleared the table, I put the bills with the checks written out for each one and I had him sign them along with the cash check that he owed me. He told me to get his glasses that were on the end table by his favorite chair. Of course, I did as I was told. He put them on and started signing. The whole time he was signing the checks, he complained, "Your momma never made me sign them. She just did it all."

I told him, "I'm not my momma! Besides, you already told me that my mother was taking all your money, which you know was a bold-faced lie. I thought you loved my mother, or do you only love her when she has money?"

Uncle Frank replied, "I do love your momma, and I guess I should have known better than to lie to you."

I said, "You should never lie at all, Uncle Frank!"

After we finished paying his bills, I reconciled his checkbook. Then I picked up the stack of credit cards that had my mother's name and Uncle Frank's name on them, and asked, "Uncle Frank, why did you and Momma open up these credit cards in both your names?"

Uncle Frank took the bills from my hands—he still had his glasses on—and looked at them. After a few minutes he answered, "Oh, because we were trying to rebuild our credit, and she had my permission to do it."

I said, "Uncle Frank, I need to know which charges are yours, and which ones were my mother's charges. I need to separate them because I don't think it would be fair for you to have to pay for the things that she charged, and I shouldn't have to pay for the things that you charged."

Uncle Frank said, "Damn, girl! Like I can remember who charged what."

I went over to the telephone with the credit card bills in hand. The only way to get this mess straightened out was to call each credit card company and request a printout of all the charges for the last year. Once I was able to speak with someone, I explained that I had to separate my mother's charges from my uncle's charges. I did not give further detail. While I was on the phone, I made the minimum payments for each credit card company. I told them that once I received the statements my uncle and I would go through them to determine which ones were his, and I would make sure payments were made.

When I was finished calling the credit card companies, I asked Uncle Frank about his life insurance policy. I told him that Auntie Bea had told me the other night that my mother and Big Pete had cashed it in, but when I was going through my mother's papers, I found the policy. From her records, the policy was not cashed in, but there was a loan taken against it for the face value of the policy.

Uncle Frank scratched his head and said, "Damn it, I didn't say that to Bea. You know I owe your mother $70,000 or so for bailing me out of debt when my wife, Betty, left me with all that debt. I did that loan myself and gave the money to your mother to help pay for Bea's attorney fees for when Bea tried to file for bankruptcy. That's all I had. The only way I was going to be able to pay your momma back was when I died. I don't care how they bury me. I'll be dead and I won't care, and your momma needed the money for your auntie. She needed the money right away. The state can cremate me for all I care. Of course, I'm not going to tell Bea where the money came from. I do have pride."

As he was speaking, I just sat there, once again shaking my head in disbelief. When he was finished, I sighed and said, "Damn it, Uncle Frank, you lied again. When are you going to learn that lying gets you nowhere? After Auntie Bea talked to me about your life insurance policy, I thought that Momma was stealing from you too. Right now, I'm madder than hell at you. I have to get out of here for a while. Damn it, Uncle Frank!"

I walked out of the room and back to my room. I was so angry my head hurt, and the day was just beginning.

Once I had my temper under control, I walked back to the Florida room where Uncle Frank still sat in the same place as when I had left. I was armed with my note pad, my mother's purse, my purse, and my mother's briefcase. As I was putting my armload down on the wrought-iron sofa, I looked up. Little Pete had just pulled into the driveway. I looked over at Uncle Frank, and his face was contorted into a painful expression. I felt a slight twinge of guilt, but he had deserved the scolding. To make him feel better, I smiled at him, went over to the table where he was sitting, and kissed him on the forehead.

I said, "I'm sorry for getting so upset with you. I love you, and we will get through this somehow, at least I hope so. You and Auntie Bea need to stop fibbing about Momma. I can't help you if you are going to lie. United we stand, divided we fall."

Uncle Frank looked up at me from where he was sitting. He grabbed my hand, squeezed it, and then said, "Just don't get so angry with me, Belinda. You know how your auntie and I are. You are not going to change us."

"I know, Uncle Frank. I love both of you, but you are going to have to stop fighting me. I need you to work with me. If you want me to be effective in getting this mess straightened out, you need to work with me.

This is the only way we are going to get through this. I don't even know if my best is going to be good enough. Remember it's only me, and I'm not rich, Uncle Frank. I can only do so much. I only have a limited inventory left, and there are many people with their hands out. I have to go and pick up Jay."

Just when I said that, Uncle Frank's phone rang and he answered it. He immediately handed the phone to me. He said that it was a collect call from Jay. I took the phone. Jay told me that he was stuck at the Atlanta airport and there was a two-hour delay because of the icy conditions. I told him to stay safe and that I would be at the Snobville airport later. I told him that I would wait for him.

During my conversation with Jay, Uncle Frank had moved from the table to his favorite chair.

He looked up at me from his chair and asked, "Your brother is coming too?"

I answered, "Yes, but now I don't know about Christina. She hasn't called back yet."

Uncle Frank asked, "They are going to help us?"

I replied, "No, Uncle Frank. They are going to help me, and I am going to help you, Mom, and Auntie Bea. Do you see now why it is so important for you to be honest regarding all this? It's very important to me that you and Auntie Bea stop sugarcoating everything you say and stop making yourselves look like you are just innocent victims. Stop acting like you didn't play a role in this."

Uncle Frank replied, "I understand now, Belinda."

I think after this conversation with Uncle Frank, he and Auntie Bea were more honest with me for the remainder of my stay in Virginia. Granted they did have slip-ups and would lay blame on someone else for things they did, but the majority of the time, at least in front of me, they told the truth more accurately than before. I guess they just had to discover that my mother's children and Pete's son were honest, even though our parents were not. That the children took the responsibility for their parents' actions and were at least attempting to make things right again. Even if we failed, at least we did whatever we could.

I kissed Uncle Frank on the forehead again and said goodbye. I told him that I would see him that night.

It was a beautiful day outside. The sun was shining with just a few fluffy white clouds. I knew the road ahead of me would be long and painful.

As I was walking out the sliding glass door, I yelled over to Little Pete as he was locking up his van, "Little Pete, we're taking the 'White Beast' today." The "White Beast" was named many years prior. It was my mother's white Cadillac, and she rarely drove it. I met Little Pete over by the White Beast and handed him the keys.

He asked, "Where's the first destination?"

I replied, "The shop. I'm sure Big Pete is already there."

CHAPTER XXXII

As I suspected, Big Pete was already moving around in the shop. I could see him through the big front window. I told Little Pete to park behind the shop. We slipped into the shop through the back door. By the time we were inside, Big Pete was sitting at his desk in the back of the shop.

He greeted us, "Good morning."

Little Pete and I both replied, "Good morning."

Big Pete informed me, "The owner of the building just stepped in a little while ago. You will need to go and see him, Belinda."

I was stunned and a little confused. I asked, "Okay. Why does he need to see me?"

Big Pete simply replied, "You just better go over and speak with him."

I said, "Okay."

Big Pete then asked, "Little Pete, can you show Belinda where he is?"

Little Pete answered, "Okay."

I still had a puzzled expression on my face. Little Pete guided me through the shop to the front and out the door. Once we were outside, he pointed to a little building and a small side road leading into a dirt parking lot around the back of the shop. It looked like a guard shack to me because it was so small. I had noticed it when we parked behind the shop, but did not pay much attention to it. I walked over to the building and went inside.

There was a desk in the room with a chair in front of it. When I walked in, I saw a man seated at the desk. He stood up when I entered. I introduced myself to the man, and he told me that his name was David Jones, and he was the owner of the row of buildings that included my shop. He motioned for me to take a seat in the chair in front of his desk, and he sat back down behind the desk.

Once I was seated, he said, "Ms. Star, your mother has a bounced check for December's rent and she has not paid for this month's rent. According to Pete King, you will be handling these matters for your mother."

I stated firmly, "Mr. Jones, I am the owner of this shop. My mother was an employee of mine. I am very embarrassed by my mother's actions, as well as those of Big Pete. In fact, he was not supposed to be in my shop at all. I wanted to settle this matter immediately because I do not conduct business like this. I sincerely apologize for the bounced check, and I would like to rectify the situation immediately. I would also like to pay for the next two months in advance right now. I need to liquidate my inventory because I cannot run a shop from Europe. I have no idea how long it will take. My mother never provided any information regarding the rent contract for this building, nor could I find anything in her records. I would like a copy of the contract."

He looked at me with a puzzled expression and said in a belittling tone, "The reason you did not find a contract is because there was no written one. I do not need to conduct business so formally. Your mother and I had a verbal contract, nothing more. As far as I'm concerned, this agreement was between your mother and me, not you. From my understanding, Big Pete and your mother own the shop. It will be fine to pay in cash for this month, the next two months, in addition to the bounced check."

I sat there thinking, *What an arrogant pompous asshole he is.* I said in a very professional tone, "I'm truly sorry, sir, that you were misled regarding ownership. My mother was representing me, not herself. Big Pete has absolutely nothing to do with my business." I picked up my briefcase, laid it on his desk, opened it, and showed him all my legal documentation proving that the shop was legally mine including all inventory. I made sure that he saw that there were no other names on the documentation. Then I said, "So you see, sir, I'm sole proprietor of Cognac's Run. I really would like more insight as to how you came to the conclusion that Big Pete was even party to this." I looked straight at David Jones' face as I spoke to him. I saw him slowly turn beet red.

When he spoke again, he stuttered a little. "I, umm, I don't—umm understand. Your mother said it was her shop. Big Pete just said it was his shop now that your mother is in jail. He told me that you came from Germany to work for him as an employee, and that you will take care of all finances because your mother was stealing from him. Everything he said made sense to me. That's why I believed him."

I put the papers back into the briefcase, closed it, and put it on the floor by my chair. I sat back into my chair and sadly shook my head. I could not believe the number of lies that I had heard in the past few days. I let out a sigh before I spoke and said, "Sir, I'm truly sorry for this, and I hope that you will show me sympathy. Big Pete is a crook and a very, very good liar, which I know you now realize from firsthand experience. I'm sure you know from reading the newspapers what Big Pete has done. I promise that as soon as I'm able and the opportunity presents itself, I will have Big Pete removed from the premises so that these scandalous activities do not affect your establishments any further. I am not party to any of these criminal activities and never have been. I'm here, sir, to clean up as much of the mess as I can and to make as much restitution to my mother's victims. I am also trying to clear her name as much as possible by making as much restitution. I have been the wind beneath my mother's wings for a very long, long time. If it gave her self-importance to give the illusion that it was her shop and not mine, does it really matter as long as I keep the verbal contract that you made with her?"

Mr. Jones' eyes were as large as saucers. I guess he was in shock that Big Pete had so easily duped him, despite the fact that he already knew from reading the newspaper what Big Pete was.

Mr. Jones said, "Ms. Star, I'm sorry for my attitude towards you earlier. Big Pete had me convinced that it was your mother, not him, that did all these nasty things, and gave me the impression that you had taken all this money that she had stolen from his clients back to Europe and now you were coming to take what little bit he had left. I feel so stupid because his story was so out there, but he told it so detailed and just somehow made it make sense. Well, back to business, and don't worry about the fees for the bounced check."

He gave me the total of what was already owed him plus the two months I was going to pay in advance.

I said, "Thank you, sir, for your kindness and candor. Don't worry; I will not say anything to Big Pete about our discovery. I think it is best for all concerned parties, and I'm referring to my great-aunt and great-uncle, that you and I act as if this conversation never took place. I do fear for their safety, but I'm not going to go into detail regarding that. I will need to go to the bank and get the cash so I can pay you. I will be back shortly to finish our business, if that is okay with you?"

Mr. Jones chuckled and said, "You know money always does the talking. I will be here waiting for your return. Again I'm sorry I acted like an asshole towards you."

I said as I was picking up the briefcase, "You're forgiven. I completely understand your motives." I then left the building and walked back over to my shop.

As I was walking back to the shop, it took every ounce of self-discipline to contain my outrage over the entire incident. I imagined my husband holding Big Pete down as I cut his lying tongue out of his mouth. Of course, I had no intention of giving in to my basic rage, but fantasies can be fun. I lit a cigarette, stood outside on the sidewalk, and smoked it before going back into my shop. It took the edge off, but not nearly enough.

When I walked into my store, Little Pete was talking to Big Pete. I said, "Okay, Little Pete, it's time to go."

I then looked at Big Pete with faked concern and politeness, and said, "Big Pete, I have twenty $1 bills in the cash box for change. Please write out a receipt for each sale, and please leave all the cash in the box. I can get into trouble for that with the taxman, and I believe in paying my taxes. It makes it hard to know what's been sold from the inventory and reconciling if there are no receipts."

Big Pete said, "Okay, I haven't taken any money from the cash box. I noticed you have a password on the computer and I can't get into your momma's computer."

I said, "Big Pete, you don't need to worry yourself over the recon. I'm quite capable of doing it, and there is no need for you to look at my shop's computer. I'm not snooping through your computer so please don't do it with mine."

He said, "Okay."

I opened my mother's briefcase, handed Big Pete the insurance forms and policy that he had been paying on Auntie Bea, and said, "I believe this is yours. You can cash it now or keep it. I have explained to Auntie Bea that it is not hers, and she doesn't want to continue paying on it because she cannot afford the premiums."

Big Pete took it from me with a smile on his face and said, "Are you sure your auntie is okay with this?"

I said, "I will call her right now so you can hear for yourself, even though she has already filled out the forms and signed them for you."

He said, "Okay, call her."

I called Auntie Bea and told her I was putting Big Pete on the phone so she could tell him about the insurance policy. Big Pete took the phone and talked with Auntie Bea for a few minutes. When he hung up the phone he said, "Thank you, Belinda."

I said, "That should cover you for the next few months if you spend it wisely."

Big Pete said, "It's only a few thousand dollars."

I simply stated, "Good, it should cover you for the next few months. We have to go and take care of more business."

Little Pete and I went out the back door and got into the White Beast. I thought for a moment that Little Pete was two-faced and was actually helping Big Pete. What I saw when the two of them were talking, every instinct in my body told me that Little Pete could not be trusted. I had learned to trust my instincts, so I asked, "Little Pete, what were you and Big Pete talking about?"

Little Pete said, "Oh, I told him that Jay was coming into town and that Christina might be coming as well."

I knew my instincts were true on the dollar and I said, "Little Pete, I can't believe that you told him about my personal business! It is none of his business! It is up to Jay to tell him, not you. I would appreciate it if you would stop telling him my business."

Little Pete said, "Big Pete is Jay's father."

I said, "So what. Jay hates his father's guts."

Little Pete said, "Oh, I didn't know that."

I said, "There is a lot you don't know, Little Pete. You need to take me to the bank so I can pay the rent on the shop."

Little Pete said, "Okay."

I knew right then and there that, without a doubt, Little Pete was just as much of a liar as everyone else involved in this big mess. I just didn't know the extent of his involvement. I knew he was keeping secrets for Big Pete, but I just didn't know why. I knew I was going to have to find out sooner rather than later. From that moment on, I did not trust Little Pete.

We pulled into the bank's parking lot, and I told Little Pete to wait for me because I would be just a few minutes. I went into the bank and reluctantly pulled out my charge card from my wallet. I stood in line for a few minutes. When the bank teller greeted me, I told her I needed to make a charge for cash. She helped me and gave me the cash. I put the cash into my wallet, and walked back out to the White Beast where Little Pete was waiting for me.

I got back in the car, and after putting my seatbelt on, I told Little Pete that I needed to go to the airport after I paid the rent on the shop, but I wanted him to go back to Mom and Big Pete's house. I told him that I needed him to start taking apart my mother's bedroom furniture because we would have to move it. I said that I would go and pick up Jay by myself while he was doing that. I told him that Jay and I would meet him at Mom and Pete's house.

On the way back to the Daisy house, Little Pete stopped at the little building where my landlord was waiting to be paid. I rushed into the building, paid him, and took the receipt he gave. He stated if there was anything I needed regarding the building to let him know, and I told him that I would.

I got back into the White Beast, and we drove back to the Daisy house. Little Pete got into his van and left. I was getting ready to pull out as well when I saw Uncle Frank at the sliding glass door yelling something at me. I stopped the car, put it into park, got out of the car, and met Uncle Frank at the sliding glass door.

He said, "Belinda, it's your sister on the phone."

I said, "Oh, shit, I have to . . . oh here, let me get it." I picked up the phone and said, "Hello, Christina." I heard Christina's voice. I was so excited because I thought she was on her way.

Christina said, "Yes, Belinda, it's me. I'm going to try to make flight arrangements for tomorrow. I haven't called because I couldn't get a cheap flight out and I've been trying to get a seat that I can afford."

I asked, "Do you need me to pay for it?"

She replied, "No, let's wait and see if I can get on this flight without it costing me an arm and a leg. I will call you again tomorrow. Do you have time to fill me in?"

I said, "No, I'm on my way to pick up Jay now."

Christina asked, "What? Jay is already there?"

I answered, "Yes, or he will be, but his flight was late because of the weather."

She said, "Well, I better let you go. Call me tonight and tell me what's going on."

I said, "I will, and I'm glad you called. I need to correct some of the accusations I made against our mother. I was wrong on some of them, but I will explain tonight."

Christina said, "Okay. I love you, Belinda; hang in there. Tell Mom I love her. Oh, did you get her medication to her?"

I said, "I think so, but I don't know. As soon as I pick up Jay, I'm taking him straight to the jail so he can see her. I will find out then. I love you, Christina, but I have to go; I don't want Jay waiting at the airport. You know that's no fun."

I laughed and she giggled too. "I love you too, Sissy. Call me when you can."

I said, "I will. I love you, goodbye." I hung the phone up and Uncle Frank was looking at me with a questioning look. I said, "I've got to go, Uncle Frank. I will fill you in tonight."

I heard him say, "Okay," as I was walking out the sliding glass door. I got into the White Beast, which was still running, and drove to the Snobville Airport to pick up Jay. I was sure he was already there and waiting on me. I hate to make people wait.

CHAPTER XXXIII

While I was driving to the airport, I started thinking about Jay. I remembered many years ago when I babysat for Mom and Big Pete so they could go to a football game. I guess Jay was about seven years old, if that. I think I was on leave, and I had just finished basic training. It was so long ago. I do remember telling him that you do not call a soldier's weapon a gun, you call it a weapon, and you have to be able to take it apart and put it back together again in just a few minutes, and little trivia stuff of that nature because he was always intrigued that his new big sister was in the Army.

I had learned that over the years Jay had written numerous school papers about me being a soldier and his hero. He was always so proud that I was his sister. Jay was a scrawny little boy. He didn't sprout up until he was about fifteen. He was always much smaller than the other little boys until he finally started to grow. I never really knew who Jay was because I was far, far away in the military.

I remembered one time in my early years in the Army I would call my mother periodically to let her know I was okay and would ask about everyone in the family and if they were all doing okay. Mom told me during one of these phone conversations a story about Jay and two school bullies. I learned during this conversation that these two much bigger bullies were making Jay and many other little boys and girls, give them lunch money every day. Jay had seen them beat up several little boys and girls. Jay was sick of them taking his lunch money and told them that his bigger sister was a soldier, and if he told her what they were doing to him, she would come to this school with her weapon, an M16, and hand grenades and kill the two little boys and their families. He scared the two bullies so badly that one of them urinated his pants before they both ran away from Jay's table in the school cafeteria.

Apparently, they were so scared that they told their parents, and the parents called the principal at the school. They told the principal what Jay had said, and they were afraid that it might be true and feared for their children's lives. The principal in turn called my mother and Big Pete, and he discovered I would never do such a thing and that I never said anything of the sort to Jay.

After Mom told me the story, she asked if I told Jay anything like that. I replied, "No, but the first time I babysat him when he was a small child, I told him you don't call a soldier's weapon a gun, you call it a weapon, or an M16. I guess I did tell him about qualifying for using the hand grenades. I didn't think I had said anything that would make him think to threaten someone!"

Mom said, "Belinda, you should have never talked about the military to Jay. He is too young to understand it, even if it was just trivial facts. Now it makes sense where he learned it."

I did not reply, but I did wonder how I was supposed to know he would make something out of nothing. I guess I shouldn't have told him anything, but he enjoyed it so much. I thought it was just boring stuff.

Jay's mother drugged him repeatedly when he was an infant and a toddler. His mother was a nurse, and she would give him medication so he would sleep while she was at work. His father scared the crap out of him all his life. I remember Mom telling me a story about Jay because she thought it was funny. Mom and Big Pete sent him to summer camp; he would not take his clothes off to change or even to take a shower the entire time he was at camp. I didn't think it was funny at all.

I then remembered a happy time when Thomas and I were stationed in Hawaii. It was about a year or so before Desert Storm. Mom called to ask if Jay could stay with us for a couple of days. Chris, my sister's first husband, was taking Jay on his aircraft carrier. He would pick Jay up at his last port of call before docking back at home port in California and then take him to California.

From my understanding, these were called Tiger cruises, and the naval personnel are allowed to take one family member from their last port of call before docking at their home port of call. I'm sure I had the naval terminology incorrect, but that's how I understood it. It was up to the naval men to provide transportation for the family member to the last port of call before traveling back. Mom and Big Pete wanted to fly Jay to Hawaii, have Thomas and me pick him up, and have him stay with us for a few nights. That way he would be able to visit with us and visit with Chris as well.

This was fine with Thomas and me because we were living in naval housing about ten minutes from Pearl Harbor. The Army and Navy and even the Air Force shared their housing in Hawaii. A few days later, we went to pick up Jay from the airport. We were waiting for him where he was to pick up his luggage. The airport was huge! We were lucky and parked underground next to the doors where airplane passengers retrieved their luggage. As soon as he saw us, Jay came running toward us and practically jumped up into my arms. He was so happy to see us. Jay was just a few inches shorter than I was at this time. I had already put a small party together with Air Force, Navy, and Army friends—a mixture of officers and enlisted—for Chris.

Chris was a Navy pilot, and he flew an F-15. Chris was one of my heroes. I was very sad when he and Christina split up, but I expected it from the day they married. He joined the Navy because they had the best top gun program, even better than the Air Force. His goal was to become an astronaut, and his dream was someday to walk on the moon. I truly believed he was well on the way to making his dream come true. Chris was over six feet tall, and he barely made it because of his height. Apparently, he even had to undergo psychological testing because if he had to eject from the aircraft because of his height and the position of his head from the top of the cockpit, it would tear his head from his body immediately. In fact, Chris watched two of his friends, who were in the air with him, crash into each other and plummet to their deaths.

Chris was a typical flyboy. He lived in the moment. He drank a lot and did pretty much whatever he wanted to do without common courtesy to others that were around him. I understood this way of thinking because as someone on the front line, you never knew if you would die tomorrow or not. At this point in time, he and Christina had been married for five years. I could not believe that their marriage had lasted that long. Christina was studying to be a psychologist and Chris had become a flyboy. He was gone for six months at a time. I just couldn't figure out how they were making it work. Little did I know that their marriage was not working out. I generally liked Chris. He had the social skills of a fourteen-year-old when he was off duty, but he was very intelligent and truly deserved to be in the top gun program.

Chris had a master's degree in meteorology. My mother had introduced Christina to Chris at a fraternity party. My mother was invited to the party after a football game because she was an alumnus. After Thomas and I picked up Jay, we took him back to our apartment. Our friends had already started showing up for the party. We knew Chris's carrier was docked because we drove by it after picking up Jay. We took Jay to the naval base. We drove around, but we could not find Chris.

One of the naval officers who showed up early for the party gave me a number to call to track him, and the officer took the phone from me and did it himself. Chris had apparently already left the carrier and was already on R&R. Everyone we had invited, plus a few extra people, showed up. Poor Jay was confused and didn't know what was going on. In retrospect, I'm glad he didn't know that the party was for Chris because it would have just hurt his feelings.

Our naval friends said they were going to go find him, but it was already 7:30 p.m., and Chris has been missing since noon when we were supposed to pick him up. Thomas asked if he needed to go with them. They said no, that they had their own ways of dealing with this without causing too much of a stir.

A few hours later, there was a knock on the door. Our friends were now in their Navy uniforms. They had two Navy police officers with them, and Chris was between them.

I asked, "Chris's not in any trouble is he?"

One of our friends said, "No, but if you and Thomas were not his family he would be, for just the principle of it."

Chris was so drunk he could barely stand up. We put him in the guest room, and he passed out immediately. I put the trashcan beside the bed and hoped that if he got sick he would use it.

Thomas, the MPs, and our two officer friends went back outside. I followed them. I decided that the rest of our friends could fend for themselves. Our friends said that they had found him shacked up in a hotel next to the Navy base with some woman that he had met in the officer's club on base. They stated that he could easily be prosecuted for that. They had discovered him because his other pilot friends were still in the officer's club getting drunk. They had loose tongues and several of them told them the hotel he was going to with the woman he had picked up. Even though it wasn't really a big deal, he could be prosecuted for adultery if they chose to do so.

They all made the decision to bring him straight to our place, and because it really wasn't a big deal, they would not say anything. The only reason they even went to look for him was because I had gone to so much trouble preparing for his arrival. Thomas and I were their friends. Our two friends told us they were going back to change into their civilian clothes, and for us to tell their wives they would be back shortly. Thomas and I thanked them and told them that we were very grateful that they found him.

We had the party while the guest of honor was passed out in our guest bedroom. Everyone left around 11:30 p.m. After the last person walked out the door, the telephone rang. Thomas picked up the phone as I was walking into the kitchen with dirty glasses and dishes.

He said, "Oh, hi, Christina." His eyes got huge as he was looking at me. "Here, let me put Belinda on the phone."

I told Thomas that I would take the call in the bedroom. I ran into our bedroom, picked up the phone, and said, "I got it, Thomas. Hi, Christina; how are you?"

Christina asked with concern laced in her voice, "Is Chris there? He hasn't called me in over a week."

I lied to my sister, "Oh, no, Christina, they haven't gotten here yet. From my understanding, they are delayed for some reason. I only know this because one of our friends is a Navy officer and he found out for us. We haven't heard from Chris either, but I promise as soon as he arrives I'll have him call you ASAP."

Christina asked, "Are you sure? I called the carrier and someone picked up the phone and said they were already docked."

I replied, "Well, Christina, I'll call my friend and find out what is going on. They may have just gotten into dock, but its late here and maybe Chris figured he would call us in the morning."

Christina said, "Oh, that's probably why he hasn't called. I guess he just wants to surprise me or something."

I said, "Yeah, you're probably right. I love you and don't worry. I'm sure Chris will call you in the morning." We said our goodbyes, and I hung up the phone.

Thomas had already walked into the bedroom and closed the door behind him.

I whispered, "Where's Jay?"

Thomas whispered, "He's in the living room watching something on the TV. Don't worry, Belinda, he doesn't know what's going on."

I said, "I hope you're right. If Christina finds out about this it will hurt her, and I don't want to hurt my sister."

Thomas replied in a more hostile tone, "You and your sister don't even get along. She treats you like a piece of crap like the rest of your family does. In fact, this is the first time she has ever called you since we have been married. Who cares if she finds out? She deserves it."

I whispered angrily, "You may be right, Thomas, but I'm not going to be the one to stoop myself to that level and deliberately hurt her as she does to me. I may not like her or the way that she treats me, but I do love her."

Thomas said in a softer tone, "All right, Belinda, I'm sorry."

We finished cleaning up the mess from the party and went to bed exhausted from everything that had happened that evening. The next day, I made Chris call Christina as soon as he was awake, and then we took Chris and Jay sightseeing around the island. Chris took us on the aircraft carrier and gave us a tour before we left him and Jay there. As I was walking off the ship, I hung back. I made sure that Jay was with Thomas out of hearing range.

I said to Chris in a very nasty tone, "If you ever fuck another girl while you are married to my sister I will hunt you down like the mangy dog you are and cut off your balls. Have I made myself clear?"

Chris looked at me in total shock with his eyes big as saucers. "Yes, ma'am, but, Belinda, I was drunk and didn't know what I was doing. I'm sorry; it will never happen again. Are you going to tell your sister on me?"

I said, "Listen here, you sorry-ass creep, I will never mention this to my sister, and you're damn lucky you're not going to be punished as severely as you could be. They are just going to smack your hand this time because of Thomas and me. This is not a threat; it's a promise. If you ever do this again, I will make sure you will be sorry for the rest of your life."

Chris looked at me as if he were studying me. Without saying another word, he turned around and walked away.

CHAPTER XXXIV

I arrived at the Snobville Airport about twenty minutes after I left the Daisy house, and as I suspected, Jay was waiting for me in front of the airport. I quickly drove to where he was waiting, opened the trunk, and got out of the car to help him put his luggage into the trunk. This was the first time I had seen Jay in years, and he had sprouted up. I guess he was about six feet now. He was still skinny with no muscles on his arms, but he turned out okay. He had just graduated from college. I was jealous because Mom and Big Pete gave him the all-American dream and an upper-middle-class lifestyle—something that I never really had. Uncle Sam paid for my college, and I served the Army to see the world. Everything was handed to Jay on a silver platter. I guess it's because he was a boy. Who knows. I now know everything that was given to him was stolen for him. I wondered if he had realized that yet.

We hugged each other and I said, "I want to take you to go see Mom first because I'm sure she has instructions for you."

We both started laughing because no matter what the circumstances, my mother would still try to control and boss everyone around, even from the jailhouse. When I opened the trunk to the White Beast for Jay to put his luggage in, it was the first time I had opened it. Jay and I discovered a large cloth handbag in it. I took it out and looked inside, and there was jewelry in it.

"We'll deal with this later," I said, and we both put Jay's luggage into the trunk.

Jay looked at me and said, "Let me drive."

I said, "Okay. Do you know a shortcut from here to get to the county jail since it's almost two hours from here?"

Jay said, "Yes, but it's mostly on the back roads, and it's still going to take a good hour."

I said, "Good. Let's go, but first stop at the first country store we see so I can get some water and soda. Are you thirsty too?"

Jay said, "Yes, but you need to tell me what the hell is going on."

I said, "I will."

Jay said, "On second thought, wait until after we get our sodas and I get out of the airport and the traffic around here. I'm afraid I'm going to get upset and crash."

I laughed and said, "Okay."

Within a few minutes, Jay pulled into a country store. We both got out of the White Beast and went inside the store. I got some water and a fountain soda. Jay got a sandwich, a bag of chips, and a large bottled soda. He put it on the counter with mine. I looked up at him with one eyebrow cocked up, and he said, "I don't have any money, Belinda. For Pete's sake, I'm still working at the pizza place. They only gave me a week off, and I was lucky to get that." So I paid for everything.

We got back into the White Beast and Jay said, "I guess I'm going to go first. Dad has been beating on your mom and me for years. I was too scared to tell you, and Christina about anything because I knew he would kill me. Your mom and my dad asked me to go to this insurance class and be certified to sell insurance so that my dad could continue running his insurance business by using my name. I was in college, which I know you knew about through the Air Force ROTC program. I couldn't hack the PT and other crap and dropped out of it. I was told I wouldn't have to pay it back, but my credit report shows that I owe them $5,000. Your mom said she would take care of it, but now all this has happened. The classic Mustang that your mom and my dad bought me four years ago is broken down, and I don't have the money to fix it. I don't even have enough money to pay for rent. I hate my father's guts, and I want to kill him for this. I'm not even twenty-three years old and my credit is ruined."

I didn't say a word as I listened to Jay go on and on about all his problems, and what Big Pete had done to him over the years. I just sat in the passenger's seat with the window down smoking my cigarette and sipping my soda as I listened to Jay tell me all the things he had never told anyone else. I decided it was best I didn't tell him anything that I knew. It was for the best. I don't think he could handle it, and I knew he would follow me to the end of the earth for his vengeance against his father. I think in his own way, Jay loved Christina and me. I also knew that at this moment, in his mind we were all he had.

After Jay had gotten it all out in the open, I simply asked one question. "Jay, why didn't you call Christina or me?"

As I watched him look down at his soda bottle, he answered with shame, "Because I am a coward, Belinda. That is why I'm here to help you, to try to make up for me being a coward, to do right by your mother, your sister, me, and especially you. I know now that you would have come and saved your mother and me because you are here right now."

I just looked at him and shook my head in sadness for what this poor boy had to endure alone. I let out a sigh and said, "You have put too much faith in me. Well, let's go and see the old jailbird before it becomes too late today. We will not think about all this or worry about this today, Jay. We will save our thoughts and energy to deal with it some other day."

Jay nodded in agreement, as he started up the White Beast. We chatted as we drove through the countryside. Most of our conversation was about Jay and college. He told me about his girlfriend and other girls he thought were pretty and liked to meet. He just chatted away, and I'm glad he did. He appeared to be very relieved that he had gotten all the trials and tribulations off his shoulders and was able to tell me the truth finally. Before I knew it, Jay was pulling up into the parking lot of the jail and his eyes were wide as saucers. He looked over at me and said, "This is going to be harder than I thought."

I said, "I know, but you can do it."

I asked him if he had his driver's license and airplane ticket. Jay said he did and it was in his backpack in the trunk.

We walked through the front doors and up to the window. The same snot-nosed guard was sitting there behind the window. His attitude toward me was completely different from my last encounter with him. He was polite and pleasant. He actually smiled at us during the whole process. I told him who Jay was, and Jay put his driver's license and airplane ticket in the slot under the window. I put my military ID and airplane ticket in the slot with his. The police officer took the items, wrote the information he needed into a large green signature book, and put the book in the slot and asked for both of us to sign it and date it for him. After we signed the book and put it into the slot again, the officer told us to have a seat and someone would get my mother and then call us. Jay and I both thanked him and sat in the chairs in the waiting room.

About ten minutes later, Ms. Green, the same female guard who had treated my mother and me so rudely during my last visit, came through the door as the buzzer sounded. She called our names. This time, her uniform fit her properly, and she looked very attractive with a proper fitting uniform. I thought, *Wow, how different she looks; very attractive even if she is a larger woman.* I was very glad that I had told her superior the other day that I considered her clothing offensive because it was so tight on her. Today, her attitude was friendly and pleasant as she greeted the two of us. She even apologized to me for being rude the other day. Of course, I gladly accepted her apology. She escorted us to the same room with the booths in it.

As we walked in, I looked over to Jay and he was fighting back tears already. I knew he loved my mother as if she were his. My mother helped raise him and gave him opportunities that I know he would not have had if it weren't for her. I wished my mother had treated me like that, but that's water under the bridge.

Jay and I stood for what seemed like forever as we waited for my mother to come in. I kept checking my watch, and it was actually only three and a half minutes before we saw the door on the other side start to open. Our eyes lit up when we saw my mother come through the door on the other side of the booths. Her eyes lit up the second she saw Jay standing beside me. We both rushed over to the booth where Ms. Green escorted my mother, and this time Ms. Green left the room. We were alone. I never expected such privacy. I let Jay sit in the chair and speak to my mother with the phone set first.

I watched as they both picked up their phones and started speaking. I could not hear my mother. All I could see was her mouth moving. Jay said hello and was silent after that. He just shook his head as if he were agreeing to whatever she was saying. I heard him say, "I love you," and then he hung up the receiver on the wall of the booth. I was standing beside him during their conversation.

When he was done, he looked up at me and said, "She wants to talk to you now." He stood up and moved aside so I could sit down in the chair. Mom was still holding the phone. She looked like she was ready to talk the second my phone was in hearing proximity. I picked up the phone and said, "Hello."

Mom told me what she instructed Jay to do and informed me she expected me to make sure that her orders were followed to the letter. She started to talk about Ed Weird. This was the first time I ever heard of him. Mom told me that Ed Weird had invested some money for her in Jay's name and I was to make sure Jay called him to arrange to pick the money up. Jay was then supposed to give all the proceeds to me so I could use that to pay on this mess that she had created. She also said Big Pete had already given his Rolex watch to Jay. She wanted Jay to hock it, and I was to help him do so. Again, Jay was to give me the proceeds from that. She said the watch was in the trunk of the White Beast. I told her Jay and I had found it when I picked him up from the airport. She put her hand on the glass divider and I put my open hand on it as if we had our hands touching, but the glass divider cruelly separated us. Jay followed suit and put his hand on it as well. Mom then told us she loved both of us and she was sorry for all the bad things that she had done. I looked over at Jay and the tears were flowing down his cheeks. I asked her about her medication. She told me they had been delivered to the jail from the pharmacy, but still they refused to give them to her.

She was afraid she might have a stroke or worse because it had now been several days since she had taken her cholesterol medication. I looked at her and knew exactly how she felt. I was also scared for my mother's health at that point. I knew I was going to have to call Christina again and have her intervene. Mom also told me that her therapist had tried to visit her but was refused entrance. I told her I would take care of it ASAP. She then told me that she had made threats to kill herself. I told her not to threaten to commit suicide while she was incarcerated because it would just make things worse for her. I sternly scolded her for making the threats. She promised she would obey me and not cause any trouble while she was in there. I was not going to hold my breath on that one though. Mom was famous for breaking her promises to me.

I warned her to stay away from the other female inmates and to keep her head down at all times. Never, ever look someone in the eye. The less threatening you appear and the more you blend in, the better your chances are for avoiding unpleasant encounters with inmates who may be mentally ill or just looking for a fight. She nodded her head in agreement and said she would do everything I told her. I looked at the door and saw Ms. Green standing there. I knew our time was up. I looked at my watch and realized that we had been allowed forty minutes to visit. Wow, that was definitely a bend of the rules.

We said, "I love you" and "goodbye."

I looked at Ms. Green, and said, "Thank you." She nodded slightly.

Once Mom was out of sight, we walked out of the room, back to the waiting room, unescorted. It seemed to me that the jail personnel were starting to trust us slightly. Things had certainly changed since my first visit. We walked out of the jail and into the parking lot. As Jay unlocked the doors, I lit a cigarette. I was overcome with emotions. I was embarrassed and humiliated by having my mother in jail, but at the same time, my heart was breaking. I was also emotionally drained. It was almost all I could do to hold my head high and stay emotionally strong for Jay, Auntie Bea, and Uncle Frank. After he had unlocked the car doors, Jay reached in on the driver's side and grabbed our sodas. He walked around to the passenger's side where I was leaning up against the car smoking and handed mine to me. He stood next to me leaning on the car. We both stared at the jail. I looked at the building as if I were trying to absorb it somehow.

Jay asked, "Do you think she will survive this?"

I sadly replied, "I don't know. I know she can be a tough old cookie if she wants to be. I think if she really wants to get through this, she will, but I truly don't know if she has that desire."

Jay stated harshly, "I hate my father more than I ever have right now for what he has done to all of us, especially to your mother. What are we going to do, Belinda?"

I answered, "I'm playing it by ear, Jay. I don't really have a plan yet. More and more problems keep coming out into the open. We cannot trust Little Pete, but I can't let him go yet because I do not know everything yet."

Jay said, "What do you mean you don't trust him? Is he part of this somehow?"

I answered truthfully, "I think he is. I just can't put my finger on it. My gut instinct tells me he is not what he appears to be. Only time will tell us about him, and I'm afraid I will find out too late. I just pray that I figure it out before it's too late. Before he causes more trouble for us down the road. All I know is that your father is trying to lay all the blame on my mother for his actions. I will not allow that! I will die trying to make sure he is held accountable for his actions. I will not allow my mother to take full blame for his part in all this. It appears that he is getting away with it, but I just can't see our Assistant U.S. Attorney allowing that after I saw her going after Mom so vigorously. It would be nice if she put more energy into prosecuting Big Pete instead of my mother. After all, my mother is just the small fish in all of this." When I was done speaking, I looked over at Jay, and he was nodding his head in agreement with everything I had said.

Jay asked, "How are we going to make restitution to all of their victims?"

I stared at the jail as I replied, "It's humanly impossible, Jay, for the three of us to do it. If you, Christina, and I took all the money we have saved up, sold everything we owned, including our cars, and sold everything that Mom and Pete owned, we would never be able to pay it all back. It is several million dollars just for your father's clients. The only thing that's in our reach is the check kiting scheme that my mother and Auntie Bea have created and the credit card fraud against me. Other than that, we can't help Big Pete's clients at all. We can do nothing for them. I wish we were rich, but we are not. Self-preservation is going to prevent us from repaying Big Pete's clients. We cannot sacrifice everything we have to right his wrongs. We should not have to pay for the crimes that he committed. I do want to salvage our inheritance, or at least as much as possible."

I continued, "Well, let's go. I want to get to the family house before Big Pete gets there and see what Little Pete has done."

Jay said, "Okay."

We both got back into the White Beast and I let Jay drive back to our family home, where Mom and Big Pete had lived.

CHAPTER XXXV

As we pulled into the driveway, I said a silent prayer of thanks that Big Pete had not returned home yet. Little Pete's van was still in the driveway. Before we got out of the car, I warned Jay to be careful what he said around Little Pete. I emphasized that he should not discuss anything of any importance with Little Pete. Jay assured me that he would be very careful. We got out of the car and went into the house through the garage door.

As I opened the door from the garage, I yelled, "Little Pete!"

I heard him answer, "Yes, Belinda, I'm up in your momma's bedroom."

Jay and I walked upstairs. When we reached Mom's room, we saw that Little Pete had already taken my mother's bed apart and had some boxes packed. He told us that he had already packed everything that was in the basement closet where Mom kept her furs and good coats. He had put them all in wardrobe boxes. He had started packing some of her books because he was certain that Big Pete would not have an issue with that. Jay and I exchanged a glance. I could tell that he also knew intuitively that Little Pete had talked to Big Pete today about which of my mother's belongings should be packed and what Big Pete wanted to keep. I knew I had not given him any instructions regarding my mother's clothing.

I looked at my watch and said, "Little Pete, why don't you call it quits today and go on home. I'll see you at the Daisy house tomorrow morning at 8:00 a.m. sharp."

He looked over at Jay for the first time. I guess he was so absorbed in what he had been doing that he didn't notice Jay standing there. Little Pete's face broke into a huge smile as he warmly greeted Jay. Jay returned his greeting, and they hugged each other. Jay and I started walking down the stairs, subtly trying to get Little Pete out of the house. Little Pete kept talking to Jay and asking questions. He was trying to get information out of him, but Jay followed my request and told him nothing. We continued to walk toward the garage door, forcing Little Pete to follow us as he talked. We finally got him out of the garage, into his van, and on his way.

Once Little Pete was gone, Jay and I went back into the house and went down into the basement. I grabbed a beer from the bar refrigerator and told Jay that we need to pack all of Momma's photo albums, family pictures, negatives, etcetera, so that they would be ready for us to move tomorrow. I went back upstairs to get some moving boxes because Little Pete had already packed all the empty boxes that had been in the basement closet. We went upstairs to Mom's office and then to the Florida room where she had the rest of her belongings stored and displayed. I told Jay to start packing up the Florida room, and I started packing up the office. It didn't take us very long to get everything packed. When we were done, we had about fifteen or twenty book boxes.

When I had finished packing up the office, I went back down to the basement to get another beer. When I walked into the basement, Jay was pouring his father's vodka down the sink.

I yelled, "Jay, stop it! I'm not ready to get into a confrontation with your father yet. Please, Jay, stop it."

Jay stopped and put the now half-empty bottle down on the bar. Jay became emotional as he spoke, "He's nothing but a drunk, Belinda! I have watched him get drunk every day most of my life. I hate his guts!"

I walked over to Jay and hugged him. "I know, Jay, but our vengeance will be to use him as he has used us. Do you understand? We have to play this nasty game to win the battle. Don't you know, Jay, the good guys always come out on top?"

I knew as the words were coming out of my mouth that I was lying to my brother. Unfortunately, the good guys only come out on top in the movies. In real life, the good guys usually come in last.

As I was hugging him, Jay clung to me and started sobbing. The words were barely coming out between sobs, "Our lives are ruined! My credit is destroyed before I even had a chance to live! My reputation is gone before I even had the chance to create one, and it is all because of that fat slob!"

By now, I had tears flowing down my cheeks too. "Jay, you're young, and I promise you will get through this. I promise you that you will have the chance to live your life, build your own reputation, and have nice things someday. When you're ready, you will have a wonderful wife and beautiful kids to boot. Your credit can be restored. This is not the end of your life. Your reputation is not destroyed. No one will bother to connect the dots and figure out that you're his son. You live in another state. You're safe, Jay. Granted, none of us will be able to come back to Snobville because of the two-faced snobs that live in this town, but that's okay. None of us live here, and none of us wants to live here anymore. There's nothing here for us. We will do something to keep Big Pete from continuing to conduct business in your name. I promise. I will fix everything, and you know I will."

He let go of me and started wiping his tears away with his hand. I handed him a paper towel to blow his noise. When he was done, he said, "You're right, I know you will. I'm sorry I'm crying like a spoiled brat."

I laughed and said, "I think all three of us are spoiled brats. We will get through this, Jay."

He said, "I know."

I said, "We better get out of here before Big Pete gets back. It's getting late. I'll lock up down here. You make sure all the doors upstairs are locked, except for the door to the garage. I'll meet you outside."

He said, "Okay."

I watched Jay as he walked up the stairs. I then quickly went up to the kitchen. I grabbed my wallet out of my purse and took a $100 bill out that I had from when I cashed Uncle Frank's check earlier in the day. I went back down to the basement. I found a small piece of paper and pen. I put the money on the bar with my empty bottle of beer on top of it. I wrote on the note to Big Pete that I had gotten thirsty and took a beer from the refrigerator. I also wrote that I thought he could use the cash until his check came in from the insurance company. I checked the French doors to the basement to make sure they were locked and went upstairs. I set the alarm and locked the door to the garage. Jay was already in the White Beast waiting for me. I closed the garage door as I walked through it with the remote I had taken from the White Beast. I got into the car and we left.

I asked Jay to stop at the grocery store before going on to the Daisy house. I picked up two packs of chicken fryer parts, potatoes, and some vegetables. After I had all the food I wanted, I picked out a bottle of White Zinfandel. I now had everything that I needed to make the dinner that I promised for Uncle Frank. When we pulled into his driveway, Uncle Frank opened the door and started yelling something to me.

I got out of the car and yelled back, "Just wait a minute. I can't hear you!"

Jay and I walked to the door with our hands full. I had the groceries, and Jay had his luggage.

I repeated, "Wait a minute, Uncle Frank. I didn't hear a word you just said. Let me get the groceries in the kitchen first."

Uncle Frank could not wait. His voice trembled with fear as he said, "Big Pete called here, Belinda! He threatened me. He said if I didn't give his gas card back to him and pay the bill he was going to have credit card fraud charges filed against me!"

I looked over at Jay and his expression was just as bewildered as mine was. I said, "What? I must not have heard you right."

Uncle Frank said, "Big Pete is going to file credit card fraud charges against me if I don't give him his gas card back and pay the bill right away!" Uncle Frank continued, "Call your auntie right now."

I put the bags of groceries down on the kitchen counter, and Jay quickly took his things into the other spare bedroom. I went back into the Florida room, and Uncle Frank was already on the phone with Auntie Bea. As soon as I walked in, he handed the phone to me.

Before Auntie Bea could say anything, I said, "I'm sending Jay over there with Mom's car to pick you up. I want you over here so we can all eat dinner together. Then you and Uncle Frank can tell me what the hell is going on in person. Okay?"

Auntie Bea excitedly replied, "That's a great idea! I haven't eaten anything yet anyway."

I hung up the phone and yelled to Jay, "Jay, go pick up Auntie Bea right now, please!"

Jay hurried into the Florida room, grabbed the keys, and left. I went back into the kitchen and quickly took the groceries out of the bags. I put everything on the counter. I put the bottle of wine in the freezer so it would chill faster. I looked around the kitchen for everything I would need. I found a few spices, some flour, and a frying pan in the kitchen cabinets. I prepped the chicken and started frying it. Uncle Frank finally came into the kitchen as I was peeling the potatoes. I watched him as he picked up his whiskey bottle, opened the lid, and took a large swallow of it.

I said, "Uncle Frank, you better hide that bottle before Auntie Bea gets here. You are in the same clothes you were in yesterday! You had better go take a shower quickly before she gets here. You know what will happen."

He glared at me and said, "Damn it, you're right." He took the bottle and put it up in one of the kitchen cabinets. He hurried back into his bedroom, which had a private bathroom. By now, everything was cooking and under control. I went into the Florida room and peeked out a window just as Jay was pulling in the driveway in the White Beast. I quickly set the table in the dining room and checked on the food that was cooking on the stove. By then, Auntie Bea and Jay had made it into the house.

Jay came into the kitchen and asked if there was anything he could do to help. I asked him to get the wine out of the freezer and pour it into the glasses that I had already placed on the dining room table. I also asked him to help Auntie Bea into the dining room. Of course, Auntie Bea was fussing that she didn't need any help because she had her trusted cane in tow. We all laughed with her. I finished preparing the dinner, dished it up, carried it into the dining room, and placed everything on the table. Uncle Frank came out of his bedroom with clean clothes on, his face clean-shaven and with his hair still wet.

Jay gave the blessing, and we all started to eat. Over dinner, Auntie Bea and Uncle Frank told us about the telephone conversations they had with Big Pete earlier in the day. Auntie Bea said she thought that he was drunk out of his mind because his words were slurred and she could barely understand him. We all decided to ignore his threat and wait to see what tomorrow brought.

After dinner, Auntie Bea, Uncle Frank, and Jay went into the living room and visited while I cleaned up the mess from dinner. After about thirty minutes, Jay came into the kitchen and said that Auntie Bea was ready to go. He was going to drive her back over to her house. I said that sounded like a good idea.

After Jay had left with Auntie Bea, Uncle Frank came into the kitchen. I was still washing the dishes. He said it had been a tiring day, and he was going to bed. I said goodnight and finished the dishes. When I was done with the dishes, I went into the Florida room and called Christina. I told her that I was wrong about Auntie Bea's land and told her more about the credit card fraud. She said she had followed my instructions and accessed her personal credit report. It seemed fine; nothing had been opened in her name, and she felt blessed. I told her about what Big Pete had done to Jay, but I didn't tell her about what Big Pete had done today. I still left Auntie Bea's name out of the check scheme because I felt she would not come at all if she knew both Mom and Auntie Bea were involved in it. I told her about the medication problem regarding Mom, and gave her the telephone numbers I had for the jail. She said she could handle that over the telephone. She said it looked like she wouldn't be able to get a flight out until Friday. I assured her that would be fine and that I hoped I would see her then.

Jay walked in just as I was hanging up the phone. He said he was beat and was going to bed. I told him that was my plan also. We both locked up the house and closed it down for the night.

CHAPTER XXXVI

I woke up at 5:00 a.m. on the button. I grabbed a clean set of clothing and got ready for a new day.

I knocked on Jay's bedroom door. "Hey, lazy, wake up! We have a lot to do today. You need to get up and get ready. I'm getting ready to do some laundry for Uncle Frank and myself. Do you have anything that needs to be washed?"

Jay opened his door and handed me an armful of clothing.

My washer and dryer were in storage in the basement. I had allowed my mother and Uncle Frank to use them for the time being. The door to the basement was kept locked because of Uncle Frank. A little less than a year earlier, while he was drunk, he had fallen down the basement stairs. He suffered no major injuries, just a sprained wrist and a slight concussion. Ever since then, however, Mom and Auntie Bea kept the door locked. I dropped the laundry by the basement door and went to get the key. Once I had it, I unlocked the door, shoved the key into my pocket, opened the door, and picked up the laundry again. This would be the first time I had been in the basement. It had one area with plumbing and a dryer outlet and we called it the "mudroom." That's where I had my washer and dryer. The rest of the basement was unfinished and was used for storage.

I hit the light switch with my elbow and carefully walked down the steps. I headed right for the washer and put in the first load. Once it was started, I walked back to the bottom of the stairs. I looked around the storage section of the basement to see how much room was left to store my mom's things. One quick glance told me there was no more room left in the basement to store anything. I looked around and saw a small pathway running the length of the basement.

It was lined with over fifty boxes. This small pathway was the only area left to move around in the unfinished basement. All the other space was packed to the ceiling with furniture and boxes. Several of the boxes caught my eye. In large black letters were the words: "WINE. THOMAS AND BELINDA." I had forgotten that Thomas and I had bought Mom and Pete's wine collection a little over a year earlier. Then I realized this must have been part of the charges on the credit card that I had allowed my mother to use around then.

I found an old box cutter and opened several of them. They were all professionally packed with the cardboard slots in them for each bottle of wine to be stored. There were twelve bottles of wine in each box. I ended up opening all of them and realized all the expensive wines were not there, but every bottle there was nicely aged, average quality wine. Each bottle must have been worth around twenty to fifty dollars. When Thomas and I bought it from my mother, we did not pay but a small fraction of the value. I knew I would have to sell it to help pay for all the debt and restitution that my mother owed. I hoped that I could sell this wine collection to a local winery or wine store. I stood at the bottom of the stairs and let my gaze wander around the basement some more. I noticed there was a lot of office furniture and equipment. There were a couple of large industrial copiers, a large window air conditioners, four old computers, and three beautiful, large safes. I became excited. I could sell most of these items! The safes alone would bring a good price. I did feel a little sad when I realized that I would have to move most of Thomas and my belongings out. As I stood there looking things over and thinking, I heard the washing machine buzzer go off. I didn't realize I had been down there that long.

I walked back to the mudroom area and put the clean clothes into the dryer. I put the second and last load into the washing machine and started it. I glanced to my left and saw two metal shelving units that were packed full of unused cleaning supplies. I knew that I could sell those as well. I would have to go through all the china barrels, but I could see there was quite a bit I could sell just from the Daisy house's basement. I made the decision to start with the basement. I would clean it out, sell as much as possible to make money to pay Mom's debts, and then move in the things from her house because all the property was mine now. I went back up the stairs and was pleasantly surprised because Jay had made breakfast. Uncle Frank was up and was fussing about the hard scrambled eggs Jay had cooked. Even as he sat there complaining, he was greedily shoving them in his mouth. I thanked Jay for making breakfast and fixed myself a plate. Why waste food? When we were done eating, Jay and I cleaned up and washed the dishes. When we were done cleaning the kitchen, we finished the laundry.

As we were finishing up the clothes, I said, "Jay, you need to call that Ed Weird character now, so we can have the check from those funds in our hands this morning."

Jay asked, "Yes, I will do that right now. Do you have Mom's address book?"

I answered, "Yes, I'll get it for you."

Jay called Ed Weird and told me Mr. Weird would have the check ready for us this morning. He showed me the address that he had written down on a small piece of paper and said we could pick it up at that location.

I said, "Good; that will be our first mission of the day. Jay, can you go out to the White Beast and bring in that bag we found yesterday in the trunk?"

Jay replied, "Sure."

As Jay was walking out to the car, Uncle Frank said he was headed to the bathroom to take a shower. I decided it was time for me to call Mom's attorney. I went into the Florida room and looked out the sliding glass door. There was Little Pete pulling up into the driveway right on time. I decided to call Mom's attorney anyway. Little Pete could let himself in. I proceeded to dial the attorney's phone number. It was about 8:30 a.m. I knew it was a bit early to call, but to my surprise, the receptionist answered. I asked to speak with the attorney, and she informed me that it must be my lucky day. She said he was in the office early and asked if I could hold.

I said, "Of course." I was on hold for a few minutes before he answered the phone. I told him I needed his advice on what to do about my mother's credit card fraud. He told me that it would be a conflict of interest, even though I would be the one footing my mother's attorney fees. He said I would have to find another attorney. He told me that I had only two choices: I could either file charges against her or pay the charges myself. If I filed charges against her, she would face even more jail time and I would make it harder for her.

I decided it was my daughter's duty to suck it up and pay them. It would be hard to fix my credit if I filed charges against her anyway. As it stood now, it was going to take a long time for me to rebuild my personal credit. My mother had destroyed it. After I told the attorney my decision, he told me I would still need to hire my own attorney. He also suggested I get power of attorney over my mother so that I could more easily take care of her affairs. I agreed and thanked him for his time and invaluable advice. After I hung up the phone, I looked out the door. I saw Jay and Little Pete were no longer outside. I assumed they went over to Auntie Bea's house. The night before at dinner, she had told us there was something wrong with her side door.

I looked at the digital clock on Uncle Frank's phone. It was already after 9:00. I found Uncle Frank's phone book under the table and started looking up law firms. I ended up making numerous calls. It seemed like every attorney in the area had at one time worked for my mother, Big Pete, or some other member of my twisted family. I finally found one who had never worked with my family, and her name was Miss Patson.

I must have talked to her for at least forty minutes, and she still wanted more details. She felt it would be more productive if we would discuss the situation face to face. She asked me if I could come to her office. Then, we could sit and talk everything through. I agreed. She asked if I could come in later that day, and she gave me a time to be there.

I decided I needed to call my father who lived in Pennsylvania. My mother and father had been divorced since I was nine years old. He and I had an up-and-down relationship most of my life, but I truly needed someone to help me get out of this financial mess. I knew in my heart that he wouldn't help me, but maybe he could help store my things. I needed someone I could trust to be a specialized power of attorney for me—just in case something happened to both Thomas and me. I also needed someone whom I could trust as the executor of my estate in the event that something happened to us. I had just come to realize that I really didn't have anyone. My father, the man that I had called Daddy my whole life, was a very religious person. He was a retired Mennonite minister and missionary. He was a missionary for several years in a third world country, and even after he returned to the United States, he continued missionary work with immigrants. He was naturally an introvert, but if he felt accepted, he came out of his shell.

He was a good man and did his best to follow his beliefs. I let out a sigh, and with the last glimmer of hope I had left, I picked the phone up to call him. I made the decision that I would not get into an argument with him. It just wasn't worth it. I knew how he was. By this time, Uncle Frank was in the Florida room with a fresh cup of coffee. He sat down at the table. He watched me as I called my father, and I knew that he was listening to every word I said. Daddy's second wife answered the phone. I told her hello, and we exchanged pleasantries before I asked if I could speak with him. When Daddy picked up the phone, we briefly exchanged pleasantries, and I told him some of what was going on.

He informed me that I didn't really know any of these people any longer, and I should not be involved in my mother's mess. He told me that I needed to move Thomas and my things out of the Daisy house and go back to Germany.

I asked him if I could store our things with him.

He immediately said, "No."

I asked if I rented a storage unit close to where he lives if he would keep an eye on my belongings, and again, he said, "No."

He gave the same response when I asked about being my power of attorney and executor of my estate. Because the conversation was going nowhere, I changed the subject. We chatted a few minutes longer, but I was fighting back tears. I never expected him to be so cruel and heartless about the situation.

As I hung up the phone, the tears would no longer be held back. I looked over at Uncle Frank with tears flowing down my face. He was frowning.

"He's a bum, Belinda. He wasn't even worth a minute of your time."

I said, "I know, but it was worth a try anyway." I made myself stop crying. I swallowed the hurt and disappointment and told myself, as I have many times in my life, *Swallow it, Belinda, and turn it into something else.*

By this time, Little Pete and Jay had returned from Auntie Bea's house.

I forced a smile and said, "Hello, Little Pete."

Little Pete said, "Good morning, Belinda. What's on the schedule for today?"

I handed him a piece of paper and said, "We need to go to this address. Do you know where this is?"

Little Pete looked at the piece of paper that Jay had given me earlier and replied, "Yes. I know exactly where it is. I can take you guys there, but doesn't Jay want to stop off at the shop first and see his father?" He looked over at Jay.

Jay answered, "No. We have too much to do today, and I'm only in town for a little while."

Little Pete said, "Oh."

I said, "We need to go now. I have another stop to make after this one."

Little Pete asked, "Okay. Are we taking the White Beast?"

I answered, "Yes." I nodded and gathered my things together. While I was doing that, which only took a minute, Little Pete and Jay went out and got into the car. As soon as I got in and shut my door, we took off. Jay passed me the bag that we found in the trunk the day before, and we looked at each other for a moment.

While Little Pete was driving us to the address that I had given him, I asked him if he knew where my mother's post office boxes were. I told him that I needed to close them, and I wanted to do that as well.

He said she had several, but he knew where they all were. He said that he would drive us to all of them. He didn't even glance at the addressed envelopes that Big Pete had given to me yesterday morning. At our first stop, Jay retrieved the check. Next, Little Pete drove to the office of the attorney that I was hiring to protect me. I needed her to make sure I didn't step on the U.S. Attorney's toes while I was trying to undo, as much as possible, the crimes that Auntie Bea and my mother had committed—the ones the U.S. Attorney did not know about yet.

Little Pete pulled into the parking lot of the attorney's office building. As I was getting out of the car, Jay asked, "Do you want us to wait here?"

I answered, "No, I would like you to come with me, Jay." I leaned through the opened passenger's side window and asked, "Little Pete, do you mind waiting for us?"

Little Pete answered, "I have no problem waiting for you, but why does Jay need to be involved?"

I replied, "Because he is my brother." I looked at Jay, who was now standing beside me, and he looked at me with pride.

When we walked into the building, Jay and I stopped to look at the office-building directory. We saw that we needed to go to the fifth floor. We took the elevator, and when we stepped off, we were right in front of the attorney's office. We walked through the glass double doors into the reception area. I told the receptionist who I was and with whom I had an appointment. She instructed us to have a seat and said that my attorney would be with me in a few minutes.

It was only a few minutes later when Miss Patson, the attorney, who I spoke with earlier that morning, came into the reception area. She graciously greeted Jay and me. I was very impressed. She appeared young and must have been in her late twenties or early thirties. She was wearing a navy blue suit. She had short curly light brown hair and brown eyes. She was a few inches shorter than I was, and she wore flat comfortable shoes. She was an attractive woman. When I spoke with her on the telephone, I thought she was at least fifty years old. I was very impressed with her sophistication, confidence, and intelligence; it was rare for someone of her age. I was already pleased.

I looked over at Jay as he greeted her, and he was acting as if he'd never seen such a cute woman before. He was actually stuttering as he talked to her and giggling like a schoolboy. My little brother was so transparent! I shook my head and stifled a groan. *Men!* I'm sure that if she had not been so young and cute, he never would have acted like that. She motioned for us to walk through the door behind the reception area. We followed her down a hallway to her office, and she gestured for us to have a seat in the chairs in front of her desk. She asked if we would like anything to drink, and I noticed that her secretary had joined us and was standing beside the desk. I said no, but Jay asked for a soda. The secretary promptly left the room to get Jay a soda.

Once she left, Miss Patson sat down at her desk, folded her hands on top of her desk, leaned forward toward us, and asked, "Ms. Star, have you decided on which course of action you would like to take first?"

Miss Patson's secretary came back into the office before I had a chance to answer. She handed Jay an opened can of soda and a glass of ice. Thank God he remembered his manners and said thank you, but he then just put the glass of ice on the corner of Miss Patson's desk. I quietly took a tissue from her tissue box; I folded it into a square and handed it to him. He looked at me with a puzzled expression. I pointed to his glass of ice on the corner of her desk. He looked at Miss Patton, and his face turned bright red. He put the folded tissue under the glass.

I replied, "Yes. First, I want to become my mother's power of attorney because it will be easier for me to settle her affairs. I want her to have a new will written; one that does not have Big Pete in it."

Ms. Patson nodded in agreement and said, "Yes, I will get that typed up today, and I will also speak with your mother today to make the arrangements. When I go to the jail to have her sign them, I will be able to take you with me. That way you can see her without a divider between you, and your conversation will not be recorded."

I asked, "Oh, you can do that?"

She commented, "There are advantages to being an attorney. I also suggest that you do a full power of attorney, not a specialized one, because you will be dealing with her husband, but as we discussed during our conversation earlier today, I will have to speak with your mother regarding her wishes."

I nodded in agreement and said, "I totally agree, but my mother wants a specialized power of attorney. I completely understand where she is coming from because with a general power of attorney it gives me a lot of power regarding her affairs."

Ms. Patson said, "I know, but in your situation, you will be dealing with her husband. With a general power of attorney, you can break the window to their home if you choose to do so, because if she can do it, you can do it as well. In other words, Mrs. Star, you are going to butt heads with Big Pete eventually. It is very similar to a married couple going through a divorce when trying to separate the marital property. You are going to be your mother's proxy. From my experience, even though both of them have given you everything they own, he is still going to fight when you start trying to sell and move the marital property. I don't know when or how, but I can guarantee he is not going to let you have everything without a fight. Also, you have no idea what your mother has or has not done. You are hiring me to protect you as well and that's what I'm trying to do."

I said, "I agree. That's what we will do, the quicker the better. The second thing I need to take care of is getting Pete King out of my shop. How can I do that? He has been stealing money from my cash box, selling valuable items from my shop and pocketing the money, but I'm not ready yet to start the fight with him."

She said, "That will be no problem, Ms. Star, all we have to do is threaten to call the police on him. Can you prove that he has been doing that?"

I answered, "Yes, I have the crumbled-up cash sale invoices I found in his trash can in my shop, and there was no money for them in the cash box."

She said, "Good," as she nodded her head in affirmation. She continued, "We will hold onto that ace until you are ready to play it."

I said, "Good. The third thing is that Big Pete is running his business using Jay's name, and we don't know what to do about it. It is my understanding that since he is not allowed to be involved in any business regarding insurance and retirements, he conned Jay to take a course to become a certified insurance agent. Jay did this, and now Big Pete is running his business in my shop without my permission and doing God knows what using Jay's name."

Miss Patson looked over in Jay's direction and asked, "Is this true?"

Jay nodded in agreement as he answered, "Yes."

She looked at him and asked him to tell the story about how and when this came into play. Jay began telling her the story.

She shook her head in disbelief and said, "I'm going to have to check into this problem and decide what the best course of action is. The two of you are not ready to take action regarding this problem yet, are you?"

Jay replied, "No, we are not ready to take any action yet, at least I don't think so." He looked at me for the final decision.

I said, "I agree with Jay. We are not ready to take on Big Pete yet."

Miss Patson said, "Good. That will give me time to research and decide what will be the best course of action for this problem. We don't want Jay to get into any trouble for making such a bad error in judgment."

I said, "The next problem is the credit card fraud issue. I have already made my decision not to have charges brought against my mother for them. I have decided I will pay them so she doesn't get into any more trouble with the law. I feel her going to jail for the other crimes is more than enough punishment for her, but is there any way I can get Big Pete for this as well? He benefited from the credit card fraud also, and I have the statements of charges to prove it. I requested the statements for the last year for all the cards that my mother had, and he has profited off of it more than Auntie Bea or my mother." I handed her all the statements I had. I continued, "Also, regarding the check kiting, I can prove Big Pete profited off of it as much as Auntie Bea did." I handed her the bank statements I had found in my mother's belongings.

Miss Patson looked through them, shook her head in total disbelief, and asked, "My God, Ms. Star, what else have your mother and great-aunt done to you? No, you cannot do anything to him, but you do have your great-aunt in a nutshell because she deposited the checks into her account. Plus, according to the paper trail, it appears she helped your mother commit the fraud."

I looked at her, confused. I did not understand because that was not what I saw when I reviewed everything. I said, "No, Auntie Bea just took the money."

Miss Patson replied, "No, Ms. Star. She did more than that. Come over here and take a look at the deposit slips with cash and the withdrawal slips from the fraudulent monies from this other account."

I stood up and leaned over her desk. I took the slips from her hand and took a good look at them. I let out a gasp of horror. I had been so tired when I looked at them before that I didn't catch the checking account numbers; they were different. I looked at the top of the withdrawal slip, and it had my sister's name on it with Auntie Bea's address. In fact, it had the date and time of the withdrawal and the same date and about a half hour later in time on the stamped deposit slip of Auntie Bea's. I looked over at Jay, and he was leaning over her desk as well trying to see the same thing I saw. We both looked at each other. I knew he was thinking the same thing I was.

No wonder Momma was so adamant about me picking up the bad checks that were left because the kite was stopped after she was arrested. Auntie knew exactly what she was doing. No wonder Auntie Bea asked me first if she was in any trouble. She knew exactly what she was doing, and she didn't care who she was hurting. I knew the truth now, and so did Jay. I instinctively put my open hand over my mouth.

Miss Patson looked up at me from her desk and asked, "Do you see?"

I simply answered with disappointment, "Yes." I was shaking my head in total disbelief. "I have already promised my mother and Auntie Bea I would do everything in my power to keep her from being in a jail cell next to my mother. Even though I know the complete truth now, I would still protect her and make restitution to Mom and Auntie Bea's victims regarding the check kiting. Auntie Bea is an old woman. She would not survive jail as well as my mother would. My mother is younger than my auntie was after all. My mother made the decision to take the fall for Auntie Bea. I will respect her wishes and honor my word."

Miss Patson's facial expression was one of complete amazement. She stood up from her desk, came around it, and hugged me. Jay was looking at us; he appeared to be every bit as confused as I was.

Miss Patson said, "Mrs. Star, you are the most honorable client I have ever had the pleasure of representing. I know the words 'unconditional love,' but I have never encountered it before in my life regarding a client. After all that has been done to you by your own family, you are still standing by your convictions. You are treating them with love instead of judging them. You seem to understand why they did it and even sympathize with them even though it was done to you and your siblings. Even though you know their guilt and the crimes that they committed against you and others, you are trying to make things right with their victims as well as for them. You have one sibling standing here before me standing by your side and accepting every decision that you make." She let go of me, looked me straight in the eyes, and said, "It truly is an honor to help you in this ugly twisted legal mess that your family is going through, but, Ms. Star, you primarily hired me to protect you from them. You are going to have to let me do what is necessary when the time comes, if it does."

I said, "Miss Patson, you have too much faith in me. I'm just as fickle as the next person is. I have turned my cheek for the last time regarding my mother, great-aunt, and great-uncle. I have sworn to all of them that I will not turn my cheek again if they ever steal from me again. I do stand by my word."

Miss Patson laughed and said, "I can tell that you stand by your word; not many people do that nowadays."

My serious attitude melted and I laughed with her and said, "I guess I can be overdramatic at times. I wonder where I got that from."

Jay couldn't help but to start laughing with the two of us. Miss Patson walked back to the other side of her desk and sat down; Jay and I followed suit and sat back into our chairs. She leaned forward until her elbows were resting on the center of her desk. She looked me in the eye and murmured with a smile on her face, "Do I dare ask if there is any more?"

I looked at her with a smile on my face and answered, "Yes." We all burst into laughter because of my ironic situation. I don't think Miss Patson had any idea of what the hell she was getting into taking me on as a client!

I said, "About a year ago, my husband and I signed a promissory note for a very expensive criminal defense attorney. We had agreed to sign it for my mother only, but when we received the note to sign, Big Pete's name was on it also. I refused to sign it because Big Pete's name was still on it. Big Pete was supposedly hiring another attorney. My mother and I made a verbal agreement that his name would be removed once I sent it back. We signed it and mailed it back, but Thomas and I never received an amended promissory note that had only my mother on it. I do not know if Big Pete was actually removed from the note we signed. My mother has waived her right to trial because she is guilty. I do not know how much is left on the bill, and I am afraid to ask about it."

Miss Patson answered, "Don't worry about it until you receive the bill. If this attorney did not amend it, then I want you to call him after you receive the bill. Tell him Big Pete was not part of it, and make sure you tell him you are not paying for Big Pete. Also, you need to tell him you want the bill reduced because your mother waived her right to trial. I'm sure if he is an honorable attorney, he will have no problem doing that. Also, make sure you explain to him how you came about signing that original note. Again, I believe he will reduce it without any problems if there are monies still due. If he doesn't, call me and I will speak with him."

I replied, "Okay. There is another problem that I have. Right now, I'm a few steps ahead of the Assistant U.S. Attorney's office regarding victims. I'm in the process of accumulating funds to make restitution to these victims. In other words, I'm trying to undo the crimes that my auntie and my mother did before the U.S. Attorney's office discovers them. I don't want to step on their toes. Will you be able to protect me or guide me to make sure I stay out of their way? I do not want to break any laws trying to make restitution to victims that have not filed charges yet, and I want to pick up all these bad checks."

Miss Patson answered, "You're not breaking any laws or stepping on anyone's toes by making restitution on behalf of your mother and great-aunt. You have nothing to worry about, but if they ask for evidence such as files or some type of paper trail regarding your mother, you must cooperate with them one hundred percent. Do not deter their investigation in any form; do whatever they request from you. If they do ask for something, and you feel uncomfortable or you are unable to do what they request from you, call me immediately. They would not ask anything of you directly. They should be going through your mother's attorney. In case they do come to you directly, remind them that they must come through me for any information. I believe your mother's attorney will make sure they stay within the rules because you have nothing to do with what your mother and Big Pete did. Things they may request from you are truly a courtesy that you are bestowing to them on behalf of your mother."

I said, "Okay. That's about it for major issues at this time. I guess when more comes up, I will call you."

She replied, "Yes, I want you to call immediately with any questions or concerns of any nature regarding this mess. That's what you are paying me for. I will start working on the power of attorney and will for your mother after I have spoken with her. I will then need to meet with you.

We may be able to get it signed and you in to see her at the end of this week or the beginning of next week."

I calmly stated, "That would be fine."

Jay and I both hugged Miss Patson, and she escorted us out to the reception area. We all said our goodbyes, and she told us that she would be in touch with both of us as soon as she could.

As Jay and I stood there waiting for the elevator, Jay asked, "Wow! Do you think Miss Patson knows what she's getting into?"

I answered, "I think she thinks it's going to be cut and dry. You know we didn't tell about the other issues we are going to have in the future. I was afraid we might overwhelm her, plus she doesn't know yet what a pain in the ass Auntie Bea and our mother can be."

Jay and I exchanged looks, and we both started laughing.

Jay said, "I know, Auntie Bea will tell her lies, Uncle Frank will tell even bigger ones, and your mother just twists the truth whenever it suits her; or one may tell part of the truth and another lies. You know Mom will be pestering the crap out of Miss Patson so Mom can get her way."

I replied, "I know. I wonder how long Miss Patson's patience will last before she is yelling at me about the other three. You know every time one of them talks to her I will have to drill Miss Patson on what they said to her so I can make sure she has the truth." I chuckled slightly, and so did Jay.

After we were on the elevator, Jay spoke his thoughts, "I wonder what charming lies my father will tell her once we decide to start making him hurt a little more?"

I answered with a facetious smile on my face, "God only knows, and she will probably believe him, but then again, she is working for us, not him, so maybe she will not buy his lies."

Jay chuckled. "I think she will believe our truth over his lies."

"I think so too."

As we were walking out to the car, I began thinking. After talking with this attorney, I knew that the faster I worked to undo as many of Auntie Bea and Mom's crimes, the better things would be for both of them. My mother wasn't in any position to wheel and deal with the U.S. attorney's office regarding my Auntie Bea or for herself for that matter. It was going to be up to me to make as much restitution as I possibly could before more charges were brought forth from the victims to the U.S. Attorney's office.

I hoped my attorney didn't lose her cool with my mother, but I feared that would be impossible to accomplish for one so young.

Little Pete was waiting for us in the car. He had parked under a big tree for the shade and was sitting behind the steering wheel. He had his reading glasses on and was reading a newspaper. Jay opened the back door and got into the backseat as I opened the front door to the passenger side and got into the car.

Little Pete folded up his newspaper and took off his reading glasses. "Well, what did you ask the attorney, and why did you need to see the attorney?"

Jay had his arms across the back of the front seat as if he was holding himself in place between the two of us so he could hear everything we were saying and be part of the conversation.

I told Little Pete, "Oh, we don't know if I'm going to hire this attorney or not." I purposely did not answer his questions.

Little Pete looked at me, and Jay was looking at Little Pete. Little Pete asked with a puzzled expression on his face, "Oh, then why were you guys in there for so long?" as he started the car up and started to drive out of the parking lot.

I answered, "Well, Mr. Romeo here was trying to pick up the attorney because she was so young and pretty."

Jay started laughing really hard. When he finally got control of himself and was able to follow along with me he said, "I was not! I was just interested in her because she was so young and smart."

Little Pete looked over his shoulder for a moment with one eyebrow cocked and said to Jay, "You're damn lucky, boy, that the woman didn't charge you for that," and Little Pete couldn't contain his laughter.

Jay looked at me for a moment, I looked at him, and we both knew we got away with my twisted truth. Well, I guess Jay and I were taught by the best liars in the country. I assumed Jay was thinking the same thing I was, but we really didn't have a choice. I just did not trust Little Pete any longer.

As we were driving, I thought that Little Pete must have sensed that Jay and I did not trust him. Out of the blue and in front of Jay he said, "Belinda, I have to come clean and tell you that Bea and I helped your mother with the check scam. She could not have pulled it off without the help of the two of us. That is one main reason I'm sticking it out to ensure my name is not dragged into this. I did it for your mother and for my paycheck. I'm admitting it to you, but if you tell anyone else, I will deny it."

I said in a deadly tone, "Pull over, Little Pete."

Little Pete looked at me with fear in his eyes, as if he had said too much.

Jay looked at me and then at Little Pete. Jay didn't say a word. I immediately started barking orders as soon as Little Pete pulled over to one side of the road, "Get out of the car, Little Pete, and get into the passenger seat! Jay, get behind the wheel and start driving! Little Pete, you can direct him to the first post office where my mother has a PO box. You will also show us where Big Pete has his PO boxes." Both men did exactly as I ordered, immediately and without saying a word. I sat directly behind Little Pete, and I spoke in a serious and deadly tone, "Well, Little Pete, why don't you start telling Jay and me all about it?"

Little Pete started telling me the entire story, or at least his version of it. He was stuttering, and he kept straining his neck as he tried to twist around to look at me from the front seat. The longer he spoke, the more of the blame he placed on Auntie Bea. I just sat there watching him and listening to him.

I remembered a lesson I learned long ago from my grandmother about the difference between a strong, righteous person and a weak one. Is this how I looked to my grandmother when I tattled on John? Was she able to see what I would be like in the future if she did not intervene? I now understood why my grandmother switched me. I had stood there and watched John do the things he did without trying to stop him. Instead, I ran away and placed all the blame on John, when in fact, my sister and my cousins were also to blame for their misconduct in that situation. I should have stopped it. It was the same as now. Instead, this time an adult was trying to lay the blame of his actions solely on my mother and Auntie Bea. If he had any integrity, he should have said no and quit. He should be taking blame for his own actions. I understood now what my grandmother, in her own way, was trying to teach me; basically, there is a right way to report something and a wrong way. There is a time to take action instantly, and there are times when it should be reported instead. I suddenly wondered if I had been putting my grandmother's lesson into practice my whole life. I wondered if this was the reason I was trying to help Auntie Bea and my mother, rather than forcing their prosecution. Is this lesson of life instilled in me and I just hadn't realized it?

Little Pete began spilling more truth as he tried to make light of the situation. He gave a cowardly laugh as he told Jay and me that my mother would apply for a credit card using Uncle Frank's name jointly with her name and then would have him get on the phone pretending to be Uncle Frank. I didn't say a word. I just put my open hand over my mouth. Uncle Frank lied to me to protect my mother, or did he? He did not give her permission regarding this, or did he? I knew I was going to have to confront Uncle Frank about this, immediately. We arrived at the first post office. I went inside, picked up a few change-of-address cards, and filled them out. When I was finished with them, I went to the clerk and asked what else I needed to do to close the post office box. She asked for the key to the box, took the change-of-address card, and that was it. We drove to three other locations and did the same thing. Little Pete stated that Big Pete's post office was close to my mother and Big Pete's house, and he would show me the next time we go to their house.

We were close to the county jail and we went there next so that we could visit with my mother. This time, they let all three of us visit with her. As we were leaving, the warden stopped me in the hallway and asked if he could speak with me. He gestured for me to step into his office. He began telling me that my sister bullying and threatening their medical staff about my mother's medication was not going to change their procedures.

I became very upset and broke down. The tears started to flow, and I could not stop them. With the tears streaming down my cheeks, I simply stated, "I will tell you this, sir, if my mother has a stroke, or something else happens to her because she was not given her medication, I swear to my God that my sister and I will sue! We will sue you personally as well as this jail. If I do not receive a phone call from my mother this evening reporting that she has finally received her medication, I promise you, sir, you will be very, very sorry. This is not a threat, but a promise, and I always keep my word! I want you to understand what I am saying. You need to take my sister's bullying and threats very seriously. She is not just another prisoner's family member; she is also part of this system, and when she says she can and will do something, you better believe she will." I didn't even give him a chance to respond. I simply said, "Good day to you, sir."

I walked out of his office and out of the building.

While I was speaking with the warden, Little Pete and Jay walked out to the car. They were standing by the car looking at me with puzzled expressions on their faces when I walked out.

Little Pete asked, "What happened?"

I said, "Never mind, Little Pete, it's not even worth talking about."

We all got into the car. This time, I allowed Little Pete to drive, and Jay sat in the passenger seat.

As we were pulling out of the parking lot, I said, "Little Pete, please stop at a convenience store so I can get us all something to drink and eat on the way back to Greenville. I also would like you to stop at a pawn shop, and I want to stop at the shop so Jay can see and speak with his father."

Before he had a chance to respond, Jay looked at me and said, "What?! I don't want to talk—"

I cut him off before he could say another word in front of Little Pete. "Jay, remember what we talked about?"

Jay turned around and stared out the windshield. He didn't say another word. We all drove back in silence.

Little Pete pulled into a parking lot of a strip mall that had a pawnshop. We all got out of the car and went inside. I carried in the bag of jewelry that Jay and I had found in the trunk. There was a middle-aged man standing behind the counter. I headed straight to the counter, put the bag on it, and opened it. Little Pete leaned on the counter on one side of me, and Jay leaned on the counter on the other side of me. I pulled out the Rolex watch that had belonged to Big Pete.

I stated, "I would like to sell this. How much are you willing to pay for it?"

The man replied, "This is a man's watch; does this belong to you?"

I answered, "No, it belongs to my brother who is standing beside me."

The man looked at Jay with an accusing look as he was taking the back off the watch. He asked Jay, "Are you sure this is your watch? What is your social security number?"

Jay answered, "Yes, this is my watch. It was given to me by my father."

Then Jay gave the man his social security number.

The man said, "That is not the social security number that's engraved inside the watch's back."

Jay said, "Because it was my father's and he gave it to me." The man immediately picked up the telephone and called someone.

While Jay was taking care of the watch, I spotted an older black man at the other counter where the women's jewelry was located in the glass counter. I went over to him and said, "I have another piece we are interested in selling."

I pulled out a fifty-dollar gold piece that had diamonds all around the outer edge that were held in place by a gold band with a gold loop. The pendant hung on a 14k gold long chain.

The man's eyes grew wide, and he snatched the necklace from my hand like the greedy old miser that he was. He had a small magnifying glass and inspected the pendant very carefully. He looked up at me and said, "I'll give you fifty dollars for it."

I looked at him, and I could feel my blood pressure rising. I was able to keep my voice calm as I said, "You know damn well that's worth a lot more!" I snatched it back out of his hand.

He looked at me as if he were trying to study me. He said with a light chuckle, "Well, you can't blame a man for trying. I'll give you half the value."

I knew that was about all I was going to get out of him and I said, "We'll take it."

That old man grabbed that pendant back out of my hand with lightning speed, and he had already walked back to the other counter where Jay and Little Pete were.

Thank God I had returned to the counter before any transaction was done. I could not believe my ears when I heard that man offered Jay only pennies on the dollar for a gold-and-diamond watch. I jumped in immediately and said, "Hell, no! You, sir, are a scammer. You know damn well that watch is worth much, much more. It is not for sale for just that."

The man started chuckling and said, "Well, you can't blame me for trying. Okay, okay. Since the big sister is involved, I'll give you this for it," as he wrote the number on a piece of paper.

I said, "That's more like it. Sold!"

I knew that we were damn lucky to be offered as much as we were. People always take advantage of others when they are desperate enough to sell their prized possessions. They are all like vultures scavenging the one that's down on their luck, and they pick the person's flesh off until they hit the bone. In my opinion, people who prey on others are just as crooked and evil as Big Pete. I knew this was just the beginning of what I was going to encounter while I was liquidating the shop's inventory as well as family items, especially since I had to do it quickly. I knew it was going to come to a point where I would have to take pennies on the dollar to clean up this mess, and I could do nothing to keep the vultures from eating my flesh to the bones to generate enough cash quickly. I knew Thomas and I were going to have to sacrifice much to save ourselves, the victims, Auntie Bea, Uncle Frank, Jay, my sister, and most of all, more jail time that my mother possibility could get.

As we were getting into the White Beast Jay said, "Wow! Belinda, I guess Mom was telling the truth about you being able to sell the shoes off of a dead bum and make a profit off it."

I just shook my head, leaned my arms across the front seat where Jay was sitting, and calmly said, "No, Jay, that is not true. We lost a lot of money in that transaction, but it was better than nothing at all. We were damn lucky that those men are greedy and did not know our circumstances; the only reason that they gave us that much was because they still will turn a big profit off those two pieces."

As Little Pete was driving, he was nodding his head in agreement with me. Little Pete pulled around the back of my shop and parked beside Big Pete's van.

Jay grabbed me by my forearm and jerked me until I faced him. He bent down and whispered in my ear, "Belinda, I don't want to do this."

I looked up at him and said, "Yes, Jay, you will. This is one of the rules of engagement. So play two-faced and be thankful you're not really on a battlefield with a weapon in your hand. Do you understand me?"

Jay became angry. "Okay, I'll play it your way."

I said, "Thank you. It's for the common good. The longer we can keep him off my back, the better off we all will be. Never underestimate your enemy. You know how the old saying goes, 'keep your friends close and your enemy even closer.'"

All of a sudden, I remembered an old funny song that my grandmother and mother would sing to us when I was a teenager. "A black cat shit in the shavings; a black cat shit in the shavings and the yellow cat licked it up; the yellow cat licked it up . . . ." I understood the meaning all too well and I truly felt like the "yellow cat" at this point. In fact, I had felt like the yellow cat most of my life. How much more crap could I endure without becoming sick from it? I understood how Jay felt, but this was something we had to do. We were going to have to continue eating Big Pete's crap, along with everyone else's, to make things right again for all parties concerned.

We all walked in the back door to my shop. Big Pete was on the phone at his desk. As soon as he saw his son, his eyes lit up from the smile on his face. He told the person he was talking to that he had to go because his son had just arrived in town. He walked briskly over to Jay and hugged him. Jay just looked at me as if he were being stabbed repeatedly. He stood there with his arms to his sides. Big Pete didn't even notice, or if he did, he did not show it.

Big Pete said, "I can't believe it! You came to help me."

Jay looked at his father as if he were a fly that needed to be swatted and said, "No, Father, I did not come to help you. I came because Belinda asked me to help her, and that is why I'm here."

Big Pete turned around and looked at me. If looks could have killed, I would have been dead then. Big Pete turned back towards his son and said, "Well if you came per Belinda's request then you are here to help me too."

Jay just shrugged his shoulders and said, "If you want to look at it that way, okay."

Big Pete said, "Well, Belinda's here, she can run the shop. Why don't you and I go get a bite to eat and catch up? I need to talk to you in private anyway."

Jay looked at me with a questioning look on his face, and Big Pete noticed and turned his glance over toward me with his eyes squinted and a furrowed brow.

I said in a calm, nonchalant way, "That's up to you, Jay. I think that would be a great idea for you to speak with your father."

Jay said, "Okay, Belinda's right, but we'll take Mom's car and I will drive."

Jay looked over at me and I said, "That will be fine. Just don't stay out too late, Jay, because you know how Auntie Bea and Uncle Frank are. You can drop off Little Pete and me at the Daisy house. I'll go ahead and lock up now since I know business will be slow today."

When I got back "home," Uncle Frank was sitting in the chair by the phone in the Florida room smoking a cigarette.

When I entered the house he said, "Hi, baby girl, your mother called and wanted me to tell you she got her medications finally and said she would try and call back later if she could to talk with you more. Also, Auntie Bea wants you to come over and speak with her. She got a phone call from someone but didn't go into detail regarding it. Also, my life insurance called about not receiving this month's payment on that loan I did for your mom and your auntie."

I said, "Okay, what do you want me to do about the loan? Do you want me to try and pay it off, or just make payments?"

Uncle Frank answered, "No, I don't want you to pay it off, just make the payments while you are here and I will make the payments when you go back to Germany. I already told you I didn't care how they bury me. I owe your momma big time."

I said, "Okay. I will do it. While we are on the subject, Uncle Frank, did you lie to me about your knowledge and giving your permission for Mom to open credit cards in her name and your name? I want the truth, Uncle Frank! You know I have an uncanny way of finding out the truth."

Uncle Frank became angry and replied, "Belinda, why on earth would I lie about that? I told you I used those cards too, and your mother made charges on them for my benefit. If I wanted to I could lie so you would pick up the entire bill for it, but I didn't, for once in my life I told you the truth."

I said, "Okay, Uncle Frank, I'm sorry, I believe you. I just wanted to be sure because Little Pete was the one that helped Mom open those credit card accounts."

Uncle Frank said, "I already knew that. I already told you, I told your momma it was okay and to open them for us."

I asked, "Okay, Uncle Frank. Do you want to go and see Momma tomorrow?"

Uncle Frank answered, "No, I'm fine talking with her on the phone. I just can't see your momma like that. Not yet anyway."

I didn't push my great-uncle on the subject and said, "Okay, but before I do anything else I'm going to take a hot bath. I'm mentally exhausted. If Christina or Momma calls yell for me and I will take the call."

Be damned if I wasn't in the bathtub more than three minutes when Uncle Frank started yelling for me. I barely heard him say it was Christina on the phone. I jumped up and almost fell trying to get out of the bathtub as quickly as I could. I threw my pajamas on while I was still wet and a bathrobe over top of that and walked very quickly to the telephone in Uncle Frank's bedroom, dripping water everywhere. He was still chatting to my sister. I think Uncle Frank enjoyed people calling and being in the house with him because everyone had neglected him for so long. I waited a few minutes so he could enjoy talking with my sister. I finally chimed in and said, "I got it, Uncle Frank, you can hang up the phone."

Christina and I waited for a few seconds, and Uncle Frank still did not hang his phone up.

Christina said, "Uncle Frank, Belinda is on the phone now. You can hang up."

Uncle Frank replied, "Oh, okay," and he finally hung the phone up; we knew because we heard it click.

Christina and I were both giggling over Uncle Frank because we both knew he was going to try to eavesdrop on our conversation. Christina started to speak; her voice was flooded with disappointment. "Belinda, I did my very best today to get them to give Momma her medications, but they gave me the runaround and I don't believe they are going to give them to her until next week because the doctor only comes to the jail every other week. I swear I tried."

Knowing the role that I had played earlier today regarding our mother's medications, I allowed Christina to take all the glory for a victory that she didn't know she had won.

I said, "Oh Christina, I don't know what you did or said, but Momma called earlier and she told Uncle Frank that she had finally received her medication. She said that they will be giving it to her daily from now on, or until the doctor says otherwise. Thank you so much for taking that very important battle on and winning it. When are you coming home?"

Christina's voiced turned to pure excitement, bewilderment, and said, "What? I can't believe they did a 180-degree turnaround. I'll keep helping you regarding our mother's physical well-being, but I can't come home and help you. I will continue helping you via telephone. You can call me whenever you want to, and I will listen to you as well."

I guess she thought that would be a good enough excuse for me, but she knows me better than that. I would not allow her to get away with it. I wondered if she had spoken with our father today about this. I turned very angry and lashed out at my sister, "What? You said you were coming. You said even though she was guilty you were going to help me fix our other relatives. Why are you not coming home?"

Christina started to stutter and said in a cowardly tone, "Umm, because you and I would do nothing but fight with each other. You know more of what is going on than I do. Momma did not call me so she doesn't need me or want me." Christina became indignant as she continued, "All my life when she was in trouble or needed someone she always, always went to you, never me. She got herself into this mess along with everyone else. I would have come home if you had not corrected yourself regarding Auntie Bea's land and trying to make Momma look good for her actions."

My voice became louder as I angrily responded, "What a pure bunch of bullshit, Christina. What in the hell is the matter with you? You were always the one that she treated as a friend and daughter, and I have always been treated like a piece of shit. She only came running to me when her pocketbook was empty and when we needed food on the table since our father would not provide for us. She has bailed us out of trouble many, many times in our youth and never judged us, except for the times she scolded us, and now when she needs us, you're nowhere to be found.

"Momma is guilty, so what?! She stole, but are we to stop loving her and supporting her because she made a stupid, nasty mistake? You know our mother doesn't think about the consequences of her actions. She lives her life in a fairy tale and you know it. You also know she has bipolar disorder with manic episodes, and that is just part of who she is, and we have to accept that as well. I was not making her look like some kind of saint! Our mother is a crook—period! I just wasn't going to blame her for other people's actions. She did enough herself; and do you think for one minute that I will so easily forgive her again, or anyone else who is involved in this? Hell no, Christina, because I'm not Jesus Christ, and I will not turn my cheek again! I have told them all that to their faces. You're just as self-serving as she is. You don't give a damn about anyone except for your selfish self. I seem to be saying this repeatedly since I arrived, 'United we stand, divided we fall,' and believe me, sister, when I say that, we all will lose in the end, we will. Oh, I forgot you're a therapist! Can you psychoanalyze that?"

Christina jumped in and angrily retorted, "I'm not coming, and that's my final decision! So bullying me like you always do, Belinda, and trying to make me feel bad isn't going to work this time. It hasn't worked for a very, very long time. You don't need me, except for the mental part, and I have told you I would support you on that and that alone. You're just a damn self-righteous bully, Belinda Denise, and whenever you think you're right you shove it down everyone else's throats."

I let go of my anger at that point, and said in a much calmer voice, "Okay, Christina Lee, you made your point and you are right, I am a bully," then my voice turned angry again, "but I only bully people when I know I'm right. To make them do the right thing. Yes, Christina, I guess I am only two-dimensional and you see much, much more since you are the only three-dimensional person between the two of us without one bit of common sense. Having that entire book sense should make your brain hurt from time to time. Since I seem to see the black and white between the gray lines, and you don't because all you have is three-dimensional book sense. What does the word 'family' mean to you? Oh, of course, screwing them over and over again. Isn't that what everyone in our family is all about, Christina Lee? What makes you any better than them? Fine, Christina, I have said enough hurtful shit and so have you. I accept your cowardly decision, and I will just say one last hurtful thing for you to brew over. The real reason you are not coming is your precious reputation. You are embarrassed and ashamed because of what our mother has done. How do I know this? Because I feel the same way, but that isn't stopping me from trying to do right by all parties involved. I still love you, Christina, but I am very disappointed in you. I am your sister, and you have hurt me once again by never standing by my side. Fighting amongst ourselves isn't going to change the fact that our mother is a crook. If I could pull a time machine out of my ass and turn back time to stop her, I would. If anything, you could have come home for me, but you chose not to, and I will have to accept it."

Christina replied in a calmer tone, and I could hear her tears, "I love you too, Belinda, and maybe you are right a little bit, but that's the way it is. I'm hanging up now because I just can't take any more of your mental bullying. You seem to be able to wear a strong-willed person down to their knees, and know how to push all the buttons to set me off. Did you think for just one moment, Belinda, that I just might not be as strong as you are?"

With that, she hung up the phone.

I have to give my sister credit, at least this time she warned me that she was hanging up the phone. She at least gave me the respect to tell me first. I felt bad because I knew I hurt her feelings, and I guess I let my temper get the best of me. I was so disappointed that she would not at least be here with me. Maybe I was a little bit wrong too. After all, this is America and everyone has the right to make his or her own choices in life.

As I hung up the phone, I realized that I had a horrible headache. Stress tends to do that to me. I sat there and rubbed my forehead and eyes. When I looked up, there was Uncle Frank with a cigarette in his hand, standing in the doorway to his bedroom. He was giving me a very judgmental look. I knew he was angry with me, and I sat there on the side of his bed expecting him to start badgering me, which, of course, he did without hesitation.

He said in a half-angry voice, "Belinda! What the hell have you done?"

I said in a tired voice, "Uncle Frank, please, not now."

Uncle Frank said, "Girl, I heard you, or at least part of it. You know damn well that your sister is not tough like you are and can't handle all this. I'm amazed that she is even supporting you on the telephone; and you just keep pushing and pushing everyone. It doesn't matter that you are doing good things, Belinda, but you have to slow down so the rest of us can catch up. I'm an old man now and your auntie is an old woman."

I looked up at Uncle Frank, let out a sigh, and said in a frustrated voice, "Uncle Frank, Uncle Frank. My sister is very far from being weaker than I am. This conversation was not about you in any way, shape, or form. I know you think that my mother is weak also. Believe me, Uncle Frank, I have a different relationship with my sister and mother than you do. I have seen how they really are, and there is not a weak bone in their bodies." I stood up and started walking toward his bedroom door, and Uncle Frank stumbled down the hallway in front of me. I could tell he was beginning to get drunk.

As I was walking behind him I said, "Uncle Frank, you are right about Auntie Bea and you. I have been pushing the two of you too hard, but please understand that I am doing that only because the time I have to help you will be limited. I'm sorry; I didn't mean to hurt you."

We were now in the dining room, and Uncle Frank said, "You know, baby girl, you are Margaret's granddaughter and Queenie's daughter. I see all the good of them in you." Then his voice started to get a little angry. "Except for that damn time you drove my truck with a flat tire." Then he just started laughing.

I knew that Queenie was a nickname that my Uncle Frank gave my mother when she was just a little girl, but this was the first time I had heard him use it. I walked back into the bathroom and pulled the stopper out of the drain so the now cold water would drain from the bathtub. I would finish my relaxing bath later. I walked into the Florida room, picked up the phone, and called Auntie Bea. When she answered it, I asked, "Who called, Auntie Bea?"

Auntie Bea answered, "Oh, it's about my property taxes and a bounced check that your mother wrote. I will talk more with you about it in the morning. Can you come over in the morning? I'm already in bed. I ate your sub you left in the fridge. I hope you didn't mind, but I need to go to the grocery store."

I replied, "No problem, Auntie Bea. Do you need me to take you to the grocery store tomorrow?"

She answered, "No, I'm quite capable of doing it myself, thank you."

I walked down the hall towards the bathroom. As I was walking, I could hear Uncle Frank snoring. I peeked into his bedroom and saw that he left his light on. I turned his light off and closed his bedroom door. I walked back into the bathroom and turned on the water again so I could finish taking a hot bath. I let the tub fill up with nice warm water until it was half-full. I turned the water off, got into the tub, and just let myself relax. After about an hour, I got out. This time I was able to dry off and then got into my now dry pajamas. I decided I wanted a nice cup of hot chocolate. I remembered seeing hot chocolate mix in one of Uncle Frank's kitchen cabinets.

I found the mix without difficulty, made myself a cup, and went into the Florida room to wait for Jay. I hoped I didn't send him into the lion's den too soon; after all, Jay was very young, and he was very bitter toward his father. I truly did not blame him at all.

I decided to total all the credit card bills to find out the total amount of the credit card fraud. I felt comfortable enough to believe I now had all the statements, and later I would discover that I was correct. When I added all the statements, the unpaid balances, and seeing the grand total I wanted to cry. The credit card debt between Uncle Frank and my mother was thousands of dollars. The debt with credit cards that had been created in my deceased grandparents' names was a few thousand dollars as well. I knew my grandparents were gone, and I was going to have to let this go. I had to focus on the living.

I tried to calculate how much the total debt was. I assumed there were more attorney fees owed, but I did not know yet what the attorney was going to do regarding Pete and my mother waiving her right to trial. There were also all the expenses I had to charge for myself since I had arrived. At this point, I was looking at thousands and thousands of dollars I needed to gather, and there were still the bad checks I would have to cover. In addition, I did not know what the closing fees would be for the mortgage, and I was still waiting to see if I had been approved. I did not even know if I would be able to afford to pay the monthly mortgage payments yet.

As the gravity of the situation overcame me, I began to cry. It hurt so much that my mother and godmother had done this to me. Even if I had decided not to get involved, these women had set me up to the point that I had no choice. I wished at this point that I had never given my word. I guess they knew I would still honor it, and I would try my best to do so. In my mind, I had no other choice but to try to pay everything that they charged in my name. I knew I wasn't the person most victimized by their deceptions. There were millions of dollars that had been stolen from Big Pete's clients. Even though my dollar amount was nothing compared to Big Pete's clients, to me, it might as well have been a million dollars.

Paying back all that debt seemed so far out of reach for me. I knew my shop's inventory would not cover it all. I was going to have to sell Mom and Big Pete's belongings. I hoped that I would be able to save our family's heirlooms, but it was beginning to look doubtful. I felt that they truly belonged to Christina, Jay, and me at this point, because Mom and Big Pete had given me everything they owned. I looked up from my papers and saw a pair of headlights pull into the driveway. I assumed it was Jay. After a few minutes, I saw Jay opening the sliding glass door and walking through it.

In a very angry voice Jay said, "I told you it was a bad idea for me to do this."

I asked, "What do you mean?"

Jay angrily answered, "I got into a damn argument with him."

I inquisitively asked, "What about?"

Jay replied, "My father plans on fighting the indictments to the bitter end, and he tried to lie to me by saying it was all your mother's fault, and that's why she was in jail. He said that *she* set *him* up! He also said not to believe anything you had to say because you are just like your mother! That you were trying to steal everything he had left and were running around town telling everyone the shop was yours. He said the shop belongs to Jane and him! He just kept going on and on and on!"

I said, "Jay, come over here. I can show you the credit card fraud."

Jay came over to the table and looked at all the statements. I said, "You see the statements have Mom and Big Pete's address on them, and you know I live in Germany."

I reached down and pulled out the legal documents that showed the owner's name of Cognac's Run.

Jay said, "You didn't have to show me. I believe you." I said,

"I know, but it's always easier for someone to believe when the evidence is in front of them."

Jay broke down and said, "I guess you're right because your mom told me when we went to see her that the shop belonged to her and Pete, not you."

I said, "See, Jay, it's much easier to prove something to you because we have so many liars among us, and unfortunately, they are our parents. All they are doing is hurting themselves and us as well. They are doing the same old same old. Divide and conquer, but this time they are not conquering anything except themselves. I guess because we are their children, we are not supposed to have anything either. I have just concluded our family just took from us because, I guess, they felt we owe them. They do not care if they hurt us or not. Maybe we owe them for giving life to us, and for putting you through college, but they stole to do that. Maybe they just thought they could control us and we would be easily manipulated. Who really knows?"

Jay said, "I totally agree with you. I just can't believe Mom lied to me like that."

I said, "Because she wants to control you, and your father wants to control you. That's all it is, either that or they *believe* you owe them." Jay said,

"I feel like I've been run over by a truck! I'm headed to bed." I said,

"I know exactly how you feel. Remember one thing about me, Jay, I'm only taking what needs to taken to pay the mess that we both agreed to pay—no more and no less. I think Christina really doesn't care what we do."

Jay asked, "Is she coming or what?"

I answered, "I talked with her tonight, and she is not coming."

Jay said, "Damn, she disappoints me."

I said, "I know."

Jay said, "Well, good night, Belinda."

I said, "Let's shut the house down for the night before we go to bed."

Jay said, "Okay."

CHAPTER XXXVII

The following morning, I woke up again at 5:00 a.m. and started the day. I made a fresh pot of coffee. Uncle Frank and Jay were still asleep. I knew I would have to be very quiet that morning because I did not want to wake them. After dressing and pouring myself a cup of coffee, I quietly turned off the alarm, opened the side door from the kitchen, walked into the Florida room, and gently closed the door behind me.

I had left the most recent credit card statements in the Florida room when I went to bed so I could call all the credit card companies again first thing in the morning. This time I was going to have the credit card companies remove the interest so I could pay the principal balance more quickly.

I picked up the stack of bills and proceeded to call the number that was listed on the statement of the bill on top of the pile. A young female answered; I told her who I was, gave the credit card number, and said, "My mother has committed credit card fraud in my name and is in jail now for other crimes. She has no means to make restitution to you. I did not make these charges, and I have been living in Germany for the past few years. I have decided that it is in everyone's best interest for me to try to pay her charges, but I feel that I should not have to pay the interest. Can you do this?"

The representative replied, "I have never had a request like this before. Normally charges are filed against the person that committed the fraud. I have never had a victim of this crime request this. I will have to speak with my manager."

I said, "That will be fine."

She said, "I will have to put you on hold for a moment."

I said, "Okay."

A few moments after being on hold, a man answered the phone. He gave his greetings and informed me who he was. He then said, "Ms. Star,

I'm truly sorry this has happened to you, especially by your own mother. We are fixing your statement at this very moment so you have no interest charges until the bill is paid off. We have no problem with this request whatsoever. What address would you like your billing statement to go to?"

I stated, "I'm staying with other relatives here in Virginia until I have cleaned this mess up to the best of my abilities, and I would greatly appreciate you sending the bills to this address." I gave him my auntie's address and thanked him for his understanding and help. I also asked, "Do you need any proof that I am telling you the truth?"

He said, "No, your statement and explanation is proof enough for me, but if my superiors need anything I will let you know. Are there other credit card accounts that your mother has used in this manner?"

I answered, "Yes."

He said, "They may want proof of your correct residency and identification, so you may want to prepare for that." I said,

"I already am. I have already set up a fax machine in my relative's home just in case I need to provide proof." It took about an hour or so for me to call all the credit card companies where fraud was committed in my name. The first manager was correct, and some companies had me fax identification to them. Every company was different. There was no consistency, but that was fine with me. After I finished with all the credit card accounts that were in my name, I started on the accounts in my mother's name and Uncle Frank's name.

Again I called the number on the statement, told the representative who I was, and gave them the credit card number.

I said, "My great-uncle and my mother opened this account together to help build their credit again because both of them have filed bankruptcy in the past. My mother now is in jail and has no means of paying this debt. My great-uncle doesn't remember what he charged, or what was charged for him, and he cannot afford to pay this debt. He is on a fixed income. I am willing to help him pay this, but I feel I should not have to pay interest regarding this borrowed money because I did not create this debt."

The representative responded, "Wow, I have never had a request like this before, and I must speak with my manager. Can I put you on hold for a few minutes so I can explain to my manager what you are requesting and why?"

I answered, "Sure, I just want to get this problem resolved."

It must have been at least ten minutes I waited on hold before a woman picked up the phone, greeted me, and told me who she was. Then she said,

"Ms. Star, do you have power of attorney over either your uncle or your mother?"

I said, "No, I do not have power of attorney over my mother yet. I have just hired an attorney and I should have it either by the end of this week or the beginning of next week. She is working on this as we speak. My great-uncle is in the bed still asleep, but I can wake him so you know that I have authority from him to request this."

She said, "That will be fine. I will need to at least speak with him."

I asked, "Can you wait a few minutes?"

She answered, "I can."

I opened the door to the kitchen, and Uncle Frank was just standing there. His hair was sticking straight up and was very messy. He scratched his back, looked at me, and asked, "What?"

I said, "Uncle Frank, I have a manager on the phone regarding the credit card debt that you and Mom have. I have explained the situation to her and she just needs you to speak with her since I do not have a power of attorney over you or Mom."

Uncle Frank said, "Damn, girl, I just woke up, and you have started already this morning. For Pete's sake, let me speak to the woman."

Uncle Frank followed me into the Florida room. He sat in the chair that I had been sitting in and picked up the phone.

He said, "Hello." Then he said, "Yes, ma'am, my goddaughter is trying to help me get out of this pickle." Then he said, "No, ma'am, I don't know what my charges are and what's not. Belinda is just going to pay off each one, one at a time." Then he said, "No, ma'am, I don't have the income to pay all this debt off. I have no clue what has been going on. I just wanted to reestablish my credit after filing bankruptcy. That's all Jane and I were doing." Then Uncle Frank looked over at me and passed me the telephone again. He got up, went back into the kitchen, and closed the door. I could tell he was very upset over the entire conversation.

I put the phone back up to my ear and said, "Yes, ma'am."

She asked, "Is there something wrong mentally with your great-uncle?"

I answered, "No, he only has a third-grade education and is not very good with money. I can tell you this, ma'am, if you do not allow me to do this you will probably never see a dime of this debt returned to you. Once I leave here, I know my great-uncle will not pay you because he is on a fixed income."

She said, "I totally agree with you that is why I'm going to go ahead and remove the interest because you are correct, you do not have to pay a dime on this. I am just grateful that you are willing to do this."

I said, "God bless you. Thank you for working this out with me. I would never be able to pay all this debt if I had the interest on it as well."

The same basic conversation repeated with the other credit cards as well. By the time we finished, Uncle Frank was so angry that his cheeks and forehead were pink.

When we were done with the last account, he said, "Those stupid dumb people. They should be thankful that they are at least going to get back the borrowed money from you because I wouldn't pay a dime. At this point, I could care less about my credit."

I said, "Uncle Frank, you act like you're not guilty in this, but you are. You were charging like there was no tomorrow, at my mother's expense. You are just as liable for this debt as my mother is. You know it, but you sit there complaining because now it's time to pay the credit card companies back. You got lucky once again because now you have another sucker to bail you out of trouble! You should be thankful that every one of those credit card companies dealt with me and agreed to drop the interest. You know, Uncle Frank, they did not have to do that. They could have left you out there to rot, and you know damn well that what you and my mother did to obtain these credit cards was fraud. I know that false information was provided to them. I also know that Little Pete was part of this."

Uncle Frank did not say a word. He took his medication with a big glass of water and looked at me. He knew the truth.

Uncle Frank, like Auntie Bea, did not grasp the fact that he could go to jail for his actions. People and companies were tired of being ripped off by people like my mother, Auntie Bea, and Uncle Frank. What my relatives did not seem to realize was that they were truly stealing from the consumers. The companies increase the interest, product, or services to retrieve their losses, so they were really stealing from the American public. I just shook my head in total disgust regarding the actions of my great-uncle, great-aunt, and my mother. It's not just me who they had stolen from.

As I watched Uncle Frank go back into the kitchen to get another cup of coffee, I thought of my sister. Christina thought that our mother was the only one who had committed crimes against her. She thought Auntie Bea and Uncle Frank had done nothing to her. I thought, *How did I come from a family like this? Jay is not even blood, but he is here. I guess I see where my sister gets her attitudes; she is positively a product of my father and mother. She only thinks of herself. How did my father put it? "It's not your concern, just go back to Germany. I'm not going to help you." He could not even help me store my things. What kind of nasty, dirty family do I have? In fact, my father has never helped me in my life. It has always been me doing for them and for everyone else in my family. Am I the nut or is everyone else in the family nuts? Who knows?*

My mind returned to the tasks at hand. I was once again sitting in the chair next to the telephone in the Florida room. I picked up the telephone again and called the credit card company that had my deceased grandparents' names on it. I again told the representative my name, what relation I was to my deceased grandparents, the credit card number, and explained to the representative that they were deceased. They all immediately closed the accounts, except for one, which requested a certified copy of the death certificates. I tried to explain to the representative that I did not have that documentation. I said I thought my Uncle Poppy had it, but was not sure. I would have to call him to see if there were any certified copies left, but they would have to close the account because they were deceased and would not be able to pay it. The representative told me they would not close the account until there was documentation.

I said, "Oh well, there really is nothing more that I can do. I am only taking care of the living, not the deceased. Thank you for your time," and I hung up the phone.

This representative was trying to obtain my personal information— social security number, address, etc. I refused to give it because it had nothing to do with the account. I believe she was going to try to attach the debt to me. *There are a lot of nasty little people in this world besides my family*, I thought.

CHAPTER XXXVIII

I smelled bacon cooking and went into the kitchen. Jay was awake and cooking breakfast again.

I said, "Good morning. It's about time you got up."

Jay laughed and said, "I can't go through a day in this mess without some type of energy."

I laughed and said, "I know the feeling, but if I ate breakfast all the time I would be ten times as fat as I am now."

We both laughed. I heard the telephone ring and heard Uncle Frank answer it. I heard him speaking to someone and assumed it was Auntie Bea. A few minutes later, Uncle Frank called my name and said, "It's your auntie; she wants to speak to you, Belinda."

I walked back into the Florida room, took the telephone, and answered, "Hello, Auntie Bea."

She said, "Belinda, I need to talk to you about my property tax, and I need my tractor fixed for this summer. It broke down last year, and your momma never fixed it for me."

At this time, I saw Little Pete's van pull up in front of the Daisy house. I said, "Okay, Auntie Bea, Little Pete has just pulled up. I will send him straight over there to fix your tractor. Also, tell him if he needs parts to do it, to go and get them. I will pay him back later today. I will be over there as soon as I finish making my phone calls."

Auntie Bea said "Okay."

Before Little Pete could get to the sliding glass door of the Florida room, I opened it and yelled to him, as he was locking up his van, "You need to go over to Auntie Bea's. She needs you to fix her tractor for this summer and have the blades sharpened. If you need any parts to fix it, please go buy them, and I will pay you back later today."

Little Pete yelled back, "Okay." Then he started walking over to Auntie Bea's house.

I thought, *That works out perfectly!* I didn't know how I was going to get Little Pete from under my shirttails. The less he knew, the better off I was.

Jay came out, sat at the table with Uncle Frank, and served him a plate of scrambled eggs and bacon.

Uncle Frank asked, "Boy, did you cook these eggs right today?"

Jay laughed. "I always cook the eggs right."

Uncle Frank just said, "Bull." After Uncle Frank got his first bite full he said, "They are hard again. How can they be cooked right?"

Jay laughed and answered, "Because that's the way I like them."

Jay and I both just started laughing.

I picked up the phone book and turned to the yellow pages. I looked through the auctioneer section as Jay and Uncle Frank were eating. I did not care for the first four; they were slightly rude and avoided my questions. The fifth auctioneer, I immediately liked. He was very professional in his greeting, he answered all my questions, and his fee was only five percent of the sale. The others wanted ten to fifteen percent. I wrote down his address and the directions he provided. I told him that my brother and I would be there later in the morning with some items that we would like to have auctioned.

I hung up the phone and said to Jay, "I guess you know what we are going to start out with today."

Jay said, "I guess I'm the moving man today."

I said, "Of course. I'd like to leave as soon as you finish eating."

Jay asked, "What are we selling?"

I answered, "I'll show you on the way."

I did not believe Uncle Frank was listening to us. He was too busy wolfing down his breakfast faster than a wild dog. Poor Uncle Frank, I did not think he ate unless the food was put right in front of him. I'd only been there a few days, and it seemed that Jay and I had put at least ten pounds on him already. I could tell this because it looked like his little belly was coming back. I was just thankful that he was gaining weight.

Jay and Uncle Frank finished eating, and I washed the dishes while Jay dried them. As we were cleaning, Uncle Frank yelled from the Florida room, "The housekeeper is here."

I asked, "What!?"

Uncle Frank said, "Oh, I forgot to tell you. Your momma has her come every Wednesday. She cleans the Daisy house first then goes and cleans your auntie's house."

I asked, "Does she, also, clean Mom and Big Pete's house?"

Uncle Frank answered, "Yes, she does their house on Tuesdays, if I remember correctly, and she doesn't speak English."

I asked, "What? What nationality is she?"

Uncle Frank answered, "I think she's Russian."

I said, "Oh, shit."

The housekeeper looked in the sliding glass door to the Florida room and saw all three of us looking at her. I immediately opened the door for her because she had a bucket with cleaning tools in it. I greeted her, and she nodded her head.

I asked, "Ma'am, I need to communicate with you. Do you have someone that speaks English who can translate to you by using the telephone?"

I pointed to the telephone and said the word English. I guess she understood me because she picked up the phone that was beside Uncle Frank's chair and called someone. She briefly spoke to the person and passed the phone to me. I asked with whom I was speaking, and the woman on the other end of the phone said she was the woman's sister.

I told her who I was and continued, "We do not need her to clean my mother's house any longer. I will pay her for this time, but after that, she will have to make arrangements with Big Pete because I will not pay for the cleaning any longer. Regarding my great-aunt and great-uncle, each one of them will be paying her after she cleans their houses each week. How much does she charge for their homes?"

I passed the telephone back to the housekeeper. My uncle was correct; it was Russian. The housekeeper passed the phone back to me and the woman on the other end of the phone answered my questions.

I said, "The day she cleans will still be every Wednesday, if that is okay with her."

I passed the phone back to the housekeeper and after speaking with her sister, she passed the phone back to me. The housekeeper's sister told me Wednesday was fine with her sister.

I wrote out a check and paid her for yesterday's work. I got Uncle Frank's checkbook, wrote a check to her for his house and had him sign it. I told Uncle Frank not to give it to her until she had finished cleaning the Daisy house.

I called Auntie Bea and told her how much the housekeeper charged to clean her house, and I told her that she would have to pay her own way.

Auntie Bea retorted, "I don't have to pay for it. Jane paid for it, so bow you will have to pay it."

I said, "No, Auntie Bea, if you want your house cleaned for you, you will have to pay for it yourself. I am not going to pay for that. I do not understand why my mother was paying for it anyway."

Auntie Bea started yelling at me, "It is your mother's responsibility to provide for me!"

I said in an angry voice, "No, Auntie Bea, it is not my mother's responsibility, nor mine to provide for you. It's time you started paying your own way. I will help you with the other problem and will be by this afternoon to talk to you about it."

Auntie was livid as she screeched at me, "You are doing everything for Frank and nothing for me! You are going to start doing what I tell you to do, girl! Do you understand me?"

I yell back over the phone, "No, Auntie Bea, you are going to do what I tell you to do, or I will not do another damn thing for you. In fact, I have a good mind to break my word and turn you over to the U.S. Attorney's office. Have I made myself clear? I will talk with you later. You give me any more grief, and I will do exactly what I threatened to do. Goodbye!"

I could not believe that my auntie thought I was going to pay for something when she could! For Pete's sake, she had four other nieces and nephews (Frank's kids) plus all the other nieces and nephews she had from the other eight siblings of hers. Totally unbelievable! I began to wonder where they were now. A family was supposed to be there for their elderly, the next generation after my auntie's, not my generation. I just could not believe this. Where was the rest of the family? Everyone should have been helping me and taking responsibility for these two elderly people. The burden shouldn't have fallen to my mother and me.

I looked over at Jay; my voice was still laced with anger as I asked, "Are you ready?"

Jay answered, "Yes."

I said, "Let's go then."

Jay asked, "Which vehicle are we taking?"

I answered, "The pickup truck. I will drive to the storage unit."

Jay said, "Okay."

We drove past the shop on the way to the storage unit, and Jay and I saw Pete standing outside. We were sure he saw us, but neither one of us waved at him and he didn't acknowledge us. I turned as if I was going to

Washington, D.C., because I did not want Big Pete to see where we were going. I drove up the highway for a few minutes then turned around to go to the storage unit. We pulled up to the storage unit, and I saw that there were larger units than the one I had. One of them had the door open, and it was empty of all contents. We went to my unit. I read the contents on the boxes, and chose five to take to auction.

I asked, "Jay, would you please put these five boxes into the back of the pickup truck? Please, please be very careful. They are very fragile, and I do not want anything chipped or broken. I need to go speak with the manager for a minute. I'll be right back."

I walked to the front office. As I opened the door the little brass bell jingled. I stepped inside and then closed the door. Patty was sitting at her desk. We exchanged greetings, and I asked, "Is it possible for me to upgrade to a larger unit? I saw that you have an empty one and I really could use more space."

She pleasantly answered, "Yes, you can, but it will cost a few more dollars for that one."

I said, "That will be fine. If no one is renting it this month can I get the lease for the beginning of next month?"

She answered, "Yes, I don't have anyone renting at this time, plus it is technically already paid for to the end of this month. The renter said for me not to worry about a refund, for me to keep it."

I said, "Oh that will work out in my favor."

We both laughed and she said, "Don't worry about the money until the first of the next month, and we will make arrangements when you are ready to move your things in that one."

I said, "Okay, thank you."

Jay was already behind the wheel of the pickup truck, ready to go to the next destination. I got into the truck, and Jay passed over the keys to the lock for the storage unit.

I said, "After we go to the auctioneer, I need to buy another lock for the storage unit. Locks usually come with two keys, and I think Little Pete may have the other. I do not trust him."

Jay said, "You're right. We will do that. Where is the auctioneer?" I pulled out the piece of paper on which I had written the address, contact, phone number, and the directions, and I showed it to Jay.

Jay said, "I know where that is. It's on the other side of Snobville. If it's where I think it is, it's a nice place."

I guess it took about an hour or so to get there. After Jay parked, we got out, and I helped him carry the boxes inside the building. A middle-aged man greeted us when we entered.

Jay said, "I'll bring in the rest of the boxes, Belinda."

I said, "Okay."

I told the auctioneer who I was, and what we had that we would like to auction. He told me when their next auction would be held and that the items I brought should fetch a good price.

I said, "That would be nice," as I started opening the boxes. The man started helping me unpack them, and he became very excited after seeing the collection, or least the small part of it that Jay and I had brought. After Jay brought in the last box and we finished unpacking them, the man started inventorying them, and he examined them very carefully.

After he had finished he said, "They are all in perfect condition!" He went over their terms and the five percent commission. I was satisfied with the terms and conditions, and I signed the forms. We said our goodbyes then Jay and I walked back out to the parking lot where the pickup truck was parked.

I asked Jay, "Are you thirsty?"

Jay answered, "Yes."

I said, "Well, stop over there at the grocery store, and we will get something to drink. After we get our drinks, we need to go see Mom next. I can get a lock later."

Jay nodded in agreement. On the way to the jail to go see Momma, we chatted and made plans to make the most out of the few days he had left here.

Before I knew it, Jay was parking the pickup truck in the parking lot of the jail. As Jay was putting the truck in park, he said, "Belinda, I think it's much easier to see her today than it was the other day. I still do not like seeing Mom like this when it should be my father. All this conflict and loss has been because of him. I know it's no consolation, but I want to say I'm sorry for his actions. I feel partly to blame that he went this far with all these crimes against so many people.

"I'm also sorry that Christina isn't here. I know she should be here to help you as well. I guess she doesn't care about wanting to try to save our inheritance, even though I'm sure there will not be much left. Our history is just as important to me as it is to you."

I said, "Jay, don't you ever apologize for the criminal actions of another. You are in no way responsible for this. I'm not responsible and neither is Christina. Even though I am angry with Christina for not being here, I am no longer as angry with her for the decision she has made. We are Americans, Jay, and that means we are not responsible for the bad choices made by another. We do not live in the dark ages, where the children are responsible and are punished for the crimes of their parents. I know it seems that way, but by being an American, we can choose to take responsibility or not. You and I decided to take responsibility for their actions; Christina chose not to do so.

"You see, Jay, this is about choice; not taking the blame for of our parents' crimes. The choice to take responsibility for their actions, but not the blame, is ours. That is why I'm not so angry with my sister anymore. She is an American. I have put myself in harm's way many times, and I have fought for this basic principle of being able to make a choice. It doesn't matter whether I agree with the other person's choice or not. What matters is that we have the freedom to choose. You and I may feel that Christina is wrong, and maybe she is, but it's her choice and no one else's. Maybe she made this choice because, like you, she could not separate accepting the responsibility without accepting the blame. She has the right. That is why so many Americans have died, for this one basic freedom and so many more."

I realized at this moment that if my country was great enough to sacrifice my life for, our justice system was worth it as well. It's not our country and our laws that are not worthy of just one life, it's the people that live in our country, and the people in our justice system that have lost or never learned what America is and what its justice system truly stands for; these are people who are not worthy.

I continued saying to my brother, "I will gladly sacrifice and die for the basic idea of greatness that our forefathers bled for, so Christina and many others like her can have this one freedom and so many more. It has always been a promise made by my father's bloodline and it is a part of me. I guess my sister and father have lost their way as well.

"Once our last forefather passed away we have slowly allowed others to chisel away many of our freedoms, but this is America, and *all* the people have to do is demand them back, but it takes all of us, not just a few. Even though we are a free nation and it should take only one voice from the millions to say no to a socialized program or to tax the individual to give it to another, it needs to be a majority. This alone is sad. Do you understand where I'm coming from? In other words, Jay, all that I'm doing is by choice, one of the last freedoms we have left. I have never, not even for a second, taken on the blame for our parents' actions, but I will *choose* to take responsibility, because I *choose* to do so.

"To explain myself further regarding this socialized crap that has seeped into our government and the people, I will tell you the real history and when it all started, and why we have lost so many freedoms. Thomas Jefferson created the Democratic-Republican Party to oppose the Federalist Party in 1792. The first democratic president, Andrew Jackson, known as 'Old Hickory,' dissolved the Democratic-Republican Party and created the Democratic Party in 1828. The sole purpose of this new Democratic party was to persuade the country to practice social equality. Keep in mind the words, 'social equality.' The Republican Party was created in 1854 to oppose slavery. So the war between freedom and socialism truly began with Old Hickory, and this is why we have lost so many freedoms."

Jay spoke with disappointment in his voice, "Yes, I do understand, but our country isn't perfect, Belinda, nor are the people. Why have not the generations before us stopped it?"

Shaking my head in disappointment at my brother I answered, "How can a person so young already have such disappointment in our great country? You are right regarding the people that live within our borders; they are not perfect. Most of the people who work in our justice system have lost their way, but I choose to believe, instead, that most of our fellow countrymen are perfect. Just look at the three of us, two of us out of three, I feel, made the right choice for all parties concerned as a family unit. So my observation of most Americans, I believe, is worth dying for.

"I do not know why the generations before us did nothing to prevent socialism in our society, but I remember something my father told me a long time ago, and I will quote him, 'Belinda, it seems to me that each generation becomes a little bit more lazier than the one before it.'"

Neither one of us said another word as we walked toward the jail in silence.

We both put our IDs and airplane tickets in the slot at the bottom of the window. The same guard that I had spoken to when I first visited my mother greeted us. After he had us sign the roster, he asked us to have a seat.

There were many family members in the waiting area this time. It was so crowded we were standing in a room packed like sardines. There were crying babies, toddlers crawling everywhere, and people standing almost shoulder-to-shoulder. Jay and I waited at least thirty-five minutes before a guard at the metal door called our names. We were only allowed ten minutes with my mother. We completely understood why. When we saw my mother walking into the other side of the dividers, our faces lit up. She looked so much better. Mom pointed at me with her index finger, so I picked up the phone on my side of the booth. She quickly told me to tell Jay that she loved him, but we didn't have enough time for her to speak with him as well.

She was back to her complete old self again, barking orders! She gave me instructions to enroll her in a book club so she could have something to read. She said there was nothing to read there, and I knew how much my mother loved to read. I promised I would get the books she requested through a book club and have them sent to her directly. That was the only way she could get books. We were not allowed to bring them to her.

She proceeded to tell me that Miss Patson had come to see her the previous afternoon. She told me she agreed with the attorney regarding a general power of attorney rather than a specialized one. She also stated that she agreed with the attorney about the will. Momma also told me to tell Jay that she was sorry for getting him involved in this mess, and she apologized to me as well. She asked if I could ever forgive her for everything she had done. I told her I was only going to forgive her this last time. If she ever stole from me again, I would break her fingers.

She looked at me through the window in shock, and she didn't say anything. I think she knew I was dead serious this time, and I was.

Uncle Frank, Auntie Bea, and my mother had gone too far this time. Jay couldn't stand it. He grabbed the phone from my hand and told my mother that he forgave her and loved her so very much and he began to sob. He told her that he hated his father for this, and of course, my mother let Jay blame everything on his father. The guard came up to my mother and tapped her on the shoulder. We quickly said goodbye.

Jay started the engine and before we headed off for our next adventure he said, "I thought it would get easier each time, but it isn't getting any easier seeing her like that."

I sighed and said, "I know, Jay, but she has to pay for her crimes. She made her choices, no one forced her to make them, and now she has to pay the piper."

Jay replied, "I know, but I wish there were an easier way for her to pay for her crimes."

I said, "You know, Jay, there are some countries where they cut your hands off for stealing; at least our justice system doesn't do that."

Jay looked at me with disgust on his face. He paled slightly and said, "Ick, Belinda, but you're right, I guess being in jail is far better than that."

I said, "Let's talk about something else. It's slightly better, but not much more pleasant. We need to move on to our next task. Why don't we head over to Mom and Big Pete's house so we can pack up Mom's reading collection. I know she has books scattered all over the house. We can also load up the photo albums and some of the other things that we already packed. While we're there, I want to call a used book dealer. Maybe we can get a few extra dollars from her books."

Jay nodded in agreement and said, "Yeah, that's a good idea." We talked more about things we needed to do, and Jay talked more about what was going on in his life. It was refreshing to have a relaxing conversation for a change.

CHAPTER XXXIX

When we arrived at Mom and Big Pete's house, we went to the garage and grabbed the boxes of books that Mom had stored there. We carried them into the house and deposited them in the living room. Next, I headed to the kitchen phone. When I got there, I picked up the phone book, turned to the yellow pages, and called the first book dealer that was listed. I told him who I was and what types of books we had for sale.

He said he was interested in what we had and asked when he could come over and check them out. I told him right now would be fine since we were at the house anyway. I gave the dealer directions, and he said he would be there within thirty minutes. I said that would be great, and we would see him then.

I only had thirty minutes to finish packing her books. I headed to her office and got started. While I was packing them, I noticed a small copier on top of a file cabinet. I had missed that earlier. I decided that I would take it to my shop because I could sell it. I lifted the cover up and checked the glass to make sure it was clean before packing it. I found a piece of paper laying face-down on the glass as if it had been copied and then forgotten. I turned the paper up and turned it around so that I could read it. I let out a gasp, fell to my knees, and started crying. It was a copy of a Virginia driver's license with my name on it. The social security number was different from mine and the picture was my mother. As I was crying I thought, *How much more has she done to me? How far does this fraud go? Will there ever be an end to this? How many more discoveries will I make of what my great-aunt and my mother have done to me and my siblings?* I started to cry even harder. Life seemed so unfair. I didn't know how much more I could take! After a few minutes of indulging in self-pity, I pulled myself together.

The doorbell rang a few minutes later. I went to the front door, and the man introduced himself as the book dealer. I let him in and escorted him to the books. He started looking through the first box of books that I had packed. He was very impressed with the collection of books and asked if he could see the others. I showed him the other two boxes.

He then asked me, "How much are you asking for them?"

I said, "I don't know. What are you offering?"

He stood there looking at the boxes of books for a few minutes and offered me a few hundred dollars. My first instinct was to ask for an additional hundred so I did.

The dealer said, "I knew you were going to do that. I swear I gave you a good offer on them."

I said, "Okay, then we will take it."

He reached in his back pants pocket, pulled out his wallet, took the cash out of his wallet, and handed it to me.

I said, "Thank you. Jay and I will help carry these boxes out to your car for you."

He said, "Thank you."

Before he left, he told me, "If you have any more books you are interested in selling please give me a call."

I said, "I will."

As he was backing out of the driveway, I said to Jay, "I liked him. He was a very nice man. I think we have some very old and rare books that belonged to Great-Grandma that Mom has in the shop. I think I may sell them to him later."

Jay said, "Are you sure we want to sell those? Why does Mom have them in the shop for sale?"

I said, "I guess because she needs money to pay all the people that have been taken advantage of."

We both walked back into the house and started moving all the boxes into the pickup truck. Of course, we could not get them all in the back of the truck, and we knew we were going to have to make several more trips just for what we had packed so far. We placed the copier that I found in Mom's office on the seat between us to keep it safe. It would also be convenient when we stopped at the shop so I could drop it off to be sold. After we had loaded the boxes, I maneuvered them so I had a bit more space. There was a two-drawer file cabinet, and I told Jay, "I want to take this file cabinet as well, but first I want to see what's inside it." Jay said, "Okay."

I opened the top drawer, and we discovered over a hundred credit cards. There were about five groups of them held together by rubber bands with at least twenty-five credit cards per bundle. There were also file folders with Christina's name, my name, and Jay's name. I opened the file folder with my name on it as Jay was opening the file folder with his name on it. We found credit card applications that had been filled out including the signatures. They were our names, but not our signatures. I opened the one with Christina's name on it and found the same thing. After Jay and I looked through them, we looked at each other. Neither one of us said a word. Jay took his and tore it up. I took Christina's and tore it up, but mine, I kept. I took the folded paper with the fraudulent driver's license copied on it from the pocket of my blue jeans, and put it into the folder. I was going to keep this file. Jay watched me do it, and asked why.

I said, "Because my mother will lie about this someday, and I want to prove it really happened."

Jay just looked at me amazed and didn't say a word.

Before we left the house, I called Big Pete at my shop. I told him we packed more books and were moving the photo albums to the Daisy house. I told him we were headed back to the Daisy house and would be dropping by the shop.

Big Pete asked, "Okay. Is Jay with you?"

I answered, "Yes. He will be with me."

Big Pete said, "Great. I'll see you guys in a bit."

Jay and I locked up the house and drove to my shop. Jay got out the copier and carried it into the shop.

Big Pete asked, "What are you doing?"

I answered, "I'm going to sell this because we already have so many copiers. Does it make any difference to you?"

Big Pete answered, "No, I guess not. You're right, we need to raise cash." Big Pete looked over at Jay and said, "I'm sorry for being an ass last night."

Jay said, "Okay."

Big Pete asked, "Do you want to go get a bite to eat again with me?"

Jay answered, "No, Belinda and I have a lot of work to do today, but I guess I could go and get a late lunch with you now."

Jay looked over at me and I said, "That would be a great idea."

I looked at Big Pete and asked, "Is business slow today?"

Big Pete replied, "Yes. Are you going to do the books today? You haven't done them in a few days."

I answered politely, "You do not need to worry about my business, but thank you for asking. I will do them right now so I can get the funds deposited today."

Big Pete said, "I took fifty dollars today because I needed it."

I irritably said, "I wish you would stop doing that."

Jay belligerently asked Big Pete, "Why do keep stealing from her? You know she is trying to pay off all the credit card fraud and everything else."

Big Pete became defensive as he answered, "This is my shop too!"

Jay said angrily, "No, it is not. Just stop lying."

Big Pete continued lying, "I told you, Jay, this is really my shop."

Jay continued arguing, "No, it isn't! Belinda showed me the paperwork that has her as owner, not you."

Big Pete stated, "A lot of this stuff in here for sale is mine."

Jay said, "No it isn't; you already gave everything to Belinda." There was no way Big Pete could continue lying because both Jay and I were standing in the same room with him.

Big Pete said, "Oh, I forgot, but Belinda, I do need money to live off of."

I said, "I have already given you a way to support yourself, so just stop taking from us. Please."

Big Pete just ignored both of us and said to Jay, "Let's just go and get some lunch."

Jay and Big Pete left, and I sat down and did the books. I put the money from the shop's sales together with the money from the checks that Jay had cashed the previous day, the cash from sales, and a check that I had. I locked up the shop, drove to the bank and deposited the funds into the checking account.

CHAPTER XL

Jay and his father must have had a quick lunch, because as I was driving to Auntie Bea's, I ended up behind Big Pete's van. He pulled the van up into the Daisy house's driveway, and I decided to pull up behind him and retrieve Jay to go to Auntie Bea's house.

Uncle Frank came out of the sliding glass door of the Florida room brandishing his shotgun. He fired a shot straight up in the air as a warning, as he was yelling and screaming at Big Pete, "If you don't get off my property, Big Pete, I'm going to blow your brains out! Do you hear me? You sorry-ass maggot! You have destroyed my Queenie; you piece of shit! She is sitting in a nasty jail cell, you yellow-belly piece of dog shit, and you are trying to make her take the blame for everything. You nasty ass wife beater! I'm going to kill you! Get off my damn property, you sorry-ass cow sucker."

I had never heard language of that extreme coming from my great-uncle. In fact, I didn't think I'd ever seen him like this before in my entire life. I had no clue what set him off at that particular moment!

Jay jumped out the van as Uncle Frank was yelling and screaming at Big Pete and ran to the pickup truck. As I was trying to get out of the truck, I fell to the ground. I don't even know how I fell. All I remembered was getting back up from the ground and running as fast as I could toward Uncle Frank.

I went straight for the firearm. I was pulling it out of Uncle Frank's hands, and he was pulling it back from me. We must have pulled back and forth for a few seconds before I got the weapon out of my great-uncle's hands. The strong smell of whiskey was just oozing from his breath. I almost choked on the strong odor. I heard the telephone ringing inside the house, and Jay was yelling something.

Big Pete had his van in the middle of the front yard. He had hit the mailbox. His back wheels were spinning gravel, and big chunks of dirt were flying everywhere as he was driving around the yard like a drunken wild man.

The driveway was a half-circle, and he was crossing all over it. He was driving in circles, backing up fast, going forward, and turning in all directions as if he were four-wheeling at high speeds. Big Pete backed up and hit my mother's pickup truck, and I saw Jay fall to the ground because Pete hit the truck so hard that the truck moved and pushed Jay to the ground. He fell hard. I knew Big Pete must have been drunk! As Pete was spinning and turning all around trying to get off the Mills farm, several of the pieces of gravel from the driveway hit me all over. Big Pete did not even realize he had hurt his son. I ran over to the van and by luck was able to open the driver's door. Big Pete started hitting my face and chest with his fists as he was trying to push me out of the van. By this time, Jay was beside me with blood dripping from the side of his face, and we both managed to pull Big Pete from behind the steering wheel and onto the ground.

Throughout the entire altercation, Uncle Frank was yelling at me, "Kill the creep! Kill him, Belinda! Kill him for what he has done to us! Give him a piece of mountain justice, Belinda! Kill him! Kill him . . ."

Big Pete must have put the van in park before he started beating me. Thank God he did because if he had not, the van could have driven itself into the main road and could have hit a passing car. Jay started kicking his father repeatedly as his father lay on the ground. He was engulfed in rage. I think he was releasing years of pent-up emotions, fueled by Uncle Frank's yelling and screaming. It took every ounce of strength I had to get Jay away from his father.

I yelled, "Enough!"

Big Pete lay on the ground for a few seconds. He was bleeding, but his wounds weren't serious. He didn't stay down for long, and when I realized he was trying to get up and continue fighting us, I yelled, "Stop it! Settle down!"

Big Pete finally came to his senses. He slowly stood up, looked at us, and bellowed, "I'm going to press charges against your great-uncle, Belinda!"

Exasperated, I stated, "You're not going to do a damn thing because you are drunk, and I will tell the judge. Just go home, Big Pete, and forget about it. No one was seriously injured. Just go home. You know Uncle

Frank is a hillbilly and we live by a different code than you do. It's a code of honor that you will never understand. Just go home!"

Big Pete said in a calmer voice to Jay, "I can't believe you kicked me. Are you okay, son? I'm sorry, I feared for our lives."

Jay glared at his father and said, "Dad, just go home and let it go. You know how Uncle Frank is. I'm sorry for kicking you, but you hurt me first. Belinda and I should not have allowed you to drop me off here. Emotions are strong right now."

Big Pete said to Jay, "You're right. I'll see you two in the morning. I love you Jay, and believe it or not, Belinda, I love you too, you're like a daughter to me."

Jay and I just nodded our agreement with him so he would leave, which he did. We didn't believe a word he said.

I remembered Uncle Frank's shotgun, which I must have dropped in the yard somewhere. Thank God Uncle Frank did not realize I had dropped it. As I picked up the shotgun and removed the last live shell, I heard a lot of yelling in the distance.

Little Pete was running across the field between the two houses, and Auntie Bea was walking with her cane as quickly as she could. I could not remember a time when I had ever seen her move so fast. I said aloud, "Oh, shit, here we go again!"

My brain went into survival instinct. I started barking orders without thinking; I had to protect my family. "Jay, drive the truck over to Auntie Bea's, and park it in one of the sheds. Make sure the doors to the shed are closed so no one can see it."

Jay looked at me with a puzzled expression, but before he had a chance to question me, I commanded, "Just do it; do it right now!"

Jay obeyed me; he got into the pickup truck and backed it out of the driveway.

Little Pete breathlessly said, "We heard a gunshot. What the hell happened? I saw Big Pete's van tearing up everything in the yard."

I said, "You must have watched the entire time. It's over. I want you to take the White Beast and park it directly behind Uncle Frank's car. Can you straighten out the mailbox since Big Pete hit it with his van? Can you fix it so it doesn't look like someone ran into it?"

Little Pete replied, "Yes, but what's the hurry?"

I said impatiently, "Little Pete, just do it; please?"

Little Pete, frustrated, asked, "Okay, where are the keys to the White Beast?"

I reached into the pocket of my blue jeans and gave him the keys to the White Beast. I asked simply, "How long will it take you to fix the mailbox?"

Little Pete answered nonchalantly, "About fifteen minutes."

I said, "Good, do it."

Auntie Bea was almost to the Daisy house with her cane in tow and that's when something shiny in her other hand caught my eyes. I remembered that I showed Auntie Bea how to fire a handgun the same time I taught my mother how to use one.

I frantically said aloud again, "Oh, shit!" I ran toward my great-aunt, and I was right, she had one of Uncle Herndon's old pistols. "Auntie Bea, give me that damn pistol, please!"

She confessed excitedly, "I heard a gunshot, looked out my window, and saw that damn Big Pete's van."

I calmly said, "Auntie Bea, it's over now. Come on inside the Daisy house. Jay and Uncle Frank will tell you everything. Just give me the pistol, please."

Auntie Bea obediently handed me the pistol. I guess she knew everything was okay now. I thought, *God only knows what will happen next.* I started to help Auntie Bea walk the remainder of the way to the Daisy house.

Jay was running across the field from Auntie Bea's house toward me.

I asked Auntie Bea, "Are you okay to walk the rest of the way by yourself? I want to give this pistol to Jay so he can put it back in your house."

She answered calmly, "Yes. Go ahead and give it to your brother to put it back up."

I said, "Thank you."

I ran toward Jay before he got any closer to the house. We met about halfway in the middle of the field that lay between Auntie Bea and Uncle Frank's houses, and I asked Jay, "Can you take this pistol back to Auntie Bea's house? She keeps it in the drawer between the two chairs in her living room."

Jay answered as he asked, "Sure, but why are we hiding the pickup truck?"

I answered, "Because I think Big Pete is going to call the cops. I think he wants to get Uncle Frank and us in trouble to get us out of the picture. That way, there will be no one to interfere in his *business affairs*. I'm not positive about this, but I'm not going to take any chances with your father."

Jay said, "You're right. It's better to be safe than sorry."

I said, "I just don't want any of us to get into any trouble with the law. If Auntie Bea and Uncle Frank get caught having unregistered weapons, they could get into a lot of trouble."

Jay said, "But it's their property, and they have the right to bear arms, Belinda, and to protect themselves."

I said, "Jay, come on, you know that's a right we lost a long time ago. The reality now is that if someone comes onto your property threatening you, and you shoot the intruder in self-defense, you are the one who will go on trial. Even if you are found innocent and you were protecting yourself, you will probably use every penny you have for the blood-sucking attorneys that defended you. It's a damned-if-you-do and damned-if-you-don't situation.

"Remember what I was telling you earlier today? You never know what type of sheriffs we will get. Remember, it's how the law enforcer interprets the law. Do you want to take that chance? And besides, Uncle Frank wasn't defending himself from anything. He started this damn mess, but I'm not going to allow Big Pete to hurt another member of my family again." I flippantly continued, "I will punish Uncle Frank in my own way. His punishment will be Auntie Bea scolding him and nagging him for days over this because I am going to give her full reign over him just for this purpose." I laughed at my mean-spirited joke and Jay joined in.

Jay commented facetiously, "Oh, that's sweet and so perfect for Uncle Frank."

We both laughed as I continued to be flippant, "Now that's the right way for mountain justice."

I picked up the old double-barrel shotgun Uncle Frank had fired from the corner of the house and hoped Little Pete didn't see me as he was fixing the mailbox.

Uncle Frank was sitting in the chair beside the telephone, and Auntie Bea was sitting on the sofa opposite Uncle Frank in the room. I interrupted their conversation. "Uncle Frank, I'm going to put this down in the basement, and I would like you to take a shower now and put on clean clothing."

Uncle Frank asked, "Why?"

I replied, "Please, Uncle Frank, just do what I ask."

Uncle Frank got up from his chair and grumbled, "Okay, but I'm not dirty."

I said, "You're dirtier than you think."

I knew exactly what I was doing because Uncle Frank had residue all over himself from firing his shotgun. I knew I did as well, but I did not think the authorities would check me because Uncle Frank was the one who had fired the gun.

I scolded Uncle Frank, "Just be thankful that no one was seriously hurt because of your impulsive actions today."

Auntie said, "Frank, just listen to Belinda, and do what she tells you to do."

Uncle Frank walked to his bedroom and I followed him until I reached the basement door. I unlocked the door, took the old shotgun down into the basement, and hid it among all the things that were already packed down there.

When I came back up the stairs, Auntie Bea was standing at the top of them.

Auntie Bea said, "Belinda, we need to talk."

I said, "I know, Auntie Bea, but let me take care of Little Pete first."

She said, "Okay" as she let me walk past her.

I met Little Pete beside the White Beast and asked, "Is it fixed?" as I pointed to the mailbox.

Little Pete replied, "Yes. It looks good again. I finally fixed your auntie's tractor, and I have the receipt for the parts I had to get." He reached in his front pocket of his pants, pulled out the receipt, and handed it to me. Then he continued, "That damn tractor was hard to fix. It had several problems with it. I had just finished fixing it when I heard a gunshot. What happened?"

I ignored his question, "Well, I'm glad you got it fixed. Let me get you the money I owe you for the parts."

After retrieving my purse and giving him the money, I said, "Thanks, Little Pete, for fixing that. I guess I'll see you in the morning, but I would like to meet up with you at Mom and Big Pete's house first thing. Jay and I packed some more today. We even moved a few things up here but could not get it all in the truck. So we are going to have to pack and move more tomorrow. I only have Jay here for a couple more days."

Little Pete said, "Okay. But what—"

He stopped because Auntie Bea walked into the room.

I thought, *Thank God,* because I was not going to answer Little Pete regarding the gunshot he heard.

Little Pete just simply said, "Well, I guess I'll be leaving now," Little Pete said.

I said, "Okay, I'll see you at Mom and Big Pete's house tomorrow morning."

Auntie Bea at this time was standing in the middle of the Florida room beside me. We both watched out the sliding glass door as Little Pete got into his van and left.

As Little Pete was leaving, Jay returned from Auntie Bea's house.

I asked, "Jay, it's getting dark; do you think we can quickly fix the grass a little from where Big Pete tore it up?"

Jay answered, "Yes, let's do that now."

We went outside and started putting the grass back in place the best we could. We got most of it fixed, and it did look better. Jay and I walked into the Florida room of the Daisy house and I said, "I better get supper started."

Auntie Bea said, "Belinda, I want to talk about everything."

I said, "I know, Auntie Bea, but I need to get us fed. Can we all talk while I'm cooking?"

Auntie Bea answered, "I guess so."

I found some cube steaks in Uncle Frank's big freezer and decided that was what I would cook that night. Jay found some biscuit mix, and we decided we would make some biscuits to dip in the gravy. I found several cans of peas and thought that would be good to go with it. Jay and I started cooking.

Uncle Frank walked into the kitchen and sarcastically asked, "Do I smell better?"

Auntie Bea laughed and said, "Yes, Frank, you smell better."

Auntie Bea saw Uncle Frank's almost empty bottle of whiskey on the counter as I was defrosting the cube steaks in the microwave.

She angrily accused Uncle Frank, "You've been drinking again, Frank. I'm dumping this crap down the drain." As she was speaking, she grabbed the bottle and carried it to the sink. Jay and I watched her pour what little bit was left down the drain.

Uncle Frank became angry and said, "Sister Bea, you do not have the right to do that!"

Auntie Bea said, "Oh, yes I do. I'm your sister and you have a problem. I'm sure that we are all in this mess with Big Pete because of you and this bottle. I also told Belinda to dump this crap down the drain, and apparently she did not obey me again. So, Belinda, I'm holding you partly to blame for this as well."

Uncle Frank looked at me as if I was supposed to do something about her actions. I just turned around and started opening the cans of peas. I heard Uncle Frank let out a loud sigh as he walked into the dining room, and I heard him say—loud enough so we could all hear him—"Women."

Auntie Bea followed him into the dining room. Jay and I grabbed the dishes and followed to make sure there was still peace between them, and we set the table. Auntie Bea was pestering Uncle Frank with questions about what had happened while Jay and I were setting the table. We did not say a word; instead, we tried to hear every word Uncle Frank and Auntie Bea said to each other. Jay and I finished making dinner, and I made some iced tea for us to all drink. Jay and I brought the dinner in and I poured the iced tea for everyone; then the doorbell rang. We all looked at each other with wide eyes.

I took charge and said, "I'll get it. Just be yourselves and start eating dinner as if nothing has happened."

I was scared to death. I knew we all were thinking the same thing: "It's the sheriffs coming to arrest us all. God only knows what charming lies Big Pete said to them."

As I walked toward the door, I realized the side of my face was hurting, and I felt as if my one eye was swollen. I realized Big Pete had hit me several times in the chest and in the face during our altercation. I knew I had not taken a shower and when I looked down at my body, I saw that my clothes were dirty. Mom had hung one of my mirrors on the hallway wall, and I decided I had better take a look at my face before I answered the door. I had blood spots from where the gravel hit me in the face and neck. My one eye was almost swollen shut, and my cheek was swollen and bruised. My arms had small bruises up and down them, exposed by my t-shirt. I saw Uncle Frank's old sweater sitting in the living room, I grabbed it and threw it on as quickly as I could. I saw a can of Lysol spray with lemon sent where the housekeeper had left it on the corner of the coffee table. I picked it up and sprayed it on myself.

Jay had already washed the blood off his face, and I guess no one said anything to me about my battered face because they thought I knew about it already. No wonder Auntie Bea was so adamant about talking with me, but no one said a word about my face. I was scared to death. I swallowed my fears and opened the front door. I don't think the front door had been used in years. Of course, I had a hard time opening it. The lock to the screen door must have been rusted in the lock position because I could not open it.

I asked through the screen door that had storm windows in it, "Officers, could you go to the sliding glass door to the side of the house? This door hasn't been used in years; the lock is stuck and I can't open it."

I pointed to the side of the house where the Florida room was located. I saw both deputy sheriffs nod their heads, and the one deputy sheriff said, "Yes, ma'am."

I let out a sigh and closed and locked the front door. I quickly walked through the living room, then the dining room. As I was looking at everyone seated at the dining room table, they all looked at me with their eyes wide. Nothing was said. I walked through the kitchen and very quickly turned the kitchen water on. I cupped my hands, filled them with water, and threw it on my face. Using my fingers, I tried to wipe some of the blood away. I grabbed the kitchen towel that was bunched on the counter and wiped my face dry. I walked very quickly through the kitchen and into the Florida room and saw the two deputy sheriffs standing at the sliding glass door. I prayed that there wasn't enough light coming into the screen door for them to have seen the blood on my face, as well as the swelling.

I slid the door opened and said, "I'm sorry about the front door, gentleman, but we haven't used that door in years. Please come in."

As the two deputy sheriffs were walking through the threshold into the Florida room, the older deputy sheriff introduced himself as well as his partner. Deputy Franklin continued, "Oh, that's okay, ma'am. We completely understand."

I said, "Well, my family and I just sat down for dinner. I think I have enough for the two of you. Would you care to join us? I can set the table for two more." I gestured with my hand toward the door through the kitchen; they both walked into the kitchen and stopped. I said, "Oh, just go through that opening." I pointed to it. It was located on the other side of the kitchen and the two deputy sheriffs walked through it and into the dining room.

Deputy Sampson said, "Oh, no thank you, we have already eaten, and we are still on duty."

They stood there observing their surroundings and my great-uncle, my great-aunt, and Jay.

Everyone gave their greetings to the deputy sheriffs, and Deputy Franklin and Sampson returned them politely.

We all talked about the weather, and it appeared that they were satisfied because I noticed them looking all around the room, and Deputy Franklin poked his head into the living room. When I saw him look into the living room, I asked if they would like a tour of the house.

Deputy Sampson said, "Yes, I would like that very much, ma'am." At this point, they still did not ask my name. I knew they were looking for my great-uncle's shotgun, but at this point, they were not sure if Big Pete exaggerated his story or not. I know they knew I was beaten, but did not ask anything about. I thought they were checking out the situation first.

I took Deputy Franklin into the living room, let him look all around and then I guided him down the hallway and showed him the bedrooms. I even opened up all the doors to the closets so he could look in them. I allowed him to take a few minutes to look inside the bathrooms as well. I chatted to him as he was doing this, giving the history of Miss Daisy's house and how the name came about.

I took the keys from my pocket and unlocked the basement door before he had a chance to ask about the locked door in the hallway. I proceeded to tell him about why we kept the door locked but left out the part about my uncle being a drunk. I figured I had no other choice but to twist the truth to my advantage like everyone else seemed to do. I had vowed to myself when I was younger that I would never do that, but I was forced to break my own vow because of my family and their evil ways. I even had to break this vow over the course of my military career numerous times for my country and the Army.

I still considered this a lie, but I knew our own justice system considered it a truth. This is one reason I do not like the people in our justice system; our laws were not meant to be like this. It should be about telling the whole truth and nothing but the truth. That is why you swear to that exact statement, but attorneys and judges take just part truths and twist it to their advantage. To me, that is still a lie, but law officers interpret the law as they wish. I knew that I would not be in trouble for lying to the law enforcer.

I proceeded to tell him the basement was unfinished and my husband and I had our possessions stored down there, but he still wanted to look, so I took him down the stairs toward the basement. He just stood on the stairs and bent down so he could see. He saw that it was packed to the ceiling with very little space to walk.

Deputy Franklin said, "Oh, I don't need to see any more. Boy, you were not kidding about it being packed to the ceiling with your stuff."

I forced a chuckle out and said, "I know. I wasn't kidding."

We went back upstairs and Deputy Franklin looked at Deputy Sampson, who was chatting with my family. He said, "Well, everything looks okay. I guess we better go."

Deputy Franklin asked me, "Ma'am, can we speak to you outside so your family can finish eating?"

I formally answered, "Yes, sir."

As we were walking through the house, I realized I would have to use my specialized training in psychological warfare to get us out of this trouble my great-uncle had caused. It was the only way I could avoid breaking any laws or more of my own vows. Nonetheless, I knew to play the game, I would have to break my own vows again somewhat.

I loathed and despised Big Pete even more for putting me in this situation. I was going to have to use my military training to do this, but then I thought, *Who better to get us out of this mess than a daughter from a family of liars and thieves?* I knew exactly what they were planning to do: take one of us outside and politely interrogate each one of us, one at a time, so the others would not know what the other said. They would end up arresting all of us or the most guilty, whichever it was. They had decided to start out with me first because they sensed I was the leader of the pack. Typical psychological games used to get information. I knew this little game all too well. My mission was to outwit these two and beat them at their own game. They had no clue that I just happened to be very well trained. I would prevent them from having the opportunity to question each one of us.

As we were walking through the Florida room, I grabbed my purse and stopped for a few seconds to grab my wallet out of it. I proceeded out the sliding glass door behind the two deputy sheriffs. They were already outside. By this time, I had already taken out my military ID and could smell the lemon smell of the Lysol spray I had sprayed on myself earlier and just chuckled.

Deputy Franklin started to speak, "Ma'am—"

I cut him off and said, "—Sirs, before you begin, I am requesting that you verify who I am and examine my identifications. Here is my military ID with my social security number on it. My name is Belinda Denise Star; my maiden name is Bishop. I am a highly decorated veteran of the United States Army. The people inside are my great-uncle and my godfather, Frank Gibbs. He is also a highly decorated veteran. He fought in World War II and the Korean War. My brother is Jay King, a recent graduate of Texas University. My great-aunt, who is also my godmother, is Bea Mills, a widow of a fine, decent man; and she is a fine and great lady herself . . . usually." I gave them a wink as I said that, and grinned.

I continued, "I stand before you with only my life's reputation of being a soldier, and I was a damn fine one at that. I believe in following the rules, and I will cooperate with you to the best of my abilities. My husband is Thomas G. Star and is still active duty in the U.S. Army, currently stationed in Germany. He has just returned from a mission in Bosnia. After you have checked me out, I request that you tell me why you are here. I know what the two of you were doing and I welcomed you into the house even though you did not state your purpose. I voluntarily helped you search my great-uncle's home for whatever it is you were looking for. I know this procedure requires a search warrant, but I had no problem allowing you to do so. All pleasantries aside, you will now need to tell me what your intent is. I know that you know that there is something amiss because of the condition of my face. I ask that you show me the same respect and honesty that I have shown you from this moment forward. But again, all that I request is you check me out before we begin and let my family eat in peace and for them to have a pleasant evening."

They both looked at me, dumbfounded. Deputy Sampson, who was the younger one of the two, just stood looking at me with my ID. His arm was still extended toward me, and my ID was clenched in his hand. At first, I thought they were frozen.

After a few seconds, Deputy Franklin said, "Well, go and check her out." The younger deputy submissively obeyed and went to their car to call my information in and check me out.

Deputy Franklin stayed behind. He said, "Well, Ms. Star, you have been more honest than most people. I thank you for allowing us to check out your great-uncle's residency without any questions."

As he was speaking to me, I could hear their police radio squawking to the other officer. I was very surprised they didn't use the radio receivers that were located on the side of their chests. Deputy Franklin continued, "Well, per your first request we have no problem obliging you. I will have to wait to ask you questions until we know who you are."

I simply replied, "Fair enough. I have no problem with that."

We both stood there in silence. To me it seemed like an eternity, but I believe it was only five minutes. Deputy Sampson walked back toward us and whispered something in the other deputy's ear. I wasn't worried because I had a very clean record.

Deputy Franklin said, "Well then, Ms. Star, it's seems you are who you say you are."

I just looked at him and shrugged my shoulders indifferently.

He continued, "I am sure you are aware from the condition of your own face that Mr. King called us and reported that Mr. Gibbs tried to kill him earlier today. He filed charges against Mr. Gibbs and we are here to investigate the allegations to see if an arrest warrant is needed. We plan to locate the firearm that was allegedly used. We were not aware of your involvement until we saw the condition of your face. I would request that you tell me the truth of the situation. Did Mr. Gibbs point a shotgun toward Mr. King and fire it?"

I guffawed before I answered, "No, sir. He did not. That is the first lie Pete King told you. Next."

Deputy Franklin asked, "Okay, Ms. Star. How did you get that black eye and the bruises on your face?"

I arrogantly answered, "That's easy. Pete King did it when Jay and I were trying to stop him from tearing up the lawn with his van. He was driving like a wild drunken man. Oh, I'm sorry, I can't prove that he was drunk—may I use the word allegedly?"

Jay had come outside and must have heard me and also stated to the deputy sheriffs, "Yes, that's true."

This was a perfect opportunity for me to stop them from interrogating each one of us at a time. I politely, and in a heavy country twang, said, "Jay, you need to go back inside. These two deputy sheriffs want to question us one at a time so they can get different stories, or at least they hope to get different stories, so that they can arrest one or all of us. I do not know which." I turned back and faced the two deputy sheriffs and asked with no accent, "Which one is it, sirs?"

They were both looking at me dumbfounded, so to ease their confusion, I said with a high pitched twang, "Oh, that's not what you're doing instead of arresting Big Pete for beating me? Oh, I forgot. I'm not filing charges against him because it would just cause more troubles for my momma and for us. Besides, sirs, what is the point in having him arrested; he is going to jail soon for stealing from his clients."

The two deputy sheriffs were still looking at me confused and not saying a word. So, I continued with my country accent, "Oh, you didn't know. I think it is eighteen counts of somethin'. My poor old mother is already sittin' in a jail cell because of what he did and is facin' the same charges he is. In fact, she was noble about it. She stopped lyin', unlike him, and started tellin' the truth, but my momma didn't steal from his clients. She was beaten into submission by her husband to help cover up the theft when she discovered it three years ago. In fact, sirs, I'm here from Europe to try and clean up the aftermath by tryin' to make restitution so some of the victims are made whole again."

I went back into my normal voice without the slang and in a deadly serious voice said, "I guess you did not do your homework. I think it's time for you to leave. I am speaking for my family as well as for myself when I say thank you for your concerns, but there will be no arrests this night because the bad guy is still fighting the charges. But he will be in jail one day. I am truly sorry that your time has been so wasted, and I hope that next time when someone files such a deadly charge, you will investigate the person who makes those allegations first before checking out the accused."

In my opinion, Deputy Franklin was very angry with me, but he was controlling his anger somewhat. In an authoritative voice, he said, "Ms. Star, why didn't you tell us about Mr. King firsthand? It has been you who has wasted our time."

I said solemnly, "No, sir, I did not waste your time; you wasted your own time by not checking out the alleged victim. I do not believe you even went to see him. If you had seen him, you would have immediately noticed that he was drunk, and if you ran his social security number as you did mine, you would have found him to be under indictment, but you did not. I gave you the chance to see what my great-uncle looks like.

I know from personal experience that Big Pete is a very good liar, and I didn't know what you were going to do to us. We feared for our very lives because ever since I've been here, I have been totally disrespected by my own brethren who wear a uniform. Admit it, sir, you wanted to make an arrest tonight, and you didn't care if it was right or wrong. You have lost your way. Both of you have. If this isn't so, why are you angry with me? I'm the one with the battered face, not Big Pete. I'm the one who will judge and decide who is guilty or innocent in my family, not you. I will be the one who lays punishment down, not you."

Deputy Franklin became extremely angry with me then. He replied in a loud, angry voice that was on the verge of a yell, "Ms. Star, no, it is not your place to decide who is guilty or not and who will be punished and how. That is my place, not yours."

I said, "Oh, yes it is, because that is another reason that I was asked to come home. This is family business, and I'm quite cable of policing my own family. If I need help or feel that someone needs to be charged for any crime, I will be the first to contact you. It will then be your job to take it from there. I am dealing with an older generation than our generation. You still have no clue what really happened here today, sir, and you never will, but I know what happened. If anyone should be arrested, it's Big Pete. I don't think it takes a rocket scientist to figure that out, but I have controlled that as well because you cannot arrest him if I don't press charges. Please, sir, just let it go. I respect you and the uniform that you are wearing. I respect our laws, and I obey them. I have even laid my life down for our laws, but you and I are just arguing over politics. I swear to you, sir, that no laws were broken here today. You are entitled to your views, and I am entitled to mine. Would you arrest a parent for disciplining their children? This is no different. I am not physically harming anyone and have no intentions of doing so, but I will protect myself and my family from those that will cause us harm."

I have no idea why Deputy Franklin stopped arguing with me, but in a softer tone he said, "I'm sorry, Ms. Star. I guess we will be leaving. Are you sure you do not want to press charges against Mr. King?"

I sadly replied, "See, that's all you want is an arrest. Believe me if I thought it would make a difference for my family, I would, but it will not. He will get out of jail tomorrow and come back to seek revenge on my family and me. I can fight my own wars, in my own way, without your involvement. I can even fight them without bloodshed. Please, officers, just let this one go."

Deputy Franklin said, "Okay, but now I want that creep for lying to us."

I did not make another comment. Jay and I just turned around and walked inside.

I felt relieved it was over. I sat down at the dining room table, and Jay did also.

Auntie Bea asked impatiently, "Well, what happened?"

I answered, "I think it's over. Big Pete may get a ticket for giving a false report or something like that, if anything. Who knows what they will do. I'm putting my foot down with the three of you. Uncle Frank, don't you ever pull out a weapon when you are drunk again, or for that matter, even if you are sober. What you did was totally uncalled for. Auntie Bea, what did you think you were going to accomplish with Uncle Herndon's old pistol? Do not talk about this ever again in front of Little Pete or tell anyone else outside this group what happened. Jay, you should be ashamed of yourself for kicking your father like that. You know better than that.

"Uncle Frank, there is no such thing as 'mountain justice.' The official term is vigilantes, and that is against the laws of our country. Our tax money pays people to uphold the law. These people have to go through special training. Whether we agree with them or not, their job is to protect us. Granted, justice does not happen all the time, but our country operates this way. If you don't like the way our justice system is run, then complain to your congressman—that's what they are there for. Our country is based on check and balances, and yes, sometimes one voice can make a difference; that is one reason our country is so great.

"Uncle Frank, I can't believe you were yelling at me to kill someone. There is a big difference between killing our country's enemy on a battlefield and killing someone in our own front yard. I think you were having some type of flashback. I know you have been in bloodier wars than I have, but I have the same memories as you do, and I do not go around acting like a barbarian. What you did today could have cost you your freedom.

"I could have been arrested and sent to jail because I tried to protect you. Jay, you could have gone to jail for beating your father the way you did. Auntie Bea, you can barely hold that pistol up, and if you had fired it, you could have hurt or killed any one of us, and you could be in jail. We were just damn lucky tonight that those deputy sheriffs believed me when I said there were no real crimes committed. I spoke my opinion, which does not make it fact. I believe that if the deputies knew what actually happened, we would all have been arrested. Uncle Frank, Mom is in jail for a reason. It may not be the right reason, but she did make bad choices and now she must pay for them. Big Pete will eventually have to pay for his crimes as well. Auntie Bea, I'm tired of you trying to blame everyone else for the choices you have made. You are responsible, no one else. Arguing with me isn't going to change a damn thing that you have done. Sitting on your butt chain smoking isn't going to make it go away. You need to get up and stand on your own two feet, no matter what your age is, and take responsibility for your own mistakes. Not only do you need to take responsibility for your mistakes, you need to do something to correct your mistakes. You always have your hand out for money. I can't help you, Auntie Bea, if you don't help yourself."

Auntie Bea said, "Belinda, I understand and I'm trying, but I don't want my name in the paper regarding my property taxes. Your momma did one of those checks, and it needs to be picked up with cash that I don't have."

I said, "Okay, Auntie Bea, how much is it?"

Auntie Bea told me the amount, and I told her that I would pick it up first thing in the morning.

Uncle Frank said, "You're right, Belinda, I acted like an idiot. I will never do that again. I'm tired and headed off to bed."

We all said our goodnights to him.

Auntie Bea said, "I'm tired too. Jay, drive me back to my house."

I gave Auntie Bea a kiss on the cheek and told her I loved her.

Jay helped her out of the house and took her back to her place. I cleaned up the mess in the kitchen, took a shower, and went straight to bed. I left a note on the kitchen table for Jay to lock up the house for the night.

CHAPTER XLI

My first waking thought was, *Another day of this mess.* I sat on the edge of the bed and tried to shake the sleep away. My head hurt, and I could barely see out of my right eye. I had not felt that way since my last special ops mission. I had gotten into plenty of scrapes because I was an exception to the rule. I had found myself somewhere a woman was not supposed to be, but I was a "she wolf," an extraordinary woman, who could do things no mortal man could do. I giggled to myself at the thought.

My mind told me I should be thankful that my current situation was nothing like that, but my body was telling me it was just as bad. At least during those deadly missions, I had friends who had my back and would do anything to prevent me from being beaten like I had the day before by my mother's nasty husband. During military combat, all you have to do is point the weapon and fire. The realization hit me that I could have been killed the day before. I truly could relate to my uncle's emotions and behavior the day before, but I knew better than to act on those feelings. I just wished I had my husband there to protect me. I was in the middle of a civilian combat, and the rules were very different.

I looked over at the clock beside my bed and gasped. It was 7:30 a.m.! I was already late for what I planned on accomplishing that day. I quickly got ready and dressed for the day. I looked into the Florida room, and Jay and Uncle Frank were reading the newspaper.

I greeted them. "Good morning. Jay, are you ready to go?"

Both men returned my greeting, and Jay answered, "Yes, let's go."

I asked Uncle Frank, "I found this lock with two keys. Can I use it?"

Uncle Frank answered, "Yes."

I said, "Thank you." Jay had already gone out to start up the pickup truck.

I told Jay that we needed to stop over at Auntie Bea's first because I needed to see what was in the safes.

I tried three times to open the safe. I felt very guilty for wanting to open them. I must not have done a good job of hiding my guilt because Jay finally said, "Belinda, they belong to you now, with all the contents. You know we have to sell what we can. Remember what you said to me, 'rule of thumb to sell as little as possible to save the most.' Here, I will open them."

Jay opened the small one first, the one that I had put my mother's large diamond engagement ring in the first day I was there. Auntie stood over us as she lit her second cigarette. I could tell that the curiosity was killing her. I think Jay knew too because he took his sweet time opening them.

After Jay had opened both of the safes, he moved out of the way and said, "It's your place to look at the contents, not mine."

I sat on the floor and said, "I'll start with the larger one. I haven't opened that one yet."

It was packed full of papers and jewelry. I pulled out the papers first. There were about $500 in saving bonds with Jay's name on them. They had Big Pete's parents listed on them as the buyers. I asked, "Do you want these?"

Jay answered, "Yes that will help with paying my rent and other things."

I handed them to him.

The next thing I looked through was a large brown envelope that had all the divorce papers from all my mother's previous marriages. I closed it back up and laid it to the side. Next was a folder that contained Big Pete's personal papers. I put that to the side as well. There was also a file with my mother's name on it. I found appraisals for numerous pieces of jewelry. I looked through the appraisals and then looked through the envelope that held several pieces of jewelry. I found three pieces of jewelry that matched the appraisal paperwork. Because I knew what they were worth, I removed them. I decided to sell those. I found my birth certificate as well as birth certificates for Christina and Jay. I removed those and asked Jay if he wanted his. He took it as well as the power of attorney papers that he and his father had drawn up that made Big Pete the power of attorney over Jay. Jay took the power of attorney paperwork and ripped it up in front of Auntie Bea and me. I put Christina's birth certificate and everything else back in the safe. I took my birth certificate and the three pieces of jewelry and laid them to the side. I closed the safe and spun the combination wheel around a couple of times. I moved to the smaller safe. I removed my mother's engagement ring and found another ring which had an appraisal.

Auntie Bea was standing directly over me watching my every move with a greedy gleam in her eyes. She frantically asked, "Belinda, your great-grandmother's wedding band is in one of these safes. Can you look for me?"

I looked through the safe and found it in one of the little jewelry storage boxes. I took the ring out and examined it. On the inside of the band, engraved in small, cursive letters was "E to M." I had not seen that ring in years! Several years ago, Mom had given it to me, but I had asked her hold onto it so I wouldn't lose it. I put it on my finger as if it would give me some type of magical power.

Auntie Bea patted my shoulder. It wasn't a gentle pat; it was more like being hit.

She said, "Belinda, give it to me. Let me see it?"

I said, "Okay." I took it off my finger and handed it to her so she could look at it. She looked directly inside it to see the engraving.

Auntie Bea asked, "Are you sure this is it, Belinda? I can't read the engraving."

I answered, "Yes, Auntie, I'm sure. Their initials are engraved in it, but it is my ring. Mom gave it to me years ago."

Jay had no idea what we were talking about.

I demanded, "Auntie Bea, give it back, now! I need to put it back in the safe so it doesn't get lost."

Auntie Bea replied, "No, this was given to Frank, not your mother!"

I demanded again, "Auntie Bea, give it back! Uncle Frank sold it to my grandmother long before I was even born, and she left it to my mother. My mother gave it to me."

Auntie Bea retorted, "That's a lie!"

I defended myself, "No it isn't! Grandma told me herself that she bought it from Uncle Frank. She showed it to me, in front of my mother, when I was a teenager. At that time, she told Momma, in front of me, that she was going to leave it to Momma, but she didn't want Christina to have it. Grandma wanted me to be next in line to receive it."

Auntie Bea said in a whiney voice, "I would like to wear it."

I said, "No, Auntie Bea, you may not!"

She whined, "Belinda, she was my mother too. Not just your grandmother."

I said, "I know that, Auntie Bea, but you have been telling lies since I arrived, and you are not worthy to wear it."

Auntie Bea's eyes grew large as she stated, "I have not been telling lies."

I said, "Yes, you have. Ever since I arrived, you have told me partial truths or twisted the truth to your advantage. That is considered lying. This is my ring, not yours."

Auntie Bea started begging, "Please, Belinda, please let me wear it! She was my mother, not yours. I have nothing else to remember her by. Please, Belinda."

I let out a sigh and said, "Okay, Auntie Bea, but you have to promise me you will not lie anymore, and you must return the ring to me as soon as I ask for it."

Auntie Bea smiled and said, "Of course, Belinda." She had a triumphant grin on her face.

I looked away and felt defeated once more. I closed the safe and put everything I had decided to keep out into the cloth handbag I had.

As Jay and I were driving up the road, I asked him to stop at the storage unit so I could change the lock. Jay stopped at the storage unit, and I changed the lock. Now I knew that those belongings would be safe from thievery.

I asked Jay to stop at the bank, and I withdrew more cash from my account. Next, Jay drove to the county clerk's office. He waited in the car as I went inside and took care of the bounced check for Auntie Bea's property tax. After that, we went to Mom and Big Pete's house where Little Pete was waiting for us. We spent the rest of the day packing and moving things to the Daisy house and the storage unit. While we were packing, the phone rang. The caller ID said Northumberland County Jail. I answered it. Mom wanted to know when we were coming to see her. She needed to talk with us as soon as possible. She said that it was extremely important. I told her that we were just finishing up for the day and we would be there shortly. After I hung up the phone, I told Little Pete it was quitting time and we would see him the same time and same place the next morning. Jay and I climbed into the pickup, which held the last load, and headed toward the jail. Jay asked if he could stop at his bank before we went to see her because it was on the way. He wanted to cash and deposit the savings bonds.

He went into the bank to take care of his business. While he was in the bank, I decided to take a walk to the pawnshop a few blocks away. When I walked in, a portly, older man who had white, thinning hair greeted me. He was friendly in his greeting, but as soon as he saw the jewelry I had, the familiar gleam of greed appeared in his eyes. I had to haggle with the man, but God was with me that day. I received close to half of the value for the jewelry. I had mixed feelings as I pawned my mother's engagement ring. I felt sad that I had to get rid of her engagement ring, but then again, it was the one from Big Pete. The only reason I was even in the pawnshop to begin with was to pay the debt that she had created with him. It was kind of fitting that their engagement ring be lost in the transaction. Ironically, I felt good about doing it. I even felt good about driving her car because she had never let me drive it before. It was as if I was punishing her for the cruelties she had committed toward me throughout my life. After all, I'm only human.

Jay was finished with his business by the time I arrived back at the truck. Our next stop was the jail. We arrived and went through the procedures. During our visit with Mom, she told me about a booth she was renting in a large shop. She told me I needed to take care of it, to go check the inventory, to see how much was left, and to restock it. She also instructed me to have the booth changed into my name. She told me that she had spoken with my attorney again, and she had instructed the attorney to make changes to her will and to her power of attorney.

I told her that I wanted to sell the wine collection that Thomas and I had purchased from her, but I did not know at that point whether I would be able to do so. She told me that if no one could or would buy it locally, I should call my cousin Mary. She said to make sure that I give her something nice for her troubles. She said that Mary would do nothing for me unless she received something for it. She spoke with Jay for a few minutes as well. We said our goodbyes and drove back to my shop. To no surprise, Big Pete was waiting for us, and he kept questioning Jay and me regarding what had happened the previous evening. I think he was trying to find out if the authorities had shown up. Jay and I acted as if nothing happened, and we told him nothing. We informed him that we were still moving stuff, and we were quitting for the day.

Big Pete said, "No problem. I will handle the shop until closing time."

Jay said, "Dad, I'm going to help Belinda unload the truck and drop her off. I'll be back before closing time. I would like to grab a bite to eat with you."

Big Pete smiled and said, "That's a great idea, son. I will see you later."

He did not say another word about the altercation of the day before. We drove back to the Daisy house, unloaded the boxes from the pickup truck, and carried them into the basement. The basement was now too full. I needed to get rid of something. I looked at my watch; it was around 2:30 p.m. I decided my next order of business would be to call some used office furniture and supply places to see if they would be interested in purchasing some or all of the office equipment in the basement. I went upstairs and looked in the phonebook. I quickly discovered that there was only one store in the area that bought and sold used office supplies. I called and was connected with the store's buyer. I briefly told her what I had, and she said she would be over within the hour to look at what I had and make an offer.

When she arrived, we introduced ourselves and I immediately took her down in the basement and showed her what I had for sale. She liked what I had and made an offer. As I expected, the offer was only a small fraction of what it was worth, but I felt I had no other choice and accepted it. She said she could have her moving people over the following morning with a check in hand. I told her that would be fine.

Next, I called Thomas. He excitedly told me that he had gotten leave and had booked a flight to Virginia for the last week of February. He gave me his flight information, and I told him I would be at the airport to pick him up. I did not tell him what had happened the previous day. I figured I would tell him when I saw him. Thomas instructed me to contact his family, briefly explain what was going on, and tell them that he would fill them in with all the details after he arrived. I told him that I could not wait to see him and that I loved him. He said that he loved me too, and we hung up.

Because I already had the phone book out, I decided to start calling the local wine shops to see if they were interested in purchasing the wine collection. I called several of them, and they all told me pretty much the same thing. I could only sell my collection to another private wine collector. Local wine stores are regulated by very strict laws and cannot make purchases from private collectors, only directly from wineries.

I completely understood and knew I was going to have to get another relative involved. It was not something I looked forward to doing.

I decided that before I dealt with Mary, I would call Thomas's family first. I picked up the phone and called Thomas's mother. I told her that Thomas was coming home on leave and gave her the date of when he would arrive. I told her a little bit of what was going on and asked her if she would be willing to take care of my mother's six dogs because she owned a kennel.

She said she might be able to but didn't know if she could afford their upkeep. I told her that Thomas and I could pay for it. She asked if I asked Thomas about this and I said no, but I would when he arrived. She said she supported Thomas and me and was very upset over my family stealing from hers because she considered me her family. When someone steals from her daughter-in-law, they are stealing from her son; therefore, they are still stealing from her family.

I called Thomas's father. I told him a little bit about what was going on, and he told me that Thomas's brothers would be on call and ready to help me with moving or anything else I needed. He told me that it was horrible that my family had stolen from his, and he made sure I knew he was there for me. He said if there was anything that he could do, just to call. He said he was looking forward to seeing his son again, no matter what the circumstances.

I called each of Thomas's three brothers and told them what I had told their parents. They were very upset and angry that my family had done this to theirs; I too was part of their family. Their anger was not directed toward me, just the rest of the family, including my father, sister, and everyone else that should be here at least to support me and help make restitution for the fraud committed in our names. As I hung up the phone, Uncle Frank walked into the Florida room.

He had been watching TV in the living room. He told me he was hungry. I looked at the clock on the phone and could not believe it was already 7:30 p.m. I told him I would go up the road and get some hamburgers. He said that would be nice. He gave me the keys to his car. I drove into town to the local fast food burger joint. I ordered three hamburger meals. On the way back to the Daisy house, I stopped in to check on Auntie Bea and give her a meal. I told her that I had picked up the check, but I was keeping it. I said good night and told her I would see her the next day.

I parked the car in front of the Daisy house, and Jay pulled up behind me in the pickup truck. He told me his father had gotten drunk again. I knew I was going to have to get Big Pete out of my shop soon. He kept on stealing the money from the sales from the shop. At this rate, I was never going to pay off the debt. I still wished my sister had come. I served Uncle Frank his food, and I ate also. After Uncle Frank was finished eating, he went to bed. I decided it was time for me to call Mary.

I called her and briefly told her some of what was going on. She said her boss was a wine collector and asked how much I wanted for it. I figured the offer I gave her was a good one because I knew the current value was much greater than what I was asking. I knew this because while I was calling local wine stores, I had asked some of them the value of the various wines in the collection. After hearing what was going on and that my mother was incarcerated, Mary said she was making flight arrangements for the next weekend. She would call me the next day with details and would be able to let me know then if her boss was interested in any or all of the collection.

She told me she was sorry for all the years of snubbing me, and told me that she had always loved me. She had acted that way because she was jealous of me. I asked why, and she said it was because I taken control of my life. I had put myself through college. I was independent. She said that Christina, the rest of the cousins, and she had to kiss my mother's hand, her husband's hand, and all the other older relatives' butts to get something from them.

I just bit my tongue. I told her that I hoped to see her soon, and I would appreciate any help that she was able to give. I told her that my mother wanted me to give her something nice for helping out, but we would talk about that another time.

Jay had been sitting next to me listening to the conversation. He told me that he wanted to talk with her, so I passed the telephone to him. To this day, I think she only really helped me because my brother spoke with her. Before that, I think she was just giving me hot air.

I decided to look at some of the bills Big Pete had given to me earlier that day. The first item I opened was a bill from my mother's attorney. As I feared, the bloodsucker had not changed the amount. I would have to call him to see if he would reduce it. In fact, I would have to call him first thing the following morning.

CHAPTER XLII

The next day the office furniture people came and took everything that I had sold to them. As promised, they had the check when they arrived. I called my mother's attorney and left a message for him to call me when he had a chance. The rest of the day was spent packing and moving things from Mom and Pete's house to the Daisy house. Jay and I went to visit Mom again at jail. Friday was pretty much the same thing. Saturday morning I drove Jay to the airport. We hugged each other and said our goodbyes. Little did I know then that I would never speak to or see my brother again. He would be lost to me forever.

After dropping Jay off, I decided to take more inventory to the shop to restock it. I went back to the Daisy house and loaded the pickup truck. I drove to the shop, and it was packed. I carried everything in and took over so Big Pete would not steal the proceeds for the day. In a single day, I sold half of what I had brought in. I guess Big Pete was not happy that I took over because he left for the day. I was unable to go visit Mom, but she called me while I was at the shop. I stopped at the grocery store on my way back to the Daisy house. We were low on almost everything.

Sunday was a repeat of Saturday. I packed up the truck with inventory and restocked the shop again. It was another great business day. My shop was packed with customers all day. After closing for the day, I did my accounting. I could not believe I had so many dealers buying from me. It was flattering, but the sales transactions were more complicated than those with regular customers. They needed to have their business ID written on the receipt because they did not pay sales taxes. I also required that they show their business ID number before I wrote it on the receipt. I also wrote their business name and address on the receipt because I did not want to have trouble with the taxman. Ninety-nine percent of the dealers were from either Washington, D.C., other counties, and other states. I decided my prices must be very good if they could buy from me and resell the items with enough of a markup to make a profit. Of course, everything was twenty percent off. I really hoped I had enough stuff to sell so that I could pay off the debts owed.

I still had a lot of inventory in the shop, but I needed to re-stock with at least three more truckloads. I knew I was going to have to do it, but I didn't want Big Pete stealing the proceeds. I made a game plan. I would restock on Friday afternoons and hopefully sell most of it by closing time on Sunday. I could do that until I paid off everything and sold most of my entire inventory. I still had a lot of inventory left to bring into the shop. I thought, *I just maybe able to do this*. I was unable to visit Mom that day, but again, she called me at the shop.

I got back to the Daisy house late. I was glad to see an empty TV dinner in the trash. That meant my great-uncle had eaten earlier. He looked exhausted.

I asked, "What's wrong, Uncle Frank?"

Uncle Frank answered irritably, "I'm pooped; that's what is wrong, Belinda Denise! I couldn't even get up to go to the bathroom because the telephone has been ringing off the hook all day. I have a ton of messages for you." He handed me a note pad page that was filled with names and messages.

I said, "Good grief," as I looked at it.

Uncle Frank said, "I've been talking on the phone all day. My ear and mouth hurt."

I just giggled at him. He was complaining, but I knew he enjoyed every minute of it. The first five phone calls were Thomas's parents and brothers. I couldn't believe it when I saw that my sister's name was on the list. Also, Mary had called. Big Pete had called three times. Of course, Mom had called. The auctioneer called—on a Sunday? My older cousin Ed Gibbs and his brother called. The name I did not recognize was Bill Bank, attorney-at-law. Who was he? That nasty Rick Cart and his brother had called. I knew these people were mooches who called themselves friends of Mom and Big Pete's. Thomas called, and of course, Auntie Bea instructed Uncle Frank to have me call her as soon as I walked in the door.

Uncle Frank said, "You better call your auntie first. I'm going to bed. I'm pooped. Oh, and Big Pete told me he was sorry for what happened."

I asked with a bit of anger, "Uncle Frank, did you tell him what had happened with the deputy sheriffs?"

Uncle Frank timidly answered, "Well, uh, not really."

I retorted, "Damn it, Uncle Frank."

I picked up the phone and called Auntie Bea. She told me that she couldn't continue accepting these collect charges from Gary, her son. She asked me if I was going to pay for her telephone bill. It was two hundred dollars! I told her I would not; it was her responsibility. She started yelling at me because my mother had paid for it all the time. I told her that she could pay for her own bills. I told her that her next bill would have charges from calls that I had made, and I would pay for them. I had not opened Uncle Frank's telephone bill yet. After speaking with Auntie Bea, I opened Uncle Frank's telephone bill and none of my phone calls were on that one either. I realized that I would have to pay for the next bills because of my phone calls. I had no problem with that at all; they should not have to pay for my phone calls, and I should not have to pay for theirs.

I called Mary next. She told me that her boss was interested in the entire collection, and she asked if I had an itemized inventory of the entire collection. I told her that I only had the list that Mom had, and I knew Big Pete sold a lot of bottles on it. I told her that I would do a physical inventory first thing in the morning and fax it to her. This was just the wine that Thomas and I had bought a year ago from Mom. They had continued selling from the collection to other people, but that was okay since they needed the money. I told her that Mom had it professionally packed and the wine had been stored in the Daisy house basement, which was a perfect condition for the wine. She told me that sounded good, and she knew my mother was an expert on storing wine. I knew my sister was about two hours behind me in time and decided to call her next.

Christina told me that she had called Big Pete because we had gotten into an argument, and she had spoken with Uncle Frank earlier that day. She was concerned because I had not called her because of our argument. She said she believed Big Pete when he told her our mother was behind the entire thing, and I had to realize that he wasn't the bad guy. He was also victimized by our mother and I needed to help him. She talked for almost twenty minutes, and I listened to her as she regurgitated all of Big Pete's lies. She believed every one of them. She spoke as if she had no problem with what he was doing. She continued to tell me she had spoken with Uncle Frank, and he told her that Mom had stolen his life insurance money and had been taking all of his money because she had control over his checkbook. She also told me that she had spoken with Auntie Bea as well, and she blamed both Mom and Big Pete for stealing Auntie Bea's land and stripping her of her million-dollar trust fund from when her husband died.

After twenty minutes of listening to my sister spew lies, I could not take it anymore. When she told me about Auntie Bea's trust fund, I burst into laughter.

I solemnly said, "You stupid little shit. If you had come home like you said you would, we would not be having this conversation at all. Everything that you have been told today by Uncle Frank, Auntie Bea, and Big Pete is a lie, and I can prove it. I don't really give a shit about what you think you know because it's all a lie. You know Uncle Frank is a pathological liar, and you know Auntie has never had two pennies to rub together. The only thing she had was the land Uncle Herndon left her, and that is not even worth a million dollars. Auntie would not have been able to afford the farm if it wasn't for Big Pete and our mother. Granted, Auntie Bea, Big Pete, and our mother are all to blame regarding the Mills farm. Mom is a crook, but so is Big Pete. Our mother stole nothing from Auntie Bea, Uncle Frank, or Big Pete. If anything, Big Pete stole from them. So, Christina, if you feel this way, and you believe this, go right ahead, but don't you ever call me here again. I will give you the same respect you gave me the other night. I'm hanging up. Goodbye."

I slammed down the phone. I was determined that it would be a long time before I spoke with my sister again. I loved her, but she was making life hard for me by talking to everyone else involved in this mess. Believing people she knew to be liars was ridiculous. What some people will do for self-importance! Especially a coward like my sister. She truly didn't have a lick of common sense. All she had to do was come to help, and she would have seen the lies for what they were. Jay saw it and lived it for several days. He was not even my blood relative. I know everyone has the right to believe what he or she wants, but I also have the right to surround myself with people who support me, instead of people who try to destroy what I am doing.

I gave myself a few minutes to calm down. I went to the kitchen, poured myself a glass of cola, and went back to the Florida room. I picked up the phone again and called Ed Gibbs. Ed Gibbs was my mother's cousin. His father was my grandmother's older brother, but Ed and my mother were very close in age. He and my mother grew up together. During my mother's youth, the family was very close. My generation was the complete opposite; we were all distant from each other. Ed Gibbs was another person in our family who pretended to be something that he was not. He has been mooching off my mother and Big Pete for decades. I had only seen him three or four times in my life before my mother married Big Pete. I never cared for him because he was such a fake. There was nothing honest, real, or genuine about him.

Now his brother, on the other hand, I liked very much. He was just a few years younger than my mother was. I always thought he was a down-to-earth person and he always seemed to tell the truth. When Ed answered his phone, I asked him what was up. He immediately started in on me about my mother and all that was going on. It was Big Pete's garbage spewing from Ed's mouth. After Ed finished, I asked him where he had gotten all his information, and he told me that he had spoken with Big Pete the night before.

I sarcastically said, "Oh really."

Ed answered, "Yes, and I believe him."

I asked as I continued being sarcastic, "Did you give the same courtesy to my mother and speak with her? Or, better yet, did you go visit her?"

He answered with irritation laced, "No, because I believe Big Pete."

I became livid and I simply blasted him out, "Ed, my mother is your blood, not Big Pete! You know my mother much better than you ever knew Big Pete. Did you ever think for just a moment that Big Pete is lying?"

I continued telling him what was really going on and what I was doing. I told him Big Pete didn't like what I was doing, and I was discovering the truth. I told him Big Pete owned nothing because he had given everything to me. I explained that I was trying to make restitution to as many of the victims as I could, but the bastard was fighting me every step of the way. I told him what Big Pete had done to his own son. I told Ed that I knew about my mother beating that he had witnessed and did nothing about, and I called him a yellow-bellied fool.

Ed interrupted me so he could accuse, "Your mother told you a lie about the beating. It never happened."

I replied, "My mother was not the one who told me."

Ed finally said he didn't know what the truth was or wasn't, and he wasn't going to get involved. I told Ed he was a sorry piece of shit. I reminded him that my mother, my auntie, and Uncle Frank are his blood and that he should be here helping me clean up the mess and supporting us, not listening to and believing Big Pete. I guess Ed and I argued for another five minutes before we both gave up. The only thing Ed would promise was that he would not get involved any further because Mom was family. He admitted that I had made some valid points. He swore to me that he would not get involved again, but he wasn't going to take responsibility for Auntie Bea and Uncle Frank either. He pointed out to me that Uncle Frank had four kids, and they should be taking care of him. He reminded me that John just lived up the street from Auntie Bea, and they should have been taking care of Auntie Bea as well. He never did understand why Frank's kids dumped Uncle Frank and Auntie Bea on my mother.

I just said, "Whatever," I said.

He told me he loved me.

I replied with, "Goodbye."

Next, I called his brother. What a difference in personality, opinions, and honesty! The first thing he asked me was if I had spoken to his older brother. I told him the truth about the phone conversation I just had with his brother and what a jerk I thought he was. My cousin laughed and agreed. He told me that Big Pete had called every family member who lived in the Crackerville area and told them everything my mother had done to him. Big Pete claimed that I was stealing and selling everything he had left. Big Pete said that I was running all over town and telling everyone that the shop belonged to me when it really belonged to him, but he didn't have the money to fight me. He told me that Big Pete told everyone that Uncle Frank had tried to kill him. Big Pete told everyone that I had turned his own son against him. My cousin told me everything Big Pete was telling everyone.

After he finished, I told him the truth. I told him everything that had happened and what I had discovered as fact. I told him that I could prove everything I had said. I told him that the shop was always mine. I told him that Big Pete had already given me everything he owned. I told him about the credit card fraud and the check kiting. I told him about the beatings Big Pete inflicted upon my mother. I told him about Ed being there during one of the beatings and how he had tried to lie to the police. I told him that my mother did not tell me any of these stories, other people had told me. I told him about Pete's business that he was running under Jay's name. I told him that Big Pete's indictments were matters of public record if anyone wanted to check on them. I told him about my sister and her attitude and failure to help.

My cousin let out a sigh and said he would take care of his older brother and the rest of the family in Crackerville. He believed me because the truth was much more believable than the lies out of Big Pete's mouth. He had known my mother his entire life. He agreed on my points of "family," but he felt that Uncle Frank, and especially Auntie Bea, did not deserve any help from them, but he would not oppose what I was doing.

He admired me for choosing to help the victims and thought I was saving taxpayer money by doing so. He supported everything I was doing, even though he would not have done it himself, but he understood where I was coming from. He said not to worry about the rest of the family in Crackerville. He swore to me that he would take care of them. He promised that everyone in Crackerville would call and check in with me to make sure that lying bastard Big Pete was kept in check. In fact, he said he would come and see me the next weekend and would go with me to show his presence and support in front of Big Pete. He said that would put an end to him calling my mother's family and telling more lies. I thanked him and gave him God's blessing.

Next I decided to call Bill Bank, attorney-at-law, before it was too late in the day. I looked at the time Uncle Frank had put beside the name and it was 6:00 p.m. I figured this was his home number. I called the number and a woman answered. I assumed she was his wife. I gave my greetings and asked if I could speak to Mr. Bank. He answered the phone and we both gave greetings.

I said, "Sir, I vaguely remember who you are. I think I've been sending Christmas cards to you every year."

He laughed. "Oh, I'm the attorney who did a power of attorney and your will when you had first joined the Army. Your mother and Big Pete are my friends."

I said, "Oh, yes, I had forgotten. That has been decades ago."

We both laughed.

I asked, "How did you get this number, and why did you call?"

His voice turned serious as he answered, "Belinda, I'm calling because I received a disturbing phone call from Big Pete earlier today. Considering I'm friends with your mother and Big Pete, I'm calling you as a favor for Big Pete, and I hope we can resolve this problem quickly because you are family to Big Pete."

I thought, *Oh, brother, here we go again.*

I said, "First of all, sir, he is not any part of my family. He is just another husband of my mother's. I know you are well aware they were married after I had already joined the Army. I never approved of the marriage from the beginning, and my entire family knows this to be true. I only gave in because the elders of my family requested I do so. I have only respected him because of my mother. I have always considered him to be a crooked person, and here we are today several decades later to prove me correct."

Bill said, "Belinda, I didn't know this, but I know Big Pete as a friend, as well as your mother. He has told me you are stealing and selling things from his shop, and I request that you stop this."

I started to become angry, but I was able to control it. "Sir, it is not his shop. It is mine and I can prove it. Do you have a fax machine at home?"

Bill answered, "Yes," and he gave me the number.

I said, "As soon as we finish our conversation I will fax the proof to you."

Bill agreed with confusion, "Umm, that will be fine."

I asked irritably, "Are there any other issues that you have concerns over?"

Bill answered, "Yes, Big Pete said you are moving things from his home without his permission and you have turned his son against him."

I said, "Sir, again you have been lied to. Big Pete and my mother have already given me everything to help pay for the debt, but now it's clear why they only said, 'You can have everything,' but they did not say the words, 'to make restitution.' Nevertheless, they have given their property to me, and it is my choice to sell it to pay the debt. I will soon have power of attorney for my mother, and I have already hired an attorney to protect me from the two of them. My mother has already told my attorney that she and Big Pete gave me everything to do with as I wish. If you would like to speak with her, I can give you her telephone number.

"As far as Jay is concerned, Big Pete burned that bridge himself. Big Pete has been running his business in Jay's name in my shop without permission. In fact, Big Pete has not even paid one penny toward the overhead. My mother was my employee, and I only agreed to open the shop on the condition that Big Pete would not be a part of it. When I arrived here from Germany, I was very unhappy to find Big Pete in that building, but I have bitten my tongue regarding my concerns."

Bill said, "Oh, I understand now. I guess because of all the stress, Big Pete has gotten confused, but if you need me for anything please contact me."

I said, "Oh, you can count on that, sir. Thank you once again for your concern."

After hanging up the phone, I faxed the documentation to him immediately.

I thought, *Well, I'm out of time now. The war has begun between Big Pete and me. Miss Patson was correct.* It appeared to me that everyone was believing his lies over my truth. No one seemed to want to take the time to check it out for themselves. They immediately chose to believe Big Pete's lies. *Does anyone bother to take the time to think for a moment, how could Belinda turn his own son against him? All they have to do is ask Jay himself.* I felt as if I were in a Twilight Zone episode. I was still in shock that my own mother had done this to me and was sitting in a jail cell. I was still humiliated and ashamed of what she had done. I felt like someone had taken a dagger and was repeatedly stabbing me in the back.

I continued thinking, *What formula is going to give me the correct results when I'm not even sure what I'm looking for? How on earth am I going to be able to fight such a cunning, evil individual?* Apparently Big Pete figured that because I had turned his son against him he would turn my family against me. I truly felt all alone in a battle that I hadn't started. I decided I wasn't even going to call the Carts. Those two brothers were not even worth my time. It was too late to call Thomas's family back. I would call them as soon as I was able. I was sure they were worried sick over Thomas and me.

I picked up the phone and called my husband. He immediately started yelling at me regarding a phone call he had received from Big Pete. He told me Big Pete had said that Uncle Frank and I tried to kill him, and he had filed charges. He told Thomas he was sorry for beating me, but he had no choice but to defend himself. He said Uncle Frank had tried to kill him with a shotgun and that I had turned his son against him. Thomas then reminded me that I was still in the Individual/Inactive Ready Reserve (IRR), plus even though I was a veteran, he was still active duty and was technically my sponsor and he would be held accountable for my actions. He asked why I would risk ruining both of our reputations and lives by losing my temper with Big Pete. He reminded me that I was still considered a lethal weapon because of my specialized training in warfare. He wanted to know what the hell was wrong with me.

I was totally disgusted with my husband. "What in the hell is the matter with you? You know damn well Big Pete is the biggest liar who ever walked the face of the earth. It did not happen that way and you should know me better than that. I'm fully aware of the consequences if I tried to kill Big Pete, and you know damn well if I had truly tried to kill him we would not be having this conversation because he would be dead and buried up in the mountains where no one could find the fat bastard. So stop giving me a load of shit, First Sergeant Star.

"I would never, ever put you into a situation like that because I love you, and I'm much smarter than that. I would let someone kill me before I would ever put you in that type of situation. I would never do anything to hurt your career, especially when I'm the one that helped you make rank to begin with. You know damn well that I believe in manipulating first to get myself out of a scrape versus violence. You know damn well that I will take a beating before I will attack someone physically. I didn't tell you about it because I let that fat bastard beat me. The only damn reason I let him beat me was because Uncle Frank had a damn shotgun that he fired up in the air as a warning to Big Pete. Big Pete was driving all around in the front yard like a drunken wild man. I can't believe you. You know damn well I did what I had to do to contain the situation before someone was hurt. He even hurt his son. So you better shut your mouth right now, TOP, before you really get a tongue lashing out of me!"

Thomas started laughing, trying to get out of trouble with me. He said he was sorry and felt very stupid for believing Big Pete's lies. He should have known better. He had forgotten how good of a liar Big Pete was. He had made the story so detailed and believable and he could just see me doing that. I reminded my husband of the psychological games that he had been trained in as well, and he knew better. We made a pact from that moment forward that Big Pete would not seep into our relationship again.

I was just hopping mad at Big Pete and realized I had totally underestimated my enemy. I felt very stupid and foolish at how much better he was at manipulating than I was, and he had no training at all. He was what I considered a person with the natural ability to play strategic mind games with others and manipulate them to his bidding. I just could not allow myself to do this to my own family, and maybe he knew it. Maybe the creep knew me better than I thought.

Yes, I thought, I could have done this same game to my sister, but my own sister? How could I do such a nasty thing to any of my family members? I just couldn't stoop to the rules of engagement that this creep had made. I knew better. How the hell was I going to fight him if I don't do the same in turn? I guess I would continue doing what was right, and let the stack of cards fall at will. I refused to fight him—not that way anyway. I would stick with the truth as my shield to protect me against his lies. The truth always has a way of seeping out someday, but for now, all I would do was stick to the truth. I refused to do what he was doing. If he won, so be it. My family then would deserve what they received.

CHAPTER XLIII

I woke up suddenly and sat straight up in the bed. I looked over at the clock beside my bed and it was only 4:30 a.m. I swung my legs over the side of the bed and sat there for a few minutes. As I was sitting there, I thought, *I can't believe that I have been here for ten nights.* Would this nightmare ever end? I even pinched my arm to be sure I was awake.

As I sat there, a multitude of emotions washed over me, but the predominant feelings were anger and disgust. I wished that the 380-pound greedy thief and liar, Big Pete, was out of my way. I despised him, but I could not allow myself to hate him. They say hate is the opposite of love. If I allowed myself to hate him, it would mean I had cared for him at one time.

Reality is something that would not be hidden for long, and I had to admit to myself that I did hate him. I hated him as much as I hated the enemies of our country who stood between freedom and tyranny. I hated him as much as if he had killed American citizens and stolen from our people or our country. I hated him because everything he was and did was the opposite of what I stood and fought for. I hated and loathed him! I wanted to have him arrested and incarcerated. I wanted to see him pay for his crimes. I wanted to see him die in jail.

My self-admission was freeing. The tears flowed down my face, and I sobbed as I released my soul's pain and torment. In my eyes, he was not even human. I considered him my enemy, someone who I wanted out of my life and out of my family's life. I viewed him as someone who needed to be plucked from society. I hated my mother for bringing him into our lives. I hated her for being a greedy self-serving individual. I was exceedingly disappointed in my great-aunt and great-uncle because they were thieves and liars. I hated my family for thinking for even one second that Big Pete was a good person! I wanted to break the promise I had made to my mother to protect Auntie Bea and Uncle Frank. I wanted to turn them in and let the law and God punish them!

As always, logic and my training ruled over my emotions. I had to think of my husband as well as myself. I knew to the core of my being that the only correct course of action was to clean up the credit card fraud and pay for all the bounced checks. The judge was correct. The best place for my mother was in jail. I could only hang on to the hope that Big Pete would also be incarcerated soon. Mom and Big Pete were a deadly combination. Both of them were very good at being able to take from people. They needed to be punished, or they would continue conning and stealing from people.

I could only hope my great-uncle and great-aunt had learned their lesson. I truly hoped, for my sake, that they would stop stealing and lying about me. My worst fear was that when I left, Uncle Frank and Auntie Bea would continue lying. I was also afraid that some lowlife would act on the lies they told and prey on them. I could only hope that their children were different from their parents.

I had an ominous feeling that because my great-aunt had not been caught or punished, she would continue to lie and steal from others. I thought she was much better at it than Mom or Big Pete. I just hoped that my intuition was wrong. That was all I could do. I put all thoughts to the side and decided to continue down the path that I had chosen. I prayed that everything would work out for all who were concerned. With that thought, I got off the bed, and I got ready for the day.

I made the decision to sell the longhorns that Thomas and I had put into storage in the Daisy house years ago. I packed them into the pickup truck and added a few other things. I covered them up with a waterproof tarp. I was not going to take any truckloads into town until Friday. I wrote out checks from my personal account for the shop's utilities. When I balanced my checkbook, I saw that I had enough money left in the account to start paying off the credit card debt. I realized I was finally developing a routine, which was good for me. I decided to call John and Ann that morning. I felt it was time that they started taking responsibility for John's father and aunt because they lived just three miles up the road from Auntie Bea and Uncle Frank. John answered the phone, "Hello."

I said, "Hello, John, it's Belinda."

John said, "Oh, Belinda, it's so good to hear your voice. Are you calling from Germany?"

I answered sadly, "No, John, I'm calling from the Daisy house. I've been here for over a week, and I need to make plans with you for you to take over your father's checkbook when I leave. I also need you to take care of Auntie Bea."

John asked with panic in his voice, "What? Where's your momma? She does all that."

I solemnly said, "John, Momma is in jail. A lot has happened. I noticed you have not called your father the entire time I have been here. And you haven't come by to see him either."

John said, "Because for the last two years all he does is complain about your mother stealing from him."

I was annoyed as I responded, "What? That's not true, but I will explain everything to you when I see you. Do you think you can come by tonight?"

John answered, "Yes, after Ann and I get off work and feed the kid, I can get Ann's mother to watch our daughter. We will be there about 6:00 p.m."

I said, "That sounds great. I will see you tonight."

Uncle Frank was out of bed. I told him, "John and Ann will be by tonight."

Uncle Frank said, "Okay."

I then asked Uncle Frank, "Why have you been lying for years about my mother stealing money from your checking account? I have already gone through all your statements, and she has never taken a dime from you. Why do you tell such nasty lies about the only person who was willing to take care of you and provide for you when you did run out of money?"

Uncle Frank just looked at me and replied, "Well, I told you that as well. Why do you think I would change my story to anyone else?"

I said, "Uncle Frank, you are going to be sad and lonely one day, and all because of your lying."

The telephone rang, and I answered it. It was the auctioneer. He said the auction went much better than he had expected, and he had a check ready for me. He told me how much we had made. I told him that sounded great, and I would be by later to pick it up. I asked him about doing large estate auctions. He told me that he did those as well. I asked how long it would take for him to set up a large estate auction, and he informed me that it depended on what I was auctioning. I told him I would come by later in the day to pick up the check. I said I could give him all the details then and we could set up a time for him to look at what I would like to auction. He agreed.

Uncle Frank asked inquisitively, "What was that all about?"

I said, "I don't know yet but will find out when I get there." I wasn't about to tell Uncle Frank my business. I knew now that Uncle Frank would lie and continue lying about anything he wanted to because he didn't care about whom he hurt. All he cared about was the attention that he received in the moment. I just prayed that when I left no one would prey on his shortcomings or believe his lies. This included Auntie Bea as well. Little Pete pulled up. I knew I could not go and see Mom that day because I was now limited to visiting on Wednesday and Saturdays. Having the visits limited to two days a week took a little bit of stress off me.

I told Little Pete I had a few things to drop off at the shop, and I wanted to start moving Thomas's and my personal stuff from the basement into the storage unit. Doing so would make more space for what I needed to pack into the basement. I told him that after the shop, I needed to go to the auctioneer. Then, I wanted to go to Mom's house so I could start trying to sell the hundreds of plants she had before they died on us. I told him that I was also hoping to make a few dollars off the plants.

I told Little Pete, "Before we do anything else, we are going to do a physical inventory of the wine down in the basement."

Little Pete became very angry and said, "Damn it, Belinda, do you know how many times your momma made me do that? At least ten times and now you're making me do it again?"

I said, "I'm sorry, Little Pete, I promise this will be the last time, but I made a commitment to do it now."

Little Pete said, "Okay, let's get it done."

I said, "Great." It took Little Pete and me about two hours to complete the inventory. When we were done, I went upstairs and faxed it to Mary's business fax number.

Little Pete went to the bathroom as we were getting ready to leave. I was waiting for him when the telephone rang. I picked it up and said, "Hello."

The voice on the other end said, "Hello, Belinda, it's Mary. I got your fax and I will be showing it to my boss later today. Do you have a good number where I can reach you after speaking with him? He may want to speak to you directly."

I replied, "Well, I don't know. When do think you will call me?"

Mary said, "Well, better yet I will call you around 8:00 p.m. tonight, if that's okay with you."

I said, "That will be perfect."

Mary said, "Oh, by the way, I will make flight arrangements for the end of the month, or maybe it will be the first part of next month, something like that."

I said, "Okay; that will be fine. In fact, Thomas will be coming in around the middle part of next month."

Mary said, "Oh, that sounds good, but I don't want to make any plans until I have talked to my boss."

I said, "That will be fine."

I knew I had lied to Mary last night about not minding my mother and Big Pete selling Thomas's and my property. We had already purchased it from them, and they had no right selling it to other people because it was not their property anymore. To me it was just something else Big Pete and my mother had stolen from me, but I felt safer not telling Mary how I truly felt. I had a suspicion that she was part of the check kiting, but I didn't have any information to prove it. I just felt that she was part of it because she was running the other office in Pennsylvania. Mary may not have had a high school education, but she was not stupid, and she was a drunk like Big Pete.

I guess thought something was fishy about her was because she did not have a high school diploma. She worked for years as a hairdresser, until eight years ago when Big Pete hired her as the manager of the office that he opened in Pennsylvania. I found that very odd. Either Big Pete hired her because she did not have an education or business background and he figured he could get away with stealing from his clients, or she was a part of the whole thing. I have always known she was never qualified for that position. I guessed I would find out when I saw her face to face. I had not heard from Miss Patson for a few days, and I decided to call her. Miss Patson told me she would arrange to have my mother sign the documents, and I could meet her the following morning at the jail. She said she had arranged for me to be with her when she met with my mother. I told her that was fine and I would see her then. I called my mother's attorney and told him my concerns with the bill I received. He said I was correct. He was defending just my mother, not Big Pete, and the correction was never made on the paperwork. He said he would have that dollar amount removed from the bill. I also brought to his attention my mother was waiving her right to trial so that should decrease the debt as well. He refused to lower it any further, so I was stuck with the remainder.

By the time I was off the phone, Little Pete was ready to go. We had already packed the small pickup truck full of Thomas's and my things along with a few items I decided to sell. We stopped off at the shop, and I carried in my horns and the other items I had.

When he saw me carry in the horns, Big Pete became very angry. "You did not ask me if you could sell these. They came out of my house!"

I said, "No, Big Pete, Thomas and I bought these, and I just brought them from the Daisy house basement. I have to put the prices on these items, and I will stop back in later this evening."

Little Pete and I unpacked the rest of the contents from the pickup truck and placed them in the storage unit. Then we went to the auction house across town. I asked Little Pete just to wait for me because I would only take a minute.

I went inside the auction house and spoke with the man after signing for my check. I told him that I didn't know when I would be ready to sell, but I had other items that I wanted him to auction. I told him that I would give him a call in the next few weeks, when I was ready to auction more things.

Little Pete and I drove to Mom and Big Pete's house. I picked up the yellow pages and began calling the plant and flower shops that were listed in addition to the nurseries. After about thirty minutes, I had a few that may be interested in purchasing them, but they needed to see the condition of them.

Little Pete and I packed up the first load of plants and went to the first place that had expressed interest. The woman bought the entire load. We went back to the house and loaded up another batch of plants. We went to the second place and they bought half of what we had. We continued going back to the house and loading up as we sold each truckload. Each place we went bought plants. We ran out of buyers before we ran out of plants. We still had two more truckloads. I decided we would take them to the Daisy house and Auntie Bea's house.

Before we sold any of the plants, I transplanted them from my mother's beloved flowerpots into plastic pots. After we had finished selling the plants, we packed her flowerpots in boxes and moved them to the Daisy house. We loaded another load of Thomas's and my things and moved them to the storage unit. It was already 5:00 p.m., and I told Little Pete it was quitting time.

I cooked dinner for Uncle Frank, Auntie Bea, and myself. I took Auntie Bea a plate of food and returned to the Daisy house.

It was about 6:30 p.m.; Uncle Frank was in the living room watching television. I pulled a computer I had brought from my mother's house and had just finished setting it up on Uncle Frank's dining room table when I heard someone knocking on the door. I guess Uncle Frank did not hear it because he didn't seem to notice. I looked over at the sliding glass door, and it was John and Ann.

I jumped up and let them in. We greeted each other with huge hugs. I said, "It's so good to see both you. John, it looks like you have lost some weight."

John said, "Yeah, I have lost a few pounds."

I said, "It's a long story. Would you like some coffee or soda before we get started?"

John said he would like a soda and Ann chimed in and requested one too.

I asked John, "Do you want me to get your father?"

John answered, "Yes, I think he better be in here too." I agreed and went into the living room. "Uncle Frank, John and Ann are here."

Uncle Frank turned off the television with the remote, got up from his recliner, and grabbed another cup of coffee.

As I stood there waiting for him, he opened the cabinet, took out a new bottle of whiskey, and poured some of it into his coffee. I did not say anything. I just went into the Florida room and sat down. Uncle Frank followed. Ann started talking about their daughter and how big she had grown.

After Uncle Frank was settled in his favorite chair, which was one of my mother's chairs, I started telling some of the story of everything that has transpired since I arrived back in the States. John and Ann were hanging on every word that came out of my mouth. They nodded their heads in affirmation as I stated my opinions and told them who I thought was to blame. I even told them about Auntie Bea, how she lost the land, and about Uncle Frank and the credit card scam. Then, I told them about my plan to get them both out of trouble. I told them how my face had been battered and what Uncle Frank had done. I told them about Jay and what Big Pete did to him. I told them about the numerous beatings that my mother endured. I told them everything.

By the time I was finished, Uncle Frank was very angry.

Uncle Frank retorted, "That's a lie, Belinda! Yes, your mother has been taking all my money and your auntie's money. They stole your auntie's land." He kept spewing the lies right in front of me.

I could feel my temper rising, and I almost lost it. Thanks to my training, however, I was able to retain a calm outward appearance. I reached for the box that contained Uncle Frank's financial documentation. As I pulled out statements and canceled checks, I calmly said, "I have his bank statements and copies of all the canceled checks for the last seven years. I can prove he is lying about my mother." I handed the pile of papers to John and Ann. They both looked through the papers and copies of the canceled checks for at least twenty minutes before they were satisfied. Neither Uncle Frank nor I said one word as they went through the statements.

After they had finished looking though Uncle Frank's records, I showed them the Daisy house papers and the mortgage documents proving Auntie Bea was the one who purchased the house originally. I showed them where she withdrew from her CD to pay for it. I showed them the mortgage papers with all three signatures. I showed them everything Auntie Bea had done with the check kiting. I started to pull out more papers when John and Ann said in unison, "That's enough."

John continued, "We believe every word you are saying." Uncle Frank started to protest, and John angrily said, "Stop it! Daddy, just stop it! You have lied enough."

Uncle Frank became angry and said he was going to bed. John calmly started telling me of several times he had seen my mother in the grocery store with sunglasses on at night, but you could still see the bruises on her face. John continued saying, "I know she had seen me but she acted as if she hadn't. I think you are a hero for what you are doing for Auntie Bea, your mother, and my father, but Ann and I are not going to run Daddy's finances because we do not want him telling lies about us as he has with your mother. You know he will do the same thing to you when you leave. We are here when you want to talk, but we are not getting involved in any of this."

Ann interrupted, "That's right, Belinda, but we will call and check up on John's father and Aunt Bea more often. But we are not getting involved in any of this or any of their finances."

I asked, "I understand, but what about Sam, Samantha, and May?"

John answered, "I don't know, Belinda. You know Samantha and Daddy haven't really spoken to each other in years after he disapproved of Billy, her husband. He told Samantha she wasn't his daughter anymore and that he did not want anything else to do with her. I don't think Samantha would even talk to him now.

"As far as May, she has always been Daddy's favorite so maybe she will take care of him, but she lives in Tennessee. Regarding Sam, he hates Daddy's guts. So I don't know. All I can tell you is that you will have to ask them. As far as I'm concerned, you know how Aunt Bea and Daddy have treated all of us over the years. I love your mother; she has done good things for me, but Ann doesn't like her because of what happened when Ann and I got married."

I said, "I know. Maybe I'm wrong in helping them."

John said, "No you're not because indirectly you are making things right for us kids."

I said, "I don't know about that, but you have to admit that Uncle Frank has been happy and so has Auntie Bea. You are right; the two of them have acted like we are dirt beneath their feet."

Ann said, "When they were doing road work up at the corner of the highway where your shop is, Big Pete called the police trying to have charges filed against the road crew. I took the call because I'm the dispatcher, and I don't think he knew it was me. He carried on like a fool, over and over again stating it was his shop. Now we know even that was a lie."

I said, "I guess you believe me now when I say Big Pete is a nasty, lying person."

Ann said, "I have always known he was that and a crook to boot. I just never said anything."

They said it was getting late and they had to leave. I walked them to the door. I hugged both of them and we said our goodbyes.

*   *   *

After they left, I sat in the Florida room, smoking a cigarette, and my mind wandered to the story of Ann and John's wedding. My mother was willing to pay for their dinner rehearsal. Mom and Big Pete were members of Farmington Country Club. My grandmother asked my mother if she would pay for the wedding. It was something my grandmother wanted to do for John, but she did not have the money to pay for it. Of course, my mother agreed to that for John and Ann. My grandmother wanted John to get married in our family church as well, but Ann refused to be married there.

To keep the peace, my mother asked about having the dinner rehearsal at Farmington. Of course, greedy Ann had no problem with that. She wanted a band and all kinds of stuff. My mother told her that she was only paying for the basics as a favor to my grandmother. It turned into a huge argument because Ann, who had no money, could not have her dream wedding.

Ann and her family were snobs and thought they were better than everyone else was. They had no class at all. They were not even remotely wealthy but considered themselves royalty.

Thomas and I were home on leave when they got married. I remembered going to the rehearsal dinner, and Ann and her family did not even show up. They ended up having a classless wedding and reception. It was their loss, not my family's loss.

To me it was not my mother's fault. Ann's parents did not have the funds to give a first-class wedding or the creativity to have a classy low-budget wedding. Everyone in my family refused to go to the wedding because Ann's family snubbed the rehearsal dinner that my mother had paid for and poor John ended up with just my mother, his mother, and Grandma at his wedding.

My grandmother raised John. His mother did not want him because he had colic and cried all the time. She was going to give him up for adoption behind Uncle Frank's back because he was gone all the time. My grandmother stated there was no way her nephew was going to live outside the family. She immediately took him in and cared for him as if he were her own child.

*   *   *

I thought, *At least Ann and John are going to check in on Uncle Frank more often. It seems to me they are even doing more to help me than my own sister is. After everything that has been said between my sister and me, I wish she would at least come here to show her support and stand by me, even if she doesn't agree with what I'm doing, but I guess that's life.*

Mary called around 10:30 p.m. I could tell she was drunk because her speech was slurred. She told me that her boss was going to buy the entire collection, and she would call me later with her flight plans and let me know when she would be here. Regarding the purchase of the wine collection, I told her that such a large sum would have to be wired into my account, but we would talk later in more detail.

After hanging up the phone, I thought it was sad that even though Thomas and I would get some of our money back on the wine, we would still lose it because I would have to pay the debts my mother created. I wanted to cry, but I was too tired to do so. I just went to bed after taking a bath.

CHAPTER XLIV

The next morning, before Little Pete and I began packing and moving things, I had him stop off at the shop so I could price the horns and the other few items that I had dropped off the previous day. They were gone. I asked Big Pete where the horns were. He told me that he had sold them and kept the money.

He looked over at Little Pete, and he told me I could have his off the wall at his house. I was furious but did not say anything. After moving several truckloads from the Daisy house to the storage unit, we went to Mom and Big Pete's house. I instructed Little Pete to continue packing. I would be back later. I had to go visit Mom. I arrived at the jail, and Miss Patson was waiting for me in the waiting room. She walked up to the window with her briefcase in hand. She waved for me to follow her. We went through the door, and the guard escorted us to a classroom. We sat there for a few minutes before Mom came through the door. I immediately got up from the desk chair I was sitting in and hugged her. We both started crying. She cupped her hands around my face and sobbed even more.

I said, "Oh, Momma, it looks worse than what it is."

Mom started asking questions, and I didn't want to tell her what happened so I said, "I have already taken care of it. So stop worrying."

Miss Patson read aloud the power of attorney. My mother and I asked several questions regarding Big Pete and if this power of attorney was strong enough to take on her husband in my mother's absence.

Miss Patson assured us, "We have purposely worded your requests not only giving Belinda full power to fight him regarding the material property, we have also done a sworn affidavit from you, her mother, stating both you and your husband gave everything you own to Belinda. She can even sell your cars if she has to. All she needs is this. Belinda can even close all the checking accounts and much, much more."

My mother and I were satisfied.

Miss Patson had my mother sign the documents and the copies of them. She notarized them and gave me two copies of each document. Miss Patson asked if we would like some privacy so we could talk and we both excitedly said in unison, "Yes!"

Mom hugged me again and kissed me on my forehead and on both cheeks.

Mom said, "Belinda, I'm so, so sorry. I'm sorry for being such a bitch. I'm sorry for shaming you. I'm sorry for everything."

I gazed into my mother's weathered sky blue eyes, and I knew she was truly sorry. I regretted for even thinking I hated her. I was angry for what she had done, but her eyes were like my sister's. They always seemed to make me melt when I looked into them; it didn't help that her eyes were sad. I knew my momma was worth fighting for, even though I thought what she had done was unconscionable. I could forgive her one day, and the next day I would be angry with her again. It had been like that my entire life. My mother did have good traits as well. Whether she deserved my help and guidance or not, she was my mother and I did love her.

We both cried, and she started telling me more of what she had done. I respected her at this moment because she wasn't quite like Uncle Frank, Auntie Bea, Big Pete, and Little Pete. She took responsibility for what she did and didn't try to blame anyone else. In fact, she didn't even mention anyone else's name. She told more about the role she played. At that moment, I admired my mother. It takes a strong woman to admit what she did was wrong and not make excuses for the bad choices she had made.

Miss Patson walked back into the classroom and said, "Belinda, it's time to go."

We walked out of the jail and into the parking lot. I had already told Miss Patson about the altercation with Big Pete and Uncle Frank. I had to do so because of the condition of my face. I had also informed her that I was not going to take any further action regarding it. She was very displeased with me because I played a nasty game with the sheriffs, but she completely understood the legal magnitude of my great-uncle's actions. She did agree that it was the best course of action, considering the type of person Big Pete was, and I still had to interact with him frequently.

Miss Patson solemnly asked, "When do you want to start on the removal of Big Pete from your shop and stopping him from conducting any further business in your brother's name?"

I answered, "We will start either next week or the beginning of the week after that; it depends. I will contact you when I'm ready to begin."

Miss Patson said, "That works for me."

We hugged each other as if we were best of friends and said our goodbyes.

I drove back to Mom and Big Pete's house, and it was late in the afternoon. Little Pete was working on removing the horns from the wall. I could tell he was physically tired. I told him just to rip them down. While he was doing that, Big Pete came home. I thought for sure we would get into a fight, but instead Big Pete acted indifferent. Because Little Pete was still on the ladder, I told him to take down the collector plates too. I said we could pack them later.

For the rest of the week, Little Pete and I moved things. I went to see my mother on Wednesday but had no intentions of seeing her on Saturday. Each evening throughout the week, I tried to call at least one of Uncle Frank's children.

CHAPTER XLV

On Wednesday evening, I called May. She was Uncle Frank's youngest daughter. She was very unattractive in every sense of the word. She had no brains, personality, or physical beauty. I guess that was why the only man that would marry her was twenty years older than she was. The last time I had seen her was a couple of decades ago; at that time, she looked as if she were twenty years older than I was. I guess all her drug addictions had taken their toll.

I dialed her number, and she answered the phone. I said, "Hi, May, it's Belinda."

May asked, "Belinda who?"

I irritably said, "Your cousin." *I thought what a dumbass she was.*

May replied, "Hi, Belinda; thank you for sending Christmas cards every year."

I had to bite my tongue because it has always angered me. None of Frank's kids ever sent a card to me or even wrote me to say they were alive. I had always had to rely on my mother to fill me in on their lives. In fact, my sister was the exact same way. I guess it took a phone call for May to acknowledge that she had received my cards.

I started to tell some of the story to May, but not very much because I did not know her as I knew Uncle Frank's other children. I told her John and Ann could fill her in on the rest of the details. I stated that I had already proven to them that I was telling the truth. I told May I would not be able to stay here forever. I told her that John and Ann did not want the responsibility, so she would have to talk to her brother John because I felt it was his place to explain his decision to her, not mine. She agreed with me and asked me to put her father on the phone because she was going to see if she could get him to move to Tennessee to live with her where she could take care of him.

Uncle Frank walked into the Florida room, and I told him that May wanted to speak with him and passed him the phone. After about twenty minutes or so, Uncle Frank passed the phone back to me. May began telling me that she could not convince her father to come and live with her. He did not want to leave Virginia. She said she would keep nagging him to see if she could change his mind. She promised she would at least start calling him every week to check up on him.

* * *

Thursday evening I called Sam and left him a message on his answering machine. I prayed that he would call me back.

I decided to go ahead and call Samantha. She answered the phone, and I gave my greetings. She told me that I needed to come and see her as soon as I could. I asked how long she thought it would take me to get there if I left right now. She thought it might be about an hour and a half. I told her that I was on my way now because it was still early. I drove Mom's car to Samantha's house. I truly wanted to see her again. I had not seen her in over a decade, and we were never alone because there were always other family members around. I took the back roads so I could get there faster.

I pulled up to the front of her trailer, and I was very proud because she now had a double wide and it was brand new. I was so happy because it appeared Samantha and Billy had finally made a comfortable living for themselves.

* * *

I sat in the car for a few minutes remembering how Samantha and Billy became a couple. It had happened back in high school. I was jealous of her new friend Patricia, whom everyone called "Pete." Samantha stopped hanging out with me and spent all her time with Pete. I remember convincing Samantha to let me come with her one weekend to visit with Pete.

Pete had dropped out of high school and immediately married. At that time, I smoked a good deal of marijuana, just like Samantha and Sam. I don't think I ever smoked it as much as they did. I rarely bought it, and if I did, it wasn't very much. I smoked it mainly at parties, or with friends that had it. Most of the time they would just give me a few joints.

My schoolwork was more important to me. I had only played hooky one time in my life, but Samantha was skipping school all the time now to hang out with Pete. I don't remember how we got to Pete's one-bedroom apartment, but I do remember Pete showing us a picture of Billy. She was planning to set up Samantha on a date with him because Samantha thought he was cute. So to try to stay in Samantha's life, I asked if she had another friend with whom she could set me up. I didn't tell Samantha or Pete, but I thought Billy was ugly. Anyway, that's how Samantha and I ended up on a double date with her future husband and his cousin, Mark. I liked Mark as a friend but never more than that.

*   *   *

I finally got out of the car. I knocked on Samantha's door, and she opened it. We must have hugged each other for over three minutes. We both had tears in our eyes. It had been so long! We went into her living room where her three children were watching television, and I couldn't believe how they had grown. In fact, I don't think I ever had met her children before then. She sat on a chair, filled a bong up with marijuana, lit it up, took a toke in front of her kids, and passed it to me. I didn't know how to respond because I hadn't smoked in decades. I never had children, so I didn't know if this was proper or not. I didn't want to insult her and really didn't mind smoking, so I took it.

I guess Samantha sensed my uneasiness and said, "Let's go in my room and close the door. You're right; we shouldn't be smoking in front of the kids."

So we went into her room and got high. I felt I had gone back in time three decades. I felt Samantha never left the '70s. She asked if I wanted a beer, and I said sure. She said she would be right back. She returned with a beer for me and a soda for herself. "Tell me what happened."

So I started telling her the entire story. She thought it was great that I was cleaning up the mess that her father, Auntie Bea, and my mother had created. She said the few times that she met Big Pete she knew he was a crook and didn't like him, but she didn't care all that much for my mother either because my mother was such a snob. Nonetheless, she realized that my mother had always been there for everyone.

Samantha continued, "Your mother, Belinda, wasn't snobby, as I remember it, until she married Big Pete. To me, she started changing into a snobby bitch a little bit at a time over the years when she was with Big Pete."

I thought about that as I sat there remembering, and Samantha was right with her observations. I wondered if my mother's attitude changed that way because Big Pete was beating her. I agreed with Samantha. I told Samantha that she was going to have to make peace with her father because I didn't think he would be around for too many more years. He hadn't been eating, and I feared there would be no one there to care for him. I asked her if he really deserved this from his kids. Samantha said she thought he did, but she agreed with me that she needed to make her peace with him for her own peace of mind. She promised that she would call him and Auntie Bea more often because she never called them now. Samantha told me her mother was living on the streets. She said the only thing she did for her mother was buy her a bag of groceries once, but she wasn't taking her in either.

I asked Samantha, "What did she do to you?"

Samantha answered, "No more than what my father has done, but she has three other children. They have just left her out on the street, but I'm not going to take the responsibility either. I have three kids to think about. Ever since we were children, Belinda, you have always done right by everyone. You are the peacemaker in the family, not your mother. You always have made people feel as if they were your equal; everyone is comfortable around you. Your mother made everyone feel inferior to her. Even my father, your sister, and Aunt Bea made everyone around them feel inferior, and the rest of us were dirt beneath their feet. Big Pete was just a piece of shit that your mother found. I can only tell you my true feelings, Belinda. They all truly deserve what life has dished out to them. All of them are greedy nasty people, and unfortunately, Belinda, they are our blood, but the point that you made to me is the fact. Anything I do will not be for my father, but for you because I owe him nothing, but I owe you so much."

She got up from the other side of her bed and said, "Enough. Let's go out into the kitchen. I think Billy's back."

As soon as he saw me, Billy came over and gave me a big old bear hug.

That's when I found out that Mark had died from cancer a few years earlier. Billy said, "Mark was married, but his dying words were about you, Belinda. He never stopped loving you."

I didn't say anything. I felt so bad! I knew I had sobered up from smoking and I said my goodbye to everyone.

CHAPTER XLVI

Late Friday afternoon, I had Little Pete help me move about three truckloads to the shop. Big Pete did not say anything. I told Little Pete that because we had worked hard all week, he could take off early after I paid him. I told Big Pete that I would take care of the shop, and there was no need for him to be in my shop this weekend. Big Pete said he had his own business to run, and he was coming in on Saturday like he always did.

Frustrated, I said, "Whatever!"

I was just thankful he left my shop that day. Friday after closing up the shop and returning to the Daisy house, I called Sam again. I guess I was lucky this time because he said I caught him just as he was walking out the door to go to a party. I told Sam where I was and that I needed to speak with him. I told him I already had talked with his brother and sisters, and he was last on my list. I told him I really wanted to see him. I told him I had saved the best for last.

Of course, Sam started laughing, but he said he didn't want to meet at the Daisy house because his father was there. I asked him if he knew where my shop was. I told him where it was, and he said that was a perfect location. He said he was canceling his plans and would meet me at my shop in an hour. I told him, "That sounds great."

I took a shower and got dressed. As I was walking out the door, Uncle Frank asked where I was going. I just simply told him the truth that I was meeting up with Sam and would see him later.

Uncle Frank became angry, and I knew he was hurt.

Uncle Frank asked, "Is he coming here? Why didn't you say something to me? I haven't seen or heard from Sam in years."

With great sadness, I replied to my great-uncle, "No, sir, he is not coming here. I am meeting him at my shop because he wants to see it. I don't know what has happened between the two of you, but I promise I will try and fix it."

Uncle Frank retorted, "I've done nothing to him, Belinda, so there is nothing to fix. Call him and tell him to meet you here so I can see my son."

I said, "Uncle Frank, I can't do that. I will talk with him tonight and I'm sure he will see you later."

Thank goodness the telephone rang right then, and Uncle Frank answered it. I watched as his face lit up with a smile when I heard him say, "Samantha!" I smiled. I was so thankful she had started communicating with her father again. I waved my hand at my great-uncle gesturing a goodbye, and he waved back at me.

I drove to my shop and parked the pickup truck in the back. I walked around to the front so Sam could see me in front of the shop. I lit up a cigarette and waited for him. About twenty minutes later, Sam pulled up in front of my shop, and I jumped in his pickup truck. I told him just a little bit of what was happening. I was becoming tired of telling the same story over and over again. I asked him if he could take over Uncle Frank's checkbook once I left. He told me he hated his father. Sam said he wasn't putting himself in that type of position because he wasn't going to allow his father to tell lies on him as his father had told lies on my mother.

Sam also said the same thing John had said. Sam warned me, "You know when you leave, Belinda, my father will be telling the same lies about you."

I just broke down and said, "That's probably what will happen, but you all know he lies. I can prove everything he said is a lie. Auntie Bea was telling lies about the farm. I can easily prove that as well."

Sam said, "You don't have to prove anything to me because I know both of them are liars."

Sam said he loved my mother because she had done so much for all of us. He didn't know about Big Pete, but he knew me and I didn't go around lying about everything. He thought what I was doing for his family was great even though he didn't think Auntie Bea or his father deserved it.

Sam stopped on a dirt road in the middle of nowhere and said, "Let's get high." He pulled out a small bag of cocaine.

I told Sam I never liked that stuff and didn't want any.

Sam asked, "Well, what about some pot? I have some of that."

I answered indifferently, "Okay."

He said, "Reach in the back seat. There is a small cooler. I put a few beers in it for us."

I grabbed a couple of beers out of his cooler. We sat in his truck, got high, and drank some beers. We must have talked for several hours. Of course, it was all about Sam, but that was okay. I'm glad he shared his life with me.

I felt it was time to talk more about his father. So I just blurted it out, "Sam, you need to make peace with your father. He loves you in his own way. Does he really deserve such a cold shoulder from you? He is all alone. Is there any way you can forgive him for whatever he has done? He is an old man now, Sam, and he is not doing so well." Sam must have sat there for several seconds, thinking over what I said.

Then he spoke after letting out a sigh. "He doesn't deserve the time of day from me. I am ashamed of him because all he does is lie, and I'm sick of it. He has treated me like I was a piece of shit all my life, but you have made good points for me to think about. I guess I could find some type of peace with him, and I guess it is time to do so. But I'm not taking care of his finances and being put into the position for him to lie about me as he has done to your mother and as he will do to you."

I said, "Oh, Sam, that takes a lot of courage on your part, and I'm glad you changed your mind somewhat. Oh, by the way, Aunt Jane and our cousin, will be at the Daisy house this Sunday. I will be working in the shop so you may want to come over."

Sam asked, "I haven't seen him in years. What about Ed, his brother?"

I replied, "No, I don't think he is coming, but I did speak to him on the phone." I told Sam about the conversation I had with Ed. Sam looked shocked and almost didn't believe me.

Sam said, "Big Pete isn't blood. Ed has known your mother since they were children. How could he even think for one second that Big Pete was telling the truth? Granted your mother stole, but she stole for Big Pete, not from him, and she stole for Aunt Bea and my father. For Pete's sake, she stole from you for them. Ed was always a freak."

I told Sam I had to go because I had another busy day.

He asked, "Are you going to show me your shop? You may have something I'd like to buy to help the cause."

I answered, "Sure, Sam."

We stopped in my shop and he looked at everything. He asked, "I do need a fax machine and a computer. How much are you selling the office stuff for?"

I showed him the prices, and he asked if he could get a discount. I gave him one.

He gave me what cash he had on him and said, "That's a deposit so you don't sell it to anyone else. I will hook up with you next week sometime and settle up, but I will be by this weekend. I'll even give Dad a call tomorrow to see how he is doing."

I said that would be fine and I would put the stuff that he was buying in the back so it wasn't sold to anyone else. We hugged each other and kissed each other on the cheeks. I locked up my shop and let out a sigh because I felt like I was back in the '70s again. Back then, everything had been so much shinier because I had my whole life in front of me. *Now look at me*, I thought. I'm in a pitiful place now. My mother, Big Pete, my great-aunt, and my great-uncle had stolen my entire future from me.

* * *

Saturday morning I was unpacking more of the inventory to display in the shop, and business started picking up with several customers.

* * *

Before I knew it, Sunday evening had come and the shop was slowly becoming bare. I did my reconciliation and the books. I had my deposit ready to be deposited in the bank first thing in the morning. I pulled up in front of the Daisy house, and there were several of my cousins talking and laughing with their children and each other. Sam and my older cousin were cooking on the grill. Everyone came over and greeted me before I had a chance to get out of the pickup. I was smiling from ear to ear. I couldn't believe it, but Ed was there too as well as John and Ann. Auntie Bea was off to the side fussing about something. Uncle Frank had a beer in his hand smiling from ear to ear. Samantha and Billy were there with their kids.

I hadn't seen my great-aunt Jane in years. I must have talked with her for a full hour nonstop. For this moment, everything seemed back to normal, except my mother and my grandmother were missing. My grandmother and mother always were the center of attention because they were the ones who always planned the family get-togethers. A few times over the years they had been able to gather the entire family together.

No one talked about the troubles at hand, but instead everyone filled everyone in on what was going on in their lives. We all pitched in and cleaned up the mess. Sam drove my Auntie Bea back to her house and left. By 10:30 p.m., everyone had gone home. Even Uncle Frank seemed happier. Uncle Frank kissed me on the cheek as he said, "I'm pooped, baby girl, and I am headed off to bed."

CHAPTER XLVII

I woke up to a new Monday and still felt like I was in some mysterious war. I really had tried to unite my family, but I knew that nothing had been accomplished. No one wanted to help me financially, not even my godparents. I started questioning myself again, so I called my husband.

Thomas said I was doing what was right for us. I was correct in selling things and paying the credit card fraud and the bounced checks because. If I did file credit card fraud charges against the various parties involved, it would hurt our credit and probably take years to be fixed. If it had not been my mother, it would have been a different story, but it was done by my own family.

Thomas said, "Babe, I know you love her, and I even like her from time to time. Whether you like it or not, Belinda, the one great thing she did was have you. Even though you do not want to admit it, she played a key role in who you are today. You are honest, you are trusted, you always try to put other people's feelings before your own, or at least until you can't take their load of bull any longer. That says you're more patient than most. Whether you try to mentally bully someone into thinking you're right and they are wrong, the point is most of the time, you are the one who is right. You have an uncanny way of simply seeing the black and white between the gray lines.

"You stand up and fight not only for your beliefs and freedoms, but also for the way you are treated as well. You have a strong back, Belinda, and you have been carrying your family's garbage for a very, very long time. I would not want to be in your shoes because you are making hard and unselfish decisions right now. I know I would not have the stomach to do it. The course of action you have taken is truly the only right way."

My husband continued to tell me that he felt sad and hurt because of what had been done to us. Whatever affects me and my name truly affects him and his name as well.

Thomas continued, "Belinda, what is truly sad, is that you and I shouldn't have to take on this burden alone, or any part of this burden. Your entire family should financially be helping us to the best of their ability. They should be united as an entire internal and external family unit. Even your father should be helping. It seems he has no problem helping other people in other countries and strangers in our own country, but when it comes time to help his own children, all he does is lay judgment on others. He should simply be helping because she is the mother of two of his children. He says he is a man of God, but he doesn't show it through his actions toward his own children. This is why it is so easy for nasty people like Big Pete and so many others to prey on your family. It is so easy for the crooks to divide, conquer, and take advantage of others when they are needy. Even though your great-aunt doesn't deserve it, we are doing right by trying to purchase the farm back. It is within our reach, and it will be our land and no one else's. Plus we will still be providing a roof over your great-aunt's head because she does not have anyone else. But the money she lost was of her own doing and it is too much money to try and recover for her."

Regarding Frank, Thomas said, "He is there, and his own children will not provide for him. All we can do is separate your mother and great-uncle financially. It is not the responsibility of another man to provide for someone else's parents, but here we are being robbed by our own government. They are taking from us to provide education for another man's children and medical care for another man's parents. Our fellow brethren throughout our great nation have lost the true meaning of, 'Charity starts in the home.' Charity shouldn't be the government stealing from one group of people to give it to another group of people. This is just one difference between your uncle and your aunt. It is the responsibility of the family to provide for your aunt because she has no one, but your uncle has four children.

"You're already there, and you have the means to do it. What you are doing is correct. Your family is not the only family unit that does not stand united. That is one reason our country is always divided on so many issues. They have lost their way and do not understand what the idea of greatness is all about. If American families cannot even stand united amongst themselves, how can our country stay united in times of need? Instead, the people of our country argue and fight amongst one another when we need to go to war or fix a wrong to make it right. They badmouth our commander-in-chief and try to lay blame on others. Our country isn't great if the people in it cannot even unite as a country. That inability stems from the core of our people and the family units and their core moral values. For Pete's sake, Belinda, you have told me this yourself. Have you forgotten so easily that you have been standing alone with me by your side now for over a decade? We are a county of many types of cultures and races, but billions of family units cannot even put their differences aside to provide support and love to one of their own who is in need. Instead, they expect it to be given to them from the government, who in turns steals from another man to give it. You may not want to believe this, Belinda, but socialism is growing in our nation. Your family is just one sad example of it. Your family is greedy, lazy, and self absorbed. They prey on others.

"You and I know what your mother has done was wrong and she truly needs to be punished. She has confessed to her crimes and now is ready to take her punishment for them. Your mother should not have to pay for crimes committed by others, and her name should not be slandered for crimes that she never committed. Your mother is a fraudster, not a fraud, even though everyone else in your family is a fraud."

I told Thomas what he said was true and correct. I was losing my way and I had lost focus on why I was there in the first place. No matter what the rest of my family may or may not have been, I was here not to judge, but to support and stand alone, stay strong, and do what was right to the best of my abilities for all concerned. I would do that even if they refused to unite. I had done the right thing for us and for our beliefs, and there was nothing more that I could do.

After hanging up with Thomas, I felt strong and confident again. I was truly questioning what this was all about. *Yes,* I thought, *I am hurt and angry for what my mother has done, and because of what everyone else has done, but at the same time, I love her and my godparents. I'm not here to judge her; God and our justice system will do that. I am not here to judge Uncle Frank and his children, Auntie Bea, my sister, Big Pete, Little Pete, Jay, my father, or anyone else. If they cannot unite and do right, then I cannot force them or bully them because it is just a waste of time. They will have to live with themselves. I am a doer and I can sleep at night.* Little did I know what other cruelties were in store for me.

* * *

I got ready for the day and heard the telephone ring. I answered it and it was Sam.

Sam said, "I'm headed off to work in a few minutes, and I would like to go ahead and pay for the stuff I bought from you the other day after work. Can I catch up to you around six or so?"

I answered as I asked, "Sure. Where do you want to meet?"

He answered, "At your shop."

I asked, "Are you sure you don't want to meet here at the Daisy house?"

Sam answered, "Okay, Belinda, but I'm not going inside. Just be out front and I will pick you up."

I said, "But Sam, you were just here yesterday."

Sam said, "Yeah, but if you noticed I didn't speak to Dad."

I said, "Okay. Then I will see you here around six or so." I must have waited for Little Pete to show up for several hours. It was 9:30, and I called him. There was no answer.

Right before I was going to start packing and moving again, the telephone rang and it was Big Pete. Big Pete told me Little Pete called in sick and would not be helping me today. I was so angry that I decided to call Little Pete and give him a piece of my mind. Before I had a chance to do so, Uncle Frank got on the phone to call Auntie Bea. He did this faithfully every morning.

I heard Uncle Frank tell my auntie that I was angry again. Uncle Frank passed me the phone. I was so angry that I did not control my tongue and started fussing over the entire thing. Auntie Bea told me to call that nasty Little Pete and remind him who paid his paycheck. Now I had my godparents all upset again, along with me. I felt terrible doing that. We all had enough stress as it was.

After hanging the phone up with my auntie, I called Little Pete. Of course, he was too much of a coward to answer the phone; so I left an unpleasant message stating I was his employer, not Big Pete. He would call me, not Big Pete. If he did this again, he should not bother showing up for work. If he felt Big Pete was his employer then he could collect a paycheck from him.

I went to the shop. I talked with Big Pete about holding a large auction. I told him we would split the proceeds 50/50. He agreed with me. I told him that I would meet him at his house first thing the next morning. I asked him to wait for me before he went to the shop so he could show me what he would like to keep. This way we would not have to worry about so much to store. Big Pete agreed with everything I had to say.

I moved a few more of our things to the storage unit. I realized we would never be able to move it all ourselves, and we would have to hire a moving team to help. I guess I hadn't realized how much property Thomas and I had accumulated over the years. I felt very blessed because we did have very nice things. I called Little Pete later in the day and told him to meet me at Mom and Big Pete's house first thing the next morning.

Sam showed up at the Daisy house around 5:30 p.m. Uncle Frank was sitting in the Florida room. I was cleaning up dishes from cooking an early dinner for Auntie Bea and Uncle Frank. I had dropped a plate off to Auntie Bea earlier so I did not know Sam was there.

Uncle Frank yelled, "Belinda, Sam's here!"

I said, "Okay."

Sam was just standing out in the yard at the corner of the house where the Florida room was looking in the windows at Uncle Frank, and Uncle Frank was sitting in the Florida room just looking at Sam. I thought how stupid these two men were. All they had to do was relate their feelings to one another, forgive each other, and make amends.

I walked outside where Sam was standing and asked, "Sam, are sure you can't take over your father's affairs? After all, Sam, look at him! All he does all day is sit in that chair, looking out the window, getting drunk."

Sam retorted, "No, I can't do it. I still hate him! I can't help it."

I gave Sam my dumb look.

He couldn't stand it and said as he was chuckling at me, "Okay, okay, Belinda. I'll go in there and speak with him for a few minutes. I hate it when you give me that damn brown-eyed puppy look with your arms and hands stretched out. I didn't think that could still work on me because you're not so young and cute anymore. I guess those big brown eyes still have it."

He just kept laughing and shaking his head. Sam and I walked back into the house, and Sam bent down and gave his father a hug as Uncle Frank stayed seated in his favorite chair.

Uncle Frank said, "It's about damn time, boy."

Sam just shrugged his shoulders once and said, "If it wasn't for Belinda I wouldn't have come in. I'm sorry."

Uncle Frank said, "I'm sorry too for being an old drunk and for everything else."

To this day, I will never know what Uncle Frank and Sam were talking about at that moment.

After we all talked for about an hour, the telephone rang. My great-uncle's face lit up again as he said, "John!"

I looked over at Sam and asked, "Are you ready?"

Sam answered, "Yeah, let's go."

On the way to the shop, Sam said, "Belinda, I am a spy. I work for the unions. What I do is secretly tape record the meetings of the employers and take the tapes back to the union so they can know what the employers are doing."

I thought, *Great, I have another cousin who is either a paranoid schizophrenic or just another pathological liar. That kind of crap comes out of Gary's mouth. I have learned over the years to allow Gary just to talk because in Gary's mind, it is all true.*

I said angrily, "Sam, what you are doing is against the law. You must have permission to tape record someone. You better not be tape recording me for any reason because you do not have my permission." I started searching his truck.

We pulled up to the back of the shop. Sam was laughing and said, "I'm not tape recording you, Belinda. I was just telling you what I do for a living."

I said, "Okay," but thought to myself, *What a creep.*

Sam gave me a check for the things he had bought, and I helped him load them into the back of his truck. Sam continued telling me his lies regarding the unions. Sam was an electrician. That was pretty much what he did when he was in the Navy before he was discharged.

CHAPTER XLVIII

The next day, I drove to Mom and Big Pete's house. I walked into the house, and Big Pete was sitting at the kitchen table drinking a cup of coffee and reading his newspaper. We greeted each other. Big Pete took me around the house and showed me everything he wanted to keep. He stated these belongings were for him to start his life over. He was only keeping enough for a small apartment. He showed me which kitchen dishes he would like to take and some pots and pans, towels, and those types of things. I agreed with everything he wanted. He asked if I would do the auction just in my name and then just give him cash. I told Big Pete that I would rather do it in both his and my name so two separate checks would be given to both of us directly because I didn't want him to be concerned that I was cheating him. I also didn't really want the sole responsibility.

Pete said the main reason he wanted to do it that way was that he didn't want the government to take anything from him. There would be no paper trail and he said, "Besides, your mother and I gave you everything anyway. I'm just thankful that you are thinking of me as well. By doing it that way there are no questions asked."

I asked him if he was sure because I didn't want him going around telling people—like he had been doing—that I was stealing from him. He said he would not do that anymore.

I said, "Okay then. I will start doing what has to be done."

I guess I should have known better because since I had been there no one in my family, including Big Pete and Little Pete, knew what it meant to give your word and a handshake and honor it. To me, that was a verbal contract. To me, this was just another prime example that people do not understand that when you give your word, and then break it, it is the same thing as lying, cheating, and stealing. What has happened to the meaning of honor? What has happened to understanding that a person's word is what defines him or her?

Big Pete asked, "Belinda, I went into your mother's office to open up the safe to get my personal papers out and the safes were gone. I didn't give you permission to take them. Where are they?"

I answered, "No, Big Pete, you didn't give me permission because my mother told me to take them the first day I was here in town. They belong to my mother, and you know this. Regarding your personal papers, I have no problem giving them to you."

He said, "My Rolex watch was in one of them, and I would like that returned to me."

I said, "No, Big Pete, it wasn't in the safe because you had already given it to your son, Jay, and he sold it when he was here."

At first I thought Big Pete was going to get angry, but he replied in an even tone, "I just wished someone had told me."

I said, "I thought Jay told you."

Big Pete said, "No, he didn't, but he is my son. I guess it was okay."

*   *   *

Wednesday morning I called the auctioneer and asked him if he wanted to take on our large auction. He told me that he would love to do it, but he was very busy with a lot of auctions going on. We both agreed to meet at Mom and Big Pete's house that afternoon to decide the best course of action and set a date for our auction.

I had Little Pete run me all around town picking up bad checks, paying debts that were owed, and going to the jail to visit Mom. When we arrived at Mom and Big Pete's house, the auctioneer was waiting for us in the driveway. I took him around the outside grounds of the house and gave him a quick look in each of the five sheds that were scattered throughout the property. I told him that we would like to auction everything in the sheds. Then I took him inside and showed him everything we wanted to auction there. I pointed out everything that my mother wanted to keep and made sure he understood that those items would not be for sale. The auctioneer asked if they could do the auction directly on the grounds and have the customers move the items themselves. I told him that sounded like a great idea. He also asked about setting up a tent right in front of the garage doors, but he said it might tear up the sides of the paved driveway. I said there would be no problem with that. He also told me there was so much to sell that we should hold the auction in three-day installments. I agreed with him. We were just wrapping up when Big Pete came storming into the kitchen.

He said, "Little Pete just called me, Belinda. You did not tell me you were doing this."

I said, "What are you talking about? Big Pete, we talked about the auction on Monday, and you knew I was making plans to do this."

Big Pete started raising his voice. "You do not have my permission to this!"

As the argument was beginning to start, the auctioneer said it would be better if he left so we could work this out. He told me I could call him when Big Pete and I reached a decision. He said we could make the arrangements later. He quickly walked to the front door and let himself out.

After the auctioneer left, Little Pete, Big Pete, and I stood in the kitchen, arguing. Before I realized it, Big Pete and I were yelling and screaming at each other.

He raised his fist to hit me, and I stated in a calm, collected, and deadly tone, "I'm not my momma. I hit back and I don't hit like a girl. The other day was a freebie."

He just stared at me, lowered his fisted hand, and threatened me, "I could kill you, Belinda."

I said, "That may be true, but before you do, I will cause you some serious pain that won't go away for a long, long time. I can say this to you, Pete King, one of us will be going to the bone yard before this is all said and done. So you better think twice before you raise your fist at me again because I will not give you the second chance to change your mind."

I looked over at Little Pete and down to the ground. Little Pete pissed his pants, and that poor old man's hands were trembling. I didn't realize I had a butcher knife in my hand.

Big Pete grunted and went into the basement. I'm sure he was going to get drunk.

I turned to Little Pete, "How dare you! Get out of my sight!"

That evening, after cooking everyone dinner, I decided to find out where my mother's friends were hiding. After what had happened between Big Pete and me this time, I wanted to see if they were truly friends of Momma's. I pulled out my mother's address book and called Brenda Lane. Brenda had been my mother's friend ever since my mother was her boss decades ago when Brenda was my mother's secretary. I spoke with Brenda, and she told me about the abuse. She told me that after a while, Big Pete would not let Mom be around her. Brenda told me that she and her husband didn't want to be involved with Big Pete and my mother, anyway, after they witnessed the severity of the abuse that went on between the two of them.

I asked her why she did not contact my sister and me at the very least to let us know what was going on.

She didn't want to get involved. Brenda asked about her daughter's wedding portrait that my mother had commissioned and paid for. Brenda said she was willing to pay for it now that she had money to do so. I told her it was between her and my mother. I told her that was not my decision to make. I hung up the phone. I called my mother's other alleged friends. I spoke with Linda and Janet. They both told the same stories. I was so angry about how cold and cruel people could be. They all gave the excuse that they didn't want to be involved, but all they had to do was either call or write Christina and me. They all had our addresses. I just could not believe my ears.

CHAPTER XLIX

Thursday morning I started the day expecting Little Pete to be gone, but to my surprise, he pulled into the driveway. I thought, *How dare he.* I went to the sliding glass door and made sure it was still locked. I stood there watching as Little Pete walked to the glass door.

Little Pete said through the glass door, "Belinda, I'm sorry. I didn't know Big Pete had already given you the green light, but that attorney you hired regarding that power of attorney doesn't give you the same rights as your mother would have regarding the property."

I asked, "Now where would you find out about this because I never told you anything?"

Little Pete answered, "Your mother."

I asked, "What?" I opened the sliding glass door and let him in.

Little Pete came in, sat on the sofa, and said, "Your mother has been calling me every night for the last couple of weeks, and I have been telling her everything you have been doing. She calls Big Pete as well. They are not in separation mode either. Big Pete calls me, and I tell him everything as well.

"I was also called as a witness for the grand jury, and I lied about my involvement because that was what I was told to say. I told them I knew nothing, but you know I did. The grand jury believed me, and I was let go.

"They don't want you to sell any of their property, and they will both lie about it, giving you anything. I am not quitting because I don't have to. You will continue paying me, or I will tell things on you, even if they are not true."

I shook my head because Little Pete didn't know about the affidavit that my attorney so wisely made my mother sign. I guess my mother had forgotten about that.

I said in a deadly tone, "I don't need you, Little Pete! I never did, but now I know what you are. If you ever tell another thing I'm doing or accept another call from my mother, I will turn over the records I have on you. I will keep you for one more month, and then it's time for you to leave."

Little Pete said, "No, I will be here until everything is done because that is what I promised Big Pete and your mother."

I said, "Okay, go in the basement and start packing, or do you plan on stealing that as well?"

Little Pete said, "I don't steal."

I said, "You better not."

I showed him what I wanted him to pack, and I told him that I would be back soon so that we could move it. I got into the White Beast and drove straight to my shop. I parked the White Beast right in front of the shop, and I walked straight in through the front door. I walked as if I were marching. Thank God there were no customers in the shop.

I barked my orders at Big Pete, "Get out of my shop right now, or I will have charges of theft brought against you. It is over!"

Big Pete angrily yelled, "I'm not going anywhere, and there isn't anything you can do about it! It is over when I say it is!"

I screeched, "Oh, yes there is!" I walked out of the shop into the next shop and asked if I could use their phone. I dialed 911. I stood outside my shop to wait for the police. I guess I was blessed that day because ten minutes later, the two deputy sheriffs who had been at the Daisy house showed up.

Deputy Sheriff Franklin said to me, "It's about damn time!"

I said, "I told you the other night if there were crimes committed that I thought needed reporting, I would do it."

He laughed. I showed them receipts and the items that were missing from my shop. They found more cash receipts crumpled up in Big Pete's trashcan along with some of the money in his pocket. He had four checks that were written out to Cognac Run. The receipts and checks totaled $1,800. I showed them my legal documents verifying the shop and its contents were mine, along with the affidavit stating that all the property at Mom and Big Pete's home was given to me. I told them that I feared he would try to hurt my family even more after this. I told them that he wasn't even supposed to be in my shop. I told them about him running his business through his son's name and gave them the telephone number of my attorney. I told them that I knew there was nothing they could do about future crimes, but I requested that they note my concerns in their report just in case.

They handcuffed him and took him away. I had forgotten to get my keys for the shop back from him. That was a huge mistake on my part! I didn't realize it until I locked up the shop and had returned to the Daisy house. I drove with Little Pete and helped him store more of our things in the storage unit. Be damned, when I went back to the shop, Big Pete was back there already!

He gave me a wicked laugh and said, "You actually thought you were going to get rid of me that easy?"

I walked out of my shop and drove back to the Daisy house. I was livid!

Little Pete said, "Belinda, I want to take you to the captain of the sheriff's office in Snobville. I think you need to talk with him regarding that power of attorney."

I said, "Okay, Little Pete." We drove in silence. I thought, *What is this little weasel up to now?*

We went into the reception area and waited a few minutes. The captain introduced himself and asked us to have a seat in the two chairs in front of his desk. He told me that Little Pete spoke with him yesterday evening regarding the altercation I had with Big Pete. He told me that my attorney and all the other stupid attorneys had it wrong regarding power of attorneys. I could not just go to Mom and Big Pete's house and take whatever I wanted. I could not just break a window because my mother could do it. If there were a physical fight, even if it ended with me lying on the ground, I would be arrested for trespassing. The captain went on and on and on.

I asked him questions. I did not understand how he could interpret the laws like that. I told him that both parties had given me their things. He continued saying it would be me who would be arrested, not Big Pete. Regarding the other issues, I would have to get an attorney, and it would be a civil matter. Because it was a she-said/he-said situation, it would be up to the judge to decide who was telling the truth and who was lying.

I looked over at the weasel, Little Pete, and he was smiling from ear to ear. The captain continued saying that every time I spoke with Big Pete or moved anything to make sure I had permission and a witness with me. I couldn't believe my ears. Little Pete set this whole thing up to make sure he was needed and would continue blackmailing me for a paycheck. I truly wanted to snap that little man's neck in two at this point! We drove back to the Daisy house in silence. I didn't even say goodbye to Little Pete. I was so angry!

I made dinner and at around 7:30 p.m. I received a phone call. It was Bill Bank again. He continued going on and on about me having charges filed against Big Pete that day. I told him that if Big Pete wasn't out of my shop by the following afternoon and the keys returned to me, I would call the sheriff's office every day reporting him as trespassing in my shop. I would slap fees against him for nonpayment of rent and utilities. I would slap a restraining order on him next, but that fat sorry-ass son of a bitch would be out of my shop for good by the following week. That I promised. He could do it either the easy way or the hard way. I didn't give a flying fuck. He started this war and I would fight him. I would fight him with my last dying breath.

After hanging up with Bill Bank, I went into the kitchen. I opened up Uncle Frank's bottle of whiskey and took a heavy swig. It was bitter and burned the whole way down my throat. At that point, I didn't care. I took another swig and then another. After the third swig, I wanted to vomit. I opened up the refrigerator and grabbed a soda. I stood there with the refrigerator open and drank the whole soda. Then, I closed the refrigerator door, went back into the Florida room, and lit a cigarette.

CHAPTER L

Friday morning I had no other choice but to find another way to sell things to pay the debts and attorney fees. I had forgotten about the booth that Mom had told me about, and I knew I would have to take care of that as well. I couldn't wait until Thomas arrived. Everyone around me was fighting against me and trying to stop me from doing what was right. All they were doing was hurting themselves and others. I called the auctioneer first thing and told him that I was sorry about the previous day. I told him that I would be by on Monday with some things I would like to auction. He said that would be fine, but I would have to sign a document stating the property was mine. I said that I would do so.

I went to the shop, and Big Pete told me that he was moving out first thing Monday morning because his attorney instructed him to do so. He acted as if nothing had happened the day before. I told him that would be fine. He swore he would not steal or take any money. I told him that I wasn't going to hold my breath.

Little Pete and I packed some of the furniture and other things that I had already gotten out of Mom and Big Pete's house. I took them to the booth located in the antique and collectibles shop. I introduced myself to the woman who ran the shop and showed her my power of attorney. I told her that I was transferring everything over to my name and paid for the December check that my mother bounced as well as January through March. I gave her a list of the new inventory that I had brought. Little Pete and I set up everything in the large booth. I told the woman I would be by every Friday to pick up a check for anything that had been sold. I dropped off Little Pete at the Daisy house and told him I would see him on Monday. I went to the shop and asked Big Pete if he would leave and stay away until he moved on Monday. I guess Big Pete wasn't in the mood to start an argument with me because I had customers in the shop, and he left without causing a scene.

This was the day that the predators came out to play in the antique and collectibles world—the people who know you are desperate for money and give you nothing for your items. They are the type of people that prey on desperate or ignorant people. Such as when someone loses a loved one and needs to auction or sell things to make money, but they auction or sell them for hardly anything. I have learned from my own experience that this type of person is just as dishonest as Big Pete. What is so sad is that no laws protect people in these situations. So I just started selling items and took what was offered because I had no other choice now that I could not auction things to pay the debts that Mom, Big Pete, Auntie Bea, and Uncle Frank had created. My auctioneer, even though he was a coward, was just one of a few dealers who were truly honest. The other hundreds of dealers, and what I considered low-class auctioneers, ripped me off to no end, but I had no choice because Mom, Little Pete, and Big Pete would not step aside so I could do the right thing.

Greed is such an ugly thing. It's like a virus that spreads through the air. I closed up the shop late to service all the customers. I returned to the Daisy house, and again Uncle Frank had several messages for me. I guess Big Pete had started again over a gas credit card that Uncle Frank had. I called Big Pete. He said if I didn't get Uncle Frank to return his gas card, he was going to have credit card fraud charges filed against him. While Big Pete was still on the phone, I asked Uncle Frank if he had the gas card. Uncle Frank said it was his gas card, not Big Pete's, and he proceeded to pull his wallet out of his back pocket.

I requested, "Just let me see it, Uncle Frank."

Lo and behold, it had Big Pete's name on it, not Uncle Frank's name. I told Big Pete that I would destroy it. Big Pete said there was a $500 debt on it.

I said, "I'm not going to pay it because there is no way Uncle Frank charged that much gas on the card. I could see you, Big Pete, incurring that much since you are driving a van."

Of course, Big Pete blackmailed me and said if I didn't pay it he would have charges filed against Uncle Frank anyway.

I said, "Fuck you, Big Pete, and the horse you rode in on. I will get the bill from you on Monday."

Big Pete said, "Fine."

I turned my attention to Uncle Frank as I angrily barked orders, "Uncle Frank, give me that damn credit card, now!"

Uncle Frank retorted, "No. Your momma gave me this card to use. I don't give a damn if Big Pete's name is on it. It's my card."

I lowered my voice as I said again, "Uncle Frank, give me the card."

The next thing I knew, Uncle Frank hit me hard on top of my head while I was bending over him trying to get the card. I became so angry, but before I lost my temper and almost decided to physically take the card from him, I grabbed my purse and left. I drove straight to Samantha's house. I told Samantha about the entire mess. She picked up the phone and started scolding her father. I went back to town and checked into a hotel. I needed a night of peace.

CHAPTER LI

I got up and checked out of the hotel the next morning. I went back to the Daisy house to put on a clean pair of clothes.

Uncle Frank was already up and started scolding me, "Where the hell have you been? You've been out all night. I've been worried sick. Just wait until your auntie gets hold of you, girl."

I retorted, "It's none of your damn business, Uncle Frank. I'm a grown woman. My goings and comings are none of your damn business. I am not sixteen years old anymore."

Uncle Frank humbly said, "Okay, okay. I'm sorry I hit you yesterday; just don't take off like that again."

He reached into his back pocket, pulled out his wallet, and took out the gas credit card with Big Pete's name on it and said, "Since you got all my kids riding my ass about it, here, take the damn thing."

I took it, grabbed a pair of scissors that were sitting on the table and immediately cut up the card.

After I did that, Uncle Frank asked, "I want my own card now. Are you going to help me get one?"

I answered, "Yes, Uncle Frank, I will stop up at the Exxon gas station up the road today and pick up an application for you."

Uncle Frank said, "I want to have Jane removed off of my checking account."

I said, "Uncle Frank, you cannot just arbitrarily remove Mom off your checking account because the banks will not allow you to do that. You must have both parties sign the documents and there is no way I'm paying an attorney to go to the jail to do that."

Uncle Frank said, "She's been stealing my money, and I want her removed."

I said, "Stop it, Uncle Frank. She has not stolen any money from you. She is in jail, and she can do nothing now anyway. You know you have

293

three retirement deposits coming from the state and federal government, and it's a pain in the ass to change your direct deposits with them."

Uncle Frank said, "I don't care. Just fix it for me."

I said, in an agitated tone, "Fine, Uncle Frank. I'll take you to your bank on Monday."

I loaded the pickup truck with another load of things to sell and took off to my shop. The day went great in terms of sales. The downside was that I knew that I was losing money because I was selling everything for much less than the true value. Throughout this liquidation I lost a small fortune.

My mother called me at the shop again. She was very upset because I could not come visit her. I told her Fridays, Saturdays, and Sundays were my best days at the shop, and I had to raise funds somehow. I became very angry regarding her calling Big Pete and Little Pete and stopping me from having an estate auction. Of course, she could not see the estate auction as being the best way. She wanted me to pay off her debts with money from the sale of my belongings, not hers. I told her that she hadn't learned anything. She said I would sell what she wanted me to sell.

I told her, "No, it will not be that way. I will sell whatever I can to make things right again." I finally caved and told her I would come visit her that afternoon. Of course, we argued until she was cut off.

I think it was still in the morning, and I was blessed because I didn't have any customers yet. Auntie came waltzing through the back door of my shop and lit up a cigarette.

I said, "Auntie Bea, you need to put that cigarette out, please."

Auntie Bea said angrily, "Belinda, don't talk to me like that! When your momma was running the store, she let me smoke in here."

It wasn't worth an argument with her so I let her do what she wanted to do.

Auntie Bea started yelling and screaming at me about the night before. She told me that only whores stayed out all night. She told me while I was there I should conduct myself like a lady. She just went on and on until I couldn't take anymore.

I yelled back at her, "First of all, Auntie Bea, I'm a grown woman! I am not sixteen years old anymore. I'm tired of you and Uncle Frank's bullshit. Get out of my shop now before you cause any more problems!"

Auntie Bea would not leave. She said I was lying about doing anything regarding her property, and she wanted her money back. She said I had been there for almost a month, and I had been doing nothing but help Frank and I had done nothing for her.

I sarcastically commented, "Oh really, Auntie Bea? Well, let's see. I've picked up thousands of dollars of your bounced checks so far, but I've done nothing for you?"

Auntie Bea said, "Your mother did those, not me."

I irritably said, "Bullshit, Auntie Bea. They were your property tax, your homeowner's insurance; several thousand dollars for some type of maintenance to your home, and credit card payments that were in your name. Shall I go on?"

Auntie Bea said, "Stop being nasty, Belinda. Enough—I'm going to do my grocery shopping."

I said, "That's a good idea, Auntie Bea; just don't write another bad check. I'm sorry for losing my temper with you. I'm scared too, Auntie Bea. I don't know any more than you do about what is going to happen. I promise as soon as I do, you will be the first to know regarding your land. I've never lied to you. Why would I start now? It doesn't get me anywhere."

Auntie Bea gave me a kiss on my cheek and said, "I'm sorry too for picking a fight with you."

As she was walking out the back door, we both saw my landlord standing there.

He said, "I will not tolerate this type of behavior in my buildings."

Neither Auntie Bea nor I said a word.

I locked up the shop early and drove to go see my mother. I noticed for over a week now a red two-door Chevy with government plates had been following me but really thought nothing of it until that day. The man had parked in the back parking lot of the shops, and he had followed me from the time I had left my shop, and I was almost at the jail.

I decided it was time to find out if he was intentionally following me, or if it had just been coincidence this week. I quickly made a right turn down a street that I knew was a dead end. I looked into my rearview mirror, and be damned if that vehicle didn't turn directly behind me. As soon as I got to the end of the road, I turned very quickly and parked the pickup truck in the middle of the road, cutting off the small road, so he could not get around me.

I jumped out of the truck, reached behind the seat, and grabbed the large crowbar that was stored there. I had my military ID in my back pocket, and I ran until I was standing directly in front of his car, after he had turned around.

The front end of his car was facing the side of the pickup truck. I stood in the middle of the road between his car and my mother's pickup truck. Either he would have to run me down or ram into the pickup truck. I was holding the crowbar loosely in my hand with my arm partly out in front of my body.

I yelled, "Get out of the vehicle now, sir. Identify yourself immediately!"

The man had trouble getting out of the vehicle because he was an older man and was about the size of Big Pete.

He stood by the driver's door and said, "I'm a private investigator for the DOL."

I said, "Give me the full name of the agency. DOL stands for many departments, sir."

He said, "Department of Labor."

I asked, "Department of Labor?"

He answered, "Yes."

I asked, "Why in the hell is the Department of Labor following me?"

Before I gave him a chance to answer, I walked toward him and asked him to show me his ID. I guess he did not have to do that, but he did. In turn, I pulled out my military ID and showed him who I was. He became embarrassed as his face became flushed.

I asked, "Do you have a warrant to do this? If so I would like to see it because I was never served."

He replied, "I wasn't aware of a warrant. I am a private investigator, and I do not need one."

I said, "You are driving a government vehicle and your ID says DOL. You maybe a private investigator, but your paycheck is GS, which therefore tells me you are a government employee, which in turns means you can only drive a government vehicle for government use, not personal use or for another job. Therefore, you must have some type of orders signed by a judge or other authority giving you authorization to follow me. This dictates to me that a judge or other authority of this nature has probable reason to violate my privacy. This is considered a constitutional right that I have given my life for to protect. I know for a fact, I'm not under investigation for any crimes because I was not told or made aware nor have I been charged with any crimes of any nature, nor have I ever committed or intend to conduct myself in any form of criminal activities, so I see no probable cause. If I catch you following me again I will take immediate action against you and your department. I will contact JAG because this would be considered their juridical authority."

His eyes grew large, and I had the feeling that he didn't know that I knew a little bit about our government agencies and some of my rights. He replied, "I will have to check into that, but I consider you threatening me with that crowbar."

I said, "Sir, I have the crowbar because I thought I had a flat tire until I realized you were following me. If I threatened you by having a crowbar in my hands because I was planning on popping the hubcap off, I'm truly sorry."

He said, "I guess this was just a misunderstanding."

I said, "I guess it was, but please go back to your department and tell them that if they suspect me regarding anything to please contact me. I will be more than happy to cooperate to the best of my abilities, but I will not have my rights violated for information that you are trying to acquire; just simply ask. Not everyone in our country is a bad person."

He said, "I will relay your message."

I said, "Thank you."

The man never followed me again.

I visited with my mother after this and told her I suspected after this encounter that she was still not cooperating with the U.S. Attorney's office. I told her that she would have to start cooperating because they were suspecting me of wrongdoing.

I told her, "You know that is not true. You need to stop fighting me regarding my property. I want you to get on the phone first thing Monday and talk with your attorney. I will not be sucked into this crap. I will pack up right now and leave."

Mom said she would stop playing games and do as I wish. I went back to the shop and caught the afternoon shoppers. I kept the shop open late to make up for lost time.

*   *   *

On Sunday, I discovered Uncle Frank's phone was tapped when I heard the familiar click that I had been trained to hear. I could not believe it as I quickly took the phone apart and discovered the small devise. I am so disappointed in the crimes that are being committed against me by my own local government. Still shocked of my discovery I put the phone back together and decided I would use this to my advantage. I made sure the people listening in heard me tell them they had better have some type of orders and probable cause. Other than that, Sunday was a peaceful day. I packed another load into the pickup truck and ran my shop all day.

CHAPTER LII

I woke up at 5:00 a.m. the next morning and could not believe that I had been there for almost a month already. I felt like I would never get back to my own life. It seemed that this nightmare would not end. I felt like vampires were sucking the blood from my veins.

I prepared for the day, just as I had done every morning since I arrived into the nightmare. I decided it was time to pay more debt now that I had obtained the funds to do so. I went into the Florida room and started writing out checks to pay some of the debt. I wanted to cry because I had such a long way to go. The telephone rang.

My mother's attorney said, "Hello, Belinda, it's me."

I recognized his voice and said, "Yes, what is going on? I didn't think attorneys started working so early."

He laughed and said, "Yes, sometimes we have to. I'm calling because the U.S. Attorney said you have to stop selling from your shop because there is some type of confusion as to who owns the property."

In a very angry voice, I said, "It is my shop, and all the contents in it are mine. Do I need to show them my documentation? If they try to stop me from conducting business, I will file a lawsuit on them faster than you can say, 'go.' Besides, how do you think you are going to be paid? Ask them how I am supposed to make restitution? What the hell is the matter with them?"

He said, "Okay. Okay. Belinda, I will call you back within the hour to let you know."

I replied, "Know what? I do not need their permission to do anything. I am an American. I will see to it that the entire country knows what they are doing."

He said, "Just let me give them a call and we will work this out."

I was angry that any government agency in *my* country would try to violate a citizen from conducting business by taking the word of crooks

Linda D. Coker

and thieves. It was bad enough that I was being followed and my uncle's phone was being illegally tapped.

Americans were going to have to do something. Our government was totally out of control and needed to be leashed once again. Now they were going after the crook's children when it was totally obvious the children had nothing to do with this. I was boiling mad again.

What in the hell do Big Pete, Little Pete, and my mother think they are going to accomplish? At this moment, I came very close to having charges filed against everyone. I was very tempted to take the documents that I had and turn Auntie Bea over as well as Uncle Frank for credit card fraud and Little Pete for blackmail and check kiting because I could prove his involvement.

About thirty minutes later, my mother's attorney called again. He told me he spoke with the U.S. Attorney, and he spoke with my mother.

"Belinda, tomorrow you need to bring the documents that your mother needs to show the paper trail that leads to Big Pete. The U.S. attorney totally agrees with you, and they want you to keep doing what you are doing. They said it doesn't really matter whether the property was yours or not because you are making restitution to as many victims as possible. It would cost them more money to fight you and then try to sell it because it was not financially worth it. They truly appreciate the sacrifices you are making, and the U.S. Attorney apologizes for offending you.

"Your mother has obtained permission to call you in twenty minutes so I am going to hang up now."

I thanked my mother's attorney.

I was still very angry with the U.S. Attorney. They apparently had been following me ever since I arrived from Germany, and they should have been able to see that I had been trying to make a right from a wrong. I would never forget what they had tried to imply. I picked up the phone and called a few moving companies. I called the company that was the cheapest for a four-man moving team. I would provide the moving U-Haul. I scheduled it for 3:00 p.m. and gave them the storage unit address.

Little Pete pulled up, and I told him we had to go to the storage unit and move some things.

We loaded up ten boxes of figurines into the pickup truck. I gave Little Pete the address of the auctioneer. I had Little Pete help me carry the boxes inside the auction house, and it took several hours for the auctioneer and me to complete the inventory. This time, he had me sign a note stating the property was mine. He planned to auction my things that weekend. Of course, the nosey Little Pete was listening to every word. He was a spy for my mother and Big Pete, and I couldn't get rid of him. I had Little Pete take me to a U-Haul dealership, and I rented a truck for the afternoon. I followed Little Pete back to the storage unit. The four men I hired were already there, waiting for me.

I had run out of room in my storage unit, so I went into the office to secure the larger unit. Patty gave me the paperwork to sign, and I paid in advance for a full year. Once I had the new unit number, I headed out. As I was having them move everything over into the new unit, Big Pete pulled up behind us in his van. Thank God I had four men working for me!

They all stopped what they were doing as soon as Big Pete started yelling at me.

"This is my stuff, you stupid bitch, and you are stealing it!"

As he was yelling, he got closer and closer until he was right in my face. The coward Little Pete just stood there, but all four of the moving men got in front of me and one lightly pushed Big Pete away from me.

The other moving man said, "Sir, I am asking you to leave before there is any trouble."

Big Pete said, "I'm ordering you to stop moving my things. This stuff isn't hers."

I believe the older man was the leader of the team because he was the one who said, "No, sir, it isn't your stuff. For Pete's sake, here is her wedding picture. Did you play girls' field hockey?" He picked up one of my field hockey sticks. "This looks like a lot of women's clothing as well."

Big Pete looked over at Little Pete and snarled as he walked quickly back to his van.

I said to the four men, "God bless you! Thank you!"

The leader of the team said, "You're more than welcome."

They all went back to work moving things from one unit to the other.

I said to Little Pete, "You can leave now. I don't think I need to pay you for standing there. You can take the pickup back to the Daisy house and give the keys to Uncle Frank before you leave. Do not expect to be paid sick leave anymore. I am only going to pay you for the hours that you work for me." I also told him, in front of everyone, that it was in his best interest to start looking for another job. Little Pete agreed with me and left.

After the moving team moved and packed everything tight in the new storage unit, we drove to the Daisy house, loaded up the U-haul, drove back to the storage unit and unloaded. After that trip, we still had a little bit of space left. I figured I could move some more things in it after Thomas arrived. I knew I could not afford another storage unit to store the rest of our belongings. I asked the leader of the team if he could follow me up the road to return the truck and give me a ride back to the Daisy house. He graciously agreed.

Uncle Frank was sitting in his chair, watching as the man dropped me off, and as soon as I walked into the house, Uncle Frank started lecturing me about taking rides with strangers, especially strange men.

He stated, "You are a married woman!"

I just ignored him and said, "I'm headed to the shop. I will be back in a few minutes."

I arrived at my shop, and Big Pete was standing outside the front door locking it. I asked, "Can I have the keys?"

Big Pete said, "Yes. You're right, Belinda, it was better that I went ahead and moved out since you're not going to have your shop for much longer."

I said, "I wish it had been different, but you are bull headed, Big Pete."

Big Pete replied, "Yeah, you're probably right. I'm sorry about the storage unit. Where did you move my things, since I realized after one of those moving men pointed it out, it was your stuff?"

I said, "Everything is secured in the basement of the Daisy house, but remember Pete, nothing belongs to you. You know you gave me everything."

Big Pete said, "Oh, okay. You're right."

I said, "Oh, before I forget, here are your personal papers. I retrieved them out of the safe the other day, and I forgot to give them to you."

Big Pete handed me the keys, took the folder, and said, "Thank you."

I told him, "I had spoken with Mom about them. She didn't want me to give them to you, but I thought it was the decent thing to do, so here they are." I glanced up at his face, and I saw a tear fall down Big Pete's face. I felt sad for him. "I just wish you would let me do what's right."

Big Pete didn't say anything as he walked away, got into his van, and left. For a few moments, it was beyond my control, but I felt empathy towards Big Pete. He had lost everything because he was so greedy. But then I remembered how he treated everyone, like we were all dirt beneath his feet, and I remembered a phrase that my grandmother and mother used to tell us all the time when we mistreated people: "As a man climbs that ladder, he should be careful of the little people that he steps on going up it because if he should fall, that will determine how hard he lands."

Now look at the mighty Big Pete. He has stolen and treated all the little people around him like dirt. He has fallen, and there was no one to catch him. He was learning a life lesson that he should have learned a long, long time ago. I knew Big Pete was angry that he lost this battle with me. We both knew that we didn't mean anything we'd said. I knew he would continue fighting me every day, and it would only get worse and worse. I knew I had to be careful because Big Pete was a professional con. It seemed that he could charm anyone. He could lie about anything, and he was believed. I knew this evil battle wasn't over, and God only knew what would come out of Pandora's Box next.

CHAPTER LIII

The next day I had Little Pete help me put the file boxes that the U.S. Attorney requested in the pickup, and we went to the courthouse. We walked through the front door into a nice waiting room. The receptionist had a glass window with a slot in it, like the one at the jail. The doors all had glass tops, but they were kept locked. They had to push a buzzer to let you into the other area. She buzzed us through the door, and we were escorted to a large conference room.

A square conference table surrounded by blue cushioned chairs was in the middle of the room. It was almost as large as the room. My mother was seated at one end of the table with the female assistant district attorney, my mother's attorney, and three other people in business suits who I did not recognize.

Mom got up from the table and hugged me. "Belinda, what would I do without you? You are the only one who cares about me!"

I hugged her back and simply said, "I love you, Momma, and you know I will help you any way I can."

After that, she went straight to the two large file boxes that Little Pete and I set on the table when we walked in.

Mom said, "Thank you, Belinda."

The female assistant U.S. attorney said, "Thank you, Mrs. Star, for your cooperation."

I looked at her confused, but said nothing. Instead, I asked, "Have you removed the illegal tap on my great-uncle's phone?"

My mother dropped the file folder she had in her hand and let out a gasp. "What?"

My mother's attorney looked at the assistant U.S. attorney with his eyes wide.

My mother's attorney asked, "What tap? Mrs. Star has nothing to do with this. Have there been any charges filed against her to warrant this?"

The assistant U.S. attorney answered, "No, there is no phone tap."

I viciously asked, "Oh really? This past weekend I caught a DOL employee following me. In fact, he has been following me for a couple of weeks. Are you going to deny that as well?"

The assistant U.S. attorney was a bit agitated and said, "Mrs. Star, I swear to you this office did not do anything of the sort. I can't speak for the DOL, but I assure you I will get to the bottom of this. I promise it will stop."

I said, "Thank you."

Mom's attorney asked if I could wait until they were finished so I could take the files back to storage. I told him I had no problem doing so. Little Pete and I waited for about two hours before we were called back in so that we could take the file boxes back to storage.

Little Pete finally spoke to me and said, "Belinda, you should not have done that. You can cause your mother more problems. If they are following you and tapping Frank's phone there is nothing you can do about it."

I didn't even try to be nice to Little Pete because he was a creep and I told him, "Shut your stupid mouth! I could care less what you think. This is none of your business."

Little Pete said, "You don't have to talk to me like that."

I asked sarcastically, "Are you looking for another job? Blackmailer. When I arrived, I thought you were my friend and ally. Instead, I have discovered you are a lying, backstabbing traitor. You care absolutely nothing for my mother or me. All you care about is what is in it for you!"

I figured Thomas would have to deal with him when he arrived. That would be the only way to get this nasty little weasel out of our lives.

Little Pete answered, "Yes, Belinda, I'm looking for another job and I am not blackmailing you. I'm not your enemy, Belinda."

I glared at him angrily. I guess there was no need to be nasty to him because it wasn't getting me anywhere. So I said, "I'm sorry for being nasty. There was no reason for it."

Little Pete said, "I understand."

We drove back in to the Daisy house in silence. Once we arrived, I told Little Pete I didn't need him because I had to take care of personal business for Uncle Frank and Auntie Bea and I would see him tomorrow. He left.

I went over to Auntie Bea's and collected her files for her taxes to take to the CPA that Mom used to do everyone's taxes. I had already gotten Uncle Frank's taxes and the shop's taxes. I drove back into town and met with the CPA. I also asked him if I would be able to do this year's taxes for the shop because I should have it closed down by the middle or end of March. He said he could handle all that as well. I told him that I would pay him now for the shop, and he would need to bill Auntie Bea and Uncle Frank for their personal taxes. He said that would be fine.

I drove back to the Daisy house and asked Uncle Frank if he wanted to go ahead and change his checking account today since I was unable to do it for him the day before. He said he didn't feel like doing it, and he would like to do it later on this week. I agreed.

I put another load of things into the pickup truck, drove it to the shop, and unloaded it. I had a bunch of dealers from other shops coming into the store to make deals. They were like sharks with their prey within reach, and I could do nothing. I put up a sign saying "Going out of business." The dealers totally cleaned out the shop that day. They bought everything that I had just brought in as well as the items that were already there.

I called Thomas and told him when he had all our tax documents together to take them to the H&R Block that was right outside the military housing and have them do our taxes that year. I asked him to make sure he had that done before he flew back to Virginia. He had no problem doing that. He asked how everything was going and I told him it was going very slowly. I told him that I would fill him in on the crap when he arrived.

CHAPTER LIV

Wednesday was another day of hell. Big Pete called first thing in the morning.

He said, "Belinda, Little Pete was here yesterday. Technically, he is still working for your mother and me. He does what we tell him to do, not you. You will pay him eight-hour days. The housekeeper's sister said I was going to have to pay her sister if I want her to clean. You will have to pay her because the house needs cleaning. I talked with your mother and she will be giving you a call. Also they have cut the electricity off and since you are using electricity to move the stuff I think it's only fair that you pay it or I will not allow you to move or take anything else out of this house."

I simply said, "I will make my decision when I speak with my mother. Goodbye."

Within a few minutes, the telephone rang again, and I answered it, "Hello."

The recording from the jail started and I accepted the call. My mother said, "Belinda?"

I said, "Yes."

My mother said, "You have to pay Little Pete for eight hours a day, Belinda, whether you need him or not. You are going to have to pay him for what he does for Big Pete."

I asked, "Is he not an independent contractor?"

Mom answered, "Well, yes he is, but that doesn't matter; you have to pay him for eight hours a day and sick time."

I said, "Oh no, I don't. If he is independent, which he is to me, and I pay him if he works for me, not you or Big Pete. He has been blackmailing me regarding you. I do not want to be around the creep. I have no other choice but to keep him on because he says he can cause you more trouble. You need to stop calling him and stop putting up blockades for me to sell all this crap and pay all these debts."

Mom said, "I'm not going to stop calling Little Pete."

I said, "Whatever Mom. You're going to do whatever anyway."

Mom said, "Belinda, one of those bounced checks I wrote went to my attorney. You are going to have to pay that as well. I gave him the shop number so I know he will be calling you later today regarding it."

I asked, "Damn, Mom, how many more bounced checks do you have?"

Mom answered, "I don't know. Also, you are going to have to pay the housekeeper as well and the electric bill."

I agreed, "Alright, Momma, how much is the electric bill?"

Mom answered, "Five hundred dollars because I was unable to pay it for the last couple of months."

I said, "That's ridiculous and I'm not going to pay it. I am positively not paying the housekeeper to clean up Big Pete's mess. If he wants a clean house then he can pay for it."

Mom said, "All you have to do is pay $100 to get the electric bill turned back on so he doesn't give us any more grief. You're right; you shouldn't have to pay the housekeeper."

I said, "Okay, Mom, I will pay the hundred dollars for the electric, but from now on he pays his own electric because we move during the day and we do not use any lights or any electricity."

We continued hashing out other issues until she was disconnected again. I saw Little Pete pull up and I told him I needed him to help me put another load of inventory into the pickup truck and help me unload it at the shop and then he needed to go to Mom and Big Pete's house and continue packing. I would catch up to him later so we could move another load. As soon as Little Pete and I started down the steps to the basement of the Daisy house the telephone rang again.

Uncle Frank yelled, "Belinda, you have a phone call."

It was Thomas's mom and she told me she had spoken with Thomas regarding the six dogs of my mother's and he agreed that she should take care of them, but Thomas and I would have to give her funds to provide for them. I told her that I had no problem with that. She then asked when I would like her to come and get the dogs. I told her I had already talked with my mother regarding them and she had no problems with it. I passed the message from my mother to Thomas's mother.

"She wanted me to tell you God bless you and thank you. My issue is going to be Big Pete so I will have to speak with him about it."

I proceeded in helping Little Pete load the pickup truck with some more store inventory. After we finished loading the pickup truck, Little Pete followed me in his van to my shop and we unloaded it. As I was unpacking and pricing the items, the telephone rang. I answered it and the woman on the phone told me she was the accountant for my mother's attorney's firm. She told me the large check that my mother paid them had bounced and she was sorry that it had taken so long to inform me because she did not know who was going to take care of it. I told her to destroy the check and to put the dollar amount back on the bill because I was only going to be able to pay her as I received the funds. I asked her if Mom's attorney told her he had lowered the previous total of the bill. She answered me saying no one told her about it. I told her she would have to fix that.

I started unpacking again and it seemed out of nowhere twenty-five people, men and women, walked into my shop all at once on a Wednesday. It seemed odd to me because it was a workday, but I thought nothing more about it because it meant potential sales. Out of the small crowd, one woman became conspicuous because she started asking me questions. This woman had dark, short hair cut in a bob. She was skinny and looked almost like a skeleton like Auntie Bea, but she was about my age or younger. She had a long straight nose with small lips and beady dark eyes. She was wearing small reading glasses.

The woman asked me, "Do you have any more of your mother's jewelry and furs?"

I answered her with a puzzled expression, "No, I do not have any jewelry or furs for sale. Why do you ask? And who do you think my mother is?"

The woman didn't answer me; instead she asked, "Is this your shop or are you running this for your parents?"

I replied, "This is my shop and my father lives in Maryland. My parents have been divorced since I was about nine. Who are you?" The woman didn't answer.

To divert my attention to her bizarre questions she purchased some things along with all the other people who seemed to know each other. They left just as quickly as they had entered my shop. I thought nothing more about it after they left and continued unpacking and pricing the items for sale.

After that, business was slow and I decided to go ahead and close the shop around 2:00 p.m. I did my banking and drove out to Mom and Big Pete's house.

I took the electric bill that Big Pete gave me, wrote out a check for $100, and called the electric company and asked them if they could go ahead and turn it back on. I had to give them another $100 today. I told them I would be there shortly.

I asked Big Pete about the dogs and he said he wanted to keep them for a while longer and he would have to talk to my mother about them. I told him that would be fine.

I told him he would have to speak with my mother because I did not have the funds to pay for the housekeeper, but to keep the peace I gave him another $100 bill and told him he could do with it as he pleased if he wanted to pay for the housekeeper or buy groceries. I knew he had funds coming in, but I just didn't know how much. I told Little Pete I would meet him at the Daisy house after I took care of the electric bill. I met Little Pete at the Daisy house and he helped me unload the truck and pack the boxes into the basement.

CHAPTER LV

Thursday at 3:00 in the morning, I heard the telephone ringing from the distance. I got out of bed quickly, ran into Uncle Frank's bedroom, and woke him when I answered the phone.

It was Thomas. He told me that he had dropped off the taxes and received the check in the mail from me to pay off the credit card that I had used when I first arrived. He told me he would pay off the credit card bill with it and I gave him the exact amount including the interest. He was just amazed I had it to the penny. I laughed at my husband and said of course I'm good because I'm an accountant. We both laughed. I did not realize it, but I sat almost on top of my great-uncle while he lay in the bed.

He must have laid there silent the entire time and said in an irritated voice, "Belinda, you're not so small anymore and I think you broke my hip. Could you please get off me now since you have hung up the phone so I can go back to sleep?"

I laughed at my Uncle Frank and said, "I'm sorry, Uncle Frank, but you are not so big anymore and I didn't see you."

I laughed as I walked out of his bedroom and heard him say, "Women!"

I believe that was Uncle Frank's favorite word as I laughed aloud, walking into the kitchen, and getting ready for a new day of hell.

I pulled out my note pad and added the new total of debt that needed to be paid and what I had paid. I felt I was slowly making it to my new goal. I just couldn't get over how expensive attorneys could be, and they just don't care as long as they take everything you own. What I could not understand was why our society needed them. Didn't our forefathers base our laws on the ten commandments? How hard was it to interpret stealing, lying, bearing false witness and so forth? Of course, mankind has to make these basic laws confusing to establish a market to take all the money from the victims as well as the villains. Isn't fraud the same thing as stealing? I was slowly learning that most people in our legal community are just as shady and crooked as the villains that they defend and prosecute. It seemed that the only people that ended up paying for it in the end were the family members of the criminals. In fact, our legal community tries to take down the innocent as well. I was very disappointed in these fellow Americans. I was sure there were a few out of a million attorneys out there that did have true honor and didn't take from the victims, bit sixty thousand dollars is pure highway robbery. In fact, attorneys seem to make more money than doctors do. How do you put a price tag on lives? What happened to the values of helping your fellow man when in need?

Uncle Frank came into the Florida room barefooted again with a cup of coffee in his hand. His toenails were long and nasty and since it was still early, I was going to take care of his nasty feet. I didn't want to do it, but it had to be done.

I went into the kitchen while he was still waking up, filled a large pot full of warm water and put some baby oil in it, came back into the Florida room, and said to Uncle Frank, "Here, Uncle Frank, let's soak your feet in this so I can clip those nasty toenails of yours. No wonder you have holes in your socks."

Uncle Frank did not give me any grief; he obediently let me put the pot under his feet, and then he put his feet in the big pot. After about five minutes or so, I took a pair of toenail clippers and started clipping his nails over the pot. It was a nasty job, but it needed doing.

I thought, *I don't have anyone that's going to take care of my godparents when I'm gone.* I knew it would be a year or so before I could come back and take care of them. I still had hope that Uncle Frank's children would take on the job.

Uncle Frank said, "Thank you, Belinda. Do you think you have time to take me to the bank today so I can get my checking account fixed? I want your mother's name removed."

I told Uncle Frank, "Like I told you the other day, Uncle Frank, you cannot just remove Mom's name like that, but I will take you so that you can see for yourself. We will leave about 8:30 this morning. I will call Little Pete and tell him I don't need him today."

I picked up the phone and called Little Pete.

I said, "Hello, Little Pete. I don't need you today because Uncle Frank wants me to take him somewhere. I will see you tomorrow morning because we have a lot to do."

Little Pete became angry. "Didn't Big Pete and your mother speak to you?"

I said, "Yes, they did, but your employment with them has nothing to do with me. If you don't like this arrangement then my advice to you is to seek new employment."

Little Pete asked, "Do you remember what I told you I would do?"

I answered, "Little Pete, I don't see the relevance of blackmailing me regarding my mother. You are going to do what you want to do, and I can't do anything about it. I do know this, Little Pete: you lied under oath and you can be held in contempt of court, plus you will be testifying against yourself regarding your involvement and I will see there is no deal cut with you. So again it's your choice."

Little Pete said, "Fine. I'll see you tomorrow."

I knew in the back of my mind that it was not over with Little Pete.

I was sure he would find something else to hold over my head. I knew I could not continue paying him. I just couldn't understand why he truly believed he could suck blood from a turnip.

Uncle Frank took a shower and got dressed so I could take him to the bank. He called Auntie Bea right before we left and told her I was taking him to the bank.

I didn't think much of this and I would regret the signs like these, even though they were in my face the entire time as to what the two of them were plotting. I guess love and trust is truly blind.

I drove Uncle Frank in his car to his bank. We arrived at the bank about 9:30. We both stood in line for the teller for about five minutes.

Uncle Frank asked, "Belinda, I'm not very good at this. Can you ask my questions for me?"

I answered, "Sure."

When we were next and we both stepped up to the counter, I said, "Hi. My name is Belinda Star and this is my great-uncle, Frank Gibbs." I gave her my military ID, my uncle's driver's license and his checkbook to look up his account. I continued, "My great-uncle would like to have Jane King's name removed from his checking account. I tried to explain to him that he couldn't just do that, but I told him we would see if we could. Can we do this?"

The lady looked up both Uncle Frank's and my name or it appeared to me that she did both our names. Her face became red and it appeared to me that she became scared of Uncle Frank and me. She didn't say anything; in fact, she ran from her station and into the back office. I looked over at Uncle Frank and he was looking at me. Both of us were totally confused why the woman reacted like that towards us. The next thing I knew, another older woman with the younger woman and two security guards came back out from the same door that the younger teller ran into. The younger lady stepped back into her station where Uncle Frank and I were standing.

The older lady had Uncle Frank's checkbook and both of our IDs in her hands and she had an angry look on her face. The two security guards had serious expressions on their faces. I became immediately scared and had no idea what this was all about.

The older lady and the security guards walked around to the line and approached us with the security guards on either side of her and said in a very serious and professional tone, "Ms. Star, Mr. Gibbs, could you please come with me?" She didn't even introduce herself.

Uncle Frank was moving to follow her, and I put my hand across his way to stop him and politely asked, "Excuse me. My name is Belinda D. Star. May I ask who are you and what this is all about before we follow you?"

She looked at the one security guard and he nodded. I guess for her to acknowledge me.

She answered, "My name is Ms. Peacock and I'm the manager of this branch. Mr. Gibbs name and your name have been flagged as fraud and the two of you have stolen a lot of money from this banking institute. The authorities have been contacted and we have been instructed to detain the two of you."

I said, "First of all, ma'am, I live in Germany because my husband is stationed there. Second of all, I have never stepped foot in any of your branches before in my life. Third of all, my great-uncle has had a checking account with you for decades. Neither one of us has ever stolen from you. Do you have a picture or a description of whoever was impersonating or using our names?"

The manager and the two security guards had puzzled expressions on their faces, and I guess we all realized we had a small crowd of customers around us at this time listening.

The manager quietly requested, "I would like to keep this private, Ms. Star." She pointed to a desk that was in front of the bank as she asked, "Can the two of you at least sit over there by that desk with me so we can figure this out?"

Uncle Frank and I obediently followed her and the security guards. After the three of us sat down, one security guard stood beside me and the other stood beside Uncle Frank. The entire situation was very intimidating. I just prayed that I was able to get Uncle Frank and myself out of this situation without having the authorities involved. I really was not sure what was taking place yet.

I looked over at Uncle Frank and noticed his hands were trembling. He was holding on to the arms of the chair for dear life. I instinctively patted his hand. He looked over at me with his eyes wide, and I smiled at him.

I said to Uncle Frank with a positive voice, "Don't worry, Uncle Frank. It's some kind of misunderstanding. I'll fix it."

I thought, *I bet Uncle Frank wishes he hadn't asked me to take him to the bank now.*

Ms. Peacock picked up the phone and called someone. Within seconds a young lady appeared by her side and gave her a file folder. Ms. Peacock opened the file folder on top of the desk in front of us. Still no one said anything. She began scanning the papers with her reading glasses on. She kept looking over at Uncle Frank's driver's license and my military ID. She looked up at the two us and said, "Well, I'm glad I didn't call the authorities because it is quite apparent these are not your signatures and not your social security numbers."

I asked, "Ma'am, do you have a picture of the people that impersonated us?"

She answered, "No, but if you can wait a few minutes I can get them faxed over."

I said, "That will be fine."

Uncle Frank said, "This is bull. I want to leave and have my checking account closed immediately, Belinda."

I said to Uncle Frank, "No, Uncle Frank. You asked me to do this and I want to get to the bottom of this now."

Uncle Frank said, "I'm going outside to smoke a cigarette."

I looked over at Ms. Peacock and she said, "Oh that will be fine because it will take a few minutes."

She got up from the desk and the one security guard asked her, "Do you still need us?"

Ms. Peacock answered, "No, I think I overreacted. I should have spoken to Ms. Star first." Ms. Peacock continued as she confessed to me, "Thank God your great-uncle has you because I would have called the authorities immediately if you had not asked the questions you did."

I didn't say anything. I just nodded in agreement with her. I got up and went outside where Uncle Frank was standing by an ashtray and joined him. I lit up a cigarette. I felt relieved that the worst part of this was over.

Uncle Frank said, "Belinda, you know it was your mother. I may have been wrong about her stealing my money, but she was stealing money from the bank using my name."

I said, "No, Uncle Frank, she is a woman and there is no way she could have done that with your name, but she could with mine. I'm not going to jump to conclusions until I see the faces."

Uncle Frank said, "Oh, I didn't think about that, but I'm totally confused about what just happened and how they did it, but it could have been Big Pete with your mother."

I said, "You may be right, but I don't think so. Big Pete is a big-time crook, not a penny-dime one. When he steals, he steals big."

I thought, *Maybe it could have been just my mother, who knows, but I have to see it for myself before I lay judgment.* I just wasn't going to be like everyone else in my family and just take the word of someone else. I would find out for myself before I ever pass judgment. What happened to you're innocent until proven guilty? Besides I wasn't here to do that anyway.

When we had finished our cigarettes, Uncle Frank and I went back inside the bank. We sat down in front of the desk again. We waited for about fifteen more minutes before Ms. Peacock returned carrying a file folder. She sat back down at the desk and opened the file. She handed me two pieces of paper. Each one had a copy of a Virginia driver's license.

She asked, "Do you know who these people are?"

I knew exactly who they were! Uncle Frank tried to take the papers from my hand. I would not let him see them yet.

I looked Ms. Peacock straight in the eyes and lied, "No, I don't know who these people are."

Then I handed the papers to Uncle Frank for him to look at. He looked over at me and I asked, "I don't think you know who these people are either, do you, Uncle Frank?"

Uncle Frank looked at me and was quiet for a few seconds. Then he looked over at Ms. Peacock and said, "No, I don't know these people either." He then handed the papers back to Ms. Peacock.

Uncle Frank and I both lied. The pictures on the copies of the driver licenses were of Auntie Bea and Little Pete. In fact it was Auntie Bea's signature. I knew her handwriting and so did Uncle Frank. If we identified Little Pete, we would have had to identify Auntie Bea. Right now, it was just better to lie. I was going to keep my promise to my mother, and I knew Uncle Frank wasn't going to turn his own sister in.

Ms. Peacock asked, "Ms. Star, this Jane King that's on your great-uncle's checking account, I know she is in jail for similar crimes. Is this why your uncle wants her removed?"

Before I had a chance to answer, Uncle Frank answered, "Yes."

I answered as well, "No, ma'am, Mrs. King was stealing to help my great-uncle."

Ms. Peacock said, "From the papers that I have scanned through, there is nothing out of the ordinary with your great-uncle's account. It doesn't appear that anyone has been stealing from him. I don't see a need in changing it because we must have both signatures in order to have her removed from his checking account."

Uncle Frank was now angry because I would not allow him to lie about my mother. Uncle Frank said, "I don't care! I want her removed from my checking account!"

Mrs. Peacock said, "Mr. Gibbs, the only thing we can do is give you a new account. We can't close this one because it is a joint account. It has your name and Jane King's name on it. You are equal partners in the account. I do not understand why you want to remove her when it is apparent that she stole *for* you, not *from* you."

Uncle Frank replied angrily, "I just would like no one else on my account, ma'am."

Ms. Peacock said, "Okay, Mr. Gibbs, we will open you a new account."

I said, "He has three direct deposits for his retirement funds, and they are all either federal or state. You know how hard it is going to be for me to change it?"

Ms. Peacock said, "I know. I guess we can set up from the old account a direct deposit from that account to the new one until you are able to change them all."

I looked over at Uncle Frank and asked, "Will that be okay?"

Uncle Frank answered, "Yes."

I said, "Well, since you don't need me to set up this new account I'm going across the street to get a cup of coffee, and I need to smoke a cigarette."

Uncle Frank replied, "Okay. Can you get me a cup as well?"

I answered, "Yes, I'll get you a cup as well."

Ms. Peacock said, "Don't be gone too long, we may still need you."

I looked at her with a puzzled expression and said, "Okay." I guess it was about fifteen to twenty minutes later when I returned and sat back down beside Uncle Frank. Ms. Peacock was typing away on her keyboard. Uncle Frank had copies of forms that he had signed earlier.

Ms. Peacock looked up from her computer and said to me, "We will have to do a specialized power of attorney regarding your uncle's account, and I will need you, Ms. Star, to sign it before we can open this new account for your great-uncle. If something—"

Uncle Frank was furious and said, "I don't need a power of attorney!"

I said, "I do not want to have any part of Uncle Frank's account because he will tell lies about me too. It's bad enough that I have to write out his checks and then beg him to sign them, but I do not want the responsibility of having my name associated with his account."

I glanced over at Uncle Frank, and he had a shocked expression on his face and he said, "Belinda!"

I said, "I'm sorry, Uncle Frank, but look what you are trying to pull regarding my mother."

Before Uncle Frank and I started to get into an argument, Ms. Peacock asked, "Well then, Mr. Gibbs, do you have anyone else that can take this responsibility? We must have a specialized power of attorney so they can write your checks and take care of your expenses if anything should happen to you. I'm sorry, but our policy is that someone of your age and your physical condition cannot open a new account without a power of attorney."

I said, "I'm going out for a cigarette."

Ms. Peacock said, "I'm joining you this time."

Uncle Frank frantically asked, "What about my account?"

Ms. Peacock said, "I will be back in a minute; it is your decision, Mr. Gibbs."

We both went outside, and Ms. Peacock asked, "Can I mooch a smoke off you? I left mine in the back office."

I answered, "Sure." I gave her my pack to take one and handed her my lighter.

After she lit her cigarette she passed my pack and lighter back to me.

After she exhaled her first puff, she looked over at me and said, "Ms. Star, I don't mean to be rude, but you know your uncle is incapable of maintaining a checking account. He needs someone. Is there anyone besides you and your mother?"

I looked at her with a frown on my face and sadly answered, "No. He has four children, and I can't get any of them to take the responsibility. They won't take care of him or provide for him in any way. I'm going back to Germany soon, and I doubt that I will be back for another year or two. After that, my husband and I will be able to take care of him."

She said, "This is so sad. What exactly has your mother done? Our records don't really say anything. I would also like to apologize for my overreaction. I'm glad I didn't take any further action. Are you sure you have no idea who that man and woman are? It's so bizarre that it was an old white lady and an older black man."

I knew she was trying to get the gossip on this now, and I said, "There are a lot of interracial couples these days. I am curious why the authorities didn't run the social security numbers, since you should have known they didn't belong to my great-uncle or me."

Ms. Peacock looked at me as if she was studying me and said, "They did, but they were invalid social security numbers. We had your names flagged because we were expecting the same crooks to use them. That is why I automatically assumed that the two of you were them, because I didn't have pictures of them at the time."

I said, "Oh, now that makes sense."

She said, "Well, let's get back in before your great-uncle has another fit." We both laughed and went back inside.

Uncle Frank had calmed down by the time we returned, and he said to Ms. Peacock, "If I have to have a power of attorney to open this checking account, it might as well be Belinda."

He looked over at me and begged, "Please, Belinda."

I rolled my eyes, smiled, and said, "Okay, I'll do it, but if you ever lie on me, Uncle Frank, I swear I will never speak to you again."

Of course Uncle Frank said, "I promise I will not tell lies on you."

I said, "We will see. I'm not going to hold my breath." We both looked over at Ms. Peacock, and she already had the specialized power of attorney filled out with our names on it. We both signed it, and she notarized it. Then she had me sign a signature card, and instead of giving the temporary checkbook to Uncle Frank, she gave it to me. I guess Uncle Frank was okay with it because he didn't say anything. I knew she was doing this to protect the banking institute in the event something would happen. This way they could not be held responsible.

I said, "Oh, Ms. Peacock, I have one other question that would help me, help Uncle Frank when I go back to Germany. Can we get Uncle Frank a debit card so he can use that for his groceries and other purchases? I have spoken to the bank that is right up the street from where he lives, and they said they had no problem reconciling his checkbook for him on a weekly basis."

Ms. Peacock said, "That's a great idea, and yes, we can do that."

I filled out the form for Uncle Frank. Ms. Peacock explained to Uncle Frank what we were doing and explained how the debit card worked. She explained all he had to do was keep his receipts, and the bank that I had talked with would reconcile his checkbook every week for him, just like I was doing now for him. He would not have to worry about me, my mother, or anyone else for that matter giving him cash on a weekly basis because the debit card works the same way. He could withdraw cash from his checking account whenever he wants, or just simply use it instead of cash. Uncle Frank seemed pleased and signed the form to order the debit card.

I felt relieved after that was all taken care of. How sad that it had come to strangers helping my great-uncle. Auntie Bea's bank even said they would do Auntie Bea's checkbook as well as Uncle Frank's.

I also felt relieved; even though Ms. Peacock was pumping me for information, I think she genuinely trusted me to some degree. I think she finally realized that Uncle Frank and I were victims regarding the check scam. I also felt she knew Uncle Frank and I were not telling the entire truth; she just didn't understand the motives of why we were holding back the truth. If she knew it was my great-aunt, Uncle Frank's sister, she would understand at least some of the reasons why we lied even though my great-aunt had victimized us. If I had not made a promise to my mother, I would have easily told her, but I knew my mother was trying to reach a plea agreement with the U.S. Attorney. I didn't have the money to do anything about what my mom and Auntie Bea had done anyway. I guess it was just better to talk with my auntie about it.

Uncle Frank and I walked silently to his car in the bank parking lot. Before I even had a chance to back the car out of the parking spot, Uncle Frank let out his anger and said, "First, baby girl, stop in that damn liquor store across the street. I want a bottle of whiskey."

I said, "Okay, Uncle Frank."

After Uncle Frank bought several bottles of whiskey and I got some beer, a bottle of vodka, and Kahlua, we sat in Uncle Frank's car in the parking lot so he could take a few swigs. I decided to open one of the beers from the six-pack that I bought. They were ice cold. I started drinking it even though I knew better because I was driving, but I thought one beer would not make me drunk so I continued drinking it anyway. I knew my great-uncle was very upset.

After taking another swig of whiskey from the bottle, Uncle Frank asked, "What the hell just happened? I'm totally confused. Were they going to arrest us? What exactly would they do to us? Why were Sister Bea and Little Pete's pictures on those driver's license copies? Did your mother have anything to do with this or not? Has Little Pete stolen money from me? Why did we lie? I want Little Pete put behind bars. Why was Sister Bea involved in this, or was it your mother? Belinda, answer me."

Uncle Frank took another swig of whiskey and lit another cigarette. I lit one with him, chugged the rest of my beer, and got another one from the back seat.

Uncle Frank asked, "Well?"

I knew he wasn't really going to understand anything, and I didn't want him running around telling lies so I simply said, "Uncle Frank, it is what it is. There is no real way of explaining to you anything. You probably will not believe me anyway, so I will just say it. Auntie Bea and Little Pete are Mom's accomplices with the check scam. Auntie Bea and Little Pete have already confessed to me. Mom is trying to do a plea agreement, leaving Auntie Bea and Little Pete out of it. She is trying to get the U.S. Attorney to allow her to take full blame. You yourself have been allowing Little Pete and my mother to give false information to credit card companies so you can have credit. That in itself is fraud, Uncle Frank. What did you plan on doing if I wasn't here? You would have lied like you have been doing by saying, 'Jane did it and I didn't know anything about it,' even though you were aware of it and even signed the credit card applications yourself. Since you lied about your income and allowed them to lie about your income, how would you have paid it back, Uncle Frank, if I weren't here? So there it is, Uncle Frank, in a nutshell. Whether you like it or not, there is always a paper trail that leads the authorities directly to the four of you, and I'm stuck right in the middle of all this crap. I guess I could get into some type of trouble by trying to lead them away from you and Auntie Bea. Even if I am making restitution for your crimes, Little Pete is benefiting from the help that I'm providing to the two of you. It's sad that I'm even involved in this entire mess.

"The only reason I'm doing this is because I gave my word to protect you and Auntie Bea and to do everything in my power to prevent you from getting into any more trouble with the law. If I had not made that promise, before I knew everything, I would not have given my word. Unlike you, Auntie Bea, my mother, and the rest of the family, I believe in honor. When I give my word to do something, I honor it no matter what—or at least to the best of my abilities."

Uncle Frank took another swig of whiskey. As I started up his car, pulled out of the parking spot, and started driving back to the Daisy house, he said, "You're right, Belinda. I don't believe a damn word out of your mouth regarding Sister Bea. She is my sister—"

I cut him off. "—see, you're ignorant, Uncle Frank, so just sit there, drink your whiskey, and don't say another word to me. If I hear one more word about this, I will say even more and uglier words to you."

To my surprise, Uncle Frank sat in the passenger seat, contentedly drinking from his bottle of whiskey like there was no tomorrow. He didn't say another word until we arrived at the Daisy house. As I unlocked the door to the Daisy house, I told Uncle Frank, "You better hide the rest of those bottles in case Auntie Bea comes over here unannounced."

Uncle Frank said, "You're right. I better hide it."

He was already drunk out of his mind and seemed to have forgotten everything that happened. After Uncle Frank was settled in his favorite chair in the Florida room, I told him I was going over to Auntie Bea's.

Uncle Frank with slurring said, "You-u-u better not get . . . into a fight with your auntie-e-e-e." Before he could say another word, he fell asleep and started snoring.

I covered him with a blanket, checked his pulse, and put a trash can next to his chair. I'd seen him worse, so I figured he was okay. I knew his drinking would kill him one day. At least for now, he was safe and in his favorite chair. There was no way he could hurt anyone. As I looked at my great-uncle for a few more minutes to be sure he was okay, I felt guilty drinking the two bottles of beer before driving. As I watched him sleeping, I vowed that I would never drink two or more beers before driving again. I knew one was okay, but chugging it was not okay. I knew I wasn't drunk, but my blood might have said something else. I knew better than that. I grabbed a couple of beers from the fridge, locked up the Daisy house, and ran across the field to Auntie Bea's house. I walked through the side door and immediately started fussing at Auntie Bea for leaving the side door unlocked.

I told her, "Auntie Bea, you can't leave your doors unlocked like the old days. There are too many crazy people out there!"

Auntie Bea then started fussing at me about the two bottles of beer I had in my hand. I just laughed at her.

She was just sitting in her chair, like she does every day, smoking her cigarettes and staring at her walls. I could tell she was happy that I came to visit with her because I had been so busy and I hadn't been over to her house for a few days to keep her company. In the back of my mind, for just a few seconds, I thought that even though my godparents lied, stole, and cheated, I couldn't help but see good in them. I loved them so very much, as well as my mother. I truly felt they were the only family I had. I guess I had been mistreated by them (and my entire family) for the majority of my life, but I still didn't realize that I was being used once again. I just didn't realize that these people truly did not care about me. They only cared about what I could do for them. I guess I still had hope that if I did something great, they would love and respect me. In some twisted way, I hoped that after this Auntie Bea, Uncle Frank, my mother, my father, my sister, and the rest of the family would love and respect me the way that I always dreamed they would.

I chatted with Auntie Bea for almost an hour before I felt comfortable enough to question her about the check fraud. For some reason it was important for me to hear what she had to say about it.

So I brought it up and said, "Auntie Bea, Uncle Frank's bank had his name and my name flagged. We were almost arrested on the spot. The manager showed me your picture with your signature. You had opened up a checking account and had written several thousand dollars worth of fraudulent checks. You never paid it back because they did not have a hold on them from another banking institute. I know you did it, Auntie Bea, but could you explain to me how this came about?"

Auntie Bea took another drag off of her cigarette and said in a calm tone, "Belinda, I already told you what I did, and I told you that I'm sorry, but I didn't do anything regarding my brother's name. I was over at your mother's house when we decided to do this. I don't remember how many checking accounts we opened through the mail, but that's how we did it. I swear to you I had nothing to do with opening an account in Frank's name."

I said, "Oh, I believe you regarding Uncle Frank, but why did you do it to me? I never asked but it's important to me to know why."

She simply said, "Because we could. You were in Europe, still playing soldier with your husband. You, Christina, and Jay should have never found out."

She said this with no remorse, but I guess I didn't hear it like that.

I simply said, "Oh, I understand," as I held back the tears, hurt, and disappointment.

Auntie Bea asked, "But your sister and Jay don't know. Do they?"

I answered, "Don't worry, Auntie Bea, they don't know about you and Uncle Frank. In fact, no one else except me knows the whole truth. Jay only knows a part of it. I think anyway."

Auntie Bea said still in a calm tone, "Good, I think its better that we just keep it that way. I know you are hurt by what we have done, Belinda, and I'm truly sorry for it, but I did it to save my land, and I'm still depending on you to make that happen. After all, Belinda, I'm the only godmother you have left. We need you, Belinda. You are all the three of us have left."

I guess my love for these people outweighed all my common sense. I guess the dreams I had of my family loving and accepting me would be my downfall because I couldn't even see that I was being conned repeatedly, and I allowed it to happen each time. All my defenses were down; my common sense and self-preservation were gone. I believed them each time they apologized. I was mentally broken down from fighting this battle on too many fronts. We chatted for a couple more hours before I left and walked back to the Daisy house.

I discovered Uncle Frank lying on the floor of the kitchen with an empty bottle of whiskey by his side. I turned him over and his hands were swollen. I pulled him up to a sitting position, reached up, and turned the kitchen water on while I held one of his hands to keep him sitting straight up. I grabbed a dirty glass that was on the counter. I filled it up with cold water with one hand and threw the water from the glass into Uncle Frank's face. He started shaking his head.

I commanded, "Get up! Get up! Uncle Frank."

He started speaking, but I could not understand a word he said. I helped him get up, and all I could think of was alcohol poisoning. I had to make him vomit, somehow. He had diabetes, and I knew his system could not take this much alcohol at once. I had no idea how long he had been lying there.

I continued to bark orders at him. "Here, Uncle Frank, lean on the sink counter and bend over a little bit. I'm going to stick this wooden spoon in your mouth, and I want you to vomit. Do you understand?"

Uncle Frank did not say anything, but he leaned closer to the sink. I had no idea if I could make him vomit or not, so I decided just to use my finger and prayed that he didn't bite me. I held his neck in one hand and stuck my index finger in his mouth. I hoped I stuck it back far enough in his mouth to make him get sick and pulled my finger out of his mouth quickly. Thank God he started vomiting profusely over the sink. He kept vomiting even though nothing else was coming up. When he was finished, I helped him into the Florida room, helped him to sit down in the chair at the table. I made him a sandwich with turkey lunchmeat, but I did not put any mayonnaise or anything on it. I gave it to him, and he drunkenly started eating it. I got a diet soda out of the fridge and asked him to drink it. He got up after he finished eating and drinking and said he was going to be sick again. I helped him into the bathroom and held him while he started vomiting again. I helped him back into the dining room because it was closer. I made him another sandwich and gave him another soda. He got up after he finished eating, went back into the bathroom, and started vomiting again. I had him eat another sandwich and drink a soda again. This time he held it down, and I think he sobered up a little bit because I could understand him better.

"Damn, girl," he said as I brought him another sandwich. "I don't want any more. I'm going to bed."

I ordered, "Eat it anyway, Uncle Frank, it will absorb the acids from your stomach."

I helped him to his bedroom and got him into the bed.

I said, "Oh, I forgot you need to take your diabetes meds, if nothing else." I went back into the Florida room, retrieved his medication, and got him a large glass of water. I was hoping he would drink the entire glass because I knew it would help flush the alcohol out of his system. He took his meds and drank the entire glass of water. I told him he should let one leg dangle off the side of the bed so he wouldn't feel like he was spinning.

He said, "I know, I know."

He went straight to sleep. I turned off the light and walked out of his bedroom.

The day was completely shot. I had not even opened up the shop, and I probably had lost some business as a result. I felt completely stupid for allowing Uncle Frank to buy all that whiskey. I decided I couldn't stop him from drinking, but I sure could control it. I walked into the kitchen; he had not hidden the other two bottles of whiskey so I took one and put it in the trunk of my mother's car.

I knew I couldn't tell Auntie Bea what had happened because she would blame me for the entire incident. For as long as I could remember Uncle Frank got drunk like that, all the time, but while I was here, I wasn't going to let my godfather drink himself to death. It was not going to happen on my watch. I had to do something. No matter what, I couldn't sit back any longer and allow this.

I thought, *What will happen to my godfather and my auntie? Mom is in jail, and I have to go back to my life. I have my husband to think about as well. What am I going to do?* I guess these thoughts scared the crap out of me, and I started crying, and I couldn't stop. I spent several hours that day in a dark depression. I cried off and on. I grabbed another beer and started drinking it. I guess I was turning into a drunk as well. It seemed to run in the family.

Somehow, I reached inside myself and pulled myself out of the depressed state. I was able to gain my inner strength once again. I said to myself, *I won't worry about this today. I will deal with it another day.* The next morning, I told Uncle Frank he could have only one bottle of whiskey a week. If he drank it before seven days were up, I was going to tell Auntie Bea, and she would deal with him. I told him he scared me, and he needed to control his drinking habit because it was out of control. He promised he would adhere to my rule. I think the only reason he agreed was because he had a hangover from hell.

Little Pete showed up on schedule, and we moved some more inventory to the shop. I had him take the pickup truck and move things from Mom and Pete's house to the Daisy house basement. I spent my day stocking shelves and selling inventory.

CHAPTER LVI

Another Monday, I thought as I rubbed my eyes to wake up. Running my shop was hard work, but business the previous weekend had been very good. I was starting to have less and less inventory as the weeks went by. I now knew that I wasn't going to have enough inventory to get out of the mess my mother and my relatives had created. I knew this week was going to be no easier than the past weeks, and I longed for my husband to be here. I only had one more week, and he would be here. I would have the strength and character I truly needed right now, physically standing beside me. I felt weak and needy as I remembered everything that had happened since I stepped off that airplane. The temptation of just calling it quits was becoming stronger and stronger with each passing day, but I had been a soldier most of my adult life and what kept pushing me was the fact that "a soldier never quits."

I thought of a great leader whom I had the honor and privilege to serve under, who had once said after returning from Iraq with me, "You can take the soldier from the Army, but you can never take the Army from the soldier. You will always be a soldier till the day you die. Whether you die on the battlefield or die of old age, no one, and I mean no one can take that honor from you . . ." After that speech, which was given by this great man during a "Hail and Farewell," six young soldiers who earlier in the week had decided not to reenlist approached him and changed their minds.

Throughout the time I had been there, I had felt like quitting my mission, but those times were fleeting. I felt stronger once I had remembered that wonderful, empowering speech. Even though I had been out of the Army for less than a year and felt like I had put on a few pounds, in reality I had not, and I still considered myself a soldier. I still believed in a soldier's mentality: "God, country, family, honor, duty, loyalty, personal sacrifice, and personal leadership." These are just a few great words that are drilled into every soldier. But these are not just words; they have deep meaning and they define characteristics of people.

Once again, I felt proud and honored to be born in this great county. Even though most of the people in our justice system are corrupt or have simply lost their way, I believed once again in our laws. I believed in our government, but not necessarily the people in it. I believed once again that there were more families in our country that united together, and that their number outweighed the dysfunctional families like my family. I am a daughter of America, and I will fight to protect my family to the best of my abilities, within the rules of engagement that are dictated to me by my great country's laws.

The tests and battles that my God had put in front of me had truly been a roller coaster of my core emotions, beliefs, and convictions. I knew that my God was not finished with me yet. Some people say God does not give us any more than we are able to handle. I must admit that a part of me wished that God did not think so highly of me.

I got up from the bed and got ready for the day. I was ready to take on any battle that was dished out to me. I would do what I believed was right and stand up for my convictions no matter the consequences.

I called my boss in Germany, and I told her some of what was going on. I told her that I still had no idea how much longer I would be here. She seemed pleased that I had taken the time to contact her and that I trusted her enough to confide in her. She told me that she didn't expect any less. She knew that I was a woman of integrity and that I had discovered many thieves within our company because of my hard work, dedication, and loyalty to her and the company. She told me that it was an honor and privilege to have someone like me who was honest, loyal, dedicated, and a true friend. She told me whatever I did here in Virginia, I had the support of her and our office. Every one of my coworkers, managers from different departments and stores were with me, and they had even started raising money for my plane ticket back home to Germany where I belonged within the military community. She considered me family, as so many other people there did too. I told her that she had too much faith in me and that I was only human.

She cut me off and said, "Your actions are much louder than your words, Belinda; that speaks for itself."

We spoke for a few minutes longer and we said our goodbyes. Tears had welled up in my eyes because of the love and generosity of my coworkers. I called Thomas next and asked if he was still coming the next week.

Thomas informed me, "Everything is still on schedule, my love. My commander, actually my whole battalion, has heard about what you are doing, and they are raising money for your lost income because you had to go back home to clean up the mess and are not making any additional income. Everyone seems to know more about what is happening to you than I do. They are all calling you a 'daughter of America.'"

I said, "Good Lord, Thomas, they have exaggerated this entire thing. They are pinning me up as some kind of hero. I'm not a hero; I'm just trying to fix another mess that my family has created. Good grief! You need to put these tall tales to rest."

Thomas laughed and said, "There is nothing I can do. You know we are a small community, and I'm kind of proud of you too."

I said, "Thomas, you would not be so proud of me if you knew some of the things I have done since I've been here. This is ridiculous."

Thomas said, "You can fill me in when I get there."

I thought, *I'm going to have to clean up these wild tales when I get back to Germany. Good grief, what does everyone think I'm doing? Battling the bad guys in our own front door by myself? I'm sure my husband had something to do with the exaggerations. Men!*

I called Auntie Bea and told her I was expecting Uncle Frank's checks in the mail sometime this week, along with a debit card that I was going to show Uncle Frank how to use. I told her I would be by after I had closed the shop for the day.

Next, I called the auctioneer. He answered the phone. I said, "Hi. How's everything going? This is Belinda."

The auctioneer in a panicky voice said, "Belinda, we cannot sell your items. You will have to come by today and pick them up."

I asked in a confused tone, "Why can't you sell my items?"

The auctioneer said, "I will explain as soon as you come and pick them up."

I said, "Okay." I was totally confused as to why he couldn't sell my things.

I called Miss Patson next. I gave her an update regarding Big Pete and told her that he had completely moved out. I told her about the DOL following me and tapping my great-uncle's phone and how I handled it. I told her something was wrong with the auctioneer, but I didn't know what was going on yet. I told her about my Auntie Bea and the checks. I told her everything that had happened.

Miss Patson was very angry regarding the captain of police, sheriff, or whatever he was. She asked me for his phone number, and I gave it to her. She said he was wrong, and she was sure Big Pete was part of that, along with Little Pete. She would need to talk with the captain. She kept stating that I did not need permission.

She was very upset with me that I lied to the bank regarding my auntie, but then at the same time she said, "But your mother is trying to make a deal with the U.S. Attorney regarding your auntie and her involvement." She told me she was going to call my mother's attorney. She would call me back later in the day to instruct me regarding those issues. She was pleased that I didn't allow Little Pete to blackmail me any longer, and she planned on calling him as well. She would do that later because she wanted to make sure he was at home when she did call him. She said that would probably take a couple of days with him.

I thought, *Thank God he gave me Miss Patson instead of all the other dishonorable attorneys in the world.* At least for now, I felt she was noble. Little Pete showed up, and we loaded another truckload of shop inventory. We dropped it off at the shop, and I had Little Pete drive me to the post office where I had opened a post office box for all the shop mail.

I retrieved the mail and instructed Little Pete to take me to the auction house since I had to retrieve the items I had planned on auctioning. He didn't seem surprised at all and didn't ask any questions. I had a strong feeling that he was behind it, but I didn't know why or how.

Before he pulled out of the post office's parking lot, an envelope from my bank caught my eye. I asked Little Pete to stop for a minute. I opened it up and could not believe it. Sam had given me a bounced check. I couldn't believe it! He knew this was one big reason that my mother was sitting in jail.

I asked Little Pete to go back to the shop before we went to the auctioneer. I said that I had to make a quick phone call. I went into the shop with anger and disappointment in my cousin building up by the second. I called, and I must have gotten lucky because he answered the phone.

Sam said, "Hello."

I said, "Hello, Sam. It's Belinda."

Sam said, "Oh, hi, Belinda. You just caught me walking out the door. What's up? You need to make it quick because I'm running late for work today."

I said, "Sam, I just got a bounced check that you wrote me for the stuff you bought. Do you know I have been accepting checks from people all across the country, and then my own flesh and blood gives me a bad check? You need to give me cash, plus fifteen dollars for the fee the bank charged me."

Sam said, "Oh, I'm sorry. I'll try and come by on Thursday. That's when I get paid."

I said, "Okay."

I locked up the shop and got back into the pickup truck where Little Pete was waiting for me.

Little Pete asked, "What's that all about?"

I answered, "Oh, nothing. I just forgot to do something, that's all." We proceeded to the auction house. Little Pete parked in the auction house parking lot, and I asked him to wait in the pickup truck. I told him that when I was ready, I would come and get him.

He said, "Okay."

I walked to the auction house door, and the auctioneer opened it for me.

He said, "I'm very glad that you came as quickly as you could."

I asked, "What's this all about?"

He answered, "Mrs. Star, you signed our form stating that this was your property."

I said, "Yes, it is."

He said, "Well, you know that this auction has been heavily advertised." I nodded in affirmation. He continued, "This past Saturday, my receptionist was answering the phone, and she was giving directions to all the folks that are coming to the auction. One gentleman called inquiring as to whom the collection belonged. It is not our policy to give this information out, but she didn't see the harm. Anyway, it was Big Pete. As soon as she told him that it was your items, he stated to my receptionist that the property belonged to him; that you stole it, and he has informed his attorney. He has told us that we may not sell it."

I said, "That's a load of crap from Big Pete! First of all, he didn't hire an attorney. He has a court-appointed one because he had been indicted on at least twenty counts of various types of fraud. May I borrow your phone?"

The auctioneer said, "Yes," as he pointed to the phone.

I called Big Pete at Mom's. When he answered, I said, "Big Pete, what the hell are you doing? You know this property doesn't belong to you and that you do not have any attorney."

Big Pete replied in an angry voice, "Yes, the property is mine, and you can't prove otherwise. My attorney is Bill Bank. Little Pete has told your mother and me all about it. In fact, it is your own mother that instructed me to stop you."

I said, "Bull. You know you don't get any more money until all the debt is paid. Why are you and Mom hurting yourselves like this?"

Big Pete said, "Okay, Belinda, I'll make a deal with you. You can go ahead and auction that stuff off, but I get half of the funds that it generates."

I said, "Okay, Big Pete, have it your way. Here, you need to tell the auctioneer." I passed the telephone to the auctioneer. The auctioneer just shook his head. He didn't say a word as he hung up.

He then said, "Mrs. Star, I'm sorry but I'm not getting involved in any of this. The contract was between you and me, not that mean, evil Big Pete. I'm not getting involved. I will help you repack all this stuff, but you will need to get this out of my auction house now."

I replied, "But you have put so much time and money into this, are you sure you don't want to go ahead and do the auction?"

The auctioneer said, "I have nothing against you, Mrs. Star, but that Big Pete scares me, and I know that if we continue with the auction, he will cause trouble for both of us. Besides, I don't want to help him in any way."

I said, "Okay."

We packed up everything, and I had Little Pete load the entire truck by himself. I was very angry with the weasel. I wanted him out of the picture entirely now. He was interfering with my life, and it had to stop! After he had the truck loaded, I made him drive to the antiques and collectibles shop where my mother had a booth. I made him wait in the truck while I went in and spoke to the owner. I asked if any of her dealers would like to buy the items I had. She told me yes, but she would first like to see everything. Again, I made Little Pete bring in all ten boxes by himself, and then sent him back out to the truck to wait. All the boxed items still had the auction house numbered tags on them. After we unpacked all the items, the owner told me that she would contact me first thing in the morning to give me an offer. I thanked her and left.

Little Pete and I went back to the Daisy house, loaded the truck with another load of inventory, drove to it to the shop, and unloaded it. I told Little Pete I didn't need him anymore and he could leave. Little Pete just stood there wringing his hands in front of himself. I watched him curiously. When he finally looked up at me, I raised an eyebrow.

The little coward said, "Belinda, I know you're not going to like this, but I was trying to wait for the right time to tell you. Your mother had me cash a check for her at my grocery store close to where I live because I had good friends that worked in the store. The sheriff just contacted me and told me I would have to pick it up with cash or I would be arrested because there is a warrant out on me regarding it. He is a friend of mine and he gave me a heads up. I need you to go and pick it up today since it was your mother that I gave the cash to."

I said, "I will need to talk with my mother before I decide to give you the money for it."

Before Little Pete had a chance to respond, the shop's telephone rang. I answered it, and it was the recording from the jail. I accepted the call and said, "Mom, you always seem to have perfect timing."

Mom asked, "Oh no, what has happened now?"

I answered as I asked, "I was about to have Little Pete leave for the day when he informed me that there is a warrant for his arrest regarding a bounced check of yours. Is this true?"

Mom answered, "Yes, it is. I thought that one cleared because that's been about three months ago. Put Little Pete on the phone." I passed the phone to Little Pete. He just nodded, agreeing with whatever my mother was telling him. He then passed the phone back to me.

I said, "Oh, and another thing. If you and Big Pete ever try and stop me from selling all this crap to pay your debt again, I will get back on an airplane and fly back to Germany. I mean it!"

Mom replied angrily, "You have plenty of other things you can sell instead of my dolls!"

I said, "No, Mother. They are my dolls, and I will sell whatever is necessary to pay this debt." Then the phone went dead. I looked over at Little Pete and said, "Let's go. Stop at the bank first so I can get the cash."

After stopping off at the bank, we pulled into a small grocery store parking lot. As Little Pete was parking, I wondered why such a small store would cash such a large check for Little Pete. We went into the store. Little Pete asked a cashier if the manager was in and said we needed to see her. I noticed a paycheck sign hanging in the store and then understood why they cashed it for him.

I followed Little Pete to the manager's office. Right before he was going to knock on the door, an older, pale, white, skinny lady opened it. It appeared she knew who he was.

We all said our greetings, and the lady asked us to have a seat. I told her who I was. I told her that I was Jane's daughter. She then told me that there was also a $50 fee because the check had bounced. I told her that I wouldn't pay the fee because I didn't have to pay for the check at all. She then reminded me that Little Pete could go to jail if I didn't. I thought, *What a nasty lady!* I thought that maybe it was time he got what he deserved, but I paid her the cash and took the bounced check from her hands.

We drove back to the shop, and Little Pete left for the day. I told him just to meet me at Mom and Big Pete's house in the morning. I knew that I had done the right thing, even though Little Pete was a weasel and a backstabber, but maybe it would have been the best thing for me to let him hang himself. On the other hand, I knew that I wouldn't be able to live with myself if I did that. I was a better person than he was. I was not going to lower myself to his level.

CHAPTER LVII

The next morning I received a phone call from the housekeeper's sister. She informed me her sister was not going to work for us anymore because of everything that had been in the newspapers. She told me that she understood that my relatives and I didn't have anything to do with it, but she felt it was better if her sister just moved on. I told her I didn't understand but I accepted her honesty. I don't know why, but I thought of my grandmother's fake bauble that my mother gave me the first night I was here. I had put it in my suitcase, which was now in my bedroom closet. I went to the closet and looked into the side pocket of the suitcase, but it was gone! I guess the housekeeper thought it was real and had stolen it. I called her sister as soon as I discovered it missing.

When she answered the phone, I said, "Hi, ma'am. It's Belinda again. My grandmother's fake bauble is missing from my suitcase. If your sister did take it, could she please give it back? It's not worth anything, but it has sentimental value to me."

She responded by yelling at me that her sister was not a thief, and that I shouldn't make accusations like that, and then she hung up on me. I knew in my gut that the housekeeper had taken my grandmother's jewel. I guess I should have been used to everyone stealing from me by then, but my tough exterior crumbled. I sat on the edge of my bed and cried. *Something else gone to the wind.*

I left and met Little Pete at Mom and Big Pete's house. Ever since I had arrived in Virginia, we had been packing up that house, but when I walked through the door, it seemed like we had not done a thing. I wished Big Pete would let me auction everything and be done with it, but it was always greedy nasty games I had to play with him.

We spent another long day going back and forth, packing, loading the pickup truck, and unloading it into the Daisy house basement. When it was getting dark, I told Little Pete it was quitting time and to meet me at the shop in the morning. I needed to be open for business, and sometimes Wednesday was a good day for sales. He agreed and left from Mom and Big Pete's house.

After he left, I drove to the antique and collectibles shop and met with the owner again. I asked her, "Well, what's the verdict?"

She answered, "I have a dealer that will give you one sixth of the value, and I have the check right here."

My jaw dropped, and I said, "What? That's highway robbery. I will take half the value for it, no less."

She replied, "Well, we found out that these items are stolen property. You even left the tags on them, and since they were stolen property we are only offering you this amount."

I retorted, "Big Pete is a crook and a liar. This is my property. How can you take the word of a known crook?"

She simply stated, "Take it or leave it."

I shook my head and said, "I guess I have no other choice but to take it because I'm trying to make restitution to the victims." I accepted the check she offered. She was smiling from ear to ear. It is amazing how many crooked people get away with these things every single day. To me, these people are no different from Big Pete.

When I pulled up in front of the Daisy house, Uncle Frank was yelling at me from the door. I parked the truck, and the second that I walked through the door, Uncle Frank handed me the telephone. I said, "Hello."

Miss Patson said, "Hi, Belinda. It's me, Miss Patson. I have spoken to your mother's attorney, the U.S. Attorney, and the DOL. You were right, the DOL had no authority. I can file a lawsuit against them if you want."

I said, "There is no point. What will it accomplish? Nothing. As long as they don't violate me again, it's over as far as I'm concerned."

She said, "You're right. Regarding Little Pete, I just spoke with him. He told me he is looking for another job. All he wants is to continue working for you until he has another job because he has a family to feed. He said he will do whatever is necessary to keep getting his paycheck from you. He said he didn't care what I thought. As far as he is concerned he still works for the Kings, and there was nothing I could do about it."

I said, "It figures he would say something like that. I will wait until my husband gets here to get rid of him."

Miss Patson said, "I don't think that's a great idea. He is still blackmailing you."

I said, "Not really. He will get his one day, so I'm not worried too much about it. What about my shop?"

Miss Patson said, "Well, your mother's attorney said he told you he took care of it, but I still spoke with the U.S. Attorney, and they promise not to interfere with your business again. Apparently, from my understanding, your mother and Big Pete caused that mess, and the U.S. Attorney felt very stupid and foolish after they realized they had been fooled. It was mainly Big Pete who created the false accusations against you, and your mother truly put her foot in her mouth because she didn't know what was going on."

I said, "That figures."

Mrs. Patson said, "Oh, the U.S. Attorney also said that they truly appreciate what you are doing, but if something else arises they must investigate. It has nothing to do with you personally. They are just doing their job."

I said, "Oh, so if Big Pete or my mother tells another lie about something, they will investigate me again?"

Mrs. Patson said, "Unfortunately, yes, but the U.S. Attorney promises they will go through your mother's attorney if something comes up."

I said, "I guess that's all I can ask for."

Miss Patson asked, "Have you heard any word regarding the mortgage for your auntie's farm?"

I answered, "No, I haven't heard anything yet. I'm still waiting, but I'm sure they will contact me soon one way or the other."

Miss Patson said, "I will help you with that as well. That will probably be the smallest of the problems we have."

I said, "I hope so."

Miss Patson then asked, "What about your auntie? I still feel you should turn her over to the U.S. Attorney."

I answered, "I just can't do that. I think, or at least hope, that I picked up the last bad check that my mother and Auntie Bea have written. I've just about paid off the credit card fraud, and I still have Uncle Frank's part so I think there is no need. At least I was able to bail out Auntie Bea. It's just the farm left."

Miss Patson said, "You know if your auntie is not punished, she could con other people and continue stealing from other victims."

I said, "I don't think she will. I think she has learned her lesson. I hope so anyway."

Miss Patson and I chatted for about fifteen minutes more. I made a meatloaf dinner with mashed potatoes and corn. I served Uncle Frank and then took a plate over to Auntie Bea. I stayed and chatted with her for a few minutes and went back to the Daisy house to eat my own supper. After eating and cleaning up the mess, I felt very tired. I decided that I would go to bed early. I was just heading back to my room when the telephone rang.

Uncle Frank called me into the Florida room and told me it was John. John told me they were going bowling and wondered if I would like to join them. He told me he could pick me up in about thirty minutes. It sounded like fun, and I told him I would love to go. True to his word, exactly twenty-nine minutes later, John and Ann picked me up. It was only a few minutes to the bowling alley. We ended up bowling for several hours. We all had a few beers and reminisced about the old days while we bowled. It was the first time I had been able to relax since I had arrived. When we left, I was tired, but I also felt refreshed.

Uncle Frank was still up when I walked into the Florida room. He said, "Oh, Belinda, I forgot to ask you if you could take me to JAG tomorrow so I can have my will changed."

I asked, "Uncle Frank, why do you need your will changed?"

He replied, "Because I want your mother removed from it."

I said, "What? Why do you want my mother removed from it? She hasn't done anything to you. You told me yourself the only way you will ever be able to pay her back was when you died. So why are you trying to cheat her?"

He just looked at the floor and didn't say a word. At this point I knew someone was behind my great-uncle's odd behavior. I just didn't know who.

He finally looked up and stated in a whiney voice, "I just want it changed. I want you as the executor of my estate because I know things will be done the way I want them. I don't want your mother on it."

I asked, "Uncle Frank, do you have your children in it?"

Uncle Frank angrily answered, "I don't want any of those brats to get anything. If I leave them the land all they will do is sell it. I'm going to leave the land to everyone that's related to us."

I said, "Uncle Frank, I don't think you can do that. You do not have any cash or assets to establish a trust to do that, but we can ask. I will take you tomorrow. You do know you are hurting my mother, right?"

Uncle Frank said, "She doesn't need to know."

I asked, "Uncle Frank, who told you that you had to change your will?"

Uncle Frank answered, "Nobody."

I looked at my great-uncle, and I knew he was lying. I just let it go and said, "Whatever. I'm going to bed."

CHAPTER LVIII

Wednesday morning I called JAG and asked if I could set an appointment up for my great-uncle. Just my luck, they had an opening first thing this morning. So much for my plans of earning some money that day. I told the E-4 (spec 4/specialist) we would be there as soon as possible. Uncle Frank got ready, and we left. I stopped at the shop on the way. It was already 8:30, and there was no sign of Little Pete. I wasn't very surprised because whoever told Uncle Frank to change his will had most likely told Little Pete I would be at JAG for the day. I drove Uncle Frank to JAG.

After showing our military IDs, we drove into the parking lot, and I parked his car. Uncle Frank started acting nervous. As we were walking into the building, I asked him what was wrong. He mumbled something to the effect that he didn't want to do this. I didn't respond. We signed in, and after waiting for a few minutes, a young lieutenant (LT) walked into the waiting area and greeted us. He escorted us into a conference room with a large table.

Uncle Frank told him, "I would like to change my will where I can leave our family land to everyone who is related to me, so they all can use and enjoy it. I do not want to leave anything to my four children. I would like to have Belinda here be the sole executor of my estate to ensure that my wishes are carried out because I have no one else I can trust."

The young JAG officer asked, "Sir, I'm sorry, but do you have some type of funds and/or assets to be able to set up a trust to do this? You will need money after you are gone to pay for taxes, upkeep, homeowner's insurance, and that type of thing. Do you have enough to last?"

Uncle Frank replied, "Well, no, I do not have any savings or funds for that. Why can't I set something up like that?"

The young officer let out a sigh and answered, "You will need to leave the land to someone who will take responsibility for the expenses."

Uncle Frank said, "My four kids don't have a pot to piss in, and I know if I leave it to them they will sell it the first chance they get. My father gave me a lifetime home on the land and the right to pass it to the next generation, but I technically don't own it. I want to set it up so no generation can have it or sell it."

I said, "Uncle Frank, first of all I will not be here to be an executor, and it would not be right to put me on it as such. Why don't you put May and Sam as co-executors, and you can put me in your will as undivided interest with all four kids. I promise the land will never be sold, and the taxes will always be paid, but you must leave it to someone because you do not have the means to create a trust, if I understand the LT correctly?"

The LT asked, "Yes, ma'am, that is correct, and it would be the best solution to the problem. Sir, do you trust your great-niece to ensure that your children don't sell the land?"

Uncle Frank answered, "Yes, I trust Belinda, but I don't trust my kids. I don't want any of them to have it."

I said, "Uncle Frank, enough. They are your children, and they are all you have. I don't understand why you treat them this way."

After the young LT and I continued talking it through with him, Uncle Frank finally agreed to put May and Sam as co-executors, and he agreed to leave all four of his children the land with undivided interest. When the LT came back with the will typed up according to Uncle Frank's wishes, he forgot to put my name on it, which was okay with me. To my shock, Uncle Frank didn't read the will! He just scanned down to where it had the names on it and started having a fit.

He said, "I told you I wanted my great-niece Belinda on this as well. Otherwise I will not do it this way."

The LT said, "I'm sorry, sir, it was a mistake. I will fix it immediately."

I just looked at my uncle, shook my head, and said, "You can hardly read but you sure didn't have any problem catching that mistake."

Uncle Frank laughed and said, "You made a promise, and I expect you to keep it even if I will not be alive to see that you carry it through."

I didn't say another word. I just shook my head again with a smile on my face as I looked at my great-uncle. I was glad he did right by his four children. I just wish he hadn't caught the mistake because, even though I wanted part of the family history, I knew it wasn't right for me to take what I considered theirs. My grandmother on her half of the family farm

341

thought nothing but revenge against my mother and didn't think of Christina or me. That was my grandmother's and mother's fault, and it would not be right to take from Uncle Frank's children, even if they were greedy drug addicts and just plain mean people. Despite all that, I loved them because they did have some of the same DNA as mine coursing through their veins. They had the same chance as I did to pursue the American dream. They didn't have to take it the way I did, but the same opportunities were there for them as well; they just needed to put forth some effort.

I truly love my country because if you want a piece of the American pie, it is there for any American that chooses to take it. It's not given to you; you must earn it and work for it, or in my case, be willing to die for it. The JAG officer gave me the certified copies and we left. I told Uncle Frank after we finished all his errands, I wanted to go see Mom since we were on that side of town. He said that would be okay, but he wasn't going in. We pulled up into the parking lot, and after I parked, I asked Uncle Frank again, "Are you sure you don't want to see her?"

Uncle Frank answered, "I just can't, baby girl. I just can't see her like that."

I said, "Okay." I grabbed the briefcase from the back seat and went inside. Of course it was packed with other family members waiting to see their loved ones.

Every time I went to see her it didn't seem to get any easier. Mom was happy to see me today because I hadn't visited her on Saturday. I told her what Uncle Frank had done, and I took one of the copies of the will out of the briefcase and to show her.

My mother started crying and asked, "Why did you do that to me?"

I answered, "Mom, I didn't do anything. Uncle Frank did, and I believe someone is telling him what to do and I don't know who it is."

I knew the original will that Uncle Frank had written was with the family attorney, and I knew that JAG did not keep copies. To make my mother feel better I ripped up the will so she could see me, even though I had two more certified copies, and I was going to honor my great-uncle's wishes. I just knew this was the easiest way to deal with this. I didn't need any more drama.

I dropped Uncle Frank off at the Daisy house and took the pickup truck over to Auntie Bea's. I put the two other certified copies of the will in the safe and told Auntie Bea where they were in case something happened to Uncle Frank.

Auntie Bea said, "Thank you for not giving Frank a hard time about it today."

I said in an angry tone, "So it was you!"

Auntie Bea said, "Of course. I don't want that convicted felon anywhere near my brother's business."

I said, "Auntie Bea, you should be ashamed of yourself! If it wasn't for me, you would be a convicted felon as well. Plus my mother has entered a plea so they won't prosecute you. Now all you have done is made sure Frank's bad kids sell the land. After all, Auntie Bea, the Hollow is your history as well."

Auntie said, "I don't care anymore, Belinda."

I said, "Whatever!" I left and went to the shop.

My nerves were shot. I did not know how much more of my godparents' hypocritical attitudes I could take. They told so many lies to make themselves look like they were the victims when the only victim in this lot seemed to be me. What greedy, narrowed-minded relatives I had! And that included my mother, Big Pete, and Little Pete, even though he technically wasn't family. I just put the entire events of that day in the back of my mind and put on a happy face as the customers started coming into the shop.

CHAPTER LIX

Thursday morning was like a blur. It was basically the same thing every day. The nightmare just continued going on and on. As I was making the first pot of coffee for the day, I heard someone knocking on the door. I peeked into the Florida room and there was Sam in front of the sliding glass door. I walked to the door and opened it.

In an angry voice Sam said, "Here, Belinda, here is your money."

I made Sam stand there while I counted it.

I said, "Sam, you need to pay for the $15 fee that I had to pay."

Sam said, "Come on, Belinda, that's all I have. You're lucky I even decided to make the check good."

I said, "Whatever."

Sam's voice then turned to friendly again and asked, "What are you doing this weekend?"

I answered, "The same old same old."

Sam said, "Let's get together, and I'll take you bar hopping just like old times."

I said, "Oh, I don't know, Sam."

Sam said, "Oh, come on, Belinda. It will be just like the old days."

I said, "Well, okay, but I don't want any trouble."

"I promise." He laughed and said, "I'll see ya Saturday around five. We can go out for dinner first."

I said, "Okay," although I wondered how he was going to pay for dinner and beer if he couldn't pay me the $15 banking fee. I went back into the kitchen to get a cup of coffee, and there was Uncle Frank with his hair messed up from sleeping.

He asked, "Baby girl, I heard you talking to someone. Who were you on the phone with?"

I answered, "No one, Uncle Frank. It was Sam. He dropped by on his way to work and asked if I would go out with him this Saturday." I didn't want Uncle Frank to know that Sam wrote me a bad check, because I would never hear the end of it.

Uncle Frank became angry and asked, "Why can't my own son take me out as well? Why does he want to hang out with you and not me?"

I answered, "I don't know, Uncle Frank, but you can ask him on Saturday."

*   *   *

Before I knew it, it was Saturday morning, and the day flew by. I locked up the shop early, around 5:00 p.m. When I got back to the Daisy house, Uncle Frank was dressed to go out with us, but I didn't know if Sam was going to be okay with that. One minute he would talk to his father, and the next he wouldn't have anything to do with him. It truly was a love/ hate relationship between them, but then again, I was the same way with my own parents. I took a quick shower and got dressed. I had just finished when I saw Sam pull up. I just decided to let the cards fall where they may.

Sam opened the sliding glass door and walked into the Florida room. Before he had a chance to say anything, Uncle Frank asked, "Boy, are you taking me out too?"

Sam looked over at me, and I just looked back at him with a curious expression.

Sam looked back over at his father and answered, "Sure, why not, but we are going out to eat, Dad."

Uncle Frank said, "That's fine. Just remember I don't have any teeth, just these fake ones."

Sam said, "Well, Belinda and I are going out for a steak dinner."

Uncle Frank said, "That's okay, I can cut the pieces into small ones."

Sam said, "Okay, it's still my treat."

I helped Sam get his father into the front passenger seat, and I got into the back seat behind Sam. Sam took us to a fancy restaurant. I didn't want to embarrass him in front of his father, but I didn't think Sam could afford it.

After eating a fine meal, Sam received the bill. He looked at it, looked up at me, and whispered in my ear, "Belinda, I don't have the money for this. Can you pay for it?"

I knew it. That deadbeat was going to sucker me into paying the bill! I looked at him with a glare and jerked the bill out of his hand. I looked down at the bill. It was $250! *How convenient,* I thought, *because that was almost the exact amount of his bounced check.* I was not about to let him get away with this.

I looked over at Uncle Frank as he was patting his stomach because he was so full and said, "Uncle Frank, Sam took us to an expensive fancy restaurant and doesn't seem to have the money to pay the bill. What do you think we should do about it?" I looked over at Sam, and his face had turned red.

Uncle Frank said, "Boy, you better pay that bill! You know you don't leave a lady holding the bill."

Uncle Frank was half drunk and was speaking louder than he should have. I looked around our table and it appeared that everyone was looking at Sam. I could tell by Sam's expression that he was very angry with me. He snatched the bill from my hand, pulled out one of his charge cards, and paid the bill.

I guess the night out on the town was off because Sam drove Uncle Frank and me back to the Daisy house in silence. He didn't even help me with pulling his father out of the truck. As soon as Uncle Frank had both feet on the ground, Sam took off. I smiled a little bit while I was unlocking the sliding glass door to the Daisy house, and thought, *What a jerk. Did he actually think I was that gullible and that I would pay the tab?* I should have known better regarding my cousin. He had mooched off the clan ever since he had become an adult. I guess all those years ago Uncle Frank was at least right about Sam. I still wasn't sure about the rest of my cousins. I still loved Sam for what he did for me all those years ago, and maybe I still was hoping it wasn't too late for him.

I looked at my watch, and it was 8:00 p.m. The phone started to ring. Uncle Frank answered it. He started arguing with someone, and then he gave up and handed me the telephone. I could hear Auntie Bea's nasty voice yelling as I put the phone up to my ear.

I said, "Auntie Bea, you should be ashamed of yourself. Are you spying on us through the window in your bedroom?" As I looked out, I could see a shadow in my auntie's bedroom across the field with the light in the background.

Auntie Bea in an angry voice answered as she asked, "Of course. Where have the two of you been? Who was that in the truck that dropped you off?"

I said, "Auntie, hush up. Uncle Frank and I are grown adults, but if you must know it was Uncle Frank's son, Sam."

There was silence on the phone for a few seconds and Auntie Bea said, "Oh. Well, good night then. I need to speak with you first thing in the morning. Can you come over?"

I answered, "Yes. You're first on my list for tomorrow."

CHAPTER LX

I went over to Auntie Bea's house first thing in the morning. I unlocked her house, and of course, she was still asleep, but I was going to teach her a lesson. I walked up to the top of her stairs and yelled in the direction of her bedroom door, "Auntie Bea! I'm here. Get out of the bed. I don't have much time."

I heard Auntie Bea fussing. I didn't quite understand her, and she yelled back at me, "Why the devil are you waking me up so early? It's not even 4:30 in the morning yet. Go back to the Daisy house, and come back in a few hours."

I said, "No, Auntie, get up right this minute. You told me first thing in the morning, and I'm here."

By then, I had walked into her bedroom and turned on her light. I looked over at her, and she had her glasses on. I could tell she was hopping mad.

She said, "You little devil. You know I didn't mean this early."

I said with a devilish smile, "No, Auntie, I think I understood your barking very clearly. You said 'first thing' in the morning. Now what do you want?"

Auntie Bea said, "Good grief! Go and make us some coffee while I get dressed, you little devil." By this time, Auntie Bea was giggling because she knew I had gotten her good.

After the coffee finished perking, I poured the first cup for myself. By then, Auntie Bea was in the kitchen and was getting a cup for herself as well. I sat down at the kitchen table watching her with the same grin on my face.

Auntie Bea turned around to look at me with her cup of coffee and said, "Let's go in the living room so I can sit in my chair."

After we both sat down, I took another sip of my coffee. Auntie Bea asked, "Belinda, how are the bad checks coming along from our check scam?"

348

I answered her, "I think I got the last one this past week."

Auntie Bea said, "Good, but did you pick up the property tax and the others that I had written? I don't want my name in the newspaper."

I said, "Yes, Auntie Bea, I picked up a total of thousands of dollars that you did alone. Mom had just a few thousand, but I'm not positive I have gotten them all because I have no way of knowing unless I am contacted."

Auntie Bea said, "Well, I'm glad that's over, and I think you pretty much got them all. I'm sorry I called your momma a convicted felon, and I guess it's easy for me to lay all the blame on her. I can't help but blame her for everything because, after all, Belinda, she brought Big Pete into our lives."

I said, "Auntie Bea, it is your choice to forgive her or not. She stole *for* you, Auntie, not *from* you, and she is in jail because of you. I hold you totally responsible for that."

Auntie Bea looked at me in total shock and said, "I'm not responsible! Your mother is a grown woman."

I said, "And so are you, Auntie Bea. So you need to stop trying to control me. If she can't, what makes you think you can? So as I have said before, united we stand, divided we fall. It's that simple, Auntie Bea. I told both of you that I would do this for you, but I would not lie, cheat, or steal for you. Look how simple it has been selling and paying off debt. The two of you could have done this easily without stealing from me and other people."

Auntie Bea just looked at me as she took another sip of her coffee.

Auntie Bea changed the subject. "What about Frank?"

I answered, "I'm dealing with the credit card debt in my name first because it is bigger than what Uncle Frank and Mom created together. Then I have an obligation to fulfill the promissory note to the attorney that Thomas and I signed. Then I will take care of Uncle Frank's debts."

Auntie Bea said, "That makes sense. What about my land?"

I answered, "I don't know the answer to that one yet. I don't even have a phone number for the finance agency, but I promise as soon as I hear from them, I will tell you. Have you heard from the Greeds?"

Auntie Bea answered, "No, and I don't have any intentions of contacting those thieves either."

I asked, "Is Mr. Greed going to honor his word if I do obtain a mortgage?"

Auntie answered, "Belinda, to be frankly honest, I don't know the man or his wife, so I don't know. All I know is what I told you already."

I said, "Oh, I see."

Auntie Bea asked, "Belinda, can you take me to church today, and do you think we can get Frank to go with us?"

I answered, "Well, what time does the service start?"

Auntie answered, "At 8:30 a.m."

I said, "Well, I don't get the churchgoer crowds until about 1:30 p.m., so yes I can take you as long as I can get back in time for that. How long does it take to get to the church from here?"

Auntie Bea answered, "About an hour and a half."

I said, "Well, we have been here chomping at the mouth for about an hour, so we had better get dressed and leave. I'll go back over to the Daisy house and see if I can't get Uncle Frank up and about, but I don't think he will go with us."

Auntie Bea said, "I don't think he will either, but ask him. I'm going to get ready now."

I ran back over to the Daisy house and tried to get Uncle Frank up out of the bed, but he told me to go to hell, so I left him alone. I knew he was hung over from drinking so much at dinner the night before.

I put my good clothes on and walked back over to Auntie Bea's. By the time I got there, she was all ready to go. She asked me to drive in her car so I did; we chatted the entire drive. We pulled up in front of the family church just a few miles up the road from the Hollow. My family had been members of this Episcopal church for over 180 years. I had been baptized there as an infant. I had gone to Sunday school there, I was confirmed there, and I had taken my first communion there. Thomas and I were married there. My mother, grandmother, great-grandmother, great-great grandmother, and so forth, were all married there. It was located in the middle of nowhere in the country just like our family hollow was. It sat on top of a hillside. It was made of stone with beautiful old stained glass and was a church of wealth from a long, long, long time ago. At the time we were there, it was struggling to stay alive because there must have been only sixteen members including me.

As we drove up the paved driveway to the church, and I was helping my great-aunt out of her car before parking it, I realized I was looking at a dead tradition. My family unit no longer existed. My mother was the last to truly be part of this heritage. I couldn't help but feel the tears stream down my face. In spite of the tears, I had one shred of hope. If Adam Greed honored his word and I was able to obtain a loan, just maybe my family could still hold on to this heritage.

All the people that were left in the church were my mother's age and older. There were no more children running around like there had been when I was a child. The people of this church were mostly hypocrites, snobs, and two-faced liars. Of course as people spoke to us before and after the service, they showed their fake smiles and empathy. I knew that as soon as we were out of earshot, they would be gossiping. All I heard were questions like: "Is your mother really guilty? Did she do this to Big Pete because he said she stole from him?" I just tuned out most of it because these people had known my mother her entire life. They had only seen Big Pete a few times a year when he went to church with my mother. As I was driving Auntie Bea back to her house after the church service I thought, *There are a lot of really stupid people in this world.*

I dropped Auntie Bea and her car off at her house, walked to the Daisy house, and changed my clothes. I then drove to the shop, opened it, and got ready for what I hoped would be another busy day.

That day, the same short, dark-haired, skinny, beady-eyed woman walked into my shop with several other people. She started asking me the same rude questions again, but this time she was much more brazen about it.

She asked, "Do you know Pete King and Jane King? Are you a veteran? Is your husband still active duty? Are you sure you don't have any of your mother's jewelry and furs for sale? Did you steal from the Kings? Why are you here?"

I just looked at this woman, and asked only one question, "Who are you?"

The woman still didn't answer, she simply asked, "Are you going to answer my questions?"

I said, "I don't know who you are. If you are not going to purchase anything, could you please leave?"

The woman left. *Who is she?* I thought.

Despite that, I had a great day—if you consider the other dealers giving me very little for my inventory a good day. Unfortunately, I had no other choice but to take what they offered. As I was locking up the shop, I thought once again, *These people are vampires that suck the blood right out of you, and they are no different from Big Pete.* I guess they were more like my cousin Sam; they were "bottom feeders."

CHAPTER LXI

It was another Monday, but this time I would be picking up my husband from the airport. I couldn't wait to see him, and I hoped things would go smoother and move more quickly with him by my side. I knew that his flight would be very long and boring. The only thing I could do was give him some excitement once he got here. Of course I wanted it to be good excitement, not just all the exciting crap that I had been going through. I bounced out of bed and went through my morning routine. I had just finished making the coffee when the telephone rang. It was Mary.

"Hi, Belinda; I finally got a flight booked. I'm flying on Saturday. The closest I could get was to Washington, D.C. Is there any way you can come pick me up?"

I answered, "Thomas will be here then. I will have to work at the shop that day, Saturday is a busy day. Thomas will be able to come get you."

Mary said, "We need to talk. I've been involved in this whole thing, too, but I want to talk about it face to face, not over the phone."

I said, "Thank you for your honesty, Mary. I don't mind waiting until you get here. It is probably best that we sit down and talk about it face to face. I look forward to seeing you."

Much to my surprise, the day flew by. Before I knew it, it was time to go and pick up Thomas from the airport. It was about 7:30 p.m. I kissed Uncle Frank on the forehead and said, "Well, I'm off to pick up Thomas from the airport. I'll be back shortly."

Uncle Frank said, "What? You didn't tell me he was coming."

I said, "Oh, I thought I did. Anyway, he will be here soon."

I was excited and as I sat in the airport waiting for his plane to land, I tried very hard to keep from pacing. I watched impatiently through the windows, looking upward at the sky, looking for his plane. His plane was thirty minutes late, and the waiting seemed like an eternity.

Finally his airplane landed. I waited by the doors, barely able to contain my excitement as the other family members were waiting for their loved ones! Finally, there he was, walking through the doors. I could not wait a second longer to greet him. I started out walking very quickly, but I wasn't moving fast enough. I broke into a run. When he saw me, he dropped his carry-on bag and held out his arms. We hugged and kissed like long-lost lovers, which we actually were.

Thomas was smiling from ear to ear. "I missed you. Where do we go to get my luggage?"

I answered him, "I missed you too. Just follow me." I grabbed his hand and held it tightly as if I were afraid that I would lose him somehow on our way to the baggage claim. We arrived before the luggage did, and we stood there silently as both of us impatiently waited for his luggage to come through the plastic strips onto the luggage carousel. Finally they came. Thomas grabbed one suitcase and I grabbed the other. He followed me as I quickly walked out of the airport to where I had Mom's pickup truck parked.

We put his luggage in the back of the pickup, and Thomas said, "Let me drive." Before I handed him the keys, I gave him another bear hug, and we exchanged another passionate kiss. I could not wait until later when we were all alone. Thomas broke off the kiss and reached for the keys. I gave them to him, and we climbed into the truck cab and headed to our temporary home. As we were driving back to the Daisy house, I told Thomas everything that had been happening since I had arrived there.

Thomas said, "Belinda, before we get to the Daisy house, I want to see where our storage unit is located. I also want to check our shop."

I said, "Okay, baby. They're both on the way, anyway."

Thomas said, "There is one more stop I want to make. That airplane food sucked, and I'm starving."

I told him, "There is a little twenty-four-hour diner close to the shop. We can stop there when we get into town." He nodded his head in agreement.

We stopped first at the storage unit. I unlocked it, and Thomas helped me open it.

He said, "We can pack this much tighter, Belinda, so we can get more stuff in here."

I said, "You are right, we can, but I'm having issues with Uncle Frank regarding our stuff that I allowed Mom to display in the top part of the

Daisy house. Uncle Frank is trying to say it's his, and it's not. Also, I can't get Auntie Bea to give me your grandfather's shotgun that Mom took from the Daisy house basement. She put your shotgun up in Auntie Bea's bedroom closet. Unfortunately, Mom didn't stop with just that one gun. She has also stashed my great-great-great-grandfather's firearm as well as many other weapons that belonged to my ancestors. They are also located in that closet of Auntie Bea's, and I want them with our things. Also, Mom has let Auntie Bea use a lot of things that have been given to us by my grandparents, and I don't know what to do about it. I've tried asking nicely and I have tried being demanding, but they both insist that these things have always belonged to them." Tears started welling up in my eyes with the frustration I had endured all alone for the past several weeks.

Thomas said, "Don't cry, baby! I'll take care of Frank, and I will talk with your great-aunt, but we will deal with one thing at a time. We'll get all our stuff back, you'll see."

I asked, "What about Big Pete?"

Thomas then put his hand to my face and gently turned it so he could see where it still had some color from being bruised. He turned my face toward the light so he could see it better and asked, "Is this what Big Pete did? You may have thought I didn't notice, but I did."

I said, "Honey, you can barely tell it now. I couldn't hit him back because I was holding on the handrail on the outside of his van, and my foot was on the step. The idiot was drunk, and he was trying to punch me off the side of the van. It was all I could do to hold on. Don't worry; Jay almost kicked him to death after we got him to the ground. He would have killed him if I hadn't stopped it."

Thomas said, "I don't care! If that creep lays another hand on you, I will hurt him so bad that he will never be able to hurt anyone else again. I promise I won't kill him, but he will be in major pain for the rest of his life so that he will never forget what he did to the one I love."

I said, "I don't think he will touch me again. Instead, he is playing nasty mind games. I hope you can help me finish this war."

Thomas said, "I'll do my best. You may think you're tough, Belinda, but Big Pete is a big man and can easily kill you even if you are very well trained. I don't want you getting into any more physical confrontations with that creep. He's a wife beater, and you have been very lucky he hasn't caused any more physical harm to you. Unfortunately, I can't stay till this is over. I won't be here to protect you."

I said, "I will do my best to protect myself."

Thomas said, "Good."

We closed up the storage unit and drove to the shop. When he saw it, his face lit up with pride, and he said, "I'm so proud of you, Belinda. We could have made a lot of money from your talents and your connections overseas. It's too bad that your relatives stole that from us."

I said, "I know. My heart breaks every time I think about it."

I took him inside and showed him the shop books so that he could see just how much my mother had profited from my talents. I also showed him what I had sold and how much more I needed.

After Thomas finished looking at the computer-generated report, he became very angry and said, "Our shop has generated a lot of money over this past year, Belinda. Granted some of this was hers, but it appears most of it was ours. We have not made one dime off of your dreams!"

I looked at him sadly and said with disappointment, "I know."

Thomas said, "Our future has gone up in smoke because of your greedy relatives!"

I said again, "I know."

Thomas said, "These creeps do not deserve this at all."

I said, "I know."

Thomas said, "But your mom made sure we had no other choice."

I said, "I know."

Thomas just became angrier as he started to see the entire picture, which was something I had lived with for many weeks. He finally got to the point where he was able to let go of his anger, as I had also done. "Well, baby, it's no need crying over spilt milk. I know you love her, and I will support you, but if any one of your family members does this to us again, I will fight them," he said.

I said, "I know; I concur. This should have never happened to us anyway."

After that, we went to dinner. I knew that Thomas was starving, and my stomach was also growling. After we placed our drink orders, I told Thomas, "Their pork chops are to die for!"

Thomas looked over the menu and said, "They serve breakfast all day too. I haven't had scrapple for years. I think I'll get breakfast."

When the waitress came back, I ordered the pork chops with a baked potato and corn. Thomas ordered his scrapple, eggs, home fries, toast, and a side order of pancakes.

I said, "My God, baby, you must be starving!"

Thomas looked up with a sheepish grin and said, "I haven't really had a decent meal since you left. I miss your down-home cooking."

I grinned, looked him over, and said, "Well, you don't look like you've been missing too many meals."

Thomas replied, "Well, I make do. You know there are a few local German restaurants I like, and some of our friends have taken pity on me and had me over for dinner a couple times."

I tried to keep from laughing as I said, "Poor baby!"

Our food came, and we were so hungry we ate without speaking. When we were done, we drove back to the Daisy house. Uncle Frank had already gone to bed. I helped Thomas carry his luggage into the bedroom where I was sleeping.

Thomas said, "That's our bed! We are moving most of our furniture out of this place. I don't care if we are trying to buy these houses back. I just don't want your family stealing from us anymore."

I said, "I don't think Auntie Bea and Uncle Frank will."

Thomas said, "I hope you are right because we cannot afford to store everything we own."

I said, "I know."

Thomas said, "I need a shower to get the airplane grime off of me."

I grinned and said, "I need one too. Uncle Frank is a sound sleeper. I'll join you." I winked at him, and he gave a wicked grin. I knew I was in for a night of rousing fun. Thomas and I whispered, laughed, and made passionate love through the early morning hours. We eventually fell asleep in each other's arms.

CHAPTER LXII

I woke up at my normal time and let Thomas continue sleeping. I carefully got out of the bed as I heard my husband snoring softly. I knew Thomas was a very light sleeper; we both were as a result of our military experiences. The battle scars on both our bodies were just small reminders of what we had endured and sacrificed for our country. As he lay there sleeping so peacefully, he appeared so innocent. I could easily forget that he was a seasoned soldier like me. I knew my military career was over, but God only knew how many battles he would be in before his career ended. I was six years older than Thomas was, and I had joined the military before he did. I guess that was one reason throughout our careers that I was always a few steps ahead of him. We had competed against each other many times, but it made us stronger and bonded our relationship to be solid and unshakable. I silently giggled as I remembered the time I had gotten Thomas a stateside swap so that he would be in my unit.

* * *

We were both young soldiers at the time. We were doing physical training (PT) and our TOP (first sergeant in command/E-8) had me setting the pace. My lower-ranking husband, just an E-4 at the time, was running directly behind me in formation when he started stepping on my heels, trying to push me up the road. Thomas, as well as many of the newer soldiers, did not know our TOP very well at all. My TOP was a marathon runner and firmly believed that it was important to keep the unit together. His personal motto was, "Leave no one behind." In addition, he was an Airborne Ranger and believed that finishing the distance was what mattered, not the speed. As a result, I was running slower than I normally would have, setting a manageable pace for the ten-mile run. My husband and the new personnel had no idea that they would be running such a long distance!

Because Thomas could not push me up the road by stepping on my heels, he started yelling in formation, "I guess we need to order a pizza." There were several other soldiers yelling at me, "Come on, Sergeant, move it. We don't want to be running all day."

Finally, TOP yelled at everyone to shut up, and he started singing another cadence. After we finished our PT for the day, TOP called both Thomas and me into his office. He blasted me out for allowing insubordination from my platoon and told me to deal with Thomas. I think that was the last time Thomas and I were ever together in the same company. We would be in the same battalion or regiment, but never in the same company or platoon. I guess I can see why the Army started doing that with married couples. I silently laughed.

*　　*　　*

Throughout the years we have seen marriages come and go. Most of the marriages were between a civilian female and a young active-duty male. The young women truly did not understand the hardships that come with marrying a soldier. I guess because Thomas and I were both soldiers, we had a better bond than most. It had been hard for me to adjust to being a civilian again when I left the military. I know that when my husband chose to retire, it would be even harder for him because he was a man. Being a soldier is not easy to endure, mentally or physically. It is a job, but anyone who wears a uniform knows it's a tough one. Even though it was a lot of "hurry up and wait." As I watched my husband lie in bed, peacefully sleeping, I thought, *If I had to do it all over again, I would do it just the same.*

I wondered if Thomas would make the same choice. I knew that I would wake my husband. He was very hard to sneak up on. Just one small noise did the trick. As I tried to open the door slowly and quietly, it squeaked just a little bit. Thomas sat straight up quicker than I could blink my eye.

He whispered, "Belinda?" as he looked in my direction.

I whispered, "Yes, honey. I'm sorry I woke you."

Thomas said in an agitated whisper, "I'm up now."

I just giggled as I crept out of the opened door and walked down the hallway toward the bathroom with my fresh clothing in hand. I started the water for a shower, and Thomas crept into the bathroom with me. He moved his eyebrows up and down with a devilish grin on his face and whispered, "Well there is no need in wasting water. Can I join you?"

I giggled softly like a little schoolgirl behaving badly and whispered to him as he was putting his arms around my naked waist, "Of course you may, First Sergeant Star, but we need to be quiet because my godfather is in the next room sleeping." I giggled devilishly.

We started kissing passionately and I whispered, "Well, we better get in the shower before there is no more hot water."

Thomas chuckled, and we stepped into the bathtub and sensually washed each other once again and made love while standing in the shower. Once the water ran cold, we got out shivering. Thomas shaved while I brushed my teeth. We finished our morning prep and got dressed for the day.

I made breakfast for us and for Uncle Frank. I was taking the frying pan off of the stove to wash it. I saw Uncle Frank standing in the kitchen, just like every other morning. He was still sleepy with his hair sticking on top of his head.

I said, "Good morning."

Uncle Frank asked, "Good morning, baby girl. Is that breakfast I smell?"

I answered, "Yes it is."

Uncle Frank asked, "Where is that husband of yours?"

Thomas walked into the kitchen from the Florida room and said, "Here I am." My husband walked to my great-uncle and gave him a hug.

Uncle Frank asked, "You've come to help Belinda clean up this mess we got ourselves into?"

Thomas smiled at my great-uncle and answered, "I sure have."

As I started washing some of the dirty dishes, Uncle Frank started walking towards the Florida room behind Thomas and asked me, "Belinda, can you bring me a cup of coffee?"

I answered, "Sure, Uncle Frank. I'll also bring the two of you a plate full of eggs and bacon."

Uncle Frank irritably asked, "They're not hard again, are they, Belinda?"

I laughed at Uncle Frank and answered, "To you, they probably are."

I heard Uncle Frank complain to Thomas about how Jay and I made our scrambled eggs. We ate breakfast and chatted as we ate. Thomas helped me finish cleaning and drying the dishes.

Thomas asked me, "Do you think your great-aunt is up yet?"

I answered, "I doubt it."

Uncle Frank said, "Here, let me call her earlier than I normally do." Uncle Frank started laughing because he knew he would wake up his sister and she would not be happy. I watched my great-uncle pull the phone away from his ear. I could hear my great-aunt fussing but couldn't understand what she was saying.

Uncle Frank passed the phone to me, and I giggled as I said, "Auntie Bea, get up out of that bed right now. Thomas is on his way over to visit with you."

Auntie Bea said, "Good grief, Belinda, you and Frank are going to be the death of me yet. Okay, I'm getting dressed now. Tell that husband of yours to give me about twenty minutes and then come on over. Is he helping us, Belinda?"

I answered, "Yes, and I'll tell him to wait. He wants to speak with you. He has already talked with Uncle Frank some. I made you some breakfast, and he is bringing you a plate over."

Auntie Bea said, "Frank and I are getting fat because of you, Belinda."

I said, "It's better to be fat than skeletons like you and Uncle Frank were when I got here."

Auntie Bea just laughed at me. Thomas went over to Auntie Bea's about a half hour later. He was gone for about two hours before he finally came back to the Daisy house. When Thomas walked through the sliding glass door to the Florida room he just asked, "Belinda, can I speak with you in the bedroom?"

I answered, "Sure."

Uncle Frank just looked at the two of us. We walked back into the bedroom and he said, "I have my grandfather's gun, but I don't want to put this in storage with our other things. I feel it would be much safer in the basement packed in a box with our other things we may have to keep here. Regarding your family firearms, you will have to get your mother to speak with your great-aunt because I don't think she believes us. I think we should just let her continue using our stuff because we are going to buy the houses and land anyway. Most of the furniture and knickknacks in the house belonged to your grandparents. If we take it all, her house will be almost bare."

I said, "I guess you're right, and this way we won't have to worry about storing it all."

Thomas said, "I can't believe how much stuff we have."

I said, "I know. Oh, I already sent Little Pete with the pickup truck to Mom and Big Pete's house to pack more and bring another load for the basement."

Thomas called his family and was making plans for them to come see us. His mother couldn't wait, and she would meet us at the shop that morning. She wanted to see our shop. My mother called, and Thomas spoke with her regarding Auntie Bea. Mom made the call short so she could call Auntie Bea regarding the family weapons. Little Pete pulled up with a truckload, and Thomas and I helped him pack it in the Daisy house basement.

We then loaded another truckload with things from the basement to sell at the shop. I told Little Pete that we would not need him for the rest of the day as we finished loading the truck. I asked him to meet Thomas at Mom and Pete's house the following morning. Thomas and I drove the pickup truck with a load of inventory to the shop. We started unloading, and Little Pete pulled up and parked beside the pickup truck. Without saying anything, he started helping us unload the truck and put the boxes in the shop.

After we finished unloading, Little Pete went to his van and came back into the shop as Thomas and I were pricing the items.

He said, "Belinda, I didn't know how to approach you with another problem I have so I will just give this to you."

He then passed me the file folder. I opened it up and it was his income tax forms. I asked with a puzzled expression, "What do your income taxes have to do with me?"

Little Pete answered, "You have been paying me every week the amount after taxes are taken out. Your mother was supposed to be paying my payroll tax. That is why my checks from you are uneven amounts. I need $1,500 to pay my taxes this year."

I said, "Little Pete that is not my problem! You agreed to this amount, and you never told me anything different. I don't have anything to do with your income taxes. Whatever went on when you worked for Mom and Big Pete is between you and them."

Little Pete became angry and his voice got louder, "Damn it, Belinda, you owe me this money!"

I said, "No I don't. You have even stated that you are still working for them. Now you are claiming that you work for me, and I owe you this. I wasn't even here in the States last year."

Thomas jumped into the argument, and before we knew it Little Pete said, "I don't even care anymore if I get into trouble. I'm going to the U.S. Attorney, and I am going to tell them more about your mother. I will even tell them that I lied regarding my involvement. I will tell them that you refused to pay my taxes. I promise you, Belinda, I will get you into some type of trouble."

Thomas said, "Little Pete, you tried to blackmail Belinda when she first got here. It didn't work, and now you are trying it again. You claim to be a friend of Belinda's mother, but you are doing everything you can to hurt her and Belinda. If Belinda and I were not paying you, where would you be? We need to let you go because we cannot continue paying you. I know that when Big Pete decides not to do right by you, you will come crying back to Belinda and try to get into her good graces again, even after the way you have been treating her. Belinda even picked up one of those bad checks that her mother wrote to you. You even stated that your friend in the police department told you that there was a warrant out for your arrest. What did Belinda and her mother do but bail you out of the trouble that you got yourself into? How much more do Belinda, her mother, and I have to pay to get you out of our lives? I do not succumb to blackmail. I think it is apparent that Belinda will not either."

Thomas continued preaching at Little Pete as the phone rang and I answered it. It was the recording from the jail, and I accepted the charges. Mom started speaking as soon as the recording was over and said, "I spoke with Auntie Bea. She will give you the rest of the guns now, or you can just leave them with her until you and Thomas come back to the States permanently."

I said, "That will be fine, and I will speak with her regarding it, but Mom, Little Pete is here saying I owe him $1,500 for taxes because you took that from his check to pay for his payroll taxes. He now says that he was not an independent contractor, but that he was an employee. He is here, in my shop trying to blackmail me again."

Mom became angry and said, "That is not true! I have never paid his taxes! When we were going under, I asked him if he would take a reduction in pay because I could not continue paying him such an exorbitant salary like I used to, but I did file his social security tax for him. I told him I could not do it for him anymore, that he would have to put the money in a savings account and do that himself at the beginning of this past year. Put him on the phone."

I passed the phone to Little Pete. I couldn't hear what my mother was saying to him, but Little Pete was arguing with her and it sounded like it had very little to do with his income.

Little Pete passed the phone back to me and my mother said, "Don't pay him another dime! He has made up his mind that he is going to make our lives a living hell. Most of the crap he is going to try to use as blackmail I have already admitted to the U.S. Attorney. The only thing I am worried about is that he can bring your great-aunt into it as well. I have no clue how he can hurt you because you were not involved in it, but the U.S. Attorney will likely investigate you anyway. So, Belinda, it is up to you and Thomas."

The phone went dead again. I let out a sigh and looked at Little Pete with disappointment. "Thomas and I will have to think about it. Little Pete, I have just one question for you. Everything you told me about Big Pete's abuse toward you when you picked me up from the airport, was any of that true?"

Little Pete looked at me for a moment before he answered, "No, not really. There was one time when he called me a nasty name, but that was pretty much it. Regarding the abuse towards your mother, that was true. Most of my behavior was for show. But I didn't really care what any of them did, as long as I got paid."

Thomas stared at Little Pete in anger. I stared at the floor. Little Pete continued, "Thomas, I'm sorry, but I'm only human, and I will milk this gravy train for as long as I can. I don't care about any of you white folk at all, and I never did. You know I work hard for my money. Both of you know that. At least I'm not outright stealing from you like Belinda's family is doing. I just want what is owed me for putting up with all this crap."

I asked Little Pete, "Then what do you call this?"

Little Pete rudely ignored me. Instead he said, "Well, I'll see you tomorrow, Thomas. At least the two of you know where I stand now. Don't think about it too long."

I looked at Thomas, and he looked at me. We both stood there looking at each other while Little Pete walked out of my shop. Thomas asked, "How many more bottom feeders are there, Belinda?"

I answered, "Hundreds—all these nasty antique and collectible dealers, as well as the pawn shop people."

Thomas just shook his head as he spoke his thoughts out loud, "This is disgusting."

I said, "I know. I have hired Miss Patson to protect me from Big Pete, Mom, Auntie Bea, and Uncle Frank, and to help me do everything within the law. I think I should call her now, see if she can speak with us today regarding this, and give some advice as to what is the best course of action."

Thomas nodded his head in agreement and said, "Call her now."

I picked up the phone and called Miss Patson. I asked if Thomas and I could see her. She agreed for us to come in that day because her schedule was clear for the rest of the afternoon. Thomas and I closed the shop and went straight to her office.

We only had to wait a few minutes before Miss Patson greeted us, and we followed her into her office. Thomas and I both told her about Little Pete, what he had been doing, and asked what would be the best course of action.

Miss Patson replied, "If you terminate him, and believe me you have grounds to do so, it will cost you more in attorney fees trying to defend yourselves regarding his false accusations. Then you have the issue with your mother. We do not know if he is bluffing, or truly means he will take action. My advice to you is just pay him off and be done with it. It sounds like this man knows how to play the system. He uses the color of his skin to manipulate people who are white. He is a very deadly force because it seems to me that he plays the victim."

Thomas and I agreed with her, and I told her that I still had the issue of clearing my brother's name because Big Pete was conducting his business using it. I was scared to take any action yet because he could blackmail me as well for trying to recover my family things from him. It seemed like everyone was trying to blackmail me in some form.

Miss Patson said, "Sadly you are right, Belinda, we have a very difficult game that we are playing here. I think the best course of action, regarding Big Pete, is to wait and see if you can get the rest of the property from that residence. I just wish your mother had called you sooner instead of waiting until the last minute. Then you would have been able to hire me sooner, and we would have been able to move more quickly. We may have been able to have these issues resolved by now, but we have to work with what we have."

I agreed with her, and then we talked about all the other issues. Ms. Patson told me that she had established the trust for my mother as I requested. She told me that she had taken the funds that I had given her and placed them in an escrow account for the trust. Everything was finished and good to go in that regard. I told her that I had just about paid off the credit card debt opened in my name, and I believed I had recovered all the bounced checks that occurred after Mom and Auntie Bea stopped their check scam. She was very pleased that we had accomplished so much in such a short time, as was I. I told her that Thomas and I had not heard anything yet regarding the mortgage, but I knew that I would be hearing from them soon. Thomas asked her if she would be able to represent me at closing. Miss Patson told us that she could, but her firm had a real estate attorney, and she would talk with them regarding this issue when it arose. We thanked her for her time and drove back to the shop.

Thomas's mother was waiting for us at the shop. She was so excited to see her son. Thomas showed her around the shop and spoke of it with pride as his mother's husband looked around and quietly listened to their conversation. She wanted to go out to dinner. I told Thomas to take her because he needed to spend some one-on-one with his mother and stepfather. I stayed at the shop and continued working until Thomas returned. My husband had thoughtfully brought a meal for me. I closed the shop and ate while I did the daily accounting. Then we went back to the Daisy house.

CHAPTER LXIII

The next morning, Thomas and I started our day at 5:00 a.m. by taking down our bedroom furniture in the guest room where we were sleeping. We loaded everything and moved it to the storage unit. We moved up an old box spring and mattress from the basement and put it in the middle of the bedroom floor. Now our bedroom furniture would be safe and available for us to use once we returned home for good. We returned to the house and started taking our knickknacks out of the curios in the living room. Uncle Frank came in as we were packing them into boxes. We were going to take the knickknacks to the shop to sell.

Uncle Frank said angrily, "What are you doing? Those are mine!"

Thomas said, "No they aren't, Frank. I bought one of these when we were stationed in Hawaii, and Belinda bought the other when we were stationed in Washington State. We moved them here with our other things when we were PCSing to Germany."

Uncle Frank started arguing with Thomas, but Thomas had reached his limit. "Stop it, Frank. It's not yours. Just go get yourself some coffee."

Uncle Frank stormed out of the room and said as he was leaving, "Belinda, I will not have anything left in the house if you and Thomas take everything."

I followed my great-uncle into the kitchen and said, "I will leave my Miss Lita's dishes, her sofa, and a few other things that belong to Mom, but when we come back to the States again, Uncle Frank, you will have to allow us to take our property."

Uncle Frank said, "That will be fine."

Thomas and I finished moving other things from the Daisy house until there was no more room in the storage unit. Thomas took his grandfather's gun and packed it with the rest of our things in the basement of the Daisy house.

While Thomas and I were talking about trying to obtain specialized orders to do a split move to military storage for the rest of our things, everything that my mother had given me, and how long it would take, Auntie Bea came down the steps to the Daisy house basement. Little Pete was right behind her.

I told Little Pete to take the pickup truck to Mom and Big Pete's house and continue packing. We would meet him there later. Thomas walked over to help Auntie Bea down the last couple of steps. Uncle Frank was at the top four steps, and Thomas helped Uncle Frank down the rest of the way.

Finally, all four of us were standing in the middle of an unorganized mess.

Auntie Bea asked, "Good grief, Belinda, what are the two of you going to do?"

I answered, "Thomas and I were just talking about him trying to get specialized orders to do a split move so we can put all this mess in storage."

Auntie Bea took my hand, in front of Thomas and Uncle Frank, started patting it, and said, "Honey, you two don't need to worry about that. You and Thomas can store everything here, plus you can store everything in my barns. There is enough room for not only your stuff but all of your momma's stuff too."

Thomas said, "Bea, we can't put the two of you in that type of situation. You know Belinda's mom has a lot of stuff."

Auntie Bea started patting my hand again, looked at me, looked at Thomas, and said, "That's the least Frank and I can do for the two of you to repay you for all that you have done for us; especially keeping me out of jail. Besides, Thomas, it will be much safer with Frank and me than in that old military storage. The only thing that we ask is that as soon as you and Belinda get back to the States, you move it all out of here. I know that the two of you are trying to get my land back, but when you get back, you should get it out of here."

Uncle Frank said, "I agree that's the easiest way to handle everything, but you aren't going to take everything from Auntie Bea and me, are you?"

I answered, "No, we will make a family decision regarding what you guys want to use and what we want to take."

Auntie Bea said, "I agree with Belinda. We will not worry about the details until the day comes to move everything out. When are you moving all of your momma's stuff out here?"

Thomas answered her, "We don't know, Bea. Big Pete is playing little nasty games with Belinda. If I can't get the rest of the stuff out, it will probably be Belinda's momma getting another relative to convince Big Pete to let us take it and store it, but we will see if I can make a difference."

Auntie Bea said, "Well, that's it. This is what we will all do."

Thomas and I helped Auntie Bea and Uncle Frank back up the stairs.

I made a fresh pot of coffee and cooked everyone a late breakfast. Thomas and I then went to Mom and Big Pete's house to meet Little Pete. We packed the rest of Mom's small jewelry boxes in with the rest of her clothing and loaded the pickup truck. Big Pete would not allow us to take the large jewelry chests that were packed full of my mother's and my grandmother's jewelry. He would not allow us to take the dogs to Thomas's mother's home either.

The next day Thomas said, "Belinda, I'm going to your mom and Big Pete's house to meet Little Pete there. You go ahead and run the shop today. Maybe without you being there, I can get Big Pete to stop fighting with us and let us do what needs to be done."

I agreed that it was worth a try.

Around 5:00 p.m. Thomas pulled up to the shop with another load of things to be stored in the Daisy house.

He walked into the shop and said, "Well, I talked with Big Pete, and I told him that the debt needed to be paid first. Then we need to sell everything else, except for the things that he and your mother want to keep to start over with. He agreed with me. So all of us will go out there tomorrow, pack, and move some more. He will not allow me to bring in a moving team, and he will not allow us to have an auction. He is playing games. I think you should just go ahead and pay Little Pete. I think we can get rid of him after that."

Friday morning, Little Pete showed up at the Daisy house. I gave him two checks, one for the past week, and one for his taxes. I told him that it would be his last day working for us. I told him that he could scream and cry all that he wanted to, but I didn't care. It was over. He could work with Thomas moving things that day or he could just leave. Either way, it did not matter to us. Little Pete said he wanted to work for his money, and he was not a thief and liar like the rest of the family. I told him he could think that, but Thomas and I knew exactly what he was.

CHAPTER LXIV

Saturday afternoon Thomas left in my mother's car to pick up Mary at the airport in Washington, D.C.

As I was closing the shop, Mary walked in with a man behind her, and Thomas was behind them. Mary introduced the man as her boyfriend David. She did not tell me David's last name. We hugged each other, and they looked around the shop. It appeared to me that Mary was trying to see how much Thomas and I were worth, but I thought it would be safer to let her think Thomas and I had money. We decided to go out to dinner. During dinner, Mary got drunk, as usual, which loosened her tongue.

She bluntly asked, "Belinda, I need to know if your mother is taking me down with her?"

I replied, "No, Mary, she is taking the full blame. Please tell me what your involvement was."

She answered, "I held the checks to the clients and knowingly sent them out late, and by late, I mean *months* late. I would give excuses that they had been lost in the mail and that I would be reissuing them. I lied to everyone that I had a college degree, but I did get my GED. I took money all the time from the petty cash, and I forged several fraudulent documents to keep the investigation away. I knew what I was doing was wrong, but I didn't want to lose my job. I guess it didn't matter because your mom and Big Pete had to file bankruptcy anyway. They paid for my apartment, and everything in it belonged to them. They came back and moved everything from the apartment, but I found this rich old sucker, and I married him. Now he is trying to divorce me. This is my new boyfriend, and he is a lawyer."

I looked over at David because she had already introduced us at the shop, but she had not told me his profession until then. I guess Mary wasn't worried about him because he was too busy talking about the military with Thomas and wasn't paying any attention to our conversation.

I asked, "What is the name of your new boss who is buying the wine?"

Mary answered, "You don't need to worry about it."

I reached into my pocketbook and gave Mary a diamond bracelet I had taken out of the safe. I handed it to her and said, "Mom and I can't pay you for being our middleman, but I hope a diamond bracelet will be enough payment instead."

Mary said, "Oh, Belinda, yes, this is more than what I expected."

I just looked at her thinking of my mother's words, that she only helped you if you paid her.

I said, "I'm glad you will accept this as payment."

Mary said, "Well, that's why we are here, to go ahead and take the wine off your back."

I asked, "Do you have a cashier's check?"

Mary answered, "No, I will wire the money to you."

I said, "No, Mary, it doesn't work that way. You must pay me first then take the wine if you think you can double your money off of it. My advice to you is not to do that because I'm not sure of the value and condition of it all."

Mary said, "Oh, I'm sure it's fine."

I said, "Well, since you are here there is no need for it to be a wasted trip. You and I can physically inventory it, and you can tell your boss that the list is correct, then wire the money to the bank next week, and return next weekend to move it."

Mary said, "Oh, that's a good idea."

Thomas and I drove Mary and David to the Holiday Inn where they wanted to stay. David checked in, and Thomas helped him take their luggage up to their room. Mary wanted to go straight to the bar and talk more with me. She told me more of the story of her involvement and more what was going on in her life. Thomas and David met us in the bar, and Thomas and I left.

Mary called the next morning for us to come pick them up around 11:30 a.m. We went, picked them up, and returned to the Daisy house. Uncle Frank was upset that I didn't tell him that Mary was in town, but he enjoyed chatting away with her and David. I took Mary down into the basement and showed her the wine. She was already drunk again and said that she didn't feel like doing the inventory. She said my list was good enough. I told Mary she should check it to make sure that I had no errors, but the silly drunk didn't want to be bothered. Her boyfriend made flight arrangements to fly out from the Snobville Airport instead of Washington, D.C. Thomas drove them to the airport, and I went to the shop.

I was assisting several customers when Thomas walked into the shop through the back door. He immediately started helping me by wrapping the items as I wrote up receipts. Once the group of customers left, Thomas said, "Your cousin has turned into a complete drunk, and that boyfriend of hers is weird."

I said, "I know."

Thomas said, "I don't trust her at all. She even had the nerve to think we were that stupid to let her take our wine and not pay for it first."

I said, "I know. I truly believe she planned on taking the wine and never paying us for it. Plus, I think she has sold it for twice as much as she paid, and I warned her I knew it was positively worth the amount I told her, but I wasn't sure that it was worth twice as much. I think she has sold it to her boss for double the amount, if there is a boss. She refused to give me his name so I could speak to him personally."

Thomas said, "Something is fishy with this whole thing."

I nodded my head in agreement. I said, "I agree something is very fishy, but I don't care, as long as we get the money for it."

Thomas said, "I agree."

We closed up the shop. We were headed back to the Daisy house when Thomas said, "Let's go out to dinner. We will take your great-aunt and great-uncle out so we know they eat."

I said, "That's a great idea. I saw a cafeteria in town. We could take them there because that shouldn't be that expensive."

Thomas said, "Yeah, that's a good idea."

We pulled into the driveway, and there were three cars parked in the driveway. Thomas got very excited and said, "Wow! My brothers are here. We will get everyone to go eat at the cafeteria together."

I said, "That sounds great."

We walked into the Florida room, and all three of his brothers, with their wives and children, and Thomas's father were piled in the Florida room. Everyone hugged and greeted us. I picked up the phone so Auntie Bea could be part of the family gathering as well and asked her if she wanted to join us. Auntie Bea told me she was tired, wasn't feeling very good, and she did not know these people. I didn't press her on it. Thomas drove Uncle Frank's car with Uncle Frank, his father, and all three of his brothers piled in. I drove the White Beast. Two of my sisters-in-law and a few of the kids rode with me, and my other sister-in-law, with the rest of the kids, drove in another car. Everyone followed me because I was the only one who knew where the restaurant was.

We put several tables together so everyone could sit as a group. We had Thomas's father at the head of the table, with Thomas on one side, and Uncle Frank. Thomas' brothers lined up across from each other next to Thomas and Uncle Frank. I sat down on the end so everyone could hear and speak with Thomas.

After everyone was settled at the table with their plates of food and drinks, Thomas's father prompted the discussion, "Thomas, tell us what the hell has happened."

Thomas let out a sigh and told his father and his family the entire story. I guess it must have taken him over an hour to tell everything. No one interrupted him at all, except for a couple of questions. The only other interruptions were when the children became restless, but my sisters-in-law took care of it.

All three brothers looked at me and swore they would support us and help out until I financially repaired everything. They all agreed, including Thomas's father, that if I got the mortgage for the Mills farm, they would all chip in to financially help us. Thomas told his father and brothers if we got it, and they wanted to have their names on the title with us, we would put their names on it as well.

We all drove back to the Daisy house, and everyone said their goodbyes outside. I unlocked the door for Uncle Frank because we could hear his telephone ringing. I grabbed the phone and it was Big Pete.

Big Pete was drunk again and spoke in a slurring voice, "It's about time you answered the phone; where have you been?"

I got angry and said, "That's none of your damn business."

Big Pete said, "I'm not going to let you and Thomas move another damn thing out of this house until you give me my wine."

I said, "What wine? You don't own any wine."

Big Pete said, "We will see about that."

By this time Thomas's family had left, and Thomas was standing at the open sliding glass door, listening. He walked towards me with his hand outstretched for me to pass him the telephone. He took it from me, and he said to Big Pete, "Listen, you sorry-ass son of a bitch, Jane already sold the wine to Belinda and me over a year ago. You do not own anything.

I'll be there tomorrow, with Belinda, to pack and move more stuff. Go to bed and sleep it off." Thomas hung the phone up. Thomas looked over at me and said, "I can't believe how stupid that sorry-ass bastard is. He has always acted like he is better than us, but he acts like a stupid drunk when someone is trying to do something right in all this mess. He will come out for the better if he stops fighting with us, and that goes for your mother as well, Belinda."

Thomas then looked over at Uncle Frank and was going to start fussing at him as well, but before Thomas uttered a word Uncle Frank said, "Now, boy, don't start in with me. I have nothing to do with that creep. I would have killed him if Belinda would have let me."

Thomas then looked over at me and said, "Maybe you should have let Frank kill him."

I said, "Thomas! We are not at war, and Uncle Frank and Big Pete were both drunk. The rules of engagement on a battlefield do not apply to civilians here at home. What the devil is the matter with you to even think of such of thing? Killing overseas is one thing, but killing a civilian in our own country is considered murder. Do you want Uncle Frank and me to destroy our lives over this?"

Thomas said, "Come on, Belinda. Jay doesn't even like his own father. It would be easy just to kill him and hide his fat corpse somewhere. Nobody would know. The U.S. Attorney would just think he took off to keep from going to jail. You have to admit it would be much easier."

Uncle Frank said, "That's a good idea, boy. I could kill him then the two of you could hide his body up in the mountains somewhere."

I looked at my great-uncle and my husband, shook my head in total disappointment, and said, "Yes, I would love to kill that creep, but unfortunately we can't do that. If we did that, what makes us any different than he is? Would we not also be thieves because we stole his life?"

Thomas asked, "I didn't look at it that way, Belinda. You're right, but admit it, would it not solve a lot of problems we are having right now?"

I answered, "No, because if we killed him, we would have to kill Auntie Bea, Uncle Frank, my sister, my mother, and everyone else because of their involvement."

Uncle Frank said, "I didn't steal from you."

Thomas said, "Yes, you did. Look at you trying to say my stuff is yours when it's not."

Uncle Frank said, "I just got confused."

Thomas said, "Bull, Frank."

I said, "I guess you understand where I'm coming from, Thomas."

Thomas said, "Yes, I do. I had to remind you that you were not here to judge, and I got sucked right into it as well. You're right it's not our place to judge or to take. Thanks for putting me back on the right path." Thomas reached over and kissed me.

Uncle Frank, with a puzzled expression on his face, said to Thomas and me, "I'm a vet as well, Belinda. I have been in bloodier battles than the two of you put together, and I don't get it. By not killing the creep, how is it going to make it any better? Remember, Belinda, it's better to kill than be killed."

Thomas answered him, "Frank, that's why you don't get it. This is not that type of war, to kill or be killed. It's about outwitting or being outwitted by the enemy. This is a mental fight, not a bloody fight. This is a different fight of good vs. evil. All of us fight with our own demons within ourselves as to what each one of us considers good and evil. I guess you call this your 'conscience.' Our world is not perfect, but our country gives us these freedoms to fight, without violence, against each other when you feel you are wronged. Our battlefields are not with a firearm, but with a pen and words, with truth and justice, and a courtroom as a battlefield, but unfortunately our country has forgotten that this freedom was for all the people, not just the wealthy and well-connected. This is just one freedom that Belinda and I have given our lives for to fight and kill, to protect our borders within, for our civilians to bask in just one of these freedoms, but now I feel the blood that has been spilled for this has been in vain. You have to pay the blackmailer because it's cheaper than having them punished; to allow these types of people like Big Pete to prey off 'family.' Well, this is just part of it, Frank.

"You have fought for some of these freedoms as well. If it wasn't for your generation of soldiers, Belinda and I wouldn't have some of the freedoms we have today. Yes, Frank, Belinda and I do get it. We have seen shit, lived it, breathed it, have been wounded for it. Our country is still great, but it's the civilians within it that have lost their way and have forgotten that you have to fight to keep it. Our justice system should be for all the people, not just the ones that can pay for it—civil or criminal. The attorneys need to have their inflated salaries contained, and judges need to be held accountable for their actions and misguided rulings. A victim shouldn't have to pay a dime for these types of crimes committed against them, but unfortunately that is not the case. I've said enough. I can go on and on, but I don't like looking at the bad spots of my country. I like to look at all its greatness and goodness.

"Unfortunately, Frank, we are all soldiers, and we know how to fight on a battlefield, but this type of war, none of us is any good at fighting. I can't speak for you, Frank, but I can speak for Belinda and myself. Belinda and I believe in honesty, and because of this I'm truly afraid we will be outwitted because we don't know how to play this type of war."

I had tears in my eyes, I kissed my husband, and he said with an irritated voice, "Ah, come on, Belinda, stop getting mushy with me. You are better at this crap than me." I just giggled at him.

I thought, *I'm blessed that my husband has a sound mind and knows how to put all the bad stuff that has happened to us during wartime in a box in the back of his head and close the door.* A lot of soldiers don't know how to do that. Even with seasoned soldiers like Thomas and me, sometimes the bad thoughts seep out of the cracks in the box.

CHAPTER LXV

I woke up and cautiously touched my husband's side of the bed to make sure he was still there and it wasn't all just a dream. To my joy and relief, his warm, firm body was lying there next to me. As I snuggled closer and wrapped my arm around him, I realized it was already Monday again, and he would be leaving this week to fly back to Germany. I thought, *He really did try to make a difference in this mess. He did his best, trying to make it better for us, but for the most part, his efforts were in vain. One good thing is, we now have Little Pete out of our lives forever, or at least I hope so. I knew it was going to get even worse with Big Pete, and he would make it even more difficult to accomplish the mission.*

I kissed my husband on the cheek ever so lightly, and I whispered to him, "It's time to rise and shine, Bear."

He slowly turned over, still in my arm that was wrapped around his side, kissed me on the mouth, and said, "Good morning, She Wolf." Thomas rubbed the sleep from his eyes by shaking his head slowly from side to side in his pillow. Thomas said, "You haven't called me Bear in a long time."

I laughed at my husband as I commented, "We haven't been at war for a long time either. I have my Bear here now to help me fight these nasty people." We made love silently in the early morning hour, and we got ready for the new day of hell.

Thomas helped me load another pickup truck full of more inventory for the shop. After we had finished loading, Little Pete pulled into the driveway in his van.

Thomas said, "That nasty little creep just will not go away!"

I said, "I have had enough of his involvement!"

Little Pete got out of his van and said, "Good morning."

Thomas asked, "What are you doing here?"

Little Pete answered, "I am here to work today."

Thomas said, "If you don't leave right this minute, I'm calling the cops."

Little Pete said, "Go ahead. I told you I was going to milk this gravy train for as long as I can."

Thomas said, "We are not paying you another dime. If you want to work, that is fine, but you're not getting another dime from Belinda and me."

Little Pete said, "Oh, yes I will. Big Pete told me to tell you Belinda's mom will call her this morning."

Thomas said, "Fine, leave until then."

Little Pete said, "No, I'll stand right here until she calls."

I asked, "Did you tell Big Pete about our wine?"

Little Pete answered, "It's not your wine, and you can't sell it."

I said, "Little Pete, you have absolutely no idea what you are talking about."

I didn't say another word to him. I went back inside and told Uncle Frank to keep his doors locked and set the alarm after we left. Under no circumstances should he allow Little Pete in the house. I called Auntie Bea and told her the same thing.

Without saying another word to Little Pete, Thomas and I got into the pickup and drove to the shop. Little Pete followed us. We couldn't believe it. As we were unloading the pickup truck, Little Pete sat in his van watching us.

The telephone rang as I was putting a box down in the shop, and I answered it. I was not one bit surprised to hear the recording from the jail. My mother started speaking as soon as it finished, before I even accepted the phone call.

She said, "Belinda, I spoke to Big Pete yesterday, and he told me Little Pete came by the house and told him you and Thomas terminated him. You must continue letting him help you move things, and you must continue paying him."

I said, "No, Mother, it's over. There is no more money to pay him, and I do not need him."

Mom asked, "How can you move furniture by yourself?"

I replied, "Big Pete is playing games. If he doesn't let me move the stuff with a moving company, then it will not happen. It's over! You'd better tell Little Pete to leave, because if he doesn't leave this second, we are calling the police. Nobody will force us to keep paying him. Have I made myself clear yet?"

Mom answered, "Okay, put him on the phone."

I asked Thomas to tell Little Pete to come into the shop. I passed the phone to Little Pete and Little Pete only said to my mother, "Yes, ma'am."

Little Pete simply said to us, "This is not over yet."

I said, "Yes, it is, Little Pete. Get out of my shop now before we call the police."

He left without saying another word.

Thomas said, "I think we better go over to your Mom and Big Pete's house again."

I said, "Let's go."

We pulled up into the driveway of their house, and Big Pete's van was gone.

I said, "Great!"

Big Pete had the alarm set, but I had the code to disarm it. We started packing as quickly as we could and loaded as much as possible into the pickup truck. We left and drove back to the Daisy house where we unloaded everything into the basement. As soon as the pickup was empty, we drove back to Mom and Big Pete's house. This time Big Pete's van was there.

Thomas and I looked at each other. Both Thomas and I went into soldier mode when we saw Big Pete's van in the driveway. Our adrenalin started pumping full force.

Thomas must have regressed to the battlefield mode because he asked, "She Wolf, how are we going to handle this?"

I answered, "Bear, get a grip. We are going to have to play this by his actions."

Thomas said, "Roger that."

We both got out of the vehicle and "assessed our surroundings" before taking any further action. I walked quickly to the garage door, and Thomas went to the side of the garage. He was peeking from the corner to where I was standing. I already had the garage door remote in my hand where I had taken it from the sun visor where it was clipped in the pickup truck. I pushed the button and stood firm in the middle and a few inches outside from the garage door as it was opening. I stood there as the door slowly opened. Before it was completely open, I saw Big Pete coming through the door from the side of the house into the garage.

He yelled, "What the hell are you doing here? I told you I want the wine. I'm not letting you take another thing from this house until I get it."

I silently stood my ground as he walked toward me. I watched him pick up a four-by-four plywood board that was resting on one side wall of the garage. He had his total visual focus on just me—a very bad mistake on his part. I continued standing there with my legs spread apart. I bent them ever so silently waiting for the forced impact that I might receive from the four-by-four that Big Pete had raised above his head. He continued coming directly at me walking very quickly. He was about half a foot from me, still slightly in the garage. Thomas ran, lunged at him, and knocked him to the ground. It only took Thomas a couple of seconds to subdue Big Pete.

I yelled at Thomas, "Sarge, put the maggot on his knees."

Thomas obeyed my command. Thomas had one leg bent with his knee toward the ground and his other leg was bent with his knee in the air with his boot firm on the ground. He had Big Pete's arms outstretched to his back and Big Pete's backside pulled tight toward the ground.

I yelled to Thomas, "TOP, make sure you don't break any bones or cause any bruises because we know this maggot is a tattletale. We just want to inflict pain at this point without anyone knowing about it except for us."

Thomas said, "No problem, TOP."

I looked down at Big Pete, spat in his face, and viciously said, "Well, maggot, what are we going to do about you without anyone finding out about it?"

I took my fist and deliberately hit him in his stomach right where his bladder was. I made sure I didn't hit him hard enough to cause any bruises. As I hoped for, it made Big Pete urinate his pants. I watched as his light-tan-colored pants turned darker around his crotch and inside of his legs. Thomas and I wickedly laughed at him.

Thomas said, "You're not so tough, are you, maggot, when you're fighting a man instead of beating on a woman?"

I said, "Yeah, that's right, you cowardly maggot. I read your discharge papers, you sorry piece of shit. You were given a general discharge because you couldn't adapt to military life, and you were an E-4 in the Navy. You never saw any action, because if you did you sure in the hell wouldn't have the attitude you have now. Sitting there telling Bear and me how a long time ago you were an E-8 in the Navy, and you saw a lot of action in Vietnam. You didn't even serve long enough to get to Vietnam, and believe me, you maggot, if you did see any action you would never be the same because there's nothing glorious about it!"

Thomas pulled Big Pete's arms backwards even harder. Big Pete screamed, as tears were flowing down his face, "I'm sorry. I'm sorry."

I said, "Sorry that you're nothing but a bottom feeder, or are you sorry for being a wife beater and a thief? You're such a coward, you even made sure my mother went to jail for you!"

Thomas started pulling on Big Pete's arms harder, and he let out more agonizing screams. I said, "You're scared, you piece of shit. You're not only fucking with people that have killed for real, you're fucking with hillbillies; you're fucking lucky, maggot, because Bear and I are not as crazy as the rest of my family. We can't be charmed with a dollar bill like the rest of them."

Pete started screaming, "Help me! Someone help me!"

Thomas and I continued humiliating him as we viciously laughed.

Thomas said, "Nobody's home to hear you."

I said, "What was it you said to me a few weeks ago? It was something like, 'You know I can kill you, Belinda.' Well let me say it to you, maggot: You know we can kill you, Big Pete, and torture you for days before doing so. So there you go, Big Pete, go ahead and play your games because the only one who will hurt in the end, is you. Thomas, let the maggot go. He's not worth it. Let's get out of here. So, Big Pete, you better always be on your guard. You never know if I decide, by myself, to come back and finish the job, to put you out of your misery—because I can."

Thomas and I stood there for a few seconds, watching Big Pete rub his forearms. When he finally spoke, he said, "I don't blame Thomas for this, Belinda. I blame you! So you and your family better watch your backs."

I laughed and said, "Maggot, please! Your threats don't scare me. They never did. I have fought bigger men than you in my life. The reason we're not killing you today is because I know Uncle Sam is going to take you down for us. If you ever lay a hand on my mother, great-aunt, or great-uncle, I will hunt you down like the mangy dog you are, cut your dick off, and shove it down your throat. I do not need my husband to do my dirty work because I can do it myself. If you knew what I was, not who I am, you wouldn't be playing this nasty mortal game with me. So fuck off and die maggot!"

Thomas and I ran to the pickup truck, jumped in, and sped out the driveway. I turned my head as we were speeding out of the driveway and saw Big Pete crying as he put his hands on his face. I looked over at my husband, put my hand on his shoulder, and said in a calm tone, "I hope that did the trick."

Thomas said, "All we did was humiliate him, Belinda, and scared him some. He's going to continue, and there is nothing more we can do about it."

"I know. I'm just glad we put him in his place, on our terms for a change. What we did was wrong, but it was bittersweet." We both started laughing, and I solemnly continued, "Thomas, thank you, but I fear I may have gotten you into trouble. We should not have let our tempers get the best of us. Do you think he thinks we are crazy burned-out soldiers?"

Thomas laughed. "Well, baby, we both know we have a little bit of shell shock in us after what we have been through over the years, but I think we are still pretty much sane. Yeah, I think the maggot thinks we are crazy now. We will see. If I get into trouble, I will deserve it because of my actions. Right or wrong I will die to protect you, and I always find myself doing stupid things to see you happy."

I asked Thomas, "Do you think he's going to report us?"

"No, but he will step up his evil games, and there is nothing we can do about it." Thomas continued, "Well, I guess we will not be able to move the rest of the crap."

I said, "I know, but we will still wait and see. You know he wants the wine even though it belongs to us, so maybe he will not be so tough now about it. Only the Shadow knows . . ." We both started laughing. I thought, *We will be okay.*

CHAPTER LXVI

Thomas was right; Big Pete started stepping up his game. After we closed up the shop for the day and went back to the Daisy house, Uncle Frank had a message for me from Mom's attorney. It sure did not take him long to start the next stage of his game.

Thomas and I already stopped at the liquor store and grocery story before returning to the Daisy house. When I was done reading the message, Thomas passed me the Jack Daniels bottle after he took a heavy swig from it. I took a big drink from it as well, but I had to have a soda to wash the bitter taste down.

Uncle Frank was sitting in his favorite chair watching us and asked as I was putting the cap back onto the bottle, "Baby girl, what about me?" I looked down at my great-uncle and immediately felt bad because what Thomas and I just did with the liquor was like eating candy in front of small child and not sharing. Thomas and I didn't think of what we had just done, so I felt I had no other choice but to pass him the bottle, and I did. I watched my great-uncle take two big swigs, and he passed the bottle back to me.

Thomas took it from me and said, "Well, if we are going to get drunk, we might as well make some bourbon and Cokes over ice."

I nodded my head in agreement with him.

Uncle Frank just blurted out, "Yeah, but that's the good stuff, and I can't afford that. Can I just have a glass full with some ice, Thomas?"

Thomas just shook his head. After a few minutes, he brought Uncle Frank and me a glass of the bourbon.

I downed the entire glass and said, "I guess I better call Mom's attorney and get it over with before it's too late. What time is it?"

Uncle Frank looked at his telephone clock and told me, "It's about 4:20 p.m."

Uncle Frank got up from his chair so I could sit as I called the attorney and put the phone on speaker so Thomas and Uncle Frank could hear the conversation as well.

After the receptionist answered the phone she transferred me to the attorney. We gave our greetings to the attorney who said, "Belinda, Big Pete called the U.S. Attorney and told them that you had over $500,000 of a wine collection that belonged to him and your mother. He reported to them that your mother was part of the scam and masterminded to sell this collection and turn it back into monies. He also said that you were going to take these funds back to Europe and put them into a Swiss bank account for your mother. He also reported to them that he wanted the collection returned so he could make some restitution to his clients. He claims he has a buyer already lined up and that would make the U.S. Attorney's job easier."

Thomas and I started laughing, and I said, "That is the biggest bunch of bull crap I have ever heard in my life. Big Pete and my mother never had a half-of-a-million-dollar collection of wine in their lives. What wine they did have, Big Pete sold most of it and I can prove it." I just continued laughing.

Mom's attorney asked, "Belinda, this is no laughing matter. How can you prove it?"

I was still laughing as I answered, "Yes, it is very funny, because I have the wine file here with Big Pete's fax receipts proving when he faxed and received offers."

Mom's attorney started chuckling. "I can't believe you have proof. Can you fax that over to me now?"

I answered, "Sure. Thank God my mother is a packrat or Big Pete would be having a field day because I would not be able to prove anything."

Mom's attorney replied, "Get that faxed to me now because I'm meeting with the U.S. Attorney first thing in the morning. I will call you after the meeting to tell you the outcome. Is it possible for you to be at this number? Can I call around 10:30 or so tomorrow morning?"

I answered, "I will have to call you because I have to drop my husband off at the airport around that time."

Mom's attorney said, "Okay, but call me as soon as you get back from the airport."

I said, "Okay."

Uncle Frank asked, "Belinda, do we have that much in wine?"

I answered, "No Uncle Frank; that was a big fat lie. He doesn't own anything, and they never had that much to begin with."

Thomas started laughing and said, "Didn't I tell you he would push his game up?"

I said, "I know you did, honey, but this one, we won because Momma is a packrat. He doesn't know I took all those files, and he probably didn't know my mother kept his paper trail."

All three of us laughed in triumph.

I asked, "Honey, can you give me that briefcase that's sitting beside you on the floor? I have the entire file because I've been working with Mary regarding selling our wine."

Thomas passed me the briefcase, and I took the file out of it. I unplugged the telephone and hooked up the fax machine. I put the papers with the fax receipts that included the dates and times on the letters going back and forth as Big Pete was selling off the wine collection. I included photocopies of the checks that Big Pete received for the wine. I faxed all of it to Mom's attorney. "That should do it," I said.

Uncle Frank said, "That deserves another drink."

Thomas and I just shook our heads smiling at Uncle Frank and I said, "Yes, I think Uncle Frank is right. Thomas, can you make us another drink? This is the first good battle that we have won."

Thomas looked at me with one eyebrow cocked up and said, "This is not the first battle we have won with Big Pete."

I said, "I know, but it is the first one we fought and won on his terms. It feels refreshing because it truly is a knockout victory, but I have a feeling this issue isn't over yet."

Thomas brought fresh drinks for everyone. In unison, Uncle Frank and I said, "Thank you."

I said, "I think we need to go over to Auntie Bea's. I want to get one of those old hand guns out of her closet for protection. If she doesn't have any good ammunition, I want to buy some tonight. I have a bad feeling Big Pete is going to do something drastic once he finds out he lost this one."

Thomas said, "I agree."

Uncle Frank said, "You don't have to worry about it, Belinda. I have several weapons, and I can protect you and Sister Bea."

Thomas laughed and said, "Frank, please. You can barely see, and you would end up shooting yourself in the foot or killing Belinda instead."

Uncle Frank laughed and said, "I promise that I won't shoot until I have my glasses on."

Thomas said, "By the time you get your glasses on it could be too late."

Uncle Frank said, "Well, then I can be Belinda's backup."

Before my husband started hurting my great-uncle's feelings any further I said, "Uncle Frank, that's a great idea. You can cover my back. Just don't shoot me in the back."

Uncle Frank laughed and said, "I know I would never do that because I can hear your big mouth a mile away."

All three of us laughed.

I said, "Well, that's settled then. Well, Uncle Frank, can you call Auntie Bea and tell her Thomas and I are on our way over to see her. There is a tub of chicken in the kitchen, and I'm taking this plate that Thomas made up over to Auntie Bea's."

Uncle Frank said, as he was getting up from one chair to go to the chair next to his telephone that I had already hooked back up, "Sure, baby girl."

Thomas and I walked across the field to Auntie Bea's house. We entered her house from the side door as always and I heard Auntie Bea talking on the phone in her living room. I put her plate of food on the kitchen table, and Thomas and I walked into her living room. Thomas gave Auntie Bea a hug, and I did the same in turn. We all sat down, and I told Auntie Bea how Thomas and I felt. I told her that we wanted to get one of the old hand guns from out of her closet. She said sure, but she didn't think she had any good bullets for it. Thomas and I went to the top of the stairs, and I opened the closet. Thomas and I went inside it after turning the light on. I found a beautiful pearl-handled.38 Colt six-barrel.

Thomas said, "Damn, Belinda, that's old."

I said, "I know. It's probably from the late 1880s or early 1900s. I'm not sure. It's in excellent condition. It just needs some cleaning, and I think it will be fine."

Thomas said, "It's beautiful, and yes I think that's all the firepower you will need. I'll clean it and make sure it's okay to use."

I laughed at my husband and thought, *Men! But I'm glad he's here because he does know much more about weapons than I do.* I said to Thomas, "I'm glad you are here. I'm rusty because I haven't fired a weapon in over a year."

Thomas giggled and said, "It's like riding a bike, Belinda, and you know it. You have been hunting and killing things all your life, just like me. That's one reason I fell in love with you—you love to hunt, fish, and play sports." He started laughing.

I said, "Well, we haven't done much of any of that in a long, long time."

Thomas said, "I know. You know it's too expensive to even fish in Germany."

We both laughed.

Thomas said, "You are so spoiled, you even make me bait your hook when we go fishing."

I said, "I know, because my daddy always did that for me, but I can do it for myself. I just like making you get angry with me, and besides, I am still a lady—at least to some degree."

We both laughed.

Thomas said, "A lady, but a very deadly one."

I said, "No I'm not because you're stronger than me."

Thomas laughed and said, "But you're smarter than me."

We both laughed.

I said, "No I'm not. I think you're smarter than me."

Thomas said, "Well, it's about damn time you admitted it." We both laughed.

We looked around to see if we could find any old gun-cleaning kits. We didn't find any and I said, "Oh, Uncle Frank has a couple. I saw them in the basement with some of his things that were never unpacked."

Thomas said, "Good. Oh, I found some ammunition. The box . . . Damn it. Look, Belinda."

I looked at the box of ammunition and the date on it was 1945.

Thomas said, "My God, look at all this."

We grabbed one of the larger boxes and started filling it with all the old ammunition we could find.

Thomas said, "I'm going to have to dispose of all this."

I said, "Yes, you better, and I don't think we will find any ammunition for this Colt. Oh, I forgot. When I was packing Mom's clothing from the closet, a .45 fell out of a shoe box and hit me in the head. I packed it in Mom's clothing, and I think the box is in the basement with Mom's other clothing. It had a brand-new box of ammunition and the .45 was not a very old one. I can use that instead."

Thomas became angry with me and said, "Damn it, woman. Why didn't you tell me that to begin with?"

I answered, "I forgot. I don't know how I forgot, but I did. I still have the knot on my head from where it fell out of the top of the closet when I was pulling stuff down."

We laughed and put everything back except for the old ammunition box.

As I was about to turn the light out, Auntie Bea yelled from the bottom of her steps, "What's taking the two of you so long?"

Thomas laughed as he walked out of the closet with the box in his hands and said, "Bea, you're going to be the death of me yet. You have old ammunition up here that I'm going to dispose of right this minute."

Auntie Bea asked, "What?"

By then, Thomas and I were at the bottom of the steps where Auntie Bea was standing.

Thomas said, "You heard me," as Auntie Bea was peeking in the box.

Auntie Bea looked at Thomas and said, "That's still good."

Thomas said, "I doubt it."

Auntie Bea said, "Oh, all right then. Herndon always took care of that type of thing."

Thomas said, "It looks like he didn't."

Auntie Bea just laughed along with us.

As we were leaving to walk back to the Daisy house, I gave my great-aunt a kiss on her cheek and said, "Now you make sure you keep this house locked up with your alarm on. If you hear something that's out of the ordinary, you call me immediately and then call the police."

Auntie Bea said, "I'll call you, and you can decide if the police need to be called."

I said, "No, Auntie Bea, its better that you call the police immediately after calling me. It's better to have a false alarm than no alarm at all, and it would be too late."

Auntie Bea said, "Okay. Good night."

As we were walking back to the Daisy house, Thomas said, "I'm not going to have time to dispose of this. When you get ready to close down the shop and get my brothers to help you move whatever is left from the shop and the booth, make sure they take this and dispose of it properly."

I said, "I will."

We went down into the Daisy house basement, and I went straight to the corner where I had my mother's clothes stored. I quickly found the box, and Thomas opened it. I pulled out the .45 and the ammunition box. Thomas and I went outside through the basement door to the back of the house after we turned the floodlights on. We had found some old empty soda cans in a trash bag. Thomas put several of them on top of the fence posts. I fired several practice shots and became familiar with the weapon. After about twenty-five minutes, Thomas was satisfied that I could hit my target. Thomas said, "See, Belinda, it's just like riding a bike."

I just laughed at my husband and said, "I hope I don't need to use it."

Thomas said seriously, "I hope you don't either." He kissed me on my forehead.

We went back inside. I found one of Uncle Frank's cleaning kits and started cleaning the weapon.

Uncle Frank had already gone to bed. Thomas and I talked about everything once again, and Thomas advised me on many of the issues that were before me. We decided the best course of action to handle them was one at a time.

CHAPTER LXVII

The next morning came too quickly. I didn't want my husband to leave me, but he had no choice. Uncle Sam's contract came before mine, and I understood that. I felt bad that my husband was even involved in any of this. If anyone found out what we had done, Thomas would be in a lot of trouble. It could hurt his career, even destroy it. Uncle Sam doesn't take too kindly to the type of behavior Thomas and I had demonstrated the day before with Big Pete, but I thought the creep deserved it. Actually, he deserved a lot more than what we had given him.

Before I knew it, it was time to take Thomas to the airport. I couldn't help myself but frown as I helped my husband put his luggage in the back of the pickup truck. I guess he saw my sour face; he turned to face me, gave me a big hug, and he kissed me.

He said, "It's going to be fine. If you can handle the Army and everything that was dished out to you then, I know you can handle your family."

I looked at him with a sad smile and said, "The Army and our country's enemies are nothing compared to my family. My family has a way of chewing me up and spitting me out without even laying a hand on me."

Thomas shook his head. "I guess I know that, but I know you're strong enough to handle it."

I said, "I hope you're right."

Thomas went through a checklist to make sure I didn't forget any of the issues at hand as we drove to the airport. He was definitely a very organized soldier and leader. He left no scenario unturned. I parked the truck and walked inside the airport. I waited as he checked in his luggage. Within an hour, they were calling the passengers to board the aircraft. I kissed him as he walked to the boarding area and watched him disappear into the concourse. I waited until I saw his plane take off before I left the airport.

When I arrived back to the Daisy house, I called my mother's attorney as promised.

Once on the phone, he proudly laughed as he said, "I was tickled to death. I caught that Assistant U.S. Attorney with her girdle wrapped around her knees. She thought she had hit the jackpot with tons of money regarding the phantom wine that Big Pete made up. She thought she had another person in some made-up conspiracy. I threw all the evidence up in her face. I never saw a woman turn red so quickly. I can't understand how Big Pete can get people to believe him so quickly. Well anyway, that Assistant U.S. Attorney had the nerve to insinuate that my faxed documents were not the originals. I told her I could call you and have you bring them as soon as possible. We had no issues producing the real McCoy. She said that would not be necessary. I just have to say, Belinda, good girl, good girl. Job well done. I have never had evidence handed to me on a silver platter like this before. Just for this I'm dropping more from your mother's bill. Just this alone shows the U.S. Attorney, or anyone for that matter, that Big Pete was the mastermind behind the fraud and embezzlement. This just proves that your mother wasn't the big fish. It was Big Pete all along. Good girl."

I said, "Well, I'm glad you lowered the bill for that one. Thank you. When are they going to sentence her? It's been almost two months now."

Mom's attorney solemnly replied, "Belinda, Big Pete is still fighting it; it could take up to a year before your mother is sentenced."

I gasped and asked, "Why so long?"

Mom's attorney replied, "Because Pete is fighting it, and they can't sentence your mother until they prosecute him."

I said, "That's just crazy."

Mom's attorney said, "I know, but that's how our justice system works. Just look at it this way, all the time she is doing now is considered time already served."

I said, "I still don't understand, but I have no other choice but to accept it."

We chatted a few more minutes as he gloated in his victory regarding the wine issue. As I hung up the phone, I thought, *He treated me like a dog with all his "good girl, good girl." I don't like being talked down to.* I realized then that my mother's attorney was a male chauvinistic pig! I didn't like him at all. As I was getting ready to go to the shop, the telephone rang. It was the recording from the jail, and of course, I accepted the call.

"Belinda, Pete is madder than hell at the two of us regarding the wine. He is using my dogs as blackmail now, and all of our family things."

I said, "Oh well, there is nothing I can do."

Mom said, "He's going to meet you at the jail so both of you visit with me at the same time tomorrow. This will be the first time he has come to see me. Maybe we can work this out."

I said, "That's fine with me, but I'm sure he is playing games. I'll be there tomorrow. I've got all your attorney fees paid now because he lowered the amount, and all the bounced checks are paid for. I still have a little ways to go on your credit card debt, and I've only got a little bit paid on your credit card fraud with Uncle Frank. I have a trust established for you for when I leave. I figure it will be a week or two before I have everything finished. I still haven't heard from the finance agency."

Before my mother had a chance to say anything, the phone was cut off. I guess they must have had a high volume of people that day because it seemed like we should have had a few more minutes to talk. Sometimes you have five minutes and sometimes you have fifteen minutes to talk, but this was the shortest call we'd had yet.

The following day I drove to the jail and was there at the precise time that my mother had instructed me to be there. As I was walking inside the jail, Big Pete opened the door for me from inside the glass doors.

Big Pete said, "Hello, Belinda."

I looked at him and nodded my head in acknowledgment. I went up to the window and gave the police officer my ID and airplane ticket. I went and sat down in one of the chairs in the waiting area. Big Pete sat down beside me and we sat in silence, waiting. When our names were called, we walked through the metal door and into the visiting room. I allowed Pete to speak with my mother first through the telephone. Then Mom spoke to me and asked me to write the following on the notepad: "I, Belinda, will give Big Pete all the wine in return for all six dogs and all the contents of the house."

She then told me to date it and sign it. Big Pete signed it as well. I just went ahead and played Mom and Big Pete's game. I had no intentions of giving my wine to Big Pete. I needed the cash to pay the debt. I didn't care about my mother's dogs, and at this point, I didn't care about the personal property either. When we were done visiting, I walked out of the jail and got into the pickup truck. I waited until Big Pete had pulled out of the parking lot, and then I took the piece of paper, ripped it up into small pieces, and put it in a McDonald's bag to throw in the trash.

I hired a temporary handyman from a temp agency for the next couple of days. Big Pete allowed the handyman and me to move more things. He still did not allow me to take the dogs and the rest of the jewelry, and he absolutely refused to allow me to hire a moving company. I told that him until he agreed to the moving company, he would not see the wine. He called my bluff and said that I could not move any more things out of his house. I guess he expected me to become upset and give him the wine, but instead I just left.

When Mom found out, she was extremely upset about her dogs and began to cry. I continued running my shop and selling things. I did try to get the veterinarian's office involved to help me convince Big Pete to release the dogs, but they would not get involved. I did not lose any sleep over it. I had done my best.

Saturday morning I received a phone call from Sam asking if he could come over and visit with me. I told him I wouldn't close the shop until around seven that night or later, depending on how many customers were in the shop. He said he could visit with me mid-morning on Monday. I told him that would be fine.

I gave Mary a call and asked her when she was wiring the money. She told me it would be the next week, and we would have to make a date for her to come move it. I told her she needed to hurry. I needed the cash soon.

I called Thomas's brothers on Sunday evening and asked if they would be able to help me close up the shop and booths. I told them it would probably be in the middle of March, if not at the end of the following week. They all told me to call them when I made a final decision, and they would be there to help me close and move everything.

CHAPTER LXVIII

Sunday evening I went to bed very early. I was so exhausted that I fell right asleep. Close to 11:30 p.m. something woke me from a dead sleep. I jumped up and threw on some clothes. I looked out my window, and I saw headlights that didn't appear to be quite right. Normally headlights shine in the bedroom windows from the road. These weren't. I grabbed the .45 from under my pillow. I quietly walked to the side window in the bedroom on the side of the house and peeked through the Venetian blinds. I saw a shadow running around the back of the house.

I ran quietly into Uncle Frank's bedroom. There was another window located at the back of the house in his bedroom. I had my forearm bent so my .45 was pointed straight up in the air. I peeked through the side of the Venetian blinds to that window. I couldn't make out who it was, but there was enough moonlight for me to see there was positively a human figure walking slowly towards the window located in the basement behind the house.

I rushed quickly and quietly to the basement door. Thank God I had forgotten to lock it! I opened it slowly and quietly. I slowly crept down the stairs with both hands on my weapon pointed towards the ground because it was pitch black and there was only a little bit of moonlight from the far end of the basement coming in.

I knew the perpetrator could not see me in the darkness. I hugged the side of the stairs as I crept down. The perpetrator didn't know there was just a small path to walk in because of everything that was packed in the basement. I heard a cracking noise as he or she broke glass, but I could not see because all the boxes and furniture were in my way. By this time, I was almost in the middle of the unfinished basement on one of the small paths I had left. I heard scuffling noises, so I made my move because I knew they couldn't see me.

I yelled, "You come one more foot, and I will kill you on the spot!"

I took the safety off and cocked my .45 to put a round in the chamber. I knew whoever it was had heard it. I heard heavy breathing and opened the basement back door. I ran out of the door. I fired two rounds up in the air and yelled, "Stop! Don't make me chase you because I can put a bullet in you right this second." The shadow froze beside the side of the house. I walked closer to the shadow and I said, "Turn around, maggot!"

He turned around, and I gasped. It was Little Pete!

Little Pete had his hands up in the air and said, "Belinda, please don't shoot. I was trying to get the boxes of wine for Big Pete."

I lowered my .45 and had it pointed to the ground. "Damn it, Little Pete! Explain to me how you were going to get fifty boxes out of the basement without me knowing about it?" Just then, I heard something crash in the basement.

I yelled, "Whoever you are in the basement, you better come out right this second before you kill yourself in there."

Little Pete said, "That's my friend, Belinda, don't kill him."

I said, "Little Pete, go turn the light on in the basement. Don't forget I have this .45 in my hand, and I know how to use it."

Little Pete yelled as he walked towards me, "Bubba, just stand still. Belinda's right, you're going to hurt yourself in there!"

I heard a deep husky voice answer Little Pete, "Okay, you didn't tell me it was full of crap. I think I hurt my leg real bad."

I shook my head in total disbelief at how stupid people could be when they give in to their greed. Little Pete turned on the light to the basement and the floodlights. The switches were located right beside the basement door. I saw his friend. He was a very tall, large, dark black man. He wasn't much younger than Little Pete, but I was sure he was much older than I was. He must have been over six feet tall. He stood there surrounded by boxes that had fallen. It appeared that he had fallen into a large old air-conditioning unit. The unit had sharp metal edges. He looked at me and simply said, "Good evening, ma'am. I'm Bubba."

Little Pete had found his way toward his friend and said to me, "Belinda, he's cut his leg real bad."

I asked Bubba, "Can you walk?"

Bubba simply answered, "Yes, ma'am."

I asked, "Little Pete, can you help him out of the basement? Take him to the Florida room so we can take a look at his leg."

Little Pete answered, "Yes, ma'am."

They walked out the basement's back door. I locked the basement door behind them, ran up the stairs, and cut the lights off from the switches that were located at the basement door at the top of the stairs.

All the commotion woke Uncle Frank. He was standing at the top of the basement stairs looking totally confused. He asked as his voice became louder and angrier, "May I ask what the hell is going on?"

I answered, "Oh, Uncle Frank, you wouldn't believe me anyway. We need to have a sensor put on the back window of the basement, and I forgot to set the alarm tonight so I'm partly to blame for this as well."

I walked into the kitchen and unlocked the door. Little Pete and his friend still had not made it up the side of the hill to the Florida room entrance. I knew now that his friend was hurt badly. I walked back into the kitchen again, and Uncle Frank was standing in the kitchen, still confused.

"Damn it, girl, tell me what the hell has just happened! I heard two gunshots!" He peeked out of the kitchen side door and said, "Who the hell is that walking up from the back?"

I took a heavy swig from a bottle of Jack Daniels I had taken out of the back of a bottom cabinet. I looked at Uncle Frank. "Do you want some?"

He answered, "Of course I do," as he took the bottle from my hand.

I asked, "Where is your first-aid kit?"

Uncle Frank answered, "It's in the big cabinet under the bathroom sink."

After Uncle Frank took a swig, I took the bottle from his hand, took another swig, and said, "Uncle Frank, please go and let Little Pete and Bubba in. They should be at the door by now."

Uncle Frank muttered, "What the hell is going on? And who in the hell is Bubba? I wish someone would tell me what's going on. It is my house after all . . ." He walked from the kitchen to the Florida room.

I walked back into the bathroom and made sure I had the safety on as I tucked the .45 into the back of my pants. I pulled my t-shirt down to cover it. I looked through the stuff in the cabinet under the bathroom sink until I found a large first-aid kit. I quickly carried it to the Florida room. Bubba had a huge, dark stain on the bottom of his pants. I asked him, "Do you care about these pants?"

Bubba answered, "No, not really. Why?"

I said, "I need to tear them, unless you want to take them off and be in just your underwear."

Bubba said, "Oh, no, ma'am, just tear them."

Uncle Frank picked up my bottle of Jack Daniels and took another swig as he was watching me. I picked up an old pocket knife that Uncle Frank had sitting on the table in the Florida room and used it to cut Bubba's pants. After a little cutting, I was able to just rip the pants up the side of his leg. Bubba turned his leg so I could see it while he was still sitting in the chair. Bubba had both hands holding on each side of the bottom of the chair for dear life. I could tell that he was in a lot of pain. I thought, *Serves him right for trying to steal from me. He's lucky I didn't shoot him dead!*

Little Pete bent over me looking at the fresh wound.

I said, "Well, Bubba, it looks like you may need some stitches and maybe a tetanus shot; it looks pretty bad to me." I had found an old bottle of peroxide when I was retrieving the first aid kit and poured it all over the open wound. Bubba starts making noises of pain and I said, "You big baby, peroxide doesn't burn."

Bubba said, "I know, but its cold, and it makes it hurt worse."

Little Pete looked at me.

I shook my head and asked Uncle Frank, "Is there any more bourbon?"

Uncle Frank answered, "Of course," and he passed me the open bottle.

I took another small swig and took the other clean towel that I had and wiped the lip of the bottle off.

I passed it to Bubba and said, "Here, take a swig."

Bubba took the bottle, took two big swigs and passed the bottle to Little Pete. Little Pete took a couple of swigs as well and passed it back to Uncle Frank.

I opened the first-aid kit and found some butterfly bandages. I took a couple of those, tried to pinch the open slash back together, and attached the butterflies to it. I found some large square gauze and put it on the wound. Then I picked up the roll of gauze, opened it, and wrapped it around Bubba's leg.

I said, "Well, that's about all I can do. Little Pete, you should take him to the hospital and get that thing stitched up."

Little Pete asked, "Can it wait until morning?"

I answered, "That's up to Bubba, I guess."

I got up, picked up the bloody towels, closed the first-aid kit, and screwed the cap back on the peroxide. I looked at Little Pete and asked, "Do you want a beer?"

Bubba answered, "Yes, ma'am."

Little Pete simply nodded.

I looked over at Uncle Frank, and he said, "No, I'm fine with this bottle."

I walked back into the kitchen, put everything on the kitchen counter by the sink, and retrieved three beers from the refrigerator. I opened each bottle, walked back into the Florida room, and passed both men a bottle of beer. Little Pete was now sitting on the sofa.

I stood there for a few seconds looking at both men shaking my head in disbelief. I took a sip of beer and glared at Little Pete. "Now do you want to explain to Uncle Frank what, or should I say who, possessed you into doing such a stupid thing?"

I watched Bubba as he just looked over at Little Pete.

Little Pete answered, "We weren't stealing anything. We had permission from Big Pete to retrieve the wine because it belongs to him. He said so. He said it was worth over $500,000, and he offered me $75,000 as a finder's fee if I recovered it for him."

I shook my head in disbelief again. I guess I shouldn't have been surprised. I put my beer down on the table, picked up my briefcase that was under the table, pulled out the wine file, and gave it to Little Pete. As Little Pete was opening it he asked, "What's this?"

I replied, "Little Pete, it's the original wine inventory. If you look at the last page of the spreadsheets, you will see the total of what Mom and Big Pete had originally."

I waited until he turned the stapled pages back to the last page. Little Pete looked up at me.

I asked, "Do you feel foolish yet? As you can see they never owned a wine collection that large. Now, Little Pete, look at the letters with the fax receipts printed on the bottom of them. I'm sure you can recognize Big Pete's signature if anything. Do you see that Big Pete himself sold all of the most valuable wines from the collection? If you look at the last faxed letters, you will see that they were from Mom to me and me back to her. You will see that Thomas and I purchased the rest of the wine. Now you know without a doubt, the wine that is in the basement is not worth that much. You can also see with your own eyes that it does not belong to Big

Pete. So therefore you were trying to steal from me. Not to mention that you both were breaking and entering. Any schoolgirl knows that."

Little Pete pulled his reading glasses from his shirt pocket and continued looking at the papers in the file. I stood there, shaking my head, and said while he was still reading, "You even brought your reading glass for the heist."

Little Pete looked up at me and said, "Yes I did, because I needed to read the boxes to make sure we took the right ones."

I started laughing. Little Pete, Uncle Frank, and Bubba joined in. I saw a small flashlight sticking out of Little Pete's shirt pocket and said as I pointed at it, "I guess you came prepared. Do you realize yet that you and your friend could go to jail for this, for a very long time?"

Little Pete and Bubba just looked at me.

Bubba broke the silence, "Ma'am, I feel like a stupid fool. I got hurt for nothing. I believe you, and I think Little Pete and I have been had. Please don't call the cops on us. We will pay for the broken window."

I looked over at Bubba, then to Little Pete, and said, "I think that's a great idea. Little Pete can work for me tomorrow helping pack and unload a few truckloads that I have left of inventory, since he wants to work for me so badly."

Little Pete looked at me and asked, "What if I don't show up?"

I answered, "It's up to you, Little Pete, to either do the right thing or the wrong thing. It's your choice, but I think you owe Uncle Frank and me an apology."

Little Pete said, "Fair enough. I'm truly sorry, and I will show up tomorrow morning. I feel like a jackass because I believed Big Pete. I know now we could have gone to prison for stealing nothing of any great value."

I said, "Well, no one was seriously hurt, and I accept your apology, but you should still take your friend to the hospital."

Uncle Frank said, "You guys are forgiven, but if I catch you around us again after tomorrow, there will be hell to pay, Little Pete."

Little Pete said, "Yes, sir."

I helped Little Pete help his friend to his van and they left. I picked up the JD bottle that had a little bit of bourbon left in it and drank it. I went into the kitchen, got myself another beer, and brought one to Uncle Frank.

I said, "I'm going to put some boxes in front of the window, and I will have someone come out here tomorrow to replace it."

Uncle Frank said, "That will be fine with me."

I stood by the sliding glass door and removed the .45 from my jeans. I took off the safety, released the round in the chamber, removed the magazine, and put the unused bullet back into the magazine. I knew it was over now.

I said to Uncle Frank, "I will take this .45 over to Auntie Bea's first thing in the morning and put it in her closet with the rest of the weapons."

Uncle Frank asked, "Are you sure this is over?"

I answered, "Yes; this part is, anyway. Big Pete is too much of a coward to do anything like this himself."

CHAPTER LXIX

I woke up with a major hangover from all the liquor I had drank the night before. I looked over at the old alarm clock that was now on the floor by the mattress, and it was 7:30 a.m. I could not believe I had slept so late. I lay there for a few minutes, reliving the previous night's events. Things had to improve soon. The stress was really taking its toll on me. I had lost at least thirty pounds since arriving, and I knew that I would lose even more. I really had no appetite. I felt like I had aged at least thirty years since my arrival, and I had been acting like an alcoholic. I smiled as I thought, *Uncle Frank is wearing off on me*. I wasn't sure how much more of the mental stress I could take before I snapped.

I heard knocking and realized that someone was knocking at the door. I threw my jeans back on. I'd been sleeping in a t-shirt since Thomas was here. I ran to the alarm system, turned it off, ran into the kitchen, and unlocked the side door.

Little Pete was standing at the sliding glass door of the Florida room. I could not believe it! He actually showed up. I unlocked the door and let him in.

I said, "I'm sorry, Little Pete, I overslept this morning. You have never showed up this early before."

Little Pete laughed, and he hugged me as he said, "I was wrong about you, Belinda. You are not a selfish little white brat. I want to say I'm truly sorry for all the wrong and hurt that I have caused you and your family. I owe you a debt of gratitude for you not getting my friend and me into trouble last night. I will never forget it. I always thought white people were just pure self-serving, but your actions last night demonstrated that is not the case."

I smiled at Little Pete and said, "That's what you get for being prejudiced, and I hope you have learned a lesson that will stick with you forever. The majority of people, no matter the color of their skin, are not bad, Little Pete. I'm just thankful that you are sorry for your actions, and I am very grateful for your apology. Thank you. I will never forget you swallowing your pride and saying so. You're just damn lucky that I didn't shoot you." Little Pete and I laughed.

Little Pete said, "While you're getting ready for the day, I want to measure that window that we broke last night because I'm going to replace it today."

With a smirk I said, "Okay, but please don't take the wine."

Little Pete laughed at me and said, "I know better this time around."

We both laughed as Uncle Frank came into the Florida room, fussing because I didn't have any coffee made yet.

Little Pete went out the Florida room entrance and around the side of the house to measure the window as I made coffee. While the coffee was brewing, I went into the bathroom, found some aspirin that had not expired yet, and took two of them with some water. I hoped it would get rid of the raging headache I had from drinking that nasty dark liquor. I vowed to myself that it would be a long time before I drank straight whiskey again.

Little Pete and I packed a truckload of inventory, and he said, "Belinda, you don't have much left. Are going to be able to finish whatever it is that you're trying to pay off?"

I answered, "I think so, or at least, I hope so."

I poured a cup of coffee and drank it in the truck as Little Pete drove the pickup truck to the shop. We unloaded it and repeated the process two more times.

Little Pete said he would be back later to replace the window. It was a standard size, and he was pretty sure he could get it installed that day. I asked him if he needed money for it. He said no because it was his fault and he would take care of it.

About twenty minutes after Little Pete had left, Sam pulled up into the driveway. He got out of his truck and was waving for me to come outside, so I did. I thought, *Here we go again with Sam's crap*. Sam met me beside his truck, gave me a big bear hug and a kiss on my cheek.

I hugged him back and said, "Okay, mister, I haven't heard from you in awhile, so what's up?"

Sam laughed and asked, "Can you get in my truck with me?"

I answered, "Okay, but why can't we go back inside the house."

Sam said, "I just want to talk in private with you for a little while."

I shrugged my shoulders and said, "Okay."

I got into his truck. He drove around to the other side of the driveway and parked the truck. I guess he did that so his father could not see. He lit up a joint and passed it to me. I took it, inhaled, and passed it back to him.

I asked, "Well, what's up?"

He picked up the file folder that was lying in the middle of the seat between us. "I owe $6,000 in taxes this year. Is there any way you can loan me the money to pay it?"

I passed the joint back to him, took the folder from his hand, and opened it. According to the paperwork I read, H&R Block had prepared his income taxes for him, and he did, indeed, owe $6,000!

I told him, "Sam, I don't have that kind of money. All the money that I'm making from selling my inventory and other personal items is going straight to all the debt that Mom, Auntie Bea, and your father had created. I'm doing my best to get them out of trouble."

Sam said, "I just thought you would have the money."

I thought for a few minutes and asked, "Have you truly made up with your father?"

Sam answered, "I'm not going to take over his checkbook, Belinda. I mean it."

I said, "Damn it, Sam, none of you will do it."

Sam said, "So what you are saying, Belinda is that you won't loan me the money if I don't take over Dad's checkbook?"

I answered, "No, Sam, I swear I don't have the money, but I do have an idea for you to get some of it."

Sam said, "Then just tell me."

I said, "You are going to have to make up with him, and I will need to speak to Uncle Frank first."

Sam said, "Okay, I will make up with him, but I'm still not doing his checkbook."

I said, "Okay, Sam. Wait here, and let me go speak to Uncle Frank."

Sam said, "Okay."

I thought, *Maybe Sam would at least start to check in on Auntie Bea and Uncle Frank when I leave. At least that would be better than nothing.*

Uncle Frank was sitting in his favorite chair, as always. As I walked into the Florida room he asked, "Now what's wrong with that boy? I thought everything was fine."

I said, "Uncle Frank, he is embarrassed because he owes $6,000 to the IRS, and he doesn't have the money to pay it. I don't have that kind of money either. I figured you had your gun collection in the other room under the bed, and you told me yourself you would never go hunting again. I thought it would be a nice gesture on your part to go ahead and give him your gun collection."

Uncle Frank looked at me for a few seconds and said, "You know what, that is a good idea! Tell that son of mine to come in here right this second."

I said, "Yes, sir."

I stepped outside the door and waved at Sam to come inside. I watched him as he got out of his truck and made sure that he was walking toward the sliding glass door before I walked back inside. I left the door open, and within a few moments, he walked into the room and slid the door closed.

Uncle Frank stood up from his chair, and the two men hugged each other.

As Uncle Frank was standing at his chair he said, "Boy, I hear you're in trouble with the IRS and need a little bit of help. You don't want to mess with the IRS."

Sam said to his father, "No, sir."

Uncle Frank said to Sam, "I want to give you something; follow me." Sam followed his father, and I followed behind as Uncle Frank led the way to the third bedroom.

Uncle Frank asked, "Belinda, can you pull that mattress off the frame? I can't bend down like I used to."

Sam said, "Here, let me help you."

We pulled the mattress and box springs from the frame and leaned them against the wall of the bedroom.

Sam said, "Dad, that's your gun collection!"

Uncle Frank said, "I know. I want you to have them. You can keep them, borrow money, or just outright sell them if you wish. They are yours now, and you can do what you wish with them. It was about damn time I gave them to you anyway. I would rather give them to you now while I'm alive."

Sam started crying and he hugged his father right there on the spot. I don't think I had ever seen Sam cry before. I knew that simple gesture made up for whatever had happened between them. I hoped it would stick this time. I had a good feeling they were friends again.

As Sam was hugging his father he looked at me and silently mouthed the words, "Thank you."

I just nodded my head, smiled, and quietly walked out of the room so they could talk in private.

I thought about their relationship as I was walking down the hall. *Their relationship is worse than the one my mom and I have, or is it? One minute we are friends, and the next we are not because my mother is always doing something bad that damages our relationship. I really hope that this time Sam and Uncle Frank will keep a positive relationship. Granted Sam and Uncle Frank are nasty people most of the time, but they are my family, and I do love them, but then most of my family is this way. I guess that's why I think it's normal. Who knows?*

I guess it was about an hour later, Uncle Frank and Sam came back into the Florida room smiling at one another and chatting away. Sam had his arms full of shotguns, and I asked Sam, "Do you need any help?"

Before Sam had a chance to answer Uncle Frank said, "Yeah, he sure does, there's a couple more handful of guns in there."

I said, "I will go get another batch."

I got an armload of guns and took them out to Sam's truck. As we were walking back into the house, Sam stopped, took me by the shoulders, hugged me again, and whispered in my ear, "You're something else, but I'm still not taking over Dad's checkbook." Then he kissed me on my cheek. We both laughed in unison.

Sam was just as stubborn as his father. I could say many more things in response, but it wasn't worth the effort.

We finished loading all of Uncle Frank's guns into Sam's truck. Sam came back inside to give his Dad a hug and a kiss on the cheek as he said, "Goodbye, Dad, and thank you."

Uncle Frank and I stood outside and waved goodbye to Sam as he pulled out of the driveway. After he was out of sight, we both walked back into the Florida room and I slid the door closed.

Uncle Frank had just flopped into his favorite chair when the telephone rang.

Uncle Frank said, "Now what?" Uncle Frank picked up the phone and said, "What the hell do you want?"

After a moment he said, "Oh, I'm sorry, Sister Bea. Belinda is killing me over here. If it's not one thing it's another. It's not even suppertime yet, and I'm pooped." Then he was silent for a few moments. He hung the phone up and said, "Belinda, your auntie wants you over at her house at once."

I asked him, "Why?"

Uncle Frank replied in a tired and angry voice, "Damn it, girl, just go over there and find out. I'm tired! I'm going to bed!"

I said, "Okay."

As I was getting ready to run over to Auntie Bea's house, Little Pete pulled into the driveway. I greeted him, and he had the new window to install. I waited around until he had that finished. Before he was done, Auntie Bea called to find out why I wasn't at her house yet. I told her Little Pete was installing a new window, and I would be over as soon as he was finished.

While I was waiting for him to finish with the window, I decided to call Miss Patson. I told her that I wanted Big Pete reported to the U.S. Attorney for conducting business in his son's name. She told me she would take care of it the following day and would call me regarding the outcome. I gave her Jay's phone number in case she wanted to speak with him directly. As soon as I hung the telephone up, it rang again. I answered it, and it was Mary.

"Belinda, I have the money. I'm at the bank ready to wire it into your checking account, but I don't have your account information to give to the teller. Hang on one second, and I'll let you speak to her." She passed the phone to the teller, and I gave the lady my information. Mary got back on the phone and told me to call her at home that night to make sure I got the money. She told me she was making arrangements to fly into the Snobville Airport Saturday in the late afternoon, and she would get a U-Haul when she got there. I told her that sounded great and I would see her then.

I felt good after hanging up the phone with Mary. I felt like I was reaching the end of this nasty nightmare. Soon it would all be over. I pulled out my checkbook and bank statements and reconciled my account. After that, I wrote checks to pay off more of the debt. I really felt like I was making headway.

I had all the bills ready to mail first thing in the morning. I looked up, and Little Pete was standing at the door. I walked outside with him, and he said, "Well, I'm finished. I guess this will be the last time I see you. I have a new job, and I start next week."

Instinctively I gave Little Pete a hug and said, "Well, make sure you stay out of trouble and make sure you don't get mixed up with people like Big Pete and my mother."

He laughed and said, "You don't have to worry about that. I positively have learned my lesson. I hope the rest of your life is blessed."

We said our goodbyes and that was the last time I heard or saw Little Pete again. After Little Pete pulled out of the driveway, I ran over to Auntie Bea's house. I walked into her living room where she was sitting in her favorite chair. I bent down, kissed her on the forehead, and asked, "What's the emergency?"

Auntie Bea said, "Belinda, sit down." She passed me a local newspaper.

This was a newspaper that was printed once or twice a month and was comprised of local news, local gossip, and events. You could pick them up free at most any local grocery store, mega-marts, gas stations, and a variety of other local businesses. It was not the city newspaper. I looked at my great-aunt with a puzzled expression.

Auntie Bea said, "Read the article on the second page."

I looked down at the newspaper, turned the page, and there was a full page article titled, "Financial Fraud in Our Community, Beware." I looked at the top of the page, and there was a picture of the reporter with her name under the picture. I gasped, looked up at Auntie Bea, and said, "This is the woman that was in my shop twice asking weird questions. She would not tell me who she was."

Auntie Bea asked, "You didn't tell her anything did you?"

I answered, "No, not anything I thought was very important."

Auntie Bea sat there in silence, smoking her cigarette and sipping on a cup of coffee as I read the full-page article.

"Well, this reporter has a scoop this month for all the readers who have been keeping up with the Kings' case. My sources wish to stay anonymous, plus my own investigation has discovered Jane King has a daughter. It appears that she came out of nowhere; like an Archangel flying with the winds on a white-winged horse to save her mother somehow. For all the readers who have not read the story of the financial menacing couple, I will fill you in. They have both been indicted on eighteen counts of different types of fraud and embezzlement. It appears Big Pete, the husband, has laid claim that the mastermind behind this was his wife, Jane King. If you readers want the full story please feel free to check out my website. The new development to this story is after the daughter came from nowhere, Jane King stopped fighting the U.S. Attorney and immediately turned herself in. She even waived her right to trial and confessed and is now helping the U.S. Attorney put the entire picture together on how and why Big Pete committed these bizarre crimes. Jane King has also confessed to what she did and it appears she did not commit the crimes, but helped conceal them after the fact, but this information is not confirmed.

"This reporter has a sneaking feeling based on reliable sources that the daughter had something to do with this regarding her mother turning herself in. The U.S. Attorney was fully prepared to take on both Kings and see they are both punished to the hilt by our own laws, but now it appears the U.S. Attorney has entered into a plea of some type with Jane King because the victims of Jane King have been dropping their charges like flies and refused to testify against her.

"As I stated earlier the daughter came out of nowhere and she has stated and proved to this reporter's sources that the Kings' shop was never really theirs; it belonged to the daughter. It has been reported that the daughter has been going all around town making restitution to many of her mother's victims and has been sincerely apologizing on her mother's behalf for the crimes that were committed against them. While these actions dictate to this reporter the daughter is truly some type of archangel for her mother, but as the case maybe, she has not even attempted to make restitution to Big Pete's victims. Sources have stated that they believe the daughter is some type of highly decorated military person and has conducted herself in the highest form of discipline. Sources have even stated that the daughter's husband has been seen helping her with whatever unseen mission these two soldiers have apparently taken on.

"It is truly amazing that Jane King appears to have raised and help form such a noble and honest individual. There is truly more than meets the eye regarding Jane King's daughter. This reporter has been attempting to obtain an interview with Big Pete. When he talked with me regarding the new developments of a daughter involved in trying to clean up their mess he became angry and called this reporter many foul names that cannot be repeated. Big Pete even threatened to kill this reporter if he were contacted again.

"The archangel who flew into town seems to have started some type of war with Pete King because he appears to be scared of her. I will keep my readers informed as this mystery unfolds."

After reading the story, I looked up at Auntie Bea with a furrowed brow and stated angrily, "This is all a bunch of bullshit. Nasty little reporters like her make their living off the misery of others."

Auntie Bea asked, "Can you sue her for this?"

I answered, "I don't think so because she did not use my name, but she did write a bunch of bullshit, and she invaded my privacy, I think."

Auntie Bea asked, "Well, she told mostly truth, didn't she?"

I answered, "Yes, but the way she wrote it makes it a pile of bullshit. Maybe I can get even with her. Have you talked with Mom regarding this?"

Auntie Bea replied, "No, I just happened to stumble on it when I went to the grocery store yesterday. It's been in stores now for the last week."

I asked Auntie Bea, "Can I have this copy of the paper?"

Auntie Bea answered, "Sure, I got several more copies."

I cocked up my eyebrows as I was looking at my auntie.

Auntie Bea said, "Well, I'm kind of proud of you and your mom."

I curled my lips up in a smile and said, "Auntie Bea!"

She laughed at me.

Auntie Bea's telephone rang and she answered it. She asked me, "It's your mother. Should we tell her about the article?"

I replied, "Yes, tell her about the article."

After Auntie Bea accepted the phone call she read the article to my mother. Then she passed me the telephone. She lit another cigarette as I put mine out.

I answered the phone, "Yes, ma'am."

Mom said, "I think I have that reporter's telephone number in my address book. I need you to call her because she has been pestering Big Pete for an interview. If you can get her to do it when you have made plans to move things and get the dogs, it will give you an opportunity to get the dogs away from Big Pete. Tell her I will even do an interview with her if that will help us."

I said, "That sounds like a great idea! I'll try."

Mom asked, "Have you heard anything from the finance agency?"

I sighed as I answered, "No, not yet."

Mom said, "Big Pete told me that they had reached him last Friday, and he gave them the Daisy house telephone number."

I looked over at Auntie Bea and said excitedly, "That's great. I will tell Auntie Bea as soon as I get off the phone."

Mom and I continued talking until the phone went dead. I told Auntie Bea that the finance agent was trying to reach me. I told Auntie Bea that Mary would be here the following Saturday, and I thought I would cook out. Auntie Bea said she would love to come over for that. I picked up the phone again and called Sam. He didn't answer so I left a message on his answering machine regarding the cookout. I asked him to call me back to let me know if he wanted to come.

I went back to the Daisy house and peeked into Uncle Frank's bedroom. He was sound asleep and snoring up a storm. He wasn't kidding when he said he was burnt out from all the events that had happened over the past two days. I saw some deer meat in the chest freezer that he kept in the Florida room. I decided to make some old fashioned stew, southern-style, of course. I used a recipe that had been passed down through my family for centuries. I hated to admit it, but it was always good. I made some homemade bread with a packet of old yeast I found in the kitchen cabinet. I prepared the stew and let it cook in the crock pot. I left a note for Uncle Frank and went to the shop.

CHAPTER LXX

The next morning, I decided to finish pricing the inventory that Little Pete and I moved to the shop, so I left very early. I left another note for Uncle Frank with the shop's phone number on it just in case someone called and needed to speak with me.

Around 9:30, I received a phone call. To my delight, it was the finance agent. I became extremely excited and said, "I didn't think you would ever call."

The finance agent laughed, and he said, "Well, Mrs. Star, you are a hard person to track down. I've been trying to get a hold of you for the last month. I couldn't figure out how to call internationally, and I called your mother's telephone number over and over again and left messages until this last Friday when your stepfather answered the phone finally. He gave me your great-aunt's number who in turn gave me your great-uncle's number and I finally got this number. Your great-aunt and uncle would not let me get off the phone this morning because they were trying to fish information out of me. It sounds like this loan is very important to your family."

I said, "Yes, sir, it is!"

He said, "Well, you got it."

I said with excitement, "What? Please repeat that."

He laughed and said, "You got it. You have been approved."

I said, "That's great. How much was is it?"

He answered, "Your mother requested $233,000, and they approved the entire amount."

I went from happy to total disappointment, and said, "But I do not need that much. I just need $192,000, plus the closing costs."

He said, "Oh, well that will not be any problem at all."

I then asked, "Does that have my shop's income on it as well?"

He said, "Well, yes it does."

I said, "Oh, no! I will be closing my shop in the next week or two to go back to Europe because I will not be able to run it now that my mother is in jail."

He said, "What? I must not have heard you correctly."

I said, "My mother is in jail. Can I still have the loan for the lesser amount and add my husband? I will be collecting rent from my great-aunt and great-uncle to help pay the monthly payment."

He said, "Oh, well, we will leave it as is and as long as you make your payments there will be no problem."

I asked, "Are you sure?"

He replied, "Yes, I'm sure. I just never had anyone so honest regarding their situation before. I truly don't know how else to respond to the new information you just gave me. We will just decrease it. We have put a lot of work in this one."

I asked, "I completely understand. Have you contacted Adam Greed?"

He asked, "Who?"

I answered, "Adam Greed is the person who picked up the notes on my great-aunt's farm and is selling it back to me."

He replied, "No. You will need to contact them and decide what day you all want to come in and settle this. Do you have a real estate agent?"

I replied, "No, but I do have an attorney. Will that do? I have never done this before, and I'm clueless."

He said, "Oh. That will be fine. Why don't you contact this Adam Greed so we can get this done as quickly as possible?"

I said, "Okay."

He gave me his telephone number and information. I told him that I would call him back as soon as I was able to reach Mr. Greed. After I hung the telephone up, I had a few customers come in. I waited on them, and once they left, I closed the shop and drove straight to the Daisy house. I practically ran into the house and grabbed my mother's address book off the table.

Before I had a chance to run back outside to the pickup truck, Uncle Frank asked, "Baby girl, did we get it?"

I breathlessly answered, "Yes, we got it, but I need to talk with Auntie Bea and call Adam Greed."

Uncle Frank excitably said, "Just go lickety-split. Your auntie is on pins and needles."

I said, "Yes, sir."

As I rushed out of the house again and got into the pickup truck I saw my great-uncle picking up the phone. I knew he couldn't stand it and was calling Auntie Bea before I had a chance to get over there. Again I practically ran into my auntie's house. She was standing in the kitchen waiting for me. I believe that old woman was about to jump up in the air.

I said as I was gasping for breath again, "Uncle Frank had to tell you already."

Auntie Bea was laughing and said, "Of course. I'm so excited I don't know what to do."

I said, "Auntie Bea, I only got this loan because it had my shop's income on it. I told the finance agent the truth, and I told him that you and Uncle Frank would have to pay rent to help me pay the monthly payments."

Auntie Bea's mouth went from smiling to a puckered frown and she said, "This land was bought and paid for. I'm not paying a dime. You better call Frank and see what he has to say before we go any further."

I went into my auntie's living room and picked up the phone. I called Uncle Frank and asked him and he said, "I'll just move back to the Hollow—that's bought and paid for. I should never have to pay rent."

As I was speaking with Uncle Frank, Auntie Bea went to sit in her chair.

I asked, "Auntie Bea, if the two of you are not going to help me, what am I going to do?"

Auntie Bea replied, "We will deal with this problem later. Just call Adam Greed."

I opened my mother's address book, found Adam Greed's telephone number, and I called it.

A woman answered the phone and I said, "Good morning, ma'am. My name is Belinda Star. Is Adam Greed available so I can speak with him?"

The woman answered, "No, he isn't. My husband just had a heart attack and is hospitalized. I'm his wife Nancy Greed; can I help you?"

I said, "Well, I guess you should know. Your husband picked up my great-aunt's farm note and made an agreement with her and my mother to sell it back to me for the same amount he paid. I have just been approved for a mortgage to buy the land back, and we need to close the transaction."

Nancy Greed asked, "Who are your aunt and mother? Your name doesn't sound familiar."

I looked over at my great-aunt as she was smoking her cigarette listening to every word I was saying. I answered, "My great-aunt is Bea Mills, and my mother is Jane King."

Mrs. Greed's voice became hostile and she asked, "Is this the same Jane King who is married to that Pete King? I think they nicknamed him 'Big Pete.'"

I answered, "Yes, ma'am."

Mrs. Greed, in an even more hostile tone, said, "I will not sell anything to anyone that is associated with that man!"

I said, "But, ma'am, my auntie and I are not associated with that creep."

Mrs. Greed said, "You said your mother was his wife, so you are."

I said, "No, ma'am, I am not; he is just the fifth husband of my mother. I have been in the Army all these years. I hardly know the man."

Before I knew it, Mrs. Greed and I were in a heated argument. I didn't know what I said, but she then said, "Okay, Belinda, okay. I will give a lifetime home to your great-aunt and great-uncle, but I will not sell the land back to you, your mother, your great-aunt or your great-uncle, or anyone else that is related to your mother and may be associated with Big Pete. That is my final decision. That is the only part of the agreement that I will honor in my husband's name."

I knew if I continued arguing with her, it would just make things worse, so I just said goodbye.

I looked over at my auntie, and she was crying and said, "We will never get my land back."

I got up from my chair, leaned over her as she sat in her chair, and said in a strong voice, "It ain't over until the fat lady sings, and I haven't sung yet."

Auntie Bea looked up at me and said, "Belinda, you are not fat. You're just big boned."

I lifted my head up in the air and laughed at my auntie's statement. I said, "Auntie Bea, there is no such thing as big boned."

Auntie Bea irritably said, "Well, you're not fat, I know that."

I told Auntie Bea, "I'm going to make another phone call." I picked up her telephone and called Miss Patson. When I was finally transferred to her extension, we exchanged greetings, and I said, "Miss Patson, you are not going to believe this!"

Miss Patson said, "Ever since I took you on as a client I have heard things beyond my wildest imagination. I probably will believe it. What has happened?"

I said, "Mrs. Greed will not honor her husband's word and sell me my great-aunt's land back. I was just contacted today by the finance agency, and they told me that I was approved for the loan." I told her about the conversation with the finance agency and Mrs. Greed. I asked, "What can I do about this?"

Miss Patson asked, "Did your auntie and mother have anything in writing?"

I answered, "No, but it was a verbal agreement with their attorneys present. They had the meeting right outside the courtroom."

Miss Patson asked, "What are the attorneys' names?"

I answered, "Hang on a minute while I ask my auntie." I looked over at my auntie and asked her their names. Auntie Bea gave me their names, and I repeated them to Miss Patson.

Miss Patson asked, "How soon can you get over here to my office?"

I answered her, "I guess about forty-five minutes."

Miss Patson ordered, "Well, leave from there right now and get over here as quick as you can. I will contact the attorneys while you are on your way. Give me this Mrs. Greed's telephone number, and I'll call her too."

I gave her Mrs. Greed's phone number and hung the phone up after saying goodbye.

Auntie Bea's eyes were as wide as saucers, and she asked with an anxious voice, "What is she going to do?"

I answered, "I don't know yet, but I have to go over to her office right now!"

As I was driving to Miss Patson's office, I thought, *Don't people honor their word anymore? What has happened to our society when a spouse refuses to honor a pledge that the other spouse has made? Why did Mrs. Greed become so hostile once I gave my mother's name? I thought they were friends. What happened to the meaning of "friends"?*

Before I knew it, I was in Miss Patson's office, and she had a glum expression. As soon as she closed her door, I asked, "Oh, no. How bad is it?"

Miss Patson was shaking her head as she answered me, "Well, Belinda, it looks like we have a very peculiar situation here. We can file a lawsuit against Adam Greed for breach of contract, but we would have to do the suit in your name. The problem is that you were not there as a witness to the verbal contract. Your information was secondhand information from your mother and auntie. This means we would have to have all the attorneys who were present during this verbal contract testify that it did occur the way you say it did; that means taking a chance that they remember it. Of course your auntie's attorney remembers it and has no problem testifying, but Adam Greed's attorney has conveniently forgotten about it.

"We have to prove that you upheld it, which you are trying to do. We would have to have your auntie testify, but because of her age, she would be considered an unreliable witness, so we would also need your mother to testify to back up your auntie's testimony. Now on that note, we do not know what is going to happen to your mother. At this point, I do not want to put her on the stand wearing prison garb. We do not have a perfect system because of the people in it. The judge would take one look at her and not believe anything she says because she is a convict, so therefore the judge would automatically not believe anything your aunt would have to say. You cannot testify regarding the contract because you were not there. The key is your mother, at this point, because she is within a fifty-mile radius of the court, and the court would not accept an affidavit from her because she can show up in court and testify. These are the rules.

"The only thing we can do now is wait to see what the court does with your mother. If they release her as time served, then she could testify. On the other hand, if they do not release her, sentence her for a longer time period, and she is transferred outside the fifty-mile marker then we can use an affidavit from her. We also have a two-year statute of limitations. If you decide that you want to sue Adam Greed for breach of contract, the other obstacle we will have to face is it will be a 50/50 chance that the judge will even rule in your favor and force Adam Greed to honor his word.

"I know you're not going to like this either, but the truth of the matter is that Adam Greed is a very wealthy and powerful person in this community, and you are an outsider. So you will be automatically stereotyped as, well, a 'stranger' who is messing with the people in this community, even though you are the one who has been wronged. The judge will not even take into consideration that you are a highly decorated veteran who has served our country and served it well. Do you understand?"

I replied, "Yes, ma'am. Do you think you can call Mrs. Greed and at least threaten her that I will take action against her if she doesn't honor Adam Greed's word? Tell her that I have no other choice but to take them on. I must do this for my great-aunt because I gave my word."

Miss Patson said, "Yes, Belinda, I will at least try, but we may have to wait as long as a year or so before your mother is sentenced, but we do have two years to file suit. I will call her right now."

Miss Patson picked up the phone and spoke with Mrs. Greed for several minutes. After she hung the phone up, she looked at me. Miss Patson told me that Mrs. Greed would call me next week and wanted to talk further regarding this.

I said, "That's better than nothing, I guess."

Miss Patson said, "I don't think she is going to change her mind, Belinda. I'm sorry we can't do anything at this point."

I said, "I know we will have to wait and take action at the appropriate time. My great-aunt is going to be very disappointed. That's why I'm going to at least try to take on these rich people, at least one time, for my aunt. No matter what my aunt has done, I love her very much, and I have to at least fight for her even if she doesn't deserve it."

I knew I was going to have to tell Auntie Bea, but I decided to wait until the next day. I went back to my shop and opened it for the rest of the day.

The following morning, my mother called at the shop, and I told her everything regarding Mrs. Greed and the finance agency. My mother told me the history of her relationship with Adam Greed. Apparently, he was a doctor and very wealthy. He had loaned Big Pete $100,000 at a 200% rate of interest. Big Pete never even attempted to pay him back. Adam Greed found out about Big Pete, the bankruptcy, and Auntie Bea, who didn't even pay her own bills. To get revenge, and to recoup his money, he picked up the two homes and ninety-nine acres for nothing. Greed did not care about Auntie Bea or my mother for that matter. It was all about getting even with Big Pete and getting his money back. I thought this was called loan sharking and was illegal in our country.

I also discovered that Mr. Greed had a mistress. Adam Greed and his mistress partied and socialized with Mom and Big Pete. Nancy Greed, Adam's wife, knew about the mistress and thought my mother was having an affair with Mr. Greed as well. This was not true, and my mother repeatedly tried to convince Nancy that it was not her. Nancy didn't

believe her and had despised my mother ever since. Adam Greed and my
mother remained friends and he had agreed to sell the land to Thomas
and me for her sake. He basically admitted that he made a mistake by
seeking vengeance on my mother because he didn't think of the other
people he was hurting.

Now it all made sense to me why Nancy Greed was so hostile toward
me when I mentioned who my mother was.

I went to the bank, made my deposit, and checked on the status of
the money Mary had wired. The full amount had been deposited in my
checking account so I could now pay more bills. I decided that I should
go talk with Auntie Bea before I reopened the shop. I told Auntie Bea that
a few problems had come up regarding the mortgage. It was the best way
I knew how to break it to her, but it did not make it any easier for her to
swallow the bad news.

After that, she changed the subject and asked for her money back. She
had given me Little Pete's last paycheck because I had asked her to pay
me back for her property taxes. Now she was demanding the money back
from me. I told Auntie Bea that she owed me at least that much because of
the thousands of dollars in bad checks I had covered for her. She threw a
temper tantrum. I decided it was not worth it, so I wrote her out another
check.

Then she started in on me about Uncle Frank paying for one week
to Little Pete's services. I told her Uncle Frank owed me for three weeks
of cash I had been giving him, and instead of him paying me directly I
had him pay Little Pete instead. I told her that was none of her business,
and she needed to behave herself. She was just being evil because she did
not get what she wanted regarding her land, and there was absolutely
nothing I could do about it until we knew what the court was going to
do to Mom.

I did not believe Auntie Bea really understood why we had to wait
before I could take legal action against Adam Greed, but I understood,
and to me, that was all that mattered. My decisions would ultimately
affect my great-aunt, my mother, and Uncle Frank. Even if I was still
holding anger toward them for their greedy ways, I did not want them
living on the street.

When I got back to the shop and opened for business again, I
immediately called Miss Patson and asked her to call my great-aunt and
explain why we had to wait to take legal action. I felt confident that she

could explain it in a simpler manner than I could. Miss Patson said she would call her that day when she had time. I called the finance agency and asked to speak to the broker. I told him that the Greeds refused to sell the land, and I would have to let the mortgage go. He apparently agreed with me and understood.

Several hours later, the shop's phone rang. I answered it and it was the finance agent again. I told him that I would have to call him back in a few minutes because I was taking care of a few customers in my shop. Within an hour, when the last customer had left, I called the finance agent back. I told him, "I'm sorry I had to cut you off earlier. Did we miss something?"

He said, "I spoke with my manager, and we still would like you to pay for the cost of our services."

I said, "What? I chose to not take the loan because the Greeds refused to sell the land. How can I owe you anything?"

He answered, "The cost for our services amount to $3,946.48. We put a lot of hard work getting you such a large loan. By your own admission, your mother is in jail, and you requested the dollar amount of the loan to be decreased because your own mother requested more than it should have been. You have admitted that you are closing your shop. From this information, we consider this to be a fraudulent application put forth by your mother."

I became livid and solemnly said, "Sir, I never admitted my mother committed fraud regarding anything. I'm sure she simply increased it to ensure I would get the dollar amount that I needed. As for my mother being in jail, this has absolutely nothing to do with my loan application. I am still running my shop as we speak. The reason I'm closing it down is because my mother is apparently unable to run it now, and I live in Germany. How dare you! Especially after you commended me for being so honest. Then you twist my words so you can blackmail me? You, sir, are the fraudster, not me. You are very close to having you ears popped."

The finance agent became angry and asked, "Are you now threatening me, ma'am?"

I laughed sarcastically and said, "That just shows how stupid you are, sir. You do not even understand the phrase 'having your ears popped.' Just to make it clear and simple for you to understand, I'm getting ready to scream and yell at you. That in turn will cause your eardrums to pop. Do you understand the meaning now?"

The next thing I knew, there was a different voice on the phone. This man introduced himself and gave his title as manager. He then began to threaten me!

I finally said, "Sir, my attorney will be contacting you shortly because I am calling her right this minute." I slammed the phone down, hard. I looked up, and I had two noisy, elderly ladies staring and listening to me.

I laughed and said, "I'm truly sorry for that outburst. I was dealing with a bottom feeder." Both ladies looked at each other, back at me, and nodded their heads, agreeing with me.

I asked, "May I help you?"

I don't know if the ladies felt sorry for me, or if they just liked what I had to sell, but they left my shop after purchasing many items. Once they left, I called Miss Patson again.

When I greeted Miss Patson she responded with, "Oh no, Belinda, now what has happened? Oh, by the way, I spoke with your great-aunt. She did not like what I had to say. She became very agitated and angry. How can you take that nasty voice of hers when she gets angry? I really wanted to reach into my phone and smack the crap out of her. It was like someone taking their fingernails down a chalkboard."

Ms. Patson had just given the perfect description of my great-aunt's angry voice, and when I heard her say it, all my anger left. I just started giggling.

Miss Patson said, "Belinda! It's not funny, especially not in my profession. It is very unprofessional to lose your self-control with a client, or even a relative of a client. Ever since I took you on as a client, I have been losing my temper with your relatives more and more."

I said, "I'm sorry, but I couldn't help myself. You have already admitted losing your temper with my mother, Big Pete, and now my great-aunt. I have to admit, Jay and I had a bet going as to how long it would take you before you got angry with all of them. The way you described Auntie Bea's angry voice was perfect."

Miss Patson started giggling too and said, "That's just not right. You and your brother set me up from the beginning. Let's see, I yelled at your mother the third time I spoke with her. I got into a yelling contest with that evil Big Pete the first conversation I had with him, but I didn't yell at your great-aunt."

We both started laughing. Miss Patson said, "So technically I have . . . Oh crap. I guess you're right."

We both just started giggling again.

I said, "But I don't hold that against you. I'm amazed you haven't quit on me yet."

She laughed and said, "I sure have come close to it. Oh, before I forget. Did I tell you the outcome of the U.S. Attorney and your brother's problem?"

I answered, "I don't think so."

She said, "Well, I called the U.S. Attorney and was able to speak with her the other day. They are going to check into it. She promised they would speak to Jay, but other than that, that was all she could really say on the matter."

I said, "Thank you. That's another issue we have gotten rid of."

Miss Patson asked, "Oh, why did you call me again?"

I replied, "You are not going to believe this one!"

Miss Patson just chuckled and said, "You always have another problem when you start out with that statement."

I laughed and told her what the finance agent had implied, and that they were demanding payment. After listening to the dreadful story, Miss Patson said, "Crap, Belinda, I have never seen so many nasty people in my life. They seem to draw to you like a moth to a flame."

I said, "Just since I came back into town this time."

Miss Patson said, "You're not going to like my advice again, but it's cheaper just to pay them so they will go away."

I said, "Damn it. No wonder this type of person gets away with so much. I'm sick and tired of being taken advantage of."

Miss Patson replied, "I know."

I asked, "Do you think you can call them and threaten them, or at least try to get them to reduce that amount?"

Miss Patson answered, "Yes, that's a good idea; give me their number."

I gave her the number and waited while she spoke and argued professionally with the person on the other line.

After she hung up she said, "They reduced it by $1,500."

I said, "Thank you, but it's still a lot of money to me."

Miss Patson said, before we hung up the phone, "I hope you don't call me again today, because every time you call we have another nasty person we have to deal with."

I said, with a frown on my face as I spoke, "I know."

CHAPTER LXXI

The next thing I knew, it was Saturday, and I was closing up the shop early so I could pick up Mary and her boyfriend. Sam had stopped by the shop earlier that day, and I had given him money to buy the meat, charcoal, beer, wine, and other things for the cookout.

I knew Sam was already at the Daisy house. I called him there, and I asked him to pick up Auntie Bea and take her to the barbeque as well. I had to admit to myself that Sam was a very good griller, and he could cook some fantastic hamburgers. He could even cook a great hot dog. He always put some secret sauce on everything.

As I was driving to the airport to pick up Mary and her boyfriend, I remembered I had not gotten Uncle Frank's debit card or the papers from the Veterans Affairs office for the retirement account that I could not transfer. I would have to fill out the papers so that all his direct deposits went straight into his new checking account. Granted, the manager had an automatic transfer from the old checking account to the new one, but I needed to fix it. I also remembered I was going to have to give another valiant try convincing Big Pete to allow me to move everything from Mom's house, and to let me take the dogs.

I put all thoughts of that to the side as I pulled into the airport. Mary and her boyfriend were standing on the curb outside the airport waiting for me. I pulled up and parked along the side of the curb.

I got out of the car and said, "I hope you guys didn't wait too long."

Mary hugged me, and I could smell the alcohol on her breath as she slurred, "Hi, cuss." She then kissed me on my cheek.

I said, "Damn, Mary, you're drunk already! Auntie Bea and Uncle Frank are at the Daisy house to see you."

Mary almost fell off the curb and said, "Damn, Belinda, you didn't tell me they were going to be there."

I said, "You didn't ask about them at all. Oh well, let's go. Sam's there too."

Mary said, "Great, we will all get high tonight."

I just rolled my eyes. Some people never change.

We chatted as we were driving back to the Daisy house, and David asked, "Oh, Belinda, we need to get a U-Haul now. Can we get one this late?"

I answered, "Sure, I know a place right up the road from Auntie Bea's and the Daisy house."

David asked, "Do you still have stuff in your shop for sale? Like your mother's desk."

I answered, "Yes."

He asked, "Can we stop there first so I can take another look at that?"

I answered, "Sure."

When I unlocked the shop, David walked straight to my mother's large desk and asked, "How much would you like for it?" I told him, and he said all he had was charge cards. He asked if it was okay if Mary just wired me the money.

I said, "There's a bank up the street, and you can do a cash advance at the ATM."

He said, "No, it's easier to have Mary send the money."

So I made the mistake of trusting him and said, "Okay. When we come back after loading the wine, Sam can help you load it into the U-Haul."

He said, "That sounds great."

We drove to the U-Haul place, and they were still open. I could not believe it, but Mary and David were trying to get me to rent it, making an issue because they didn't have their driver's licenses with them. I told them they could pay for it with their money, I could use my driver's license, and they could drive it. Lo and behold when Mary charged it, I saw her driver's license in her wallet and said, "Good, you don't need mine. There is yours, Mary. You must have overlooked it."

I thought, *Gotcha.* Then I made another mistake in telling them that I had two large wine racks, and I was only asking $50 for each. They said they wanted those also, assured me that they were good for it, and Mary would wire me the money. Of course, I never saw the money for the desk or the wine racks.

They followed me in the U-Haul back to the shop. I helped David load the two wine racks into the truck. We drove back to the Daisy house. Sam was outside cooking on the grill in front of the house. Auntie Bea and Uncle Frank were sitting in the deck chairs Sam had carried outside. We all ate and visited with each other. Sam drove Auntie Bea back to her house and then came back. He then helped David and I load the boxes of wine into the U-Haul. Mary didn't even bother to help. She was too busy continuing to drink. Once the wine was loaded, David, Sam, and I drove in the U-Haul back to my shop. Sam and David loaded the desk into the truck, drove to the storage unit, loaded the wine racks into the U-Haul, and we were finished.

Sam walked back into my shop with me, and as I was turning out the lights Sam said, "Damn, Belinda, there's still a lot of stuff in here, but it's starting to look bare."

I answered with a frown, "I know."

I turned out the lights, and we all piled back into the U-Haul and drove back to the Daisy house. We made a brief stop at Mr. Bee's convenience store because David wanted a combination lock for the back of the truck. He found what he was looking for, and we were on our way again.

After getting back, Sam and David helped me clean up the mess from the cookout, and after we washed the dirty dishes Sam said, "Well, I'm tired and it's starting to get late. I'll see you guys later. I'll talk with you again sometime this week, Belinda." He gave Mary and Uncle Frank a hug and shook David's hand.

I walked outside with Sam to his truck. He gave me a big hug and put four joints in my hand.

I asked, "What's this for?"

He replied, "You know how Mary is, she's going to want to get high, and I don't want her mad at me so you can deal with it. I don't like being around her when she's drunk like Daddy."

I replied, "Okay, but isn't this too much?"

Sam said, "I thought you deserved a blast from the past after all you have been through since you got back. I'm totally grateful that you are cleaning up the mess. I trust you, Belinda, more than I ever trusted your sister, your mom, or even my sisters and brother. I know I've been a shit toward you off and on through the years, but you somehow always came through for me whenever I needed it, and you always treated me as if I were someone important."

I looked at my cousin and said, "I didn't know you felt that way."

Sam said, "Now don't get mushy on me. You know tomorrow I may turn back into the jerk again."

I said, "Okay. I'll take care of it for you with Mary."

I kissed my cousin on the cheek and said, "Drive careful."

He said, "I will."

I walked back towards the Daisy house and thought, *That was the nicest thing Sam ever said to me.*

Uncle Frank had already gone to bed. David and Mary seemed to be having a hard time opening the combination lock. I stood there in the doorway watching them and listening to them because they didn't notice I was standing in the room with them. Mary was trying to open the lock and seemed not to understand the directions that came with the lock. She appeared to have sobered up quite a bit.

I heard David murmur, "Listen, you stupid bitch, give it to me. You're dumber than a monkey's ass."

I never heard that expression before. I watched him grab her by her lower arm right above her wrist. She moaned with pain because he gripped her wrist so hard and said, "David, you are hurting me."

David replied, "That's not all you're going to get when we get to the hotel for not obeying me, you stupid redneck piece of shit. If you want to be with me you need to start doing what I tell you!" He grabbed the lock from her hand. He said still in a half whisper, "You're nothing but a trophy to me and a good fuck."

I had seen enough! I walked closer to them on the opposite side of the large room where they were standing and I said, "Listen, you stupid fuck rod. First of all, don't you ever talk to my flesh and blood like that again, or I'll break every one of your fingers for touching her like that." I gently took Mary's wrist in my hand to look at it more closely. I could see his finger marks that left bruises on her lower part of her arm near her wrist. After examining her bruised lower arm, I looked up at my cousin, and her eyes were wide as saucers.

I said, "No matter what you are, no man has the right to speak or touch you in that manner, Mary. You are worth much more than that because you are my blood."

David grabbed my upper arm and jerked me around so that I faced him. He venomously said to me, "Don't you ever do that again. I don't give a shit who you are, bitch—" Before he had a chance to utter another word, I coldcocked him with my other fist right to the upper side of his nose. I heard the cartilage snapping, and his head tilted backwards a little, but he let go of my upper arm. He let out an agonizing scream, and he cupped both hands over his nose.

I saw blood coming out his nostrils, and he said, "You fucking bitch, you broke my nose!"

As he collapsed on the sofa, I said, "You're damn lucky that's all I did. Mary, could you please go in the kitchen and get one of the kitchen towels? Wet it with cold water, and fill it up with some ice cubes out of Uncle Frank's freezer."

Mary just looked at me for a moment with a stunned gaze and answered, "Sure."

As David was sitting there, I looked at the directions for the combination lock. That pitiful, wimpy man just sat there with his hands over his nose. Within seconds, I had the lock opened, and I held it up in his face so he could clearly see it.

I said, "Stupid redneck, lean your stupid head back to slow down the bleeding. Did you ever think for a minute that you're nothing but a half decent fuck for Mary, because I know my cousin can do much, much better than you. Oh, by the way, I didn't break your nose, you stupid fuck, move your hands."

David said in a whiny voice, "No, you're going to hurt me again."

I said, "No kidding! Move your hands, or I'll belt you again." He moved his hands, and with a firm pinch on his nose, I snapped the cartilage back into place. "Told you it wasn't broken, you pathetic excuse for a man."

He said in a grateful tone, "Oh that feels much better. I'm going to sue you when I get back."

I said, "No you're not. You're nothing but a scummy tax attorney. Don't you think my cousin already told me what you do for a living? You're not even really a true-blooded attorney, you're nothing but a bottom feeder like most other attorneys, but you're a coward as well because you go around browbeating and physically hurting women. Now I know why you have already been married three times. I know what you are." I turned around because Mary cleared her throat, so I knew she had been listening.

She said, "Here, Belinda."

I took the ice pack from her, turned around, gave it to him, and said, "Here, put this on your stupid face. Go into the living room because I'm going to speak with my cousin. If you don't like that, I think I have a corn cob in the freezer that I can shove up your ass as well."

With the ice and towel on his face and nose, David said, "Go fuck yourself."

I said, "I love fucking myself all the time. I'm sure it's a much better fuck than you can give anyone!"

As David was turning on the television in the living room, I whispered to Mary to meet me in the basement because I wasn't quite finished with this scumbag that she had as a boyfriend.

Mary whispered back and said, "No, I want to hear you finish it because he deserves it. This is not the first time he has hurt me, and I truly felt like I wasn't going to ever have another male friend again because of him. Please, Belinda, finish it in front of me."

I said, "Okay then."

We both went into the living room where he was sitting on the sofa with the remote control, and he said in an irritated voice, "You have made your point, Belinda. I'm sorry I called you names, and I'm sorry I called Mary names and hurt her. If you keep it up, Belinda, I'm going to hurt you."

I said, "Hmm, I don't think so. If you think that's the case, come on, asswipe. Let's take it outside, but before we do, I better tell you something. We're not rednecks because we don't work in the field; we are Virginian hillbillies who will kill you and put your rotting corpse where it will never be found up in the hills. So come on, motherfucker, they didn't call me She Wolf in the Army for nothing, and She Wolf does not mean a whore. You have no clue of my true bloodline, jerk off."

David just looked at me as if he were trying to study me before he got the courage up to physically fight me.

I said, "Oh, by the way, asswipe, my husband is still active duty, and if you lay a hand on me again . . . . Well, let's put it this way, you will disappear off the face of this earth. Do you understand my meaning?" His eyes grew wide, and I noticed that his hands had started to tremble. I finally had scared the maggot. Mission accomplished!

I could hear the fear in his voice, as David said, "Okay, Belinda. I'm sorry. Let's just forget about it. I promise I will never talk to Mary like that again or hurt her again because I know if you get wind of it I'm sure your husband will kill me."

I gave him a wicked grin and said, "Damn right, and don't you forget it. Oh, I forgot to mention that it will be a slow, painful death. We have both been trained in interrogation. We have ways of taking you to the edge of death, bringing you back, and repeating the process as many times as we want."

I looked at Mary and said, "Come on, Mary, I have something to show you down in the basement before you guys leave."

I turned the light on in the basement and pulled out one of the joints that Sam gave me. I walked down the stairs into the basement as Mary followed me.

As we stood in the basement, I said, "Sam wanted me to give this to you," and I pulled out two of the joints.

Mary said, "Light it up!"

I lit one up. She took the other from my hand and put it in her pants pocket. We chatted until we finished the joint.

Mary said, "It's getting late, so I guess we better get on the road and go check into a hotel. Thank you, Belinda; hopefully I will not have any more trouble with David. I will be breaking up with him when we get back home."

I said, "Mary, you better do it because he can hurt you, even kill you!"

Mary said, "I know, but I think you finally scared him tonight to at least leave me alone through this trip back."

I said, "I hope so."

We went back upstairs and walked outside. We were all standing outside by the U-Haul. Before they left, I gave my cousin a kiss on the cheek and hugged her. I extended my hand to David, and he hesitated for a few seconds before shaking my hand.

I said, "I'm sorry for hurting you, but I did fix your nose. Be good to my cousin."

David said, "I'm sorry too. Oh, what the hell, may I hug you?"

I didn't answer him; I just let him hug me. I knew what he was and always would be. All I did was shake him up a little bit. Mary climbed up in the passenger side, David got into the driver's side. He started up the truck, and they pulled out of the driveway. I stood watching as they left. I walked back inside the house, locked up for the night, and went to bed.

CHAPTER LXXII

Monday morning, I woke up at my normal time, went to the bathroom, and then I crawled back into bed. I decided to go back to sleep for a few more hours because I felt like I could start slowing down now. I was so exhausted from all the stress of the previous few weeks. I just wasn't ready to face another week. I didn't even want to think about what this new week would throw at me.

I woke up again around 8:30. This time, I felt fresh and as if a heavy weight had been lifted from my shoulders. I knew I was just about finished paying all the debt for now. I had a few more details to work out, and I could go back home again. I could return to my own life.

I got up off the mattress, dressed, and prepared for a new day. I leisurely walked into the kitchen, after doing my morning toiletries, made a fresh pot of coffee, and cooked breakfast. By now, my mornings had become a comfortable routine.

I drove over to Auntie Bea's with a plate full of food for her. I could smell the coffee as I walked in through the side door of her house. Auntie Bea walked into the kitchen from the living room when she heard me enter and said, "Well, ain't we running late today. I'm famished! I'm so used to you coming over here with breakfast much earlier than this, and Frank hasn't called me yet."

I put the plate of food on her kitchen table and said, "Uncle Frank was still sleeping when I left to come over here. I guess this nightmare has taken its toll on all of us."

Auntie Bea said, "I totally agree with you."

I said, "Enjoy your breakfast. Here is your newspaper. I grabbed it on my way in. I need to go back to the Daisy house and make some phone calls." I gave my great-aunt a kiss on her cheek and left. I pulled up into the driveway of the Daisy house, and I'd be damned if Uncle Frank wasn't standing at the door, yelling at me again.

I walked in, and Uncle Frank said in a whisper, "It's Mrs. Greed."

I said, "Damn!" I picked up the phone and said, "Yes, ma'am."

Mrs. Greed said, "Your attorney called me last week, and I told her what I stated to you before—your great-uncle and great-aunt have a lifetime home. Since I spoke with her, I did some thinking about it. I am willing to sell you back just Miss Daisy's house with the quarter acre."

I said, "I must have the entire farm back for my great-aunt." I talked with her for over thirty minutes, pleading with her to change her mind.

I said, "My godparents are on a fixed income, and they cannot afford rent."

Mrs. Greed asked, "Well, how much can they afford to pay?"

I answered, "Uncle Frank and Auntie Bea could pay about $500 maximum, but I hope you do not charge them that." We continued talking as I was trying to persuade her into selling the entire farm back to us.

She finally said, "Well, you have made some valid points, Belinda, but I will have to think about it. Please do not call me regarding it. If I change my mind I will contact you."

I knew this meant she would not change her mind ever. I knew I was going to have to fight her in court someday, and I would have to save every penny I made to fight her. I knew I could only afford to fight her one time.

Uncle Frank asked as I hung up the phone, "Well, did you change her mind?"

I replied, "No, I didn't. The only good thing out of all this is that both of you have a lifetime home."

Uncle Frank asked, "Is that a good thing?"

I answered, "Yes and no, because she is going to charge you rent."

Uncle Frank said, "Well, I would have had to pay you for a portion of the mortgage so that will be okay."

I said angrily, "No, Uncle Frank, it's not a good thing! You will be paying a stranger, not family, for something that already belonged to us." I put my face in my hands and just started crying and said, "Are there any truly decent people left in this country of ours?" I got up from Uncle Frank's favorite chair, wiped the tears from my face, and simply stated, "Auntie Bea is going to be pissed."

Uncle Frank said, "I know."

I asked, "Can you tell her, and tell her we will have to wait to fight the Greeds because of Mom's situation? She already knows because Miss Patson explained it to her last week."

Uncle Frank replied, "Sure, baby girl. We've gotten through worse hell than this, and I'm sure we will all get through this too."

I said, "Uncle Frank, I'm going to be taking on rich and powerful people. All I can do is try, but I'm afraid we are going to lose in the end. I don't think I will win that battle, but I will still try for Auntie Bea and Mom."

Uncle Frank said, "All that matters is that you try. Don't worry about Sister Bea. I will handle her."

I looked at my great-uncle and giggled. He giggled too.

"Okay, I know Sister Bea is a handful." I didn't say anything more about Auntie Bea. I simply asked, "Did you eat the breakfast I left you this morning?"

Uncle Frank answered, "Yes. My dirty dishes are in the sink."

I said, "Okay. Let me get them cleaned up because we still have some unfinished business of yours to take care of."

Uncle Frank said, "Okay," as he took another sip of his coffee.

After I finished cleaning up the dishes, I retrieved Uncle Frank's files that I had created regarding his finances. I opened up his bank file. It was easy to find because I had taped the manager's business card on the outside. I picked up the telephone and called his bank. I spoke with the same manager that I dealt with before and told her that I never received Uncle Frank's debit card. She confirmed my auntie's address, and she told me she would reissue it. If I did not receive it in seven business days, I was to call her back immediately. She stated I should have received the card over a month ago. I thanked her for her time and hung up the phone.

Uncle Frank asked, "Do you think someone stole it?"

I answered, "I don't think so, because there has been no money withdrawn from your account."

Uncle Frank said, "I guess it got lost in the mail."

I said, "I think so too."

I pulled out the file titled "Veterans Affairs" and called the number that I had found regarding one of Uncle Frank's retirement accounts. I informed the representative that over a month ago I had requested forms for my great-uncle to fill out and sign because he had a different checking account now. I stated that he never received them. They assured me they had mailed them out over a month ago according to their records. I told them it must have gotten lost in the mail. I needed to get this done quickly because I was trying to straighten out all of my great-uncle's affairs before

I returned to Germany. She said it would be four to six weeks before I received another copy for him. I thanked her and hung up the phone.

I then picked up the phone and called Thomas's father. I told him I would need Thomas's brothers to help me move things from my booth and the rest of the items that I had left in the shop so I could close it down this Saturday. Thomas's father said he would call them all that night, and he would have them call me to get directions and set up a time to meet. I thanked him and hung up the phone. Next, I called the first out of the last three credit cards of Uncle Frank and my mother's to cancel them. I had the statements in hand and was going to pay off the entire principal on each one. I called the first one, asked to be sure I had the correct principal, and requested to close the account. After hanging up the phone I took the two credit cards for that account, one was in Mom's name and one was in Uncle Frank's name, and cut them up into small pieces over the trash can. I had been doing this with each of the credit cards for the last two months as I paid them. Uncle Frank was sitting in his chair listening and watching as I worked.

The second one was a Sears' credit card. Uncle Frank asked, "Which one is that?"

I answered, "Sears."

Uncle Frank said, "No, don't cancel that one! I want to keep it."

I said, "Uncle Frank, if I pay it off it will be cancelled."

Uncle Frank asked, "No, don't pay it off. I will keep that. What is the balance?"

I answered, "Twelve hundred dollars."

He said, "I will keep that debt. Put that to the side and just make a payment from my checkbook."

I asked, "Are you sure?"

Uncle Frank replied, "Yes, that is my card. Can you have your mother's named removed?"

I answered, "I don't think so, but I can call and ask." I picked up the phone and asked the representative if I could have a person removed from the credit card account. She informed me that I couldn't do that. I asked the lady if she could hold for a moment, and I told Uncle Frank that they would not do that.

Uncle Frank said, "Well, that's okay. I still want to keep it." I thanked the lady for her help and hung up the phone. I took the credit card with my mother's name on it and cut it into small pieces over the trash can. I took the other one with Uncle Frank's name on it and passed it to him. He reached into the back pocket of his pants, removed his wallet, opened his wallet, and put the credit card inside it.

I retrieved the last file folder, and it was a Discover card. Uncle Frank asked again, "Which one is that?"

I answered, "Discover."

Uncle Frank asked, "Is that the last one of the debt?"

I answered, "Yes."

He asked, "How much debt is on that one?"

I answered, "It's $3,084.17."

Uncle Frank said, "I want that one too."

I said, "Uncle Frank, you cannot afford all this debt. I will pay half of it, and you can pay the other half. I think that would be fair."

Uncle Frank said, "Yes, that's fair because I had charged on those cards too."

I said, "But I don't think you charged as much as my mother did." I did have a gut feeling that he had charged a couple of thousand dollars so I figured I was being fair about it. I did not call that credit card company. I simply wrote out a check from my checking account for half of the amount and got the bill ready to go out in the mail with the other one that I had ready to go as well. I did the same thing. I cut up the card with my mother's name on it and passed Uncle Frank the card with his name on it.

I got Uncle Frank's checkbook, wrote out the payment amount for the Sears card, and he signed the check. I put the statement in the envelope, licked it to seal it, and put a stamp on it. I went back to my checkbook, wrote out a check for the full amount to the finance agency that they agreed to, and got that ready to go into the mail.

I calmly walked into the kitchen and got myself a beer. I opened the beer and took a good swig of it. I was very pleased with myself; all the debt was paid. It was time to celebrate!

As I walked back into the Florida room, Uncle Frank asked, "What are you so pleased with yourself for?"

I giggled as I answered, "I'm finished with all the debt. I've made restitution to almost all of my mother's victims. I did not believe I would have made it this far. Wow! I made restitution to one hundred and fifty people. Wow! My only wish was that I could have made restitution to both my mother's and Big Pete's victims, but that was so far from reach. If I were rich, I would have done just that."

Uncle Frank laughed and said, "It's about time."

I giggled.

Uncle Frank said, "I will celebrate with you. Baby girl, go and pour me a little bit of my whiskey in this coffee," as he passed me his coffee cup.

I said, "Okay, Uncle Frank, but that's just plain nasty."

It was time for me to call that newspaper reporter. I retrieved my mother's address book and looked up the woman's name. I picked up the telephone and dialed her number. She answered, "Hello. This is Ms. Weasel."

It was all I could do to contain my laughter. I said, as I almost choked trying to suppress my laughter, "Hi, Ms. Weasel. My name is Belinda Star, the one that you wrote about. I am very upset about your article."

Ms. Weasel said, "I'm sorry, Ms. Star, I was just doing my job. I didn't write anything bad about you, and I did not use your name."

I said, "You make it sound like my mother is some kind of monster. She is made of flesh and blood, just like you. She made a terrible mistake, and she is paying for it. I do not appreciate you making it sound as if she did more than what she really did."

Of course Ms. Weasel started asking questions; she was a reporter after all.

She asked, "Then can you tell me what she did?"

I replied, "I'm not at liberty to tell you at this time, but I can tell you some of the evil things Big Pete has been doing."

She said, "Oh, really."

I said, "But first I need to ask you if you ever got that interview with him after he cussed you out. From what I've heard you're going to try and sue him for calling you names and threatening your life." Of course I didn't know any of this. I was just fishing for information.

To my surprise she asked, "How did you find out that I filed a civil suit against him?"

I asked, "Didn't he threaten your life?"

Ms. Weasel answered, "Yes, he did, but I did not report that, and no one else knows except . . ."

I just answered her, "I have anonymous sources as well, Ms. Weasel, and no, Big Pete did not tell me. When is your court date?"

Ms. Weasel answered, "It will be this Friday."

I said, "Oh." I started telling her about the blackmail regarding our beloved family dogs. I knew she was a dog owner as well. I put on my drama hat and turned on the tears. I started crying about how he had blackmailed me for money by threatening to file credit card fraud charges against my Uncle Frank. I told her I ended up paying five hundred dollars on the gas card because it would have cost me a small fortune to fight him in court. I even passed the telephone to Uncle Frank so he could back up my story. Uncle Frank added to it by saying that Big Pete tried to kill him when Big Pete was drunk.

Uncle Frank passed the phone back to me, and I continued telling her little tidbits until I felt comfortable, from the sound of her voice, that she sincerely felt remorseful for writing about a family member whom she knows nothing about.

I finally asked her, "My mother said she will give you an interview and answer any questions you have. My attorney can get you access inside the prison to have a one-on-one interview with her for as long as you need. I will give you an interview myself, if you continue with this lawsuit against Big Pete because on the day you have him in court, I can go retrieve the dogs and move my family heirlooms out of his house. I have a power of attorney on my mother, and I can show it to you if you wish. I cannot get into a confrontation with Big Pete on their property because the police captain said they would have to arrest me, but I can take anything that belonged to my mother because I have power of attorney."

She said, "Wow! The hearing is at nine thirty in the morning of this coming Friday. I will help you keep Big Pete away from the house so you can do this."

I said, "If you back out, you must tell me because I will have to cancel the moving team."

She said, "You don't have to worry about that, Belinda."

I said, "God bless you! Thank you for helping my family and me." I hung up the phone and looked at Uncle Frank, and he said, "Shit, Belinda, if Big Pete catches you there will be hell to pay."

I said, "I know, but it's worth the risk. He didn't tell anyone about this lawsuit. Wow! I can't wait until Mom calls so I can tell her what I have found out."

I grabbed Uncle Frank's phonebook and looked up moving companies. I called the first one listed. They had no trouble being their no earlier than 9:15 on Friday morning. I explained some of what Big Pete was all about and told them that it was very important that they did not show up any earlier. I gave them the address and said I would meet them there on Friday. I promised that if I needed to cancel, I would contact them immediately.

As soon as I hung up the phone, it rang, and I answered it. It was the same old recording from the prison. I accepted it, and as soon as the recording finished, I said, "Mom, you are not going to believe this." I told her everything that I found out from Ms. Weasel.

Mom asked, "So are you going to do it on Friday?"

I replied, "Yes, I'm going to try, but it's all up to this Ms. Weasel."

Uncle Frank wanted to speak with Mom, so I passed the phone to him. He seemed to be just as excited as we were about this new opportunity to solve another problem.

I drove to the shop and thought if we did get everything moved from Mom and Big Pete's house, I could sell all the stuff in the sheds. Men love that stuff. I could even sell some of the linens and standard household stuff that people love buying at flea markets. I decided I would talk to the landlord regarding my shop and see if he would extend my agreement for just one more month.

I walked into the small building where he conducted business and said, "Good morning, sir. I was wondering if I could rent the building for one more month."

He said, "Positively no."

I asked, "Why?"

He answered, "All that fighting going on with your great-aunt and other relatives and just the scandal surrounding it. I want nothing to do with it."

I said, "Sir, that is so hypocritical of you. I know you saw several heated arguments with my great-aunt and Big Pete, but you have to understand that my great-aunt has been under a lot of stress."

He said, "But you allowed that old lady to smoke in a public building."

We continued debating, without either one of us raising our voices, until I finally gave up because he was not going to change his mind.

I said, "Well, I will be moved out this weekend, probably Sunday afternoon, so I can get one last weekend of sales. I will stop by your office on Monday morning to receive my refund for the other half of this month."

He said, "Okay. That will be fine."

As I was walking toward the door to leave he said, "Belinda."

I turned around to face him, and he walked toward me. He said, "I'm sorry, but the truth of the matter is I have already rented the building out for next month to someone else. I should have just told you that. I truly want to say you are a decent person, and I hate to admit it, because of all the scandal surrounding you, but somehow you did generate a lot more business over these last few months for the other shop owners and dealers. They have said so. They all have told me that you are one hell of a salesman, but you never pushed anything on anyone. I want to personally say that I wish there were more noble and honest people in the world like you. I truly mean that."

He extended his hand, and I said with a smile on my face, "It was good doing business with you, sir." I shook his hand and walked out of the building.

I just did not understand his change of attitude toward me. I did not realize that the bottom feeders thought so highly of me—probably because they were buying things from me for practically nothing. Thank God I had enough to complete the most important part of my mission. Everything else I sold will be just icing on the cake to pay this last month of bills and to put extra funds in the escrow trust account that Miss Patson had established for my mother.

The next morning, I called Thomas and told him the good news. I told him that I was going to attempt moving the property from Mom and Big Pete's house.

He simply said, "Be careful. Never trust a reporter. They just care about their own agenda. They don't care who they hurt in the process."

CHAPTER LXXIII

Before I knew it, it was Thursday morning, and there was not much left in the shop. I had even sold the metal shelving and other display cases. The shop was virtually empty. I had a couple more truckloads of other things in the basement, and I was going to see if I could sell some of it over the weekend.

The telephone rang, and I answered it. It was Ms. Weasel. She told me Big Pete called her and made a deal with her. He apologized to her and promised her an interview for this Friday if she dropped the lawsuit. She contacted her attorney yesterday, and the lawsuit had been dropped. I could not believe my ears. How does Big Pete do it?

I said, "Ms. Weasel, then all interviews with my mother and me are cancelled. I will be shocked if Big Pete actually goes through with his promise to give you an interview. So I guess Big Pete won this battle as well. I do not understand why everyone seems to be so greedy."

She said, "I know he will keep his word."

I was shocked. "You are going to accept the word of a con man, thief, and liar? What the devil is the matter with you? You would rather interview a person who will tell you lies than people who will tell you the truth?"

Ms. Weasel said, "I'm sorry, Belinda, but it has already been arranged, and I know he will honor the agreement."

I just wickedly laughed and said, "Your greed will be your downfall regarding this story. Goodbye."

I immediately called the moving company and told them I would have to cancel. I had just finished waiting on a customer, and they were walking out the door when the telephone rang. It was the recording from the jail. As soon as I accepted the call, I immediately told my mother about the reporter dropping the lawsuit and the deal she made with Big Pete. My mother became very upset and said, "We have to get the stuff out of the house, Belinda! The house is in foreclosure, and I guess Pete just plans on leaving it along with my dogs. You're going to have to call your Uncle Poppy."

I said, "I don't want to get any more people involved in all this."

Mom said, "Just call him and talk to him. I'll hang up and call you back later to see if he will help."

I had my mother's address book with me, and I called the number she had under his name. I told Uncle Poppy what Big Pete was doing. I told him about Big Pete beating my mother over the year. I told him about Big Pete threatening to hurt or kill Auntie Bea, Uncle Frank, and me. I even told him that Big Pete had threatened to hurt everyone in our family. In fact, I may have told too much because Uncle Poppy became so angry about it, he started yelling into the phone.

"I knew it! I knew that creep was no good! Nobody beats on my sister except for me or family . . ." Uncle Poppy must have ranted and raved for at least fifteen minutes before he asked, "Well, Belinda, what's your plan?"

I replied, "Well, we have a problem. I have been staking out the house for the last week in the early evening hours. I have not been able to stake the house out during the day because I have to run the shop." I told him about the reporter and the lawsuit.

I told him, "If we get all the male cousins and a large moving truck, it would still take us two full days to move all the crap. If we tie him up to a tree, according to my mother's plan, and left him alive then we would be in trouble with the law."

Uncle Poppy simply said, "Then we will kill him and burn his corpse up in the Hollow. It's that simple, Belinda."

I said, "Uncle Poppy, it's not that simple because I will be the first suspect! I'm not going to jail for the creep, and besides, we have no right to take his life."

Uncle Poppy said, "It's mountain justice for hurting a family member. It's the old way."

I replied, "That may be true, Uncle Poppy, but Aunt Janet would never speak to me again if we were caught."

Uncle Poppy said, "You're right, but I can't do anything else to help Jane. I could get Big Pete away from the house."

I said, "I don't think Big Pete is stupid enough to trust being alone with you, because after all, you are Mom's brother. Don't worry, Uncle

Poppy, this will play out eventually. We may be hillbillies, but we are not stupid."

Uncle Poppy said, "You're right, Belinda. I was not thinking this through, but I'm not a coward. I will do it if you think we can get away with it."

I said, "I know you are far from being a coward, Uncle Poppy, but seeking vengeance by murder is a bit too extreme. It seems that the crooks have more rights than the victims in today's justice system. I guess just plain old common sense is out the window."

Uncle Poppy said, "I totally agree with you, but you just let me know if you come up with a sound plan to get our family stuff out of his grip."

I said, "You know I will. Thank you, Uncle Poppy. I do love you."

Uncle Poppy said, "Girl, you know I love you, or I would not have picked so many fights with you to toughen you up over the years. I do take some credit that I help mold you into a fine soldier. I'm very proud of you. I love you as if you were one of my own kids, if not more."

Uncle Poppy is still a bully no matter how much he tries to sugarcoat it, I thought as I hung the phone up.

Of course Mom called later in the day, and I told her about my conversation with Poppy. She said, "Belinda, I can't believe you talked your uncle out of it. He would have done it for me. You are nothing but a coward. I raised you better than this."

I said, "Mom, we are being recorded you know. There is always a trail that can be discovered nowadays. Let it go. I am not a coward! I just have plain old common sense, and I do respect our laws. You are talking like a crazy person."

After being badgered by my mother until she was cut off, I thought, *Am I the only sane member of this crazy family of mine? I'm a coward because I will not commit murder over family heirlooms and personal property? Don't we have laws to protect us from monsters like Big Pete without having to go to this extreme?*

It was Sunday afternoon and there were just a few boxes of things left in the shop. I had already spoken with Thomas's brothers during the week, and they planned to meet me around 6:00 p.m. to help clean the shop and move whatever was left into storage. I started sweeping, and I heard the jingle of the brass bell ring as the front door opened. There were all three of Thomas's brothers. They all hugged and kissed me, and we exchanged our greetings. It only took us about twenty-five minutes to finish cleaning up and moving the few boxes I had left. Before we left, I took one last, slow look around the shop that had been my dream.

We dropped off the boxes at the Daisy house. I left Mom's pickup truck there because all three brothers had larger pickup trucks. We drove to the antique and collectible mall where I had a booth and loaded everything out of it onto two of his brother's trucks. I spoke with the manager and gave her my military APO address to send the check to for the things that had been sold already. I thought we could probably squeeze these items in the storage bin, and the brothers agreed to at least try to get it all into the storage unit. Two of Thomas's brothers bought a few pieces of furniture that I had in the booth and paid me cash right there on the spot for it. When I opened the storage unit, the brothers moved some things around to make more room to fit what I had from the booth into the storage unit. We got lucky, and all of it fit in the unit. After all that physical work, we were hungry. We all went to a fast food joint and chatted for a few hours. Two of Thomas's brothers left from the restaurant, and his oldest brother dropped me off at the Daisy house.

Now it was just hurry up and wait, so I could finish the little things I had left to do. If we found out soon when Mom's sentencing was I would be able to take action against the Greeds to get Auntie Bea's land back. It would be up to Mom to get everything out with Pete regarding the property in their house, and I figured it would be Jay helping to make that happen.

CHAPTER LXXIV

I woke up Monday morning around 9:30, and I did not feel guilty at all for sleeping so late. I decided that I would sleep late every day that week. I would have a yard sale Friday afternoon through Sunday, and I would finish setting up Uncle Frank's finances. I planned on having his utilities automatically paid from his checking account. I had already spoken with the pharmacy, and that bill would also be paid automatically. I already arranged for the bank up the road to help him reconcile his checkbook every week. All he had to do was take his checkbook and bank statement. I made all the necessary calls that morning to arrange for management of his finances. I went through everything and showed him how it all would work.

Then, I went over to Auntie Bea's to get the mail. I still had not received Uncle Frank's debit card, and I asked Auntie Bea, "Auntie Bea, I haven't gotten Uncle Frank's debit card yet. This is the second time I requested it. Have you received something in the mail looking like a credit card?"

Auntie Bea became agitated and answered, "I destroyed it, and stop ordering credit cards in Frank's name."

I said, "Auntie Bea, it is not a credit card, it's a debit card that looks like a credit card. Do you know you can go to jail for tampering with someone else's mail?"

Auntie Bea said, "Bull, it's coming to my address."

I said, "Auntie Bea, it doesn't matter. I am so tired of you doing everything in your power to prevent Uncle Frank from being independent!" I walked out the door because I was so furious with her ignorance. Instead of asking, she just did as she pleased with no thought to someone else's needs.

Tuesday morning I received a phone call from Mrs. Weasel. She was very upset as she told me, "Belinda, you were right! He cussed me out again and refused to do the interview. Now I have dropped my lawsuit, and I have no story. Can I still get an interview with your mother and you?"

I said, "I told you that your greed would be your downfall. You couldn't help me, so don't expect me to help you. Don't ever call me again." With that statement, I hung up the phone.

I had my yard sale over the weekend, and it was a huge success. It's amazing what people will buy. Wednesday, prior to the yard sale, I visited with my mother. She was still upset with me. She was still fussing over the property and could not understand why I could not just tie Big Pete up to a tree and take everything.

As I was sitting there, remembering my last visit with her, the telephone rang. Surprise, surprise, it was my mother again. This time there was no recording. She had a friend in the jail that had a cell phone somehow. Mom told me, "My friend that's in my cell with me has a son that will do what you won't. He will help you move everything out of the house and store it up on the Mills farm. He has about twelve buddies that will help as well, but it will cost a lot of money to do it."

I said, "Mom, you're crazy."

She replied, "Belinda, just speak with him now."

I heard button tones on the telephone, then silence, and then I was speaking with a man.

I told him, "Thank you, but no thank you. My mother is crazy. I guess she wants me sitting in a jailhouse cell with her."

The man on the other end agreed with me, and we hung up. Of course, within just a few minutes Mom called again and tried to badger me into doing it.

I said, "No! End of discussion, period." I hung up the phone.

For the next two weeks, my mother continued pestering me over and over again. In my eyes, I had done everything that I could possibly do. I had fulfilled my daughter's duty. It was time for me to leave.

Uncle Frank even said, "Belinda, it's time for you to go home to your husband. We will be fine."

Auntie Bea, with her attitude, was also trying to get me to leave.

CHAPTER LXXV

I finally listened to my godparents, and I made flight arrangements for March 30, 1999. I guess I was a coward because I did not tell my mother. I did not feel like dealing with her drama when she found out that I was going home to my husband.

Since Auntie Bea had screwed up the debit card, I took Uncle Frank's checkbook to her. I had all his bills ready to be mailed out with all the checks. I told her not to pay off the next month's utilities because they were direct deposit. All she had to do was write the amount in his checkbook. I told her about the retirement account of Uncle Frank's. I told her she had to give him $100 cash every Friday. I wrote everything down for her so she would not forget.

I kissed her on the cheek and gave her a hug goodbye. I told her that I was sure Mom would make arrangements to move everything else in the next few months. I told her I would call every other week to check up on both of them. I walked back over to the Daisy house. Uncle Frank was putting his shoes on to drive me to the airport. I gave him a blank white envelope with five $100 bills in it.

"What's this for?" he asked after opening the envelope.

I told him, "I called the telephone company to find out the total of our bill. That is to take care of my part of the bill, plus extra money to last you for a few weeks. Just remind Auntie Bea that all your bills will be paid automatically. I was going to sit down and try to figure out who called whom, but that just seemed like too much of a headache. I'm just giving you the total amount."

Uncle Frank said, "Baby girl, you think of everything."

I replied, "I try. Are you sure you two are going to be okay?"

Uncle Frank answered, "Yes. Just check up on us from time to time."

I said, "I promise I will. I will be back whenever they decide to sentence Mom. Then, Auntie Bea and I are going to file a lawsuit against the Greeds."

Uncle Frank drove me to the airport. As I had my luggage in hand, he kissed and hugged me.

He said, "Don't leave us hanging, Belinda."

I said, "Uncle Frank, when the time comes, I promise I will be back to finish the job."

I checked my luggage and asked where the nearest mailbox was. The clerk behind the counter pointed his finger in the direction of the mailbox. He answered, "It's over there, ma'am."

I said, "Thank you." I dropped a letter addressed to my mother in the slit.

I had written that I was a coward and could not tell her I was leaving face to face. I wrote that I had done all that I could and it was up to her to finish it with Big Pete.

My flight was announced for boarding, and I settled in my seat by the window on a small airplane. Two connections later, I was on the long flight back to Germany. I settled in my seat; fortunately, this one was by the window as well. It felt strange to relax and be headed back to my world after three months of pure hell. Deep in my heart of hearts, I knew I was not finished with my mission yet.

After we were airborne, the stewardess brought the can of tomato juice and a cup of ice as I requested. I looked out the window and started thinking about everything that had happened over the last three months. I wondered how long it would be before I was back on this same flight again. This flight seemed even longer than my flight three months ago. I was so anxious to get back home, to be safe in my husband's arms again. I must have fidgeted in that seat the entire flight.

Finally, we landed at the Rhine Maine Airport. I impatiently waited for the announcement that we could disembark. I grabbed my bags out of the overhead compartment as soon as we were given permission to do so. I stood in the aisle with other impatient passengers, and finally people started to move to get off the airplane. I walked through the concourse into the waiting area of the airport. There was my beloved husband smiling from ear to ear. I didn't care who saw me. I dropped all my bags and ran to him and jumped into his open arms. I wrapped my arms and legs around his firm body. I started kissing him all over his face and lips.

Thomas laughed and whispered in my ear while he was still holding me, "Is it over?"

As he was holding me, I bent backward so I could look into his face. With a frown, I replied, "No, honey, it's not over. I guess a daughter's duty is never over."

As I put my feet back on the ground and he let go of me, he said as he kissed me, "I'm just glad you're back home with me."

ABOUT THE AUTHOR

Linda D. Coker was born and raised in the surrounding valley of the Appalachian Mountains of Virginia and currently resides in the beautiful state of Colorado.

She is an honorably discharged veteran of the United States Army and has a degree in business management.

Linda was one of the first women recruited after the Women's Army Corps (WAC) was disassembled and integrated into the Army. After Linda married another soldier, it became harder for the two of them to stay stationed together; she gave up her military career so she could be by his side. She still played an active role throughout her husband's military career by volunteering her time to support the spouses and family members of her husband's fellow soldiers during many hardship deployments.

Linda was blessed during her travels with her husband, and she had the opportunity to work with many major contractors that support the troops. With these opportunities, she was still able to be part of the Army in the background and support her husband and his units in some capacity.

After her husband retired, Linda nearly died from the stress of her job; she took a three-year break from daily working and started writing stories. She considers herself to be a pretty good storyteller.